continued . . .

The Comforts of Home

JODI THOMAS

BERKLEY BOOKS, NEW YORK

THE BERKLEY PUBLISHING GROUP
Published by the Penguin Group
Penguin Group (USA) Inc.
375 Hudson Street, New York, New York 10014, USA
Penguin Group (Canada), 90 Eglinton Avenue East, Suite 700, Toronto, Ontario M4P 2Y3, Canada
(a division of Pearson Penguin Canada Inc.)
Penguin Books Ltd., 80 Strand, London WC2R 0RL, England
Penguin Group Ireland, 25 St. Stephen's Green, Dublin 2, Ireland (a division of Penguin Books Ltd.)
Penguin Group (Australia), 250 Camberwell Road, Camberwell, Victoria 3124, Australia
(a division of Pearson Australia Group Pty. Ltd.)
Penguin Books India Pvt. Ltd., 11 Community Centre, Panchsheel Park, New Delhi—110 017, India
Penguin Group (NZ), 67 Apollo Drive, Rosedale, Auckland 0632, New Zealand
(a division of Pearson New Zealand Ltd.)
Penguin Books (South Africa) (Pty.) Ltd., 24 Sturdee Avenue, Rosebank, Johannesburg 2196,
South Africa

Penguin Books Ltd., Registered Offices: 80 Strand, London WC2R 0RL, England

THE COMFORTS OF HOME

A Berkley Book / published by arrangement with the author

ISBN: 978-1-61793-278-6

BERKLEY®
Berkley Books are published by The Berkley Publishing Group,
a division of Penguin Group (USA) Inc.,
375 Hudson Street, New York, New York 10014.
BERKLEY® is a registered trademark of Penguin Group (USA) Inc.
The "B" design is a trademark of Penguin Group (USA) Inc.

PRINTED IN THE UNITED STATES OF AMERICA

There is a legend in the small town of Harmony, Texas, that one winter, where the rivers once crossed in the center of town, the waters grew muddy. For months winter storms made the waters bubble and rage, and the people of the town grew weary of looking at their distorted and pockmarked reflections.

After a time, everyone stopped looking at the mirrored river and began only to see themselves the way others saw them.

Visitors often commented that the people of Harmony grew better looking, for their beauty came not from what they saw for themselves, but from what they felt through others' eyes.

Chapter 1

TYLER WRIGHT MANEUVERED HIS NEW BLACK RANGE ROVER through the silent streets of Harmony, Texas. A light rain tapped on the windshield like a ticking clock. He knew he should still be trying to sleep, but with the dawn his life might be about to change forever, and he wanted to be ready to meet it wide awake.

He drove out of town and headed toward Amarillo's airport, warning himself to calm down. The day held no guarantees. He'd had his hopes crushed a dozen times over the years he'd known Major Kate Cummings. Almost two years ago she'd stepped back into his life, and he had no idea why she'd returned or, for that matter, why she'd left. Maybe she wasn't ready to start more than a casual relationship, maybe she never would be, but that didn't stop him from hoping. He was in midlife. He was ready.

Only, last night when she'd called asking him to meet her plane, he'd heard something different in her voice. An excitement about seeing him. A longing to come home to Harmony. This was the first time she hadn't rented a car and driven in on her own, almost as if she'd just decided to stop in town and had not come just to see him.

This time he'd pick her up and drive her to Harmony. Everyone would know she was there because of him.

Rolling down his window, Tyler smiled into the dawn. In the past two years since he and Kate had become good friends, she'd started talking about Harmony as if it were her home. It had taken him months of asking to get her to just come spend a weekend in his town. It might be 2010, but part of him knew people would talk if she stayed at his place, so Tyler always booked her a room at the Winter's Inn Bed-and-Breakfast. Surprisingly, his proper Kate and the crazy innkeeper, Martha Q Patterson, got along perfectly. Each looked at the other as a curiosity.

After that first visit, every month Tyler invited her back and every month she came. Once she was in town, they'd join friends for dinners, and go to concerts in the park or movies at the little theater where their feet always stuck to the floor. They would take walks in the cemetery where he'd tell her the stories of all the people of Harmony, and then they'd stop at the magnolia tree he had planted just because she'd told him once magnolias were her favorite tree. On each visit Tyler hoped she'd take root and stay as well.

As he drove across the flat plains of the Texas panhandle, now dressed in winter browns, he thought about how wonderful his Kate was. He might be in his midforties and more than a few pounds overweight. He might not be much of a conversationalist and he knew he was probably the world's worst dancer, but he had a perfect woman in Kate.

To the world she was Major Katherine Cummings, an arson expert with the army. To him she would always be the hazel-eyed beauty he'd met one night at Quartz Mountain Lodge during a storm, with whom he'd talked half the rainy night away. Their friendship blossomed through e-mail. Months later a fire had rolled across the open land around his town, and Major Cummings had come to help. But afterward she broke off all contact.

Then one night he'd e-mailed her of a danger the folks she had met faced and she'd responded. Their friendship seemed patched together with spiderweb thread, but with each e-mail, each visit, Tyler felt they added one more thread—one more bond.

He never asked about why she'd stopped e-mailing after the fire. He was afraid he'd hear that he wasn't half the man she thought him to be. Over the two years since, she'd stood him up almost as often as she'd come to visit. Her answer was always simply that her work kept her away.

He set no restrictions on Kate. No rules. No promises. He knew she had an important job she couldn't talk about and, as Harmony's only funeral director, he had a job he didn't want to talk about, so when they were together they talked of other things.

Tyler dreamed of what she might say if he asked her to stay with him in his apartment above the funeral home and not go to the inn tonight. She'd visited him several times. His housekeeper had even cooked them a meal one night when Kate stayed late watching a movie in his quarters. He'd felt like a teenager walking her back to the inn and saying good night on the porch.

Deep down, he knew he wouldn't ask her to stay with him this time. They didn't have that kind of relationship, not yet, maybe not ever.

The day had warmed by the time he reached the Amarillo airport. He pulled to the side of the road and cut the engine. He could go inside and wait by the luggage claim, but he'd be among strangers there. Here, he could watch the planes and wait alone with his thoughts. He glanced in the rearview mirror. Alex Matheson, the town's sheriff, had mentioned yesterday that he looked like he'd lost a few pounds. Maybe Kate would notice as well.

An hour later hunger overtook him. He gave in and drove around to a little café next to the strip called English Field.

He took his time ordering and eating. In his daydreams he was busy planning how to ask Kate to marry him someday. He thought, as a fourth-generation undertaker, it might be proper to say simply, "Kate, how would you like to be buried in the Wright family plot beside me?"

She might think it was funny. She might never come back to Harmony.

Maybe it would be best just to ask if she'd like to grow old with him by her side. They liked the same books, the same movies, even the same kinds of food. They never ran out of anything to say. Maybe they weren't as romantic as two young lovers, but she'd kissed him good-bye on the lips a few times and she never seemed to mind when he took her hand.

As Tyler drove through airport security and parked in front of the luggage pickup area, he made up his mind that after two years of talking it was time for the next step.

He'd try to keep it light. "Kate, if you're going to call my border collie your baby every time you see her, maybe we should marry and make the poor dog legit."

No, he frowned. That was too light. She'd be here for a few days. Surely he'd think of something before she left.

He stepped from the car as people began to circle around the luggage carousel. Halfway to the door, he spotted her through the glass. His Kate. She stood all straight and still like the soldier she was, but he knew her laughter and the way she talked to Little Lady as if the dog were a baby. He knew the feel of her hand in his.

Before he could reach her, she pulled her luggage from the moving ribbon. Tyler rushed forward. "I'll get that," he said, covering her fingers for a moment before she let go.

He set the suitcase down and checked the name tag. When she didn't move, he looked up into her face.

For the first time since he'd met her, Tyler saw tears in her eyes.

"What's wrong?" he whispered, not wanting to draw attention.

She pressed her lips together and slowly shook her head, then said just loud enough for him to hear, "Take me home, Ty."

Tyler knew grief. Bone-deep grief so overwhelming a person can't express it. He'd worked with it all his life. He knew how to handle it.

Without a word, he put his arm around Kate and walked her slowly to the car. When they were away from the airport, he looked at her. She sat as still as stone. He said the only thing he needed to say. "I'm here, Kate. I'm right here."

She reached across the seat and took his hand. They drove to Harmony in silence.

Chapter 2

POST OFFICE

MORNINGS IN THE MIDDLE OF FEBRUARY ALWAYS STARTED out cold, making some of the residents of Harmony want to sleep in like hibernating bears, but by midmorning the prairie sun usually warmed enough to have people shedding heavy coats in favor of sweaters and sweatshirts.

Ronelle Logan, dressed in her drab once-black-now-gray coat, left the post office and marched toward Main Street barely noticing the weather, or the people passing her. She knew them all. Strangers were as rare as chain stores in town. Ronelle could list what magazines most folks got in their mail, but she didn't want to talk to anyone. In fact, she didn't even want to look at them. People in general frightened her. One on one they were terrifying.

When they waved, Ronelle lowered her head and kept walking. She couldn't remember one day in her twenty-seven years of life that she'd wanted to talk to anyone in town. She'd been born here but didn't call one of them by name. Her mother had pulled her out of school in the second grade because, in Dallas Logan's opinion, there were far too many germs in schools.

For a few years Ronelle thought the kids were the germs her mother talked about. She made no effort to make friends with any of them. By the time she got her first and only job at eighteen, she'd developed a habit of avoiding people as if they were no more than the germs her mother harped about.

Except maybe the funeral director, Tyler Wright. He brought her crossword puzzle books from as far away as Kansas City and Albuquerque sometimes, and he'd told her how sorry he was when her father died eight years ago. All the other people who came to the funeral tried to calm her mother, but Tyler had walked right up to her and talked to her. While her mother was wailing over her father's casket, Tyler Wright gave Ronelle the last hug she'd probably ever get.

Ronelle remembered how she and the funeral director just stood quietly side-by-side while three pallbearers tried to pry three hundred pounds of weeping widow off the casket.

Ronelle shifted the box of mail in her arms and pushed the memory aside as she stepped onto the town square. She wished she'd taken the dolly to haul the mail like Mr. Donavan, the postmaster, had suggested, but her pride wouldn't let her after she saw Chatty Jerry smiling at her. He was always telling Mr. Donavan how much harder delivering the mail was than sorting it in the back like she did. Jerry seemed to think that anyone who worked for "the service," as he called it, and didn't face the weather daily was a lower life form around the office.

The old postmaster usually ignored Jerry. Everyone knew Jerry would probably be taking his place in a year or two. Ronelle figured that would be about the time she got fired. Her father and Mr. Donavan had been friends. They'd started

working together when they both returned from Vietnam.
When her father became ill and suggested she start working
in the mailroom, Mr. Donavan had welcomed the idea. In
the years she'd worked for "the service," the postmaster had
sometimes been indifferent to her, but never unkind.

Chatty Jerry, however, only frowned at her now and then.
Once he commented that if he could palm off one house
to another postman, it would be Dallas Logan's place. He'd
said it just loud enough to make sure she heard.

Ronelle wasn't surprised that Jerry, along with half the
people in town, hated her mother. Most of the time she hated
her too. Dallas Logan never had a nice thing to say about anyone, including her only child. When Ronelle's father became
ill, he probably figured he was doing her a favor getting her
the job so she could be out of the house nine hours a day.

She'd watched her father manipulating Dallas until her
mother thought a job for their only daughter was her idea.
Over the years Dallas complained, but never suggested
Ronelle quit. After all, it was Dallas's idea and she never
saw herself as wrong.

In his will, her father left the house to his wife, but he'd
added that if the place was ever sold, half of the money
would go to Ronelle.

She shifted the box of mail again, glad to be out in the
cold, fresh air for a few minutes. Special deliveries were
rare this late, but she never minded making them. If they
were heavy, Mr. Donavan delivered them after Jerry came
in from his rounds, or he'd call one of the rural postmen
on his cell and have him circle by after making his route.

But today, the postmaster was complaining of heartburn
and Jerry was whining about his feet when he stopped by
for coffee, so that left Ronelle to walk the two blocks to
an old duplex just off Main. The Mission-style building
looked like it belonged on an old movie set from the fifties
and not in small-town Texas. The foot-thick walls had been
painted so many times that the corners looked like rings of
a tree. Green over rusty red, over brown, over dull orange.

Whenever she walked past the duplex, she half expected a cartoon character to jump out.

Only this time she wouldn't just walk by. She would stop to make a delivery. She felt like a real mailman. Correction— mailwoman.

She climbed up uneven steps beside a ramp and guessed Martin Winslow in 111B must be a very old man. She walked by his place twice a week to have lunch at the diner, but she had never seen him pick up his mail. In fact, she'd never seen anyone come or go from this house.

Moving around a line of long-dead plants, she knocked on the door, hoping no one would answer. She could leave the box and take her time walking back to the post office.

Somewhere from deep inside came a yell: "What do you want?"

Ronelle hesitated. The guy didn't sound too friendly. He also didn't sound like an old man. For a moment she thought this might be the kind of trap her mother was always warning her about. At twenty-seven, she was a little old to be sold into a child prostitution ring, but the kidnapping and torture openings could come at any age. Dallas Logan loved to tell her about all the terrible things that could happen out in the world. Their dinner conversation usually consisted of Dallas reading some tragedy in the paper and mumbling, "Just when I thought people couldn't get any worse, they surprise me."

"Mail," Ronelle stuttered out. No, that wasn't right. "Special delivery," she corrected.

"Come in. The door's unlocked," the unfriendly voice snapped.

She stared at the doorknob. People usually came to the door to receive their special deliveries. Maybe somewhere in the handbook she'd been given years ago there was a proper procedure.

"I said come in!"

She pushed the door with the corner of the box. B-movie slasher music began to play in her head.

Holding the box tightly, she shoved her way inside, telling herself she was a mailwoman and the mail always gets delivered. But if she saw any detached fingers hanging like Christmas lights or smelled blood, she planned to bolt. Her mother had told her that killers take trophies of their victims and leave buckets of blood when they kill. Dallas even told her that sometimes the smell of blood never leaves the scene of a crime.

Ronelle left the door ajar.

The place was warm—too warm, she thought—and dark, almost like a cave. But on the bright side, she didn't smell blood or see any body parts hanging around.

"Mail, Mr. Winslow," she managed to say as she took another step inside and let her eyes adjust to the lack of light.

"Set it on the hall table and close the door on your way out." The unfriendly voice didn't seem to be warming any.

Ronelle took another step forward. This was as close to an adventure as she'd had in years. When she was a child, once her father left for work, she was never out of her mother's sight. When he died, she became her mother's companion whenever she wasn't working, and even going for a walk around the block wasn't worth the tantrum her mother threw when she got back. Dallas Logan seemed to think giving birth came with a right of ownership. She would have insisted Ronelle quit work, but she claimed they needed the money. Dallas thought sacrificing her daughter to the workforce was far better than going into it herself.

Ronelle took another step into the shadows, knowing she'd never mention this to her mother.

A man sat behind a massive desk. His black hair fell without a curl or wave to his shoulders. Books lined the room, but there was no other furniture. All the windows had blinds, admitting the light in thin, knife-sized slices. The glow from the computer screen in front of him made his face ghostly white. He reminded her of the vampires her mother told her existed everywhere but West Texas. His face seemed all sharp lines and shadows.

He looked up with eyes so dark they could have been

black. "I told you to leave it on the table by the door. You deaf as well as poorly dressed?"

"You have to sign for it, Mr. Winslow," she whispered, wondering what was wrong with her clothes. She'd worn sweatshirts and baggy jeans all her adult life and no one had ever commented.

He shoved back violently from his desk and moved his wheelchair around the end. "Give it to me," he snapped. "I'll sign, then I want you out of here. I don't have time for interruptions or for someone gawking at me."

She managed to make her feet move enough to hand him a clipboard. When he snapped his fingers waiting for a pen, she realized she'd forgotten to bring one.

Before she could explain, he swore, rolled backward a foot and grabbed one off the desk. "Incompetent," he mumbled under his breath.

He looked down and scribbled his name so fast she was sure no one would be able to read it, then shoved the clipboard back toward her.

Ronelle stared. She'd never met anyone who seemed to dislike people more than she did. In a strange way, she found it comforting. This man wasn't going to ask questions or want to visit. He wanted to be alone. He was alone. She was just a walking bother come to irritate him.

"What are you looking at?" He glared at her.

"A cripple." She had said the first thing that came to mind.

She turned and ran.

When she pulled the door open, she dropped the clipboard, but she didn't care. She couldn't take the time to stop.

She was out the door and halfway back to the post office before she breathed. The feeling that she'd just stepped into a lion's den washed over her. She'd not only walked in, she'd pulled the lion's tail. She'd insulted him.

Slowing her steps, she relived every detail so she could tattoo it in her mind. How the house looked. How angry he sounded. How frightened she'd been. Tonight as her mother rambled on about every soap opera she'd seen that day, Ronelle would be thinking about her adventure. She'd be remembering Mr. Winslow with his dark, dark eyes and midnight hair.

She'd met the most frightening man she'd ever seen, and she'd lived. Now when her mother told her horrible stories of people being tortured, Ronelle would have a face to put on the demon. Martin Winslow. Hauntingly handsome.

She walked into the office a few minutes later with her head held a little higher than usual. Mr. Donavan and Jerry were sitting in the back drinking coffee and complaining about the weather.

Jerry greeted her for once. "I hear you went over to the Winslow place. I would have taken the box, even with my feet hurting, if I'd known that's where you were headed. He's a hard one, girl. I hope he didn't swear at you. They say he was a world-class skier before the accident. Now he's just one angry man. He wasn't rude to you, was he?"

Ronelle shook her head, but didn't look at him. She didn't want to share her one adventure with Jerry. She didn't even share the coffeepot with him since she'd seen him take a taste from his cup, then pour the coffee back into the pot so he could reheat it.

Mr. Donavan answered the phone and Jerry lowered his voice. "There's something wrong with that guy. I'll bet he hurt his head in the accident and will never be right. Kind of like our own Howard Hughes, if you know what I mean. Course, he's not rich or old and I don't think Hughes was in a wheelchair, but he might have been. After all no one saw him, you know. He just sat up in his rich apartment and ate M&Ms. I wouldn't be surprised if that's what Winslow lives on. Somebody told me Hughes wouldn't eat the red ones, or maybe it was the brown ones. If I wasn't eating a color it would be the blue ones. I've always wondered . . ."

Ronelle stopped listening. Jerry could talk mold into evacuating. She moved to her bench in the back. She could still see them, but they seemed to always forget she was there.

Someone came in front and Jerry ran, sore feet and all,

to help a customer. He loved doing what everyone knew was Mr. Donavan's job.

She watched as Donavan hung up the phone and stood shaking his head as if a few screws were loose at the neck. She expected him to go out front, but he walked to the back. Toward her.

Ronelle kept her head down as she worked. All she had were the postcards left to sort, and she always read them first.

"That call," Mr. Donavan began. "It was from Marty Winslow. He said you forgot the clipboard."

She nodded, waiting to hear that she was fired. She didn't need the job. In the years she'd worked she'd saved most of her income each month, but the thought of having to stay home all day with her mother was terrifying.

She looked up, trying to figure out what to say to save her job when Mr. Donavan scratched his head and added, "Strangest thing. Marty Winslow told me he doesn't want anyone but you delivering his mail. He says if I send someone else, he'll complain to the state office about how we're discriminating against the handicapped."

Ronelle didn't even know there was a state office for complaints. She guessed neither did Marty Winslow. She also wasn't sure who he was thinking of as handicapped, her or him.

The postmaster glanced in the direction Jerry's voice was coming from. He seemed to be giving an in-depth weather report to someone on the other side of the counter. "Winslow is a man who likes his solitude. I can see why he'd want you making the deliveries and not Jerry." He let out a long breath. "So, if you don't mind, Ronelle, starting tomorrow you'll have a route of one house. You can stay in the back the rest of the time and go deliver his mail when it suits you. If you want to do it during your lunchtime, I'll allow you an extra fifteen minutes for lunch. Fair enough?"

Ronelle didn't raise her head, but she whispered, "I'll do it during my regular lunchtime." She usually came back early anyway.

"All right."

"Do I get a jacket?" she said as he turned away.

Mr. Donavan barked a laugh. "Sure. I got one in the back that'll fit you pretty good. Only remember, when you're wearing it you're representing the U.S. Mail. If someone stops you and asks you a question, you got to answer them. You can't just put your head down and keep on walking."

Ronelle nodded.

He stopped at the door and looked back at her. "Your dad would be proud of you," he said, then walked away.

She fought down a lump in her throat. No one had ever been proud of her. Dallas had told her all her life that her father was disappointed she wasn't a son, and she was disappointed because, to her way of thinking, Ronelle wasn't much of a daughter. Ronelle asked her mother once why they hadn't had more children. Dallas simply answered, "It wasn't worth the trouble."

That night, alone in her room next to her mother's, she thought of Marty Winslow and wondered why he'd asked that she be the only one to deliver his mail. Maybe he hated Jerry? Maybe he wanted to torture her? Maybe he recognized someone like himself?

When she'd been a child, she'd often thought that she must be an alien dropped off by accident here in Harmony. By the time she was five, she knew she wasn't like others, but was the man behind the huge desk today anything like her? In all of her life she'd never met someone of her species.

Tomorrow, when she delivered his mail, she planned to find out.

Chapter 3

❧❦

MARTHA Q PATTERSON SAT ON HER FRONT PORCH AT WIN-
ter's Inn Bed-and-Breakfast and decided she was bored. In
all the fifty-five years of her life, she'd never been bored.
From her late teens through her thirties, when she was wild,
she was always out partying every night and sleeping late
every morning. In fact, Martha didn't even remember ever
being awake in the A.M. until her fortieth birthday.

On that particular birthday, she had awakened early to
have time to dress for a day of shopping. Her sixth husband, Oliver Hannon, never bought her presents, so she
was more than happy to surprise him with the bill for a
nice gift every holiday along with surprise gifts for no reason scattered through the year. He had enough money to
afford expensive gifts, and she figured just having a wife
twenty years younger should keep him happy.

That morning she was feeling old and decided to drop by Oliver's work at the accounting firm he'd founded with his two bean-counting brothers. When the Hannons had been young men, they'd all three worked hard, but now in their sixties, they mostly just supervised and played golf. As an accountant, Oliver rarely had anyone in his office until March when folks started worrying about taxes, so he was usually free to take her to lunch on the very rare occasion she managed to get there before one.

Martha Q walked in on him with his secretary, and they didn't look to be accounting for anything including all their clothes. Oliver just stood there with one sock on and his shirt unbuttoned, asking where she wanted to go to lunch. It wouldn't have been so devastating, but the secretary was in her fifties and flat-chested. Martha was humiliated.

She'd divorced Oliver within months, taking half his money and all his socks when she left. With nowhere to go, she decided to drop by Harmony for a visit with husband number two.

Bobby Earl Patterson was the only one in the line of men who'd slept on the left side of her whom she still talked to, mostly because he fixed her car for free whenever she asked. He'd also been the only one without money. Which explained their separation. Martha Q was a woman used to being taken care of, and changing the oil from time to time just wasn't enough.

When she found Bobby Earl ill, Martha Q told herself her big heart wouldn't let him die alone, so she married him again. In truth, she loved him, but then she'd loved them all in one way or the other. Bobby Earl used to tell folks he was her twenty-seventh husband since he was both her second and her seventh.

She drove him to doctors and hospitals as cancer slowly ate away at him. They laughed about her driving and watched old movies together at night while she gained weight and he lost it. She helped him with his tire and lube business, finding she had a knack for numbers. As he seemed to grow older before her eyes, he never failed to tell her how beautiful she was, and that helped pass the time.

When Bobby Earl died, Martha Q decided to give up men and open a bed-and-breakfast. She had a good head for business and had spent a great deal of her life in bed, but knew nothing about breakfast. So she'd opened Winter's Inn and hired Mrs. Biggs, the best cook in Harmony.

Everything had been wonderful in Martha Q's world until Mrs. Biggs's two big strapping grandsons came to stay with her a few years ago. One was eighteen at the time, so he got a job in construction, but the other was still in high school and, judging from the amount of effort he was putting out, Border Biggs might be in high school for decades.

Since Martha Q didn't want Mrs. Biggs to leave, and no one in town in their right mind would rent a place to an eighteen-year-old thug and his pre-prison little brother, Martha Q decided to buy a duplex down the street from the inn. The thugs were out of her hair and her kitchen, Mrs. Biggs had somewhere to go besides the cemetery during her afternoons off, and Martha Q could take her naps in peace.

To her surprise, the other half of the duplex rented right away to a man in his thirties who'd been in a bad skiing accident. He was grouchy and altogether unpleasant, but he paid his rent on time and that was all that Martha Q cared about. To her shock, he seemed to get along with the Biggs boys. At least she thought he did. He hadn't complained.

Which was good, but left Martha Q bored. Everything in her life was running too smoothly. She'd lived in the chaos of juggling lovers and husbands as well as hair appointments all her life. Only now, she hadn't been named in a court document in years. Something just didn't feel right.

She watched as Border Biggs, the younger of Mrs. Biggs's grandsons, and one of his worthless, long-haired friends climbed out of a pickup and began raking the last of the dead leaves.

"Morning," the dark-haired friend waved. "I'm Beau Yates."

"I don't care who you are. It's about time you two got over here," Martha Q yelled back. "If you'd waited any longer, winter would be over and the grass would be fighting its way through the dead leaves."

"It's only been a week since you called," the long-haired smart aleck said with a smile. He was shorter and maybe a little younger than Border, but then everyone was shorter than the Biggs boys.

Martha Q considered how men were often built like cars. Some long and lean like sports cars, some strong and hard-working like pickups, and some, like the Biggs brothers, reminded her of diesel trucks—big, loud, and smelly.

Maybe the long-haired kid hadn't reached his full growth, even though he looked eighteen. She couldn't tell what he'd become. Maybe a trailer park heartbreaker. Maybe a cop. He had that kind of stance that said he thought he was somebody important even if he hadn't grown into his own ego yet.

"Don't talk to her, Beau," Border whispered under his breath. "Every male who ever did is dead."

"I heard that," Martha Q snapped. "It's comments like that that make me like you slightly less than I do dogs, and I hate dogs."

The long-haired one went to work, but Border leaned against his rake. "You know, Mrs. Q, you're starting to grow on me."

"I am not. And don't call me Mrs. Q. Martha Q is my first name, not my last initial."

Border thought about it a few seconds and asked, "What's your middle name? Period?"

"None of your business," she said.

Border grinned. "Must take a long time to write Mrs. Martha Q None-of-your-business. If you married old-what's-his-name, your name wouldn't fit on any driver's license."

Martha Q stood, then cursed as the porch swing hit her just behind her chubby knees. She made it halfway to the door before she added, "You think you're funny, but your jokes aren't any better than your playing on that guitar.

Maybe you'd be wise to stay off every stage you pass. Some crowd might try to kill you between sets."

"What's wrong with my playing?" Border was no longer smiling.

"Nothing a few lessons wouldn't help."

"I can't afford lessons." Border frowned.

Martha Q had enough of being nice. "Well, maybe if you got to work you'd earn that twenty dollars waiting for you when the leaves are gone and then you could take one lesson. You're at that magic spot where any practicing you do would have to help."

Border got the point. He went to work with no more than a growl in response.

Martha Q waddled to her room and changed out of her purple jogging suit into her best business clothes. She had to think of something to do besides arguing with idiots. She was too old to go dancing, too young for bingo, but somewhere she believed adventure was still calling her name.

"What's the matter, Mrs. Patterson? Something wrong?" the young housekeeper asked as Martha Q came down the stairs.

"What makes you think something is wrong, Lori?"

"Well, ma'am, you always sit on the porch till noon. Then you eat the lunch Mrs. Biggs sets out for you, then you take a nap." The housekeeper had the nerve to look proud of herself.

"I have to go out." Martha Q straightened as she reached for her coat. "In fact, unless I find something interesting to pass the time, I'm going over to the Wright Funeral Home and plan my funeral. I might as well die if all I can think of to do is sit on the porch and eat between sleeping."

Lori wasn't hired for her cleaning skills, but more accurately because she never argued. "Yes, Mrs. Patterson, that sounds like a plan."

Martha Q didn't bother to turn around. She decided she'd stop off and eat lunch with her lawyer, then have her fortune told at the bookstore. If her lifeline was up, she might as well blow all she could on a casket.

Twenty minutes later when she got to the office of Elizabeth Matheson Leary, Attorney-at-Law, the door was locked. Liz had redecorated her office and carpeted the hallway, but the place still needed something.

She smiled, thinking a lawyer in a law office would be a nice touch. Two years ago she'd been Elizabeth's first client and the office furniture wouldn't sell in a yard sale, but Liz had been so excited about being a lawyer that no one who dropped by noticed the furniture.

Martha Q swore as she stomped down the hallway. She'd worn her good shoes and now she'd have to go all the way down the stairs without having a chance to rest. Liz had promised she was going to work until her baby came. "Must be one of her doctor's visits or something," Martha Q mumbled as she headed down the stairs.

Having never had children, she didn't see much of a need for them. Kids were everywhere in abundance. Just go in Walmart day or night and you could hear a half dozen screaming, but lawyers, good ones like Elizabeth Matheson Leary, were hard to find. Next thing Martha Q expected was for Elizabeth to quit and start living out there in the canyon with that crazy husband of hers who wrote graphic novels. He always looked at Martha Q as if he half expected her to turn into a bug or something. He might be one hunk of a man, but the ink stains on his hands bothered her more than the scar along his jawline. Every woman in town thought he was a complicated man, but Martha Q considered that an oxymoron.

"What kind of way is that to make a living?" Martha Q said to herself as she reached the bottom of the stairs. "A grown man drawing superheroes and monsters all day."

"Excuse me, ma'am, were you talking to me?" a young man in a suit asked as he started up the stairs. He was slim, with light brown hair and dimples. The suit fit him as if it were tailor made.

Martha Q had always been a sucker for dimples, but today she was working on a bad mood and didn't want to be interrupted.

"No," she snapped, "I was talking to myself for lack of

any other intelligent conversation. It should be a crime for a lawyer to post business hours and then not be there."

The young man smiled. "I agree. When a person needs a lawyer, they need a lawyer. That's why I became one."

She looked at him then, really looked. He was tall, but not too tall. Maybe a touch over six feet. She wouldn't call him handsome, but he did have a way about him when he smiled. He was the kind of man who wasn't overly worried about his appearance; his hair was windblown and the sleeves of his wrinkled dress shirt were a bit too long for his suit jacket. He wasn't afraid to face people straight on, and he had nice hands, tanned and strong as they gripped an old leather briefcase.

She knew, from her vast experience, that he had the marks of a good lover.

Too bad she was twice his age and probably double his weight. Otherwise she would have taken him on as a project and moved him from good to great in the lover category.

He offered his hand. "Name's Rick Matheson. I'm Liz's cousin. I haven't taken the bar yet, but I've finished my classwork. If you just need advice on something, Mrs. Patterson, I'll do what I can. No fee involved, of course."

"So you're an almost-lawyer?" She wasn't surprised he knew who she was. She considered herself a legend in this town.

He smiled that warm smile again. "Yeah. Hopefully by the time Liz and Gabe's babies come I can take over for her for a while. I'm renting the office across the hall. I hope to intern for a year, and who knows, maybe one day be her partner."

"Babies?"

"Yes, ma'am. They're having twins. Figured everyone in town had heard by now."

Martha Q frowned. "Like there aren't enough Mathesons in this town already."

Rick laughed. "Right. My mother always says that if the other two founding families had reproduced as fast as the Mathesons, Harmony would have double the population by now. Only I guess the babies will be Learys, not Mathe-sons."

Martha Q stared at him. She liked him well enough and she was hungry, so she said, "What's your hourly rate?"

"I can't really charge until I pass the bar."

"Good." She linked her arm in his. "I'll buy you lunch and you'll give me your not-so-professional advice. Does that sound fair? What do you want for lunch?"

"Fair enough, Mrs. Patterson, and I like steak."

She grinned. "You'll make a good lawyer, boy, and call me Martha Q. I've learned never to get too attached to last names."

Chapter 4

TYLER WRIGHT DROVE HOME FROM THE AIRPORT WITH HIS Kate silent beside him. He had the feeling she was holding herself together with army starch and willpower. In all the time he'd known her, he'd never seen her like this. Sometimes he saw the major in her, sometimes the strong woman who'd made it alone in the world all her adult life, but never this.

He went straight to the funeral home and led her through the side entrance. They took the elevator up to his rooms above the business without anyone seeing them. The warm apartment was bigger than most homes in town. A blending of ancient furnishings with modern updating of carpets and tapestries, it seemed to welcome them in like an old friend in a new dress. He left her to freshen up while he went down to ask Willamina, his housekeeper, to fix a light lunch for two.

Instinct told him Kate wouldn't want to see anyone.

The old housekeeper acted like she didn't hear when he

made his request. He should have known by now that her hearing never returned until after *The Bold and the Beautiful* was over. Tyler went into the kitchen and warmed up a can of soup while he made two ham sandwiches. He had no idea if Kate would eat them, but food had always been comforting in his life.

When he returned to his apartment, he expected to find her in his large living room, or maybe on the tiny back balcony he loved in winter because it was sheltered on three sides from the wind but still caught the morning sun. When she'd visited a few times she'd said she liked both the areas. She'd even suggested he have real plants around. He didn't have the heart to tell her that he worked with flowers all day and really preferred not to see them at night.

He set the tray down on the coffee table, but Kate wasn't anywhere to be seen. He walked through the apartment that had once been big enough to house a family. The guest bathroom door was open, but she wasn't there or in the tiny kitchen area he'd never used. Finally, he wandered down to his bedroom, guessing that she'd left. From his front door she could walk anywhere in town within minutes. Maybe she'd been embarrassed at letting him see her near tears and she'd decided to walk over to the inn alone.

Tyler thought he might as well get dressed in his business suit and go downstairs to work. Kate would call him later, or he'd drop by the inn to see if she wanted to go to dinner. If she needed space, he would give her that.

When he reached his bedroom door, he froze.

The lights were off in his room, the curtains drawn, but he saw her on the bed. She'd removed her coat and shoes. She lay curled up around one of his pillows almost like a child. The border collie he called Little Lady rested at her feet. Both looked sound asleep.

"Kate?" he whispered.

She didn't answer.

He had no idea what to do. After watching her for a few minutes, he knew he had to do something, but he'd never had a woman crawl into his bed. His entire experience with women, other than casual dating, consisted of three short-lived romances in college involving lots of petting with none ending in bed and one one-night stand with a woman he met at a party. That ended in bed, leaving only regrets at dawn.

Only this wasn't a fling. This was Kate. His Kate. The woman he'd been friends with for years. The only woman who'd ever truly mattered to him. Here she was, broken by something she couldn't or wouldn't talk about. He wanted to know all about what had happened. He wanted to make it better for her. But she hadn't told him. Hadn't even talked to him.

Tyler frowned, then realized what she *had* done. She'd come home to him. Broken or hurt or sad didn't matter. She'd come home to him.

He walked back through the apartment to the door that led to a small corridor that held the stairs and the elevator. The door between his apartment and the corridor hadn't been closed in years. Hinges creaked as he pushed it across the carpet. He closed it, then shoved the bolt. No one from below could now reach the apartment.

By the time he'd backtracked to his bedroom, he'd removed his jacket. He slipped off his shoes and lifted the throw from one of the chairs by the windows. Without a sound, he climbed into bed beside Kate, pulled her back gently against his heart, and slowed his breathing to match hers.

He was surprised how small she seemed in his arms . . . and how right she felt.

Tyler held her for over an hour before he heard the low chime in the living area telling him someone had just entered the front door downstairs. Everyone who worked for him came in the side or the back. When the front door opened, sending a chime to all the nonpublic areas of the building, they knew it was business. This was Wednesday, a workday, and Tyler never missed work.

As carefully as he could, he slipped from her side. Pulling the blanket over her shoulders, he leaned and kissed her cheek. Then, silently, he pulled on his suit jacket and looped a tie around his neck. The dog waited for him at the door. Little Lady always responded to the chime. The dog must think of herself as the official greeter.

"I'm hurrying," he said as he opened the door and stepped into the corridor. By the time they reached the first floor, Tyler had tied his tie and looked respectable and sober. Just as a funeral director should look.

But inside, he couldn't stop smiling.

He went through all the motions of visiting with the children of Ida Louise Hudson. Yes, they wanted their mother's body moved from a nursing home in California to Harmony to be buried. No, they couldn't stay for a graveside, but would he have a small service just in case someone came? After all, she'd been born and married in Harmony. Someone might remember her. Yes, a simple spray of flowers and could he take care of having her death recorded on the headstone beside their father and would he mail a copy of the death certificate, along with the bill, to each?

In less than an hour all the plans were made and Tyler walked Ida Louise's children, all in their fifties he guessed, to the front steps. They each walked to their individual cars without hugging or a single tear falling and drove off. He had a feeling that Ida's family had just shattered. The Hudson children would never get together again.

When he walked back in, Calvin, one of two embalmers who worked mostly in the basement, was waiting for him.

Tyler sighed. "You guessed right about this one," he said. "When they called, I thought they might stay at least the night. One came in from Dallas, you know, another from Arkansas. Both long drives to make twice in one day. But they only want us to take care of it."

Calvin shrugged. "That's what we do, Mr. Wright." Calvin might be ten years older than Tyler, but he'd called his boss Mr. since the day Tyler's father died.

Tyler smiled. "We do. Don't have the grave dug until we know what flight she'll be coming in on. As soon as she's back home, I'll phone the minister. Maybe we can schedule the graveside at dawn tomorrow. It'll be cold, but I think she might like that."

"Which minister?"

"I asked the family that and you know what they said?"

Calvin shook his head.

"They said it didn't matter," Tyler answered. "I thought I'd call that young Methodist pastor out on North Road. He could use the money, and he'll do a nice job even if it'll only be you and me standing beside him."

Calvin agreed with his choice. "I noticed a car parked at the back gate of the cemetery last night. You want me to call the sheriff and have her check it out?"

Tyler waved the idea aside. Drunks looking for a quiet place to sleep it off sometimes thought the cemetery would be a quiet spot. "I'll check it when I lock up tonight. Don't worry about it."

Calvin turned and headed toward the back. Since they saw each other several times a day, he and Tyler had long ago given up bothering with hello or good-bye.

Tyler was suddenly in a hurry to be upstairs. He took the stairs this time, not wanting to be away from Kate a moment longer than necessary.

He felt something was wrong the moment he turned the corner in his hallway and noticed his bedroom light was on.

The pillows had been replaced. The throw tossed back in the chair by the window.

Kate had gone.

At first he didn't see the business card lying on the bed, and then he had a hard time focusing enough to read.

Three words allowed him to breathe. *Dinner at Inn?*

He ran his thumb over the writing, wishing she'd signed it, or, better yet, addressed it to *dear one*. She'd called him that once . . . only once.

Chapter 5

TRUMAN FARM ON LONE OAK ROAD

THE APPLE ORCHARD ALWAYS FASCINATED REAGAN TRU-
man in the winter months. Her uncle Jeremiah told her once
that his father had started it back before the first World War.
Now, a hundred years later, half the apple jelly in town and
most of the apple pies came from Truman apples. But it
wasn't the fruit or the trees that drew Reagan. The shadows
pulled her near like long fingers. In the summer all grew
green and beautiful, but when the weather turned cold the
bare branches crossed over one another like a framed wonderland in blacks and grays, and she had to come close.

Some people might love the spring, some the summer
or even the fall, but for Reagan her heart beat strongest in
winter. She loved the raging storms and the silent snow.
She loved her land as if she'd been born to it.

The orchard bordered Lone Oak Road on one side and
the Matheson Ranch on the other. As shadows lengthened

she walked and enjoyed her time alone. Somehow, Reagan felt she belonged here in this unfinished world with its beginnings and endings mixing together without forming a complete canopy. Her whole life seemed like that. Starts and stops forming like ribs around a body lean of meat.

Smiling, she remembered how her uncle always said she needed to grow roots. At sixteen she'd had nothing, been nothing but a runaway with no place to run to. Now, at twenty, Reagan felt like her very blood pumped through this land . . . her land. She'd poured her sweat into it along with her love. She'd even risked her life fighting a prairie fire to save this farm. It was as much a part of her as she was of it. She felt like her adopted uncle did—she'd never sell, never.

After a deep breath, she turned, knowing it was time to get back to the house. Uncle Jeremiah was probably already in the kitchen. He liked to watch her cook, though he'd grown so thin she wasn't sure he ever ate more than a few bites. His mind was still sharp, but his body was failing him. Reagan did all she could, taking over the running of the farm and the maintenance of his established orchard and her new one. Hank Matheson, the rancher next door, often told her she was doing too much. But how much was too much to give an old man who'd taken her in as his own when no one else in the world wanted her?

She'd hired a couple who were both nurses and moved them in upstairs. Foster took care of Uncle Jeremiah, doing all the things her uncle wouldn't allow her to help with, and Cindy, Foster's wife, monitored the old man's medicines. To Reagan's surprise, her uncle didn't seem to mind having them around. After a few days, he even stopped telling Foster that being a nurse wasn't a good job for a man.

As she walked toward the little golf cart–sized truck she used on the trails between the fruit trees, Reagan was mentally planning dinner when her cell phone rang.

She slid behind the wheel and flipped the phone open.

"Hi, Rea," came Noah's familiar voice. "You asleep yet?"

She laughed. "It's not even dark, Preacher, what time zone are you in and how much have you been drinking?"

"I'm in North Carolina, I think. I didn't win any money the last ride." She heard his long exhale of breath. "The rodeos aren't much fun when you don't make the eight seconds."

She didn't miss that he hadn't answered the second question. More and more when Noah called from the road, she had a feeling he wasn't sober. Maybe he only got homesick when he drank. Maybe he needed the whiskey to give him enough courage to talk about going on. Somewhere the boy she'd met in high school had lost his big dreams, and in so doing he'd lost himself.

His easy laugh came over the phone. "What are you up to, Rea? No. Let me guess. Sitting in the yard with your uncle waiting for the sunset, or maybe walking in that forest you call an orchard. One of these days you'll fall over a tree root and we won't find your bones until spring."

"You know me pretty well," she said, figuring he knew her better than anyone else alive. "You planning on making it home before spring?"

"Sorry, Rea, I don't think so, but I'll call. I promise. No matter where I am, I'll call. There's always a rodeo somewhere, and as long as I've got the gas and the fee, I'll be riding."

He was the first real friend she'd ever had. He'd been the first boy to kiss her, her first date, her first heartbreak. "Take care of yourself, Preacher."

He laughed without much humor. "No one on the circuit calls me that anymore."

They'd called him Preacher because when he rode in high school rodeos, the announcers used to say he got religion when he climbed on a thousand pounds of mean muscle. Now, four years later, Reagan knew he'd lost his religion along with the joy he had for the sport. Now he rode like it was an addiction. Only even when he won, she had a feeling the money never made it to the bank.

"Why don't you come home, Noah?" she asked, as she did almost every time he called.

"I'll think about it," he said, but his words didn't ring

true. "Got to go, it's my time to drive. I'll talk to you again soon. I promise. Good night, Rea."

Reagan closed the phone. She hadn't told him what was happening in Harmony or in her life. She had a feeling he didn't care. Even if she'd said she needed him right now, he wouldn't come, and if he promised tonight, he'd only break his word come morning.

They'd been best friends in high school, talked every night on the phone, drove all over the panhandle so he could ride in every rodeo they heard about. Then his father thought he was good enough to turn pro and Noah gave up his plans for college. The first year, he barely made enough in prize money to stay on the road. The second year he told her it looked like he might break a hundred thousand, enough to start his herd on his small ranch. But halfway through, Noah got hurt again. This time when the doctors patched him up, they seemed to have left out his love for the sport.

Noah McAllen was on a merry-go-round, not with painted wooden ponies but with huge angry bulls, and he couldn't seem to find the way off the ride.

Reagan leaned her head on her arms atop the steering wheel and cried. She feared for Noah that the ride wouldn't stop until one bull, one night, killed him.

NOAH FLIPPED HIS PHONE CLOSED AS HE WALKED AROUND his pickup, now so dirty he couldn't even tell what color it was. He slipped into the driver's seat as his buddy slid across and began building his nest for the night.

"Just head west," Don grumbled, already sounding half asleep. "We'll be lucky to make it to where we turn south by noon tomorrow. If you get sleepy, wake me."

Noah knew the routine, but he let Don ramble. They both knew they probably wouldn't be friends if it weren't for the rodeo. Though they both rode bulls, they did it for different reasons. Noah saw it as a fast way to make money,

and he had long ago become addicted to the thrill of adrenaline that jolted through his body every time he climbed
on. Don, on the other hand, rode for the thrill that surrounded the game. The wild unpredictability, the giggles of
the girls when bull riders entered a bar, the flash of camera
lights when he won. He didn't care for the sport; he liked
the parade.

Noah let Don talk himself to sleep; for once he didn't
really want to talk about what they'd face tomorrow. He just
wanted to drive and think of Reagan. He hadn't seen her in
months, and then their last words had been yelled at each
other. He'd waited two weeks before he called. He'd forgotten what they'd been arguing about and she didn't mention it.

He drove through the night, trying to remember exactly
what she looked like. Her curly red hair that wrapped around
his fingers. Her green eyes that could cut through all his
bullshit with one look. Her voice had sounded older somehow tonight. Part of him still saw her as that frightened new
kid at a school where everyone else knew one another.

She wasn't his girlfriend then or now. Maybe she never
would be. They'd grown apart, he told himself, like people
do. He'd seen best friends in high school go away to different colleges and a year later struggle to keep a conversation
going over coffee.

She was just a friend, he reminded himself. Only once
in Oklahoma City after the rodeo, the girl he was with said
he'd called her Rea when they made love.

Noah shook his head, figuring that could mean one of
two things. Either he'd have to try to get along with Reagan
and marry her, or he'd have to learn to keep his mouth shut
when the lights went out.

Chapter 6

❦

SNOW BEGAN TUMBLING DOWN IN HARMONY BEFORE dawn. Ronelle Logan made it to work, but Marty Winslow received no mail for her to deliver. On Friday the sun came back out, warming away the snow from the walks, but Marty Winslow still had no mail. She checked his box three times, hoping she'd overlooked something. The new coat had been hanging by the restroom door for two days.

Ronelle Logan felt like an inmate waiting on death row. Every morning she ate what she feared might be her last meal and waited.

She didn't know whether to thank him for not telling the postmaster that she'd called him a cripple or to worry that he might somehow make her life more miserable than it already was. Both days she ate a candy bar for lunch and worked on her online course instead of going home or over to the diner.

About three, the few special deliveries came in. Ronelle waited in the back, standing so she could see Mr. Donavan through the door as he looked them over.

"Ronelle," he yelled. "You'd better get that new coat on. You've got a letter that needs delivering."

She pulled the blue wool coat on and wished she had armor and a few weapons to stuff beneath its folds. She had a feeling she was going into battle. She looped her father's old satchel over her head so the leather crossed her chest.

Mr. Donavan handed her three envelopes when she walked to the front. "Might as well drop these two off at the fire station. It's not much out of your way."

As she stuffed the mail in the satchel, he added, "That your father's old bag?"

She nodded and left without a word.

The fire station was half a block farther than Winslow's place, but she went there first. She told herself she did it just in case he frightened her again and she had to run back to the post office.

No one was at the fire station except Bob McNabb. She'd seen him around town and knew he was married to Stella, who worked part time at the funeral home. Everyone in Harmony was interconnected like some kind of giant spiderweb.

Old Bob took the envelopes from her and said thanks without asking any questions, then went back to setting up chairs in one of the bays.

Ronelle walked away, thinking delivering the mail wasn't as hard as she thought it might be. She was almost to the duplex where Winslow lived when she saw a man sitting on a huge motorcycle out front.

He was big, over six feet, overweight, and covered in black leather. When he glanced in her direction, she saw he wasn't old, still in his teens. He looked hard, though. The kind of hard that opened fire in a public building . . . like a post office.

She looked away, focusing on the tattoos on his knuckles. Her mother told her once that men get knuckle tattoos in prison. This guy looked too young to be an ex-con, but he did have tattoos.

While she was trying to figure out if he was casing out the neighborhood to rob or just planning to start a random killing spree, he yelled, "Winslow, you got mail!"

"Thanks, Border, tell her to bring it on in."

The guy raised an eyebrow at her and nodded toward the door.

Ronelle almost ran up the steps and into the house. This Border was more frightening than the man in the wheelchair. A dragon guarding the entrance to an ogre's cave.

She walked into the room, empty except for the desk and of course the man behind it.

She laid down the mail.

"Thanks," he said, without looking up.

She nodded and took a step backward.

Now he lifted his head and looked her straight in the eyes. "I'm not going to bite you, you know." A corner of his mouth lifted. "At least until I know you better."

She backed toward the door without breathing. *Was he kidding?* Turning, she bolted, far more afraid of the honesty in his eyes than anything her imagination could dream up. People never saw her, not really, and they never, *never*, teased her.

The guy on the motorcycle was gone. Ronelle hurried back to the post office, trying to shake the feeling that Marty Winslow was still watching her.

When she entered the back of the office, she took off her blue coat and worked an hour before slipping into her old black-gray coat.

Jerry poked his head into the back room where she stood pulling on her gloves. "Got a few wild plans this weekend, Ronelle. I think there's a dance over at Buffalo's tomorrow night . . . live music." He laughed like he was the only one who caught the joke. "You could pick yourself up a fellow."

"Leave her alone," Mr. Donavan yelled.

"I'm not doing anything but talking. She hasn't said ten words to me since she came here." Jerry acted like he was counting on his fingers. "Let's see, that comes out to about one word a year."

"She doesn't have to talk to you." Donavan pulled on his coat. "Besides, it seems to me you talk enough for all of us around the place."

Jerry shrugged. "Sorry, Ronelle, you do what you want to do."

She passed him without a word and left. She had to act exactly the same, she decided, or her mother would notice and ask questions. No one could know that Marty Winslow had seen her, really seen her. Maybe it wouldn't matter to anyone, not even him, but for her the world had shifted and might never be the same again.

Chapter 7

FRIDAY
FEBRUARY 19
LEARY LAW OFFICE

REAGAN TRUMAN SAT IN ELIZABETH LEARY'S OFFICE AND
fought back tears. For the past three months she'd been living
in limbo. Meals, even sleep lost their rhythm as she moved
through the days and nights like the sole passenger on a
never-ending train ride. Thanksgiving, Christmas, even her
twentieth birthday had come and gone with her not really
paying much attention.

The only relative she had, her uncle Jeremiah Truman,
had suffered his fourth heart attack in early October. He
was leaving her, not all at once, but an inch at a time. A
week before his ninetieth birthday he almost left her in the
night while she wasn't watching.

Slowly he'd recovered—maybe, she reasoned, simply
because God knew she wasn't ready to let him go. She

had no memory of her parents, no person who'd loved her before him. No one in the world had even loved her until Jeremiah Truman.

This morning, while tears floated in her eyes, he'd told her to go see the lawyer. There were papers to be signed, he'd insisted. Reagan knew the old man was taking care of her even as she tried to help him.

Foster Garrison was looking after him while she was in town. Foster had been a medic in the army twenty years before and recently lost his job at a clinic because of cutbacks. His wife was picking up shifts now and then at the hospital, but they needed the money Reagan paid.

Uncle Jeremiah's harsh manner seemed to suit Foster fine. He didn't waste any words babying the old man or bother listening when Jeremiah fired him at least once a week. Foster's wife, Cindy, had a kind heart and won the old man over with her ginger-apple pancakes.

Reagan felt like they melted into the house as if they'd always been there. She enjoyed the company and loved knowing Uncle Jeremiah was in good hands when she had to leave the house.

When Jeremiah came home, weak and tired, Reagan moved her desk into the front parlor beside his bed, and moved her bed into what had been a study downstairs. While he napped in the afternoons, she worked on her homework from the classes she took a few nights a week at Clifton College. She spent the mornings running the business, the afternoons studying, and the nights worrying about what would happen when he left her.

Every day when he woke he'd grin as if pleased to be alive and back on his land, and then he'd complain that she should be out with people her age and not watching over him like a hawk.

She'd shake her head. "I'm right where I want to be. After all this time, you're not thinking about kicking me out, are you?"

He'd smile then, and she knew they were both remembering when she'd been sixteen and he found her sleeping in the hammock in his yard. He'd offered her breakfast and ended up taking her in to raise. No one in town knew he wasn't her real uncle.

On her eighteenth birthday he'd planted a second group of apple trees in the west field behind the house. He called it the pie orchard and said it would provide apples for more pies than she could ever bake. He'd also had her name legally changed to Truman and the farm transferred to her. His way of telling her that it would always be hers. For a child who'd grown up without ever having a home, he'd given her the world.

When she'd been little and foster parents took her in, she'd believed that maybe, just maybe, this time they'd want her forever. But they never did. Jeremiah had been the first to see the value in her. He complained about everything under the sun—but her. If he wanted her to see the lawyer, she'd see Elizabeth Leary.

The door to the office opened and a very pregnant Liz Leary waddled in. Reagan had always thought she was beautiful, but now Liz seemed to glow, and with her large middle she could understand why Jeremiah thought it couldn't wait.

Liz circled to her desk. "Thanks for seeing me, Reagan. I know it was hard for you to leave your uncle, but as you can see, I may not be in the office long."

"How's that husband of yours holding up?" Reagan asked, not wanting to be reminded of how frail Jeremiah was right now. People who never spoke to her were stopping her on the street and in the grocery to ask about him. She'd rather hear about how Gabe, Liz's husband, was doing. Reagan thought of him as her guardian angel. He'd saved her life one night.

Everyone knew the little lawyer's husband had gone nuts since he found out he was going to be a father. If Gabriel Leary could, he'd build a ten-foot fence around his property and never let anyone in.

"He's still adjusting to the idea of two babies." She

laughed. "Once, I asked Gabe if he liked kids and his answer was, 'I don't know any.' Since I've been pregnant I realize he has no idea what to do with children, and babies frighten him. The best way I can think to describe it is, he seems to be preparing for an alien invasion. I don't dare tell him I want lots of kids; he's already begging his friend Denver to take a week off and help him knock the wall of the nursery out so they can double it. Then I reminded him my sister Claire would want to paint it and he reconsidered."

"Maybe give him time to get used to these two babies." Reagan winked. "I'm not sure he'll ever get used to having your famous sister Claire around. She still painting those strange paintings?"

"That's another problem for another day."

Liz might be in her thirties and Reagan had just stepped into her twenties, but Reagan felt certain they'd be friends for years to come. Even pregnant, Liz, with her blond hair and green eyes, looked like a china doll, while Reagan, with her wild rust-colored curls and old jeans, looked like a dry land farmer on hard times. Still, there was a bond between them.

Liz nodded, silently asking permission to begin, as she opened a thick file on her desk. Her face grew serious, and Reagan knew the time for chatting was over.

"Your uncle asked me to inform you of a few facts. He seems to think it might have some bearing on decisions you have to make in the future."

Reagan turned her head toward the long windows in the office. Jeremiah would say he was just facing facts, but for her, she wished she could face the future when it arrived. Evidently, he wasn't giving her that choice.

"I know the land is valuable and we both know I'll never sell." Reagan wanted to say it because she knew the people of Harmony were probably already talking about what the Truman kid would do after her uncle was gone. The founding families—the Mathesons, the McAllens, and the Trumans—never sold land unless they had to, but would the girl be able to make enough to keep the place going after the old man died?

Liz grinned. "Never is a long time."

Reagan shrugged. "I've got old bonds in the safe-deposit box that will pay the taxes for years. Even if I don't make a dime on the apples, I could live."

"Reagan, stop worrying about bad times and listen to the three things he wanted you to know about while he's still alive to answer any questions."

Reagan straightened and waited.

The lawyer began. "He called me the night before he was released from the hospital. He asked me to draw up an airtight will for him. After he passes, he wants no one thinking they have a claim to the farm but you."

Reagan understood.

"Second," Liz continued, "he wants you to cash in a few of those bonds and do some good. He decided he wants to be around to see what he can do to help the people of Harmony, but he doesn't want anyone to know where the money comes from. He asked me to give you a list of ideas, but it's your decision."

Reagan sat back. "I can't wait for number three."

Liz didn't smile this time. "I argued with him over the third thing he wanted to tell you, but he insisted you know. When he had your name changed before you turned eighteen, he hired an agency. It took them two years . . . but they found your mother." Liz paused for a moment to look at Reagan before going on. "He didn't know if you'd want to see her, so he told me to tell you about her, but he wants you to understand that he knows no more than what is in the report and he doesn't want to talk about it. Reagan, I think this report reminds him that you're not truly kin and that's one thing he doesn't want to think about."

Reagan looked out the window, watching people passing by across the street. Suddenly she realized she was doing what she'd always done as a child—staring at faces of strangers, looking for a resemblance, looking for something she might remember of a mother. Only now, she didn't want to see anything in a stranger's face.

"I don't want to meet her. Not ever." Reagan stood. "She's dead to me. I'm a Truman now. You keep the report. I don't even want to see it."

Liz shrugged. "I'll lock up the report. We can talk about it at a later date if you like. Or, it will lie in the bottom of my safe forever." She thought for a moment and added, "This is the one file I will not pass on to my cousin, Rick Matheson. While I'm out with the babies, you'll have to wait if you need legal work on this subject. Is that all right?"

"You can burn it for all I care. I'll never ask to see it."

Liz nodded. "I think this last heart attack really frightened the tough old man. I assured him you shouldn't have any trouble when the time comes. The farm is already in your name, you can sign on all accounts, and I'll be in your corner if there is ever a problem."

AFTER REAGAN LEFT THE OFFICE, SHE CLIMBED INTO HER old pickup and cried all the way home. When Foster saw her he knew something was wrong, but he didn't ask any questions. He just filled her in on Jeremiah's day and said they should celebrate; her uncle was growing stronger.

That night, curled up in her bed, Reagan cried silently. Change was coming. Jeremiah knew it and she felt it. He'd held her hand a little tighter when he said good night. "I can't lose him," she whispered. "I can't be alone."

Reagan tried to think of all the people who were her friends. Who would come and help if something happened? Then she thought of her best friend, Noah.

If she called and asked him, he might come, but if he didn't, Reagan wasn't sure she could stand to hear her own heart breaking.

That night she dreamed of a woman with rust-colored hair chasing her, pulling at her skin as if she could pull a piece of flesh off her.

When her own cries woke her, Reagan curled into the

covers. The word *mother* had always been nothing but a word. Knowing that the woman who had given birth to her was still alive meant little, but questions whispered in the aftermath of the nightmare. Would her mother have the same color hair? Had she ever tried to find the child she'd left at the hospital? Did Reagan ever cross her mind?

Reagan reached for her phone and hit speed dial for Noah McAllen. After several rings, he picked up.

"What's the matter, Rea?" he said, still sounding half asleep.

"What makes you think . . . ?"

"You wouldn't have called this late unless you need to talk. Give me a minute to pull my jeans on and I'll go out in the hallway so I won't wake the other guys."

Reagan heard several men moan or swear in the background. When times were good, Noah had a room to himself, but when times were bad in the rodeo game he'd sometimes bunk on the floor in someone else's room.

"I'm listening," he said after a minute. "Shoot."

She wanted to hear his voice more than talk, but that would sound strange, so she told him about her dream and how frightened she'd been.

"I wish I were there to hug you, Rea. We could cuddle up. You could tell me everything while I slept."

"I wish you were too." Neither one said anything for a few breaths, and then she whispered, "I miss you so much sometimes." They'd probably never be as close as they'd been in high school. He was a different man and she'd changed as well, but she still missed the Noah who was half kid, half man.

"What are you wearing?" he whispered, and for a moment she swore she could hear him smiling.

"Shut up."

He laughed. "Just asking. Who knows, one night I might get lucky and you'd be just out of the shower."

"You never give up trying to make me blush." Her bad mood had vanished.

"Come on, Rea, give me a break. I've been wondering

what you look like naked for years. If I ever get too old to wonder, I hope you just shoot me."

"Go to bed, Noah."

"Good night, Rea. Maybe when you go back to dreaming, you'll dream of me."

"Not likely." She closed the phone, thinking how he always had enough magic in his pocket to change her mood even if he didn't have enough to change his dreams.

Chapter 8

SATURDAY
FEBRUARY 20
DALLAS, TEXAS

DENVER SIMS CHECKED INTO THE HYATT AT THE DALLAS–
Fort Worth airport. The desk clerk on duty called him by
name before he looked at the card. "One night or two this
time, Mr. Sims?"

"Only one," he answered, fighting not to let his disappointment show. He was an air marshal who flew all over
the world. He should be living a grand life, but for the past
two years, every time he got a few days off, he'd been building a house on land a friend sold him just outside Harmony.
Denver thought the place would somehow ground him,
make him feel like he belonged somewhere, but it hadn't. It
didn't seem to matter how many square feet he had, he still
felt like no place was home.

Shoving the second key in an envelope, he passed it back

to the desk clerk. "For Claire," he said, feeling the slow smile that always crossed his face when he said her name.

"I remember, sir. I'll keep an eye out for your lady."

Denver turned away, wanting to tell the man that Claire wasn't his lady. Maybe she never would be. He took the elevator and thought about how he used to love this life on the road. Always having his laundry delivered to his hotel room, eating out, meeting new people constantly, making love to a woman while knowing he'd never see her after a night or two.

Lately he felt the need to settle, maybe put down roots, maybe have a family, but the one woman he wanted only had time for a one-night stand. If he added up all the nights they'd spent together, it wouldn't total a month. Once in a while he had the feeling she was his hell. Payback for all the affairs he'd had and walked away.

If he had to watch her walk away the same number of times he'd left women, Denver figured he had a few more years of torture to come.

He opened the door to his room and noticed that the flowers he always ordered when Claire joined him were already by the bed. A meal would be delivered at nine. Her favorites. He'd learned what she preferred from every menu in every hotel where they'd stayed.

Only the details didn't hide the fact that they were in a hotel room again. He was close enough to her to walk from his house to hers in Harmony, but she would meet him only in hotel rooms. He could understand why he'd never been asked to stay at her place; Claire Matheson lived in a rambling old ranch house with her mother, her daughter, and her two great-aunts. The place had so many guests and relatives and ranch hands dropping by he was surprised it didn't have a revolving door. Claire's art studio was on the third floor, in what had been the attic. He'd have to get through two floors of relatives to even see her. She was right, the hotels probably were easier.

Denver figured he wouldn't be welcome at the ranch for breakfast and they'd probably shoot him if he tried to leave in the middle of the night. When Hank Matheson, the only male on the ranch, married and moved out, the women had Denver's friend and army buddy, Gabe Leary, put in a first-class security system. Denver knew he could slip through the system, but their having it wasn't exactly a welcome mat.

Claire could come to his place, though. Maybe not for the night, but for a few hours. He'd built on a huge kitchen and a master bedroom bigger than most apartments he'd rented. His place looked nothing like the old farmhouse he'd bought two years ago. Only Claire had never been there.

Putting his Glock in the safe, he pulled the drapes open and watched planes take off and land. She'd said she was landing twenty minutes after him, but she didn't want him to be at the gate. As always, she wanted him to meet her alone, away from everyone. He'd attended her art shows in a dozen places, eaten meals with her family when they were both in Harmony, and stood near when she'd won awards for her paintings, but their affair had to remain a secret from everyone. Denver couldn't even tell his best friend, Gabe Leary, because Gabe was married to Claire's sister.

This was one hell of a mess where affairs were concerned. He felt like they were flying under the radar and it was just a matter of time before the blip showed up.

Denver barked a laugh and turned to pour his first whiskey. What they had wasn't an affair. He hadn't looked at another woman for two years. He didn't need a band on his left hand to know they belonged together. Claire wasn't a passing fancy, she was his life, and it hurt all the way to his core to know he was no more than an accessory in hers.

He watched his reflection in the crystal glass. He saw a man distorted. Parts. No whole.

The door lock clicked. Denver turned, bracing for the beauty of her to hit him like a tropical storm.

She didn't disappoint. Dressed in black with only a touch of white collar showing, she stepped into the room.

Her long, wine-red hair was tied in a knot at the back of her neck, but he could feel it in his hands already. She looked at him with bottomless brown eyes and smiled. His heart started up again. Sometimes he felt like those characters in *Brigadoon*. He lived only when she was with him; the rest of the time was just existing. They'd seen each other a few times that first year, and each time had been wild, like a lost moment in time and reality. The second year they couldn't get enough of each other. Every month their paths crossed, always at hotels near airports. She left him fulfilled, satisfied, and planning the next encounter.

Only lately, once a month wasn't enough, not nearly enough for him, and he still wasn't sure she really liked him . . . or even knew him, but he had no doubt she needed him.

She'd given up telling him how much she hated him and all men after they'd made love in New York for the first time. She'd been setting up for a big show and he'd had a three-day layover. They'd spent it in bed unable to get enough. He'd added *love, Denver* to his texts and whispered how he adored every part of her, but he'd never told her straight out. He wasn't sure how he'd react when she didn't answer back.

Each month she seemed to be more popular in the art world. Her paintings of men dying horrible deaths seemed to have caught on. Apparently every woman knew at least one man she'd like to see barbecued over an open fire or hanged from the Empire State Building by a rope made from ugly ties. As her legend grew, she met him less and less in public, even for a drink or coffee, until finally this fall she hadn't even joined him for breakfast when they both happened to be in Harmony. But when she e-mailed him her flight schedule, he knew to book a room if he could get there for the layover.

"Hello, darlin'," he said now, as if it had been only hours and not more than a month since they'd seen each other. "You look beautiful, as always."

She turned and closed the door. Then without a word,

she slipped out of her heels as she pulled her hair free of the bun. The long strands danced to her waist.

He didn't move. He couldn't even breathe. All he could do was watch. In all his life he'd never had a woman affect him so completely. He didn't just want to touch her, he wanted to breathe her in, watch her every move, listen to the way she breathed when she slept or how she sighed when he ran his hands over her gently.

She let her black jacket fall to the floor, then unbuttoned her tailored trousers and let them pool at her feet so she could step free.

Standing in only her white blouse, she waited. Still no greeting.

Denver swallowed the last of his whiskey and moved toward her. He'd meant to talk first. Wanted to catch up on how her world was going. He knew her, maybe better than she knew herself. He knew she didn't care much about her success even though that was mainly what she talked about when she was around people. He also knew that beneath the perfect mask was a shattered woman whose husband had ended her world years ago, and she'd barely been able to tape the fragments together. She was a mother, a daughter, a sister, and an artist, but she wasn't his. He sometimes asked himself the question that if this was all he could have of her—one wild night now and then—was it enough?

When he raised one finger and slid it down the V of her blouse, she jerked slightly and closed her eyes. "I said hello," he whispered in a low voice as he kissed his way from her ear to her mouth while his hands slid beneath her shirttail and cupped her hips.

She sighed and backed a step away.

He moved close again, barely touching her as he freed the first few buttons of her blouse. "I don't care if you talk to me, darlin'. I know what you want."

She backed away again, her breath coming quickly. Each movement shifted the cotton top just enough that he saw she wore no bra.

"And you know what I want." He wasn't holding her, just touching.

She stepped away again, her eyes wide.

He let a foot remain between them as he slowly pushed his hand between the starched white cotton of her blouse and brushed his fingers around her breast.

She shut her eyes and gulped deep breaths as he finished unbuttoning her blouse and pushed it off her shoulders.

"You are so beautiful, Claire," he whispered as his hand gently moved over her.

She backed to the door and he closed the distance between them as he pressed his body over the length of hers. He held her head in his hands as he kissed her full out for several minutes before breaking the kiss so that he could stare into her eyes.

She wasn't a woman many people touched, and he knew no man had touched her but him in a long time. "You planning on talking to me tonight, Claire?"

"No," she answered, trying to turn her head away.

"Fine," he said, then pulled her mouth to his again. "We'll have to find another way to communicate." He kissed her until he felt her give up any resistance.

When he broke the kiss, she leaned her head back against his arm, her mouth still slightly open. He swore the woman melted into his skin every time she came close, but the first few moments were always a sparring match before she surrendered to what they both wanted.

"Are you glad to see me?" he whispered as he bit lightly against her bottom lip. When she didn't answer, he moved his hand over her middle, then up, taking his time exploring her flesh. His hands grew bolder. He smiled, loving the little sounds she made, purring to his touch.

"Yes," she whispered finally. "Yes."

He picked her up and carried her to bed. As she stretched atop the sheets, he pulled the drapes, turning the room and his life into shadows.

All the things he'd planned to say vanished as he spread out beside her. He didn't just need her, he was addicted to her. The time for words was over. Tomorrow after they'd made love until they were exhausted, then slept until noon, he'd order breakfast and they'd talk while they ate.

Then, he knew they'd make love one more time. He'd roll over and act like he was asleep while she showered, dressed, and left. She'd know he was awake just as he'd know she knew, but they'd learned months ago that neither one knew how to say good-bye.

Chapter 9

TYLER WRIGHT SAT IN THE WINTER'S INN BED-AND-Breakfast pretending to eat. Three days had passed since he'd picked up his Kate at the Amarillo airport and she'd slept in his arms. Three days and they'd yet to talk about anything important. Why was she sad? Would she be interested in marrying him? Nothing.

In fact, they'd barely been alone with each other. At the bed-and-breakfast, Martha Q was always around. She seemed to think Kate came to town just to visit with her. Tyler had long ago decided that Martha Q had probably talked at least half her husbands to death. She'd been married so many times folks played a drinking game in the local bar of trying to name the men in order. Tyler had heard it was more popular than naming the seven dwarves.

Martha Q's latest crazy plan was to start a once-a-week meeting of a "lonely hearts club" that came, for a price, with instructions for how to find and catch a man. Martha

Q saw herself as an expert in this field. She'd talked one of the Mathesons, an almost-lawyer by the name of Rick, into helping any of the women, pro bono, of course, if they should need any advice on handling their money or land before going into a new marriage. Martha Q even said Rick would help with ending the present, unhappy union if they needed him.

Tyler thought the whole idea sounded one inch short of insane, but on a scale with her other ideas it was about par.

Mrs. Biggs, the cook at Winter's Inn, wasn't much better at allowing him time alone with Kate. She'd spent an hour yesterday teaching Kate to make Italian bread. They'd made so much they decided to make lasagna to go with it and invite over everyone Kate knew.

Tyler felt like he was being selfish, not wanting to share Kate's time. Yesterday, when he had to leave to work, he'd hurried back to find she'd gone to lunch with the sheriff, Alexandra McAllen-Matheson. When Kate returned late in the afternoon, Tyler asked what the two women had talked about, but Kate had simply said, "An old police matter."

Talking to everyone in town about everything seemed more important than talking to him. Tyler felt forgotten, and mad at himself for being selfish of her time. He knew she was fitting in and loving it.

When Alexandra and her husband, Hank Matheson, came over for the lasagna, Tyler was happy to see his best friend, but part of him wanted to stand on a chair and yell that it was time for everyone to go home so he could be alone with Kate. After all, he was the reason she had come to Harmony this week.

He worried he was neglecting work too, which was rare. Tyler had managed to get Ida Louise buried, but he still hadn't checked out the car parked at the back of the cemetery. It had disappeared Friday, and then Calvin told him it was back this morning. Tyler liked everything in his life in order, and even a car parked out of place bothered that order. But this week the car was only one of many things that didn't settle right.

Having a funeral where no family bothered to attend always upset him. Then he had Willamina to deal with, or more accurately, not to deal with. His housekeeper, who'd worked for the Wright family most of his life, had left him a letter saying she was taking her vacation days, eighty-three to be exact, and then going into retirement. When he tried to contact her, Willamina's sister, Dottie, told him she'd gone on a cruise. He'd be more likely to believe that the two old women in their seventies got in a fight and Dottie killed her. Willamina usually left town to visit her children on her days off and, to his knowledge, never took her sister along or *ever* went anywhere else.

Now he was worried about Willamina and what it would be like to cook his own meals, do his own laundry, clean his own kitchen. He could easily survive the weekends alone or even a week now and then, but eighty-three days?

He decided the only thing to do was forget about it until Kate left. Willamina had threatened to quit every time he asked her to make liver and onions. Surely she hadn't gotten mad when he interrupted her soap opera on Wednesday? Or maybe he'd left everything out on the counter when he made Kate a sandwich? At Willamina's age, it wasn't likely that she ran off with a man, so everything would probably be back to normal in a few weeks. Nothing really ever changed in his life.

"You worried about something?" Kate interrupted his thoughts when she noticed that everyone, except him, had moved to the living room with their coffee and dessert.

"No, just thinking."

She laughed, that laugh he loved. "Well, stop thinking and give a hand with the dishes."

He did, thinking about how he might be washing dishes at home soon. Maybe he should buy paper plates and cups to weather Willamina's absence. Who knows, maybe the woman had planned her escape for years. For all he knew she was dancing on some island right now with nothing on but a grass skirt.

Finally, everyone left and the dishes were done. Martha Q climbed the stairs to her bed and Mrs. Biggs went to her room beyond the kitchen.

Tyler knew it was late, but he poured two glasses of wine and sat down on the couch. He tried to hide his disappointment when Kate joined him and took the chair to his right. He smiled and passed her one of the glasses.

"That was a wonderful meal," he said for the fourth time.

"Friends made it so," she said, then took a sip. "I never get to cook like that when I'm working. Never in a place long enough to settle in and buy the groceries."

"But you have friends?"

She shook her head. "Not like I do here. They see me as this dumpy middle-aged woman who's an expert on arson fires. If we do share a meal, it's usually to talk about a case." She ran a hand through her short graying hair, and it all fell softly back into place as if perfectly trained.

"You're not dumpy," he said, thinking she made him feel tall. "And you're not middle-aged. You're still young, Kate, barely out of your thirties."

She shook her head, then smiled. "That's why I love being here with you. You make me feel like who I am inside and not just what I do."

He didn't know how to direct the conversation to where he wanted to go, so he just jumped in. "Kate, I liked holding you while you slept."

The parlor lights were too low to tell if she blushed. He didn't know if he should say more, so he waited.

Finally, after she took another drink, she lifted her chin slightly and whispered, "I'm sorry about the way I came in. I'd been sleeping on planes and in airports for three days. I was exhausted and hadn't had time to shove all I saw at the last site out of my head. I called you to come get me when I laid over an hour in New York because I knew I didn't have the strength left to drive." She stared at her glass, then added, "I should have taken the time to sleep a few days before . . ."

"No," he said. "You did the right thing. You came here."

"Well, thanks for picking me up."

"Any time," he said, wishing he'd said *Every time.*

She leaned over and patted his knee. "It's late. I'd better turn in."

"Walk me to the porch steps," he said as he stood.

He bundled in his coat and she wrapped a shawl that Martha Q kept by the door around her shoulders. They walked out, hand in hand, onto the porch. The air was damp and crisp. A low wind crackled in the bare branches surrounding the inn. For Tyler the place was beautiful and lonely at the same time. The old house stood in the middle of town but had the feel of being alone. He'd felt like that most of his life.

"Good night," he said as he raised his arms.

She moved into them and for a long while they just hugged.

When she pulled away, he tried to keep his voice casual as he said, "You can come over to my house for a nap any time, Kate."

"And you'll make me soup and ham sandwiches?"

"I don't have to. We didn't eat the other ones. They're still in the fridge."

She made a face and he kissed her on the nose. Something he was sure no one ever did to the major.

She smiled and rushed inside, saying she was freezing.

On his way home he stopped by the cemetery. He rarely asked anyone to lock the cemetery at dusk for him, and even though he knew Calvin or one of the groundsmen would have, he liked to be the one who made the final check. It was his responsibility. It had been since his father handed him the keys to his first car.

The old Ford Mustang was parked by the back gate again. In the dark he couldn't even tell the color. Dark blue? Black? Tyler decided it was far too cold to walk across the cemetery to check it out tonight, and the back road was too muddy to risk getting stuck.

He'd come back tomorrow morning before he took Kate

back to Amarillo to catch her flight. She didn't go to work until Monday, but she'd explained that she needed a day to unpack. He didn't much like the idea that unpacking ranked above spending an extra day with him, but he told himself he understood.

Chapter 10

❧

MIDNIGHT

REAGAN TRUMAN'S CELL PHONE CLAMORED IN THE DARKness. It took several rings for her to find it.

"Hello," she mumbled, hoping she didn't wake her uncle in the next room.

"Rea, this is Noah."

"It's late, Noah." She pulled the string on an old Tiffany-style lamp that was probably five times her age. Something was wrong; not even Noah called this late.

"I know, Rea, but I need to talk to you."

She shoved her hair out of her face and tried to force sleep away. "All right, what's up?"

"I'm in the hospital, Rea. I was hurt tonight in Memphis."

"How bad?" She laughed nervously. She'd almost asked if he was still alive.

There was a long pause on the line. "I don't know. Bad. Broken arm, two ribs, but it's my back that has me worried."

He didn't speak for a moment. When he began again, he sounded more like a frightened boy than a man of twenty. "I'm hurt bad enough to maybe kick me off the circuit. When I hit the dirt, I was out cold. They said I kept yelling your name in the ambulance, but I don't remember. All I remember is the pain."

"Noah, what can I do? Do you want me to go over to your folks' house? I think they're in town. I could call your sister, Alex."

"No, I don't want them to worry. I know Mom. She'll freak out and Dad will start lecturing me like I'm still a kid. I don't want them to know anything until I know how serious it is. They're not telling me much yet." He paused, and she knew he was fighting to keep his voice calm. "Rea, I got to face this before I ask them to. If it's nothing, they don't even need to know. If it's crippling, I got to have a plan."

She understood. Noah had always been their positive, sunny child. The McAllens had already lost one son eight years ago. She'd seen the panic in their eyes once when Noah had been admitted to the hospital after an accident. She understood why he'd want to save them pain. "What can I do?"

He was silent for a moment, and then he said simply, "Come get me. No matter how bad it is, I want you near when I find out."

She slid out of bed and paced to the window. He was asking her to leave her uncle. Noah was alone in a place without friends or family. "I'll try," she whispered. "Call me tomorrow."

Rea fought back tears. She felt she couldn't go and she couldn't stay.

The light came on across the hallway in the parlor that had become her uncle's room since his last heart attack.

Reagan scrubbed her cheek with her palm before checking on him.

Jeremiah pulled himself up in bed and looked like he was waiting for a report when she walked in. The harsh frown he always greeted everyone with hadn't frightened her since the day she met him. "Well, girl, something's upset you. Might as well talk about it. I'm as awake as I'll ever be."

"I got a call from Noah. He was hurt at the rodeo tonight." She didn't bother with details. Her uncle saw life as clean cut, without emotion.

"If he called, I'm guessing he's not dead. If he called you, I'm thinking he doesn't want his folks to know."

"He wants me to bring him home here to recover, but it's a long way to Memphis. I'd have to leave you."

Jeremiah raised one eyebrow and studied her a moment before snorting and saying, "Go get that boy and bring him here to heal. Hell, the place is turning into a hospital anyway."

"But . . ."

"No *but*s about it. You care about him, don't you?

"Yes, but I care about you."

The old man smiled. "I know you do, but before long I'll be part of your past. That boy, he's part of your future."

Reagan lowered her head onto the covers of his bed and cried.

The old man placed his hand on her hair and patted lightly. "You're the best thing that ever came along in my life, kid, and you'll probably be the best thing in his, but you should know that I plan to be around for a while to remind him."

Reagan raised her head. "But . . . we're just friends."

He smiled as if he knew a secret and patted her head one more time before he pulled away. "I know, girl. Now pack your bags and go get your friend. Foster and Cindy will be here to watch over me."

Reagan kissed his cheek as he tried, not too hard, to wave her away.

Chapter 11

❧

HARMONY FIRE STATION

DALLAS LOGAN SAW IT AS HER CIVIC DUTY TO ATTEND every public function in Harmony even if no one else seemed to want her there. In Ronelle's mother's opinion, the town would go to hell in a hatbox if she, and her daughter, weren't present.

Ronelle had no more luck persuading her mother to stay home or go alone than she did at correcting the mixed metaphor. As far as Dallas was concerned, if her daughter wasn't at the post office working, she should be by her side.

So, Saturday morning, they were off to the meeting at the fire station. Of course, Dallas drove; she saw no reason for Ronelle to even learn. After all, Ronelle was young; she could walk anywhere she needed to go—the post office, the store, or the diner. As long as Dallas held the keys, she held the power, and they both knew it.

The paper stated that the talk would center on how

the county was going to afford another fire truck. No one seemed to have an answer, but that wouldn't stop them from hashing it over in great detail.

Ronelle hated town meetings. She never said a word. In fact, she usually took her crossword puzzle books and timed herself to see how many she could get done in an hour.

They arrived later than her mother would have liked. Dallas didn't get to talk to anyone because the meeting was being called to order. They also had to take a seat near the back, and nothing bothered Dallas Logan more than not being seen.

Ronelle lost interest in the meeting within minutes. She slid down in her chair and began a crossword puzzle. Halfway through it, she heard a familiar voice. A voice she'd never forget. Marty Winslow.

Looking between the two overweight women in front of her, she watched as Marty presented a plan. He sat in his wheelchair, his black hair pulled back, almost making him look like he'd cut it. He rattled off numbers while someone flipped charts behind him.

"Who is that?" Ronelle whispered to her mother.

"Some high-powered financial planner," Dallas answered in her not-so-low voice. "Must not be too good. Don't even look like he can afford a haircut."

One of the two heavyweights in front of them turned around and glared at Dallas.

Dallas huffed at the woman as if to say *Mind your own business.* The woman had the good sense to turn back around.

"Don't pay him no mind, that man who obviously thinks he's a genius." Dallas pointed with her head toward Winslow. "Everybody knows those financial types are always telling other people how to spend their money and then committing suicide when they can't handle their own. I bet it'll be hard for him to jump from a window with that wheelchair. He looks more like the kind to blow his brains out with a forty-five. Then what good will they do him splattered all over the wall like so much ground liver."

Ronelle closed her eyes. She knew without looking that

every person within five feet of them was staring at her mother with that drop-dead-lady look in their eyes.

Thank goodness Hank Matheson stepped to the mic and said, "Let's give Marty Winslow a round of applause for all the work he's done. This looks like a plan we can make happen if we all head in the same direction."

One old man yelled, "Yeah, if we live long enough," but everyone else clapped.

Ronelle slipped out the side door. She knew the minute the crowd broke someone would confront Dallas, and that was her mother's favorite time. She'd debate the existence of hell with the devil himself.

Standing in the cold, Ronelle tried to make herself invisible, and as usual it worked. When she'd been little she used to believe that if she didn't see people, they couldn't see her. She'd practice moving through stores without looking at anyone. Now, she pressed her shoulders against the wall and wished she were thin and flat-chested so she could mold against the building unseen.

The two firemen huddled by a booth set up to sell chili didn't notice her. One was Willie Davis. He was younger than Ronelle, but she knew him because he was the one who usually came out to fix the streetlight by her house. Her mother always tried to give him a hard time about why he didn't try to catch the criminal shooting out the light and not just keep coming by to fix it, but Willie Davis just smiled and said, "Yes, ma'am, you're right."

This infuriated Dallas. People agreeing with her left little room for argument.

The other fireman beside Davis was a big guy of about the same age: twenty, maybe twenty-one. He reminded her of the man she'd seen on the motorcycle outside Marty Winslow's house, but he looked a little older and not quite as frightening.

He might live here, but he seemed like an outsider, like her. When she glanced back at him, he caught her eye for a moment and gave a slight nod as if to say that he recognized someone who didn't fit in. They might never talk, but Ronelle decided she would say hello to him if he ever addressed her first.

She couldn't see any tattoos, but he might have them. Everyone under forty had them but Ronelle. Her mother told her once that if Ronelle ever got a tattoo she'd cut it off her skin with a potato peeler. The threat hadn't frightened her because she'd never considered it seriously, but the knowledge that her mother was serious about the potato peeler did.

Someone inside the fire station opened the bay door and people poured out. Bowls of chili were sold for three dollars, and a long table had been set up for baked goods. Ronelle wasn't much with numbers, but she figured it would take longer than one lifetime to save up for a fire truck with money from bake sales.

"Stop standing there like a doorstop," Dallas snapped from behind Ronelle. "We might as well go home. All these folks are interested in is food. I've never seen such a basket of nuts."

Ronelle knew Dallas would not stay to eat. She often reminded Ronelle never to eat anything at potluck dinners or bake sales. One person hating the town could wipe out the entire population with poison.

Looking around, she saw everyone eating and had a horrible thought. If they all died, that would leave only her mother and her in town. While her mother stopped to talk to Willie Davis, Ronelle slipped a piece of corn bread into her pocket. It would be all in crumbs by the time she got home, but she planned to eat it. Just in case.

Chapter 12

SUNDAY
FEBRUARY 21
WINTER'S INN BED-AND-BREAKFAST

TYLER HOPED TO LEAVE EARLY ENOUGH TO HAVE LUNCH with Kate in Amarillo before her flight, but when he got to the bed-and-breakfast to pick her up, Mrs. Biggs had a huge breakfast cooked. There was little in the way of food that Tyler could resist, and homemade cinnamon rolls with nuts on top would never make the list.

Kate shrugged as if to say she couldn't hurt their feelings and invited him to join her. Of course Martha Q sat down across from them, ending any chance of private conversation.

The innkeeper wanted help with the wording for a flyer about her lonely hearts club. "I need a name that doesn't sound sad," she complained.

"Don't look at me," Tyler said. "I only write obituaries."

Kate laughed and patted his knee under the table. "I'm no more help."

"Well, *Want to hook up* sounds too modern." Martha Q tapped her head with her pencil. "*Singles club* sounds like a bar. *Finding the right one* sounds too vague."

Tyler nibbled on a cinnamon roll he'd pulled from the platter placed in the center of the table. He didn't know if they were the centerpiece or the appetizers, but he couldn't resist them when they were hot out of the oven with the buttery sugar mixture still dripping. While he tasted, he tried to keep his mind on the conversation. "Do you think many people find the right one?"

Martha Q frowned at him. "Of course. I did several times."

"How about *Ending loneliness*?" He tried again. He had little faith that any club Martha Q started would last longer than bananas in the sun.

Both women shook their heads. Kate sighed. "It needs to be something uplifting. Something like *Embracing change in your life.*"

Martha Q thumped her forehead with the pencil a few more times. "We'd get as many women wanting to divorce as we'd get ones looking to marry. It's been my observation that some of the loneliest people in the word are lingering in bad relationships."

"It would be like a swap meet. One woman's bum might be someone else's Prince Charming." Tyler was proud of his idea until he saw both women glaring at him. After that, he decided he'd just eat his breakfast and let them figure it out.

While the women talked, he did what he often did in the presence of people he didn't particularly like; he began planning Martha Q's funeral. Finally, when it was time to go, he stood and said, "You ladies will have to continue your dreaming and scheming another day."

"That's it!" Martha Q yelled. "We'll call the club Dreaming and Scheming."

Apparently, to Tyler's surprise, women didn't consider scheming a derogatory trait in looking for a man.

When he and Kate were finally in the car heading toward

Amarillo, she was in a talkative mood, wanting to know all about Martha Q's colorful past. Tyler told her what he knew, but he wasn't good at coloring. His father had taught him two things: Never judge and never gossip. It was hard to talk about Martha Q without doing one or the other.

When the conversation slowed, Kate began to talk about her work. She described three burned bodies she'd had to maneuver around in the last arson fire she investigated and how horrible they smelled.

Tyler didn't need details. He'd picked up bodies burned to death before, but he let her talk. He told himself he should be glad she was confiding in him. She probably had no one to just talk to. He tried to listen to every word she said, but the hope of how he thought this weekend could have gone kept drifting though his mind like deadwood on a midnight lake, shadowing reality with what might have been.

They were at the airport before he realized he hadn't said anything he'd meant to say to her. He wanted to ask her to wait a while before rushing for the security check, but she seemed in a hurry and talked about all she had to do when she got back to the office. By the time he unloaded her bag, she was on the phone, already back in her world.

"Good-bye," she said, shuffling her carry-on bag to her shoulder.

"I'll see you next time." He tried to smile.

She kissed his cheek. "Of course. E-mail me."

She was gone before he could answer. He watched her moving through the maze, checking in, showing her ID, tugging off her shoes.

He watched, wondering if his Kate was running toward or away from something.

His feet felt heavy as he walked back to his car. By the time he drove out of the airport, snow had begun to fall. He knew he should stay on the main roads, but he veered off onto a farm-to-market two-lane. Nothing helped him think better than driving in the country. It would take him an hour longer to get home this way, but he didn't care. No one was waiting for him. Not even his housekeeper.

Tyler was a man who never allowed himself self-pity. He knew from the time he could reason that he was the only son of an aging funeral director. He would be expected to take over the responsibilities of a family business and, to his surprise, he loved them. When he wasn't thinking about being alone or why Kate didn't want to see him more than once every few months, he stayed busy. He helped people. He was there when they needed him.

He'd ask Kate to stay with him the next time she came. Or, he wouldn't. Passion was not something either one of them seemed to have in their lives, so why expect it now? They were both beyond the years of thinking about having children, so time could drift for a while. Maybe all they were meant to be was friends. Maybe they'd find a quiet kind of love in their later years.

That was all he could hope for. A quiet kind of love.

Tyler pulled off at a small gas station and got a few snacks. Even in winter, he liked ice cream. The kind with chocolate wrapped around it. Since he knew there would be no meal waiting for him later, he picked up a dozen home-made tamales and hot sauce. Remembering he hadn't gotten anything green, he grabbed a large bag of M&Ms, figuring he'd eat the green ones first and have the others for dessert.

Laughing at his own joke, he walked to the car and thought he'd have the greens right now with his Dr Pepper.

By the time he passed Lone Oak Road it was getting dark, but Tyler had had a long talk with himself. He'd even decided he wouldn't e-mail Kate tonight to check if she made it home. He'd never been all that special to any-one; why would he have thought he would be to Kate? He should be happy with what he did have. Good friends, a job he loved, and long drives to clear his head.

Tyler smiled, thinking of the people who did think he was something. Saralynn, Hank's niece. She might be only eight, but she thought he was her knight. Hank, his best friend, always called if he didn't make breakfast at the diner every Tuesday. A good-looking rancher and a chubby undertaker might look like a strange pair to be friends, but it worked. Tyler thought it was because they both cared about people.

Names, one after the other, came to him as he drove toward the cemetery. People who'd cried on his shoulder and told him they couldn't have made it without him. The guys at the fire station, who depended on him to man the phones when there was an emergency. Tyler decided he might live alone above his office, but he had a whole town for family. Maybe he should just be thankful for what he had and stop wishing for more.

He circled by to lock up the cemetery and noticed that the old Ford was still out by the back gate. Since he was in his Rover, he plowed down the dirt road to have a look.

The banged-up car looked like it hadn't been moved all day. Judging from the shape it was in, it might have been abandoned.

Tyler's four-wheel drive might have held the icy road steady, but his leather dress shoes almost slipped beneath him as he climbed out to take a closer look. A thin layer of snow had settled over a sheet of ice. Halfway to the car, he thought of turning back to the warmth of his Rover, but he felt like this was one thing in his life he could get settled tonight. Clicking on his flashlight, he moved forward.

He checked the doors. Both locked, but he could see what looked like a woman's purse on the passenger side. Abandoned cars didn't usually come with purses.

Shoving more snow off the window, he tried to see inside, looking for any information that would help him figure out who owned this piece of junk.

Something moved in the backseat.

Tyler jumped back, holding his flashlight as a weapon.

After taking a few deep breaths, he looked again, telling himself an animal might have crawled inside the car looking for shelter from the freezing wind and been trapped.

He thought he saw a tennis shoe. Then another. He rapped on the window. "Is anyone in there? This is private property; you can't stay here."

Tyler remembered hearing his father tell about hobos

camping out in the back of the cemetery, and now and then Tyler had caught kids sneaking in on a dare. Only this time, he had no idea what he faced.

Pulling out his cell, he dialed 911.

The dispatcher picked up on the first ring.

"This is Tyler Wright," Tyler said as he watched someone moving around in the cramped backseat. "I'm at the back gate of the cemetery. Could you send someone? I have a trespasser."

"We're on our way, Mr. Wright. Do not confront. I repeat. Do not confront."

Tyler smiled, guessing the dispatcher was reading from a book. What did the man think he was going to do, tackle the guy in the car and hold him down until help arrived? Flipping the phone closed, he waited. When whoever was sleeping in the car climbed out, he didn't plan to do anything but talk. If the stranger tried to drive off, he would simply get out of the way. After all, all Tyler wanted was the car gone.

It took a few minutes, but finally the passenger door flew open and long thin legs appeared. Then hair. Half a bushel of curly sand-colored hair almost brushed the ground as the intruder leaned forward and planted tennis shoes in the snow.

In the beam of the flashlight, he couldn't be sure, but the moment she flipped her hair back, Tyler realized the squatter was a girl.

"What do you want, you idiot?" She didn't sound very friendly. "You woke me up."

"You're parked in the cemetery." Tyler said the obvious.

"I haven't heard any of the neighbors complain."

Her clothes were wrinkled, her fist clenched, but he didn't miss the sparkle of fear in her eyes as his flashlight turned on her face. "I've already called the police." He tried to sound calm, but nerves made him yell.

"Don't threaten me," she shouted as she moved forward. "And get that damn light out of my face."

Her hand swung at the flashlight.

Tyler stepped backward, avoiding her advance. Her arm

hit the flashlight. Tyler jumped, almost dropping it. His feet went flying out from under him. He hit the cold ground with a hard thud. His head seemed to bounce against something and hit a second time before the flashlight vaulted from his hand and slammed against his forehead.

The world had turned to one giant snow globe in his mind, but he thought he heard a squeal a moment before the woman landed on top of him.

In all of Tyler's life he'd never been a fighter. In fact, he thought, generations of possum blood must run in his family, because their first and only line of defense seemed to be to roll over and play dead.

The woman tried to shove herself off him as the sound of a siren filled the air. Tyler closed his eyes, letting pain rattle through his entire body while the night grew even darker.

In what seemed like only a blink's worth of time passing, Tyler found himself in an ambulance with an EMT who had *Charles* written across his chest pocket telling him he was going to live.

Tyler pushed the man away. "Of course I'm going to live."

Charles looked as if Tyler had just moved from the victim line to the nutcase line. "You must not remember, Mr. Wright. You were violently attacked at the back gate of the cemetery. Deputy Phil Gentry has the woman in the back of his squad car. He'll have her locked up by the time we get you to the hospital. She was one yelling screaming ball of mad when we pulled her off you."

Tyler felt his throbbing headache getting worse. "She didn't attack me," he said as he pieced everything together. "I frightened her. She yelled at me and I slipped on the ice. I must have hit her when I went down because a moment after I fell, she landed on top of me."

The EMT leaned closer. "You sure about that, sir? It sure looked like she was pounding on you when we pulled up."

"I'm sure, Charles. Get a hold of Phil and have him bring her to the hospital. She's as likely to have injuries as I am."

The EMT hesitated. "It was so dark. We thought . . ."

Tyler nodded, then regretted it. No matter how bad he felt, he couldn't let some poor woman spend the night in jail because of what was as much his fault as hers. He shouldn't have yelled at her like he did. Shining the light in her face must have scared her to death. And telling her the police were on their way probably didn't do much good either.

If his head weren't pounding, he'd say he was sorry. Instead, he closed his eyes and listened to the EMT trying to explain everything to the deputy. Apparently, they hadn't saved his life, they'd just picked up two people who'd fallen on the ice.

He made an effort to free himself from the gurney, but the EMT had to help him. A few minutes later, Tyler walked into the emergency room. A nurse showed him to a room, and within an hour the doctor released him. He had a mild concussion, a bad bruise on his left hip, and a knot on his forehead the size of a golf ball from the flashlight.

When he walked to the desk to wait for Calvin to come pick him up, Tyler asked about the woman. She'd been admitted. Besides bruises, she was dehydrated and running a fever.

Tyler stepped outside when Calvin pulled up in the old station wagon they always used to pick up bodies from the hospital. Much less obvious than a hearse. Tyler thought of climbing in the back and lying down. The way his head hurt, he was at least half dead. Plus, he felt like somehow all the injuries, his and hers, had been his fault tonight. She probably didn't have any money and was just looking for a quiet place to sleep. He should have waited until afternoon to check the back gate. If she had been still there, then they could have talked.

Calvin drove home so slowly that Tyler could have walked beside the car.

The third time Tyler assured Calvin that he was all right, the older man dialed Beth, the funeral home receptionist and bookkeeper. "He's hurt," Calvin whispered, as if Tyler couldn't hear, "but he's going to be all right. Call the others. I'm inbound now."

Tyler wasn't surprised they were all waiting for him when he got home. Calvin and Dave, who did work on the cemetery grounds, tried to help him inside. Beth and Stella, the night host, asked him questions all the way up the front steps.

He finally turned to the four of them and smiled. "I'm all right. I swear. I don't need help getting upstairs or someone to stay with me." He smiled at Stella McNabb, who looked like she might cry. "I could use some cocoa, though, and maybe a few of your cookies."

The women hurried off, happy to have something to do.

Calvin and Dave walked him up the stairs anyway, wanting to know details of the accident.

By the time Tyler had finished, the women were there with cocoa and cookies. As they each said good night and offered to come in a moment's notice if he needed anything, Tyler added four more people in the world that he mattered to.

Chapter 13

THE HOSPITAL IN MEMPHIS LOOKED HUGE AS REAGAN paid the cabdriver and walked inside. She'd tossed a few changes of clothes and a toothbrush in her bag along with her computer. Over the months she'd learned that when she entered a hospital, she never knew how long it would be until she walked out.

The nurse at the desk pointed her toward the ICU but didn't seem overly friendly. Maybe it was because Reagan looked more like a homeless person than a visitor. She'd grabbed her work coat by mistake and on the plane noticed it had a rip along the pocket and stains on both sleeves.

She'd checked on Uncle Jeremiah, then left the farm before daylight. Foster explained over and over how he'd never leave Jeremiah's side while she was gone. If the old man took one step downhill in his recovery, they'd call her right away. Cindy drove her to Amarillo to catch a plane, telling her everything she could do to help Noah.

From Amarillo she'd gone to Dallas and waited two hours for a flight to Memphis. All in all she figured it had taken her almost as long to fly as it would have taken her to drive. She'd called Noah's phone twice, but there'd been no answer.

Once Reagan found the ICU, she made a corner of the waiting room home and watched the wall clock for the fifteen minutes of visitation every two hours. Noah was asleep the first time she saw him. The nurse warned her not to wake him. Besides bruised and broken, he looked thinner and older than he'd been last summer.

Reagan stared at the man and remembered the boy. He'd been almost seventeen when he'd walked up to her in the school courtyard at lunch. He was all legs and hat and full of bull. He'd told her that first day they met that he would be a hunk someday.

She smiled, brushed her hand along the cast on his arm, and thought how he'd been right. His long muscles had hardened into a powerful body, and the jaw, now bruised and covered in whiskers, was clenched tight, fighting the pain. If he'd been an actor on the screen he would have broken hearts, because he looked like the perfect image of a real western cowboy come to life.

Reagan didn't try to stop the tears as she started remembering all the times he'd been hurt and how every time he fought back. But now it might not be as easy. Broken bones and bruises would heal, but tubes running to him told her there was more wrong this time. Internal injuries, maybe, or a back that might never be strong again.

"If you called me to come to watch you die," she whispered, "I swear I'll never forgive you."

He didn't move, but the beeps and rhythm of the machine frightened her. She took his hand. A man's hand, strong and scarred. "I've come to take you home, Noah. I don't think I can make it without you for a friend right now."

She wasn't sure, but she thought she felt his fingers tighten.

Before she could say more, the nurse told her it was time to go.

Reagan smiled and whispered, "See you soon."

The first night she slept in the waiting room. The second day he was out having tests run during every visiting time. As far as she could tell, no one had tried to see him except her, and no one had called to ask the volunteer at the main desk about his condition. His family didn't know, and the cowboys he'd been traveling with had moved on to the next rodeo. Knowing Noah, he'd probably told them he was fine and family was on their way.

She was asleep, her second night in the waiting room, when a nurse came out and said he was awake. "I'll sneak you in, but only for a few minutes. It'll make him feel better just knowing you're here."

Reagan scrambled. She didn't even bother putting on her shoes; she just followed the nurse.

Noah's eyes were open—at least one of them; the other was swollen closed, and varying shades of purple striped the lid like a bad makeup job.

"Hi, Rea. Nice to see you." He gripped her hand tightly, saying far more with his touch than with his words.

She smiled. "It's good to see you too."

"The nurse told me some scrappy girl was out in the waiting room. Been giving them hell for two days wanting to know what's happening." He groaned when she laughed. "I knew it had to be you."

Rea looked down at her once-clean shirt. She'd spilled her drink on it yesterday, but hardly noticed the stain until now. "I was planning to clean up in the morning before I saw you."

"You look great just the way you are. Thanks for coming. I probably shouldn't have called, but I didn't want to go through this alone."

"I don't look great. You can't see well, or maybe this time you really did take one too many blows to the head."

He squeezed her fingers.

"I haven't been much help either. Since I'm not kin,

the doctors won't talk to me. In fact, I've pestered one so much, he runs when he sees me coming."

"You've been more help than you know just being there." He suddenly looked very tired. "One of the nurses said they'll be moving me to a room tomorrow. I'm just sleeping here for tonight since they're not full. Why don't you go find a real place to sleep and I'll see you in the morning."

"Are you sure?"

"Sure. I promise I won't die on you."

Tears rolled unchecked down her cheeks, but he didn't see them.

The nurse moved beside him. "He'll rest now." She smiled at Reagan. "You'd best get some sleep too, honey, or you'll be checking into this place."

Reagan didn't want to leave, but she needed a bath and a change of clothes. She grabbed her bag and walked to the main entrance. A guard on the night desk agreed to call her a cab.

Walking out into the cold night to wait, she thought about how much she hated hospitals. She felt like a miner who'd been trapped in bad air for days. If they brought canaries into hospital hallways, the birds would be dead within minutes. Everything in the place smelled of cleaning fluid, even the popcorn she'd had hours ago for supper.

When the cab pulled up, Reagan realized she hadn't stayed in a hotel since she'd been about ten and a caseworker had to take her to a group home a few hundred miles away. They'd been caught in a storm and pulled off at a Hilton. The caseworker complained she'd never get her money back, but for Reagan it was like walking into a palace.

"Where to, miss?" the cabdriver said in a tired, bland voice.

"The nearest Hilton." Reagan leaned back in the seat, hoping it wasn't twenty miles away.

As it turned out, it was almost within sight of the hospital. She tipped the guy ten dollars and walked into the lobby.

The clerk didn't look much older than her. "How may I help you?" Her smile was wide, but not friendly.

"I need a room for the night."

"Smoking or nonsmoking?"

"Non."

"King or queen?"

"Queen." Reagan guessed she was talking about the bed size.

"We're out of queen, but we have a king."

"All right, king." Reagan was beginning to think this was some kind of surprise game show.

"Fill this out, please, and I'll need to see a driver's license and a credit card."

Reagan pulled out her driver's license and the credit card she used for ordering on the Internet.

The clerk wrote down her room number on a folded envelope and passed it to her along with a card.

When Reagan raised an eyebrow, the girl whispered, "Your key."

Reagan took the card and decided she could figure it out. She took a step, looking around the lobby, then backstepped to face the girl again. "Is there a place to get a meal?"

"Room service is open until eleven. They mostly have sandwiches this late. You can charge it to your room."

"Good. Send up a meal of soup, sandwich, and milk."

"What kind?"

"Any kind. Whatever the cook has handy."

Reagan picked up her card key and walked away. In the elevator, she read how to unlock her door, then broke into a smile when she stepped inside. The room looked like it belonged in a fancy decorating magazine. Within minutes, she'd stripped and stepped into the shower.

After she'd washed her hair and slipped on a white robe, she walked out into the room and found a tray of food waiting for her. As she ate, Reagan decided her one luxury from now on in life would be that every time she traveled, she'd stay in fancy hotels. Since this was only her second hotel in twenty years, the rule wasn't likely to bankrupt her.

She slept until eight. Her first thought was of Noah when she woke. She called the hospital and was told he'd be undergoing more testing most of the morning. Reagan got dressed and went downstairs for breakfast.

She bought a wool jacket from the gift shop and took a cab back to the hospital, wanting to be waiting in his room when he got finished.

When they rolled him into his private room, he was asleep. Reagan waited more than an hour before he finally opened his eyes.

"You look better," he said.

"You still look terrible." She laughed. "But then, they didn't have much but bones and muscle to work with. I've never seen you looking so thin."

"I know. They've been running tests all morning and not letting me eat. I keep telling them every part of my body hurts and they keep saying, 'Isn't that wonderful.' Problem is, when I tell them how bad my back hurts the docs say they can't find the reason."

"You've got feeling in your legs?"

"Yeah. The bull did some damage, but he didn't break my back. I guess I'm lucky. They want to keep an eye on me for two or three more days, and then they said I can go home. I'll have a few months of therapy, and then if everything goes well I'll be back in the saddle by summer. I've still got a ways to go to fill my card."

Reagan didn't want to hear it. She was thankful he would recover, but the idea that he planned to go back to trying to kill himself almost broke her heart. Rodeo cowboys paid more than a hundred dollars for a pro card, then made a point for every dollar they won in prize money. A thousand dollars got the pro standing. Then it was big rides at big rodeos for big money.

A nurse came in and asked her if she would leave for a few minutes.

Reagan didn't even want to know why. She almost ran from the room. If he didn't have so many breaks and bruises already, she would have tried to kick some sense into him. All he could think about was rodeo even after it almost killed him.

Standing by the window, she phoned home. Uncle Jeremiah was giving Foster all kinds of hell, which the retired medic claimed was grand. He'd had the old man up walking twice since dawn, and with luck he'd be out of the wheelchair within a month.

One load lifted off her shoulders. Maybe she'd have time to talk some sense into Noah while he was recovering. She wanted her best friend back before the thrill and the danger claimed him.

After walking the halls for a while, she wandered into the coffee shop and sat thinking. Having Noah for a friend was like knowing an addict who wouldn't quit no matter how bad the fall. She thought of calling that TV show that did interventions. Maybe if all of Noah's friends and family got together and promised never to speak to him again if he didn't stop the riding, he'd quit before he died in the mud.

No, she realized. His family loved the rodeo. They'd never go along with her plan. His father was a national champion. His friends were all the buddies he traveled with from town to town. They loved the thrills. They'd only look at her as if she were crazy for trying to make him stop.

She took a cab, went back to the Hilton, and booked another room for the night. Reagan knew she had to calm down before she talked to Noah again, otherwise they'd just fight.

NOAH WATCHED THE NURSE CHANGE HIS BANDAGES. He knew Reagan wouldn't be back for a while. They were one step away from an argument. He wished he could find the moment in his memory when things stopped being perfect between them. They'd been so close once he swore he could read her thoughts. He didn't know all the reasons why she didn't want to be touched, but he told himself he'd wait. He'd go slow.

But he hadn't waited. He'd decided all she wanted was to be friends. They'd never talked of love; neither was ready for that kind of commitment. She was focused on her farm and taking care of her uncle. He'd hit the road at eighteen. For a while it was like some kind of crazy party. The rush of the rides, the drinking to calm down, the girls knocking on his door when he won.

The nurse asked him if he needed a pain pill and he said yes, knowing a pill wouldn't end the hurt inside him. He and Rea could never be more than friends. He tried to make himself believe that he could accept it.

Only, how would he get her out of his thoughts? When he imagined making love, it was Reagan in his arms and no other. She was one petite little girl of a woman who didn't have a single sexy thing about her, but she was the only woman he'd ever longed for. He'd spent a few hundred hours figuring out just what he'd do with every part of her body. Thoughts she'd probably kill him for thinking.

He didn't deserve her.

Closing his eyes, he knew it had been a mistake to call her. She was like a mirror of what he could be, held up to show him how little he'd made of himself.

Only he'd break his other arm and both legs before he'd tell her to go.

Chapter 14

TYLER WRIGHT SLID INTO THE BOOTH ACROSS FROM HANK Matheson at the Blue Moon Diner. Even though Hank had finally married and built Alex, his bride, a house on his ranch that overlooked both their properties, he still dropped by the main ranch house every Tuesday and Thursday morning to pick up his niece. He took her to breakfast and then school.

Saralynn was in grade school now and managed quite well with her leg braces and crutches, but she still loved it when her uncle carried her.

The diner was packed with locals and a few tables of truckers who'd discovered the place.

"How are you this morning?" Tyler addressed Saralynn first.

"It would be better if it was Saturday. Mom's taking me to Oklahoma City then." Saralynn made a face. "I wish it was Saturday." She waved her hand and looked disappointed when the world didn't change.

"Sorry, Princess." Tyler smiled. "Give it time. Saturday will come. No use wishing your life away."

She put her chin on her palms and sighed before turning back to the menu.

Tyler nodded in Hank's direction. "How about you? Staying out of trouble, I hope." He smiled at Hank. "Wouldn't do to have your own wife arrest you."

Hank Matheson grinned. "It might be interesting to see her try."

Saralynn, unaware there was a conversation going on, spoke up. "I forgot to say I'm fine today, Sir Knight." She might be all grown up at eight years old, but she still called Tyler the name she'd given him when she was four.

"That's good to hear, Princess." Tyler handed her a set of art pencils he'd picked up at the hobby store the last time he'd been in Dallas. "I thought you might need a few more drawing pencils."

She laughed. "Thanks." Flipping her paper placemat over, she set to work.

Tyler leaned close. "Want to tell me what you're planning to draw? They say you gifted folks see the picture in your head even when you look at a blank canvas."

She didn't look up as she worked. "It's a cave lit only by diamonds. A place where only fairies live."

Hank folded up his newspaper, ordered, then turned his attention back to his friend. "I blame you for her wild imagination. You've always played along with her dreams. I swear, her make-believe world is so real sometimes I wonder if I'm not part of the fantasy world just living in her mind."

Tyler laughed. "Right. It's all my fault. Your family being so grounded and all."

Hank shrugged. With his mother a potter who rarely remembered what month it was much less what day, his sister an artist who only painted pictures of men suffering horrible deaths, and his other sister married to a graphic artist who wanted to name their children after superheroes, Hank had no room to talk about daydreams. At the Matheson place creativity must seep through the soil. It was no wonder Saralynn was off the charts with talent. "Forget my family," Hank said. "You look like you fell off the hearse and the family car ran over you."

Tyler touched the dark bruise on his face. "You should see the one on my hip."

Hank laughed. "No thanks. I can miss that showing."

Both men laughed, knowing the girl was no longer listening to them. They settled into their routine of talking frankly with one another over coffee.

"How's her legs?" Tyler said, pointing with his head toward Saralynn.

"This new doctor seems to know what he's doing. Another few weeks the braces come off, and maybe this time they'll stay off. The guy who looks after Jeremiah Truman's recovery is living out on his place. He said he'd come over every afternoon and check on her once the therapy starts."

Tyler nodded. He'd met Foster and Cindy Garrison. He seemed like a nice man, and his wife, Cindy, was as gentle and kind as they come. Some folks in town claimed that old Jeremiah wouldn't have made it through his last spell if Foster hadn't been there.

Hank studied the dark bruise on the funeral director's forehead. "I heard about your accident from Alex. Got attacked by a flashlight, right?"

"Right." Tyler sighed, owning his own stupidity. "But the bruises don't hurt near as much as having to eat my own cooking. It doesn't look like Willamina's coming back. Her sister called me yesterday and told me she got a postcard from Saint Thomas. Apparently seventy-two is not too old to go native. Said she'd been skinny-dipping in the ocean."

"I don't even want to think about seeing that."

Tyler agreed. "I don't understand it. The woman spent forty years watching TV in my kitchen, never smiling or even talking to me, and then she takes off without even saying good-bye."

"What do you think set her off?"

"I have no idea," Tyler lied. He'd figured it out from something the sister had said about two women around the place being one too many. The old cook must have thought Kate was there to stay the day she slept on his bed. "I'll manage, though."

"You don't want her to come back?"

Tyler shook his head. "To tell the truth, I don't think she liked me all that much. Mom said I used to pester her when I was a boy and she first came to work for the family. I don't think she ever forgave me. When I first took over I used to make a list of what I wanted for dinner every night. The only thing I could always depend on was that nothing on that list would be served."

"So you'll get along without her?"

"I've already hired Three Sweeping Maids to come once a week and clean the place. In two hours they do more cleaning than she did all week. I eat breakfast out, make a sandwich for lunch, and have frozen food for supper. Who knows, I might even lose a little weight now that she's gone. To Willamina the four food groups all started with *S*. Sugar, starch, salt, and shortening."

Hank leaned back as the waitress slapped their plates on the table. "As long as Kate doesn't show up too often and cook like she did last week, you'll probably be healthier without Willamina. That meal Saturday night at the inn was great."

"Yeah." Tyler acted interested in his breakfast. He didn't want to talk, or think, about Kate. When he hadn't e-mailed Sunday night after his trip to the hospital, he had a headache all day Monday and didn't even go down to his office. This morning, when he finally checked, she hadn't written. Their friendship seemed like a dance, one step forward two steps back.

The realization that she meant a great deal more to him than he meant to her settled in around his heart like cold blood. He might as well be living in Saralynn's fairy cave for all the reality he saw. Kate was a friend, and to wish for more would only lead him to more hurt.

"I heard the woman you found out back in the cemetery is still in the hospital." Hank broke into Tyler's thoughts. "They say she was pretty sick. Running a fever, getting dehydrated. You know, Tyler, she might have died if you hadn't gone out to check on her Sunday night."

Tyler looked up. "Really?"

"For real. The doc told Alex that the girl thought she could just crawl in the back of her car and sleep till the fever broke, but she'd been there almost a week and was only getting worse. With it below freezing last weekend, she could have frozen, or come down with pneumonia. She's lucky you came along."

Tyler didn't know what to say. He'd thought he'd done everything wrong that night. Frightened her. Shone the light in her face. Bullied her. Now to find out that something he'd done might actually have been good made him feel better. "I might drop by and see her if she's still in the hospital. I need to say I'm sorry for frightening her."

"That'd be nice," Hank said. "I don't think she has any family around these parts."

"Sir Knight?" Saralynn lifted her head from her work of art.

"Yes, dear," Tyler answered in his most courtly fashion.

"You can have my picture if you like. I made it of the lady you helped."

Tyler looked down at a giant holding a fairy with bright green wings. "Thank you. But isn't she a little small in the picture?" He remembered her falling on him and she was no small woman.

Saralynn shook her head. "She's a fairy in disguise. They do that sometimes just so they can walk among us and we won't step on them by accident. Don't ever let her eat okra or she'll go back to her real size."

Tyler held the picture up as if it were a great work of art. In truth, it was rather amazing. "Do you like okra, Princess?"

"No," she answered as she put her drawing pencils in their case. "I never eat the stuff."

Before either man could comment, she looked at her uncle Hank and said, "It's time to take me to school."

Hank frowned. "You didn't eat your eggs and biscuit."

She split the biscuit in half, gulped down a forkful of eggs while she added honey to the biscuit, then wrapped it in her napkin. "I'll eat it later."

Hank carried Saralynn out while Tyler ordered a cup of coffee and a roll for dessert. He wondered why the breakfast specials never came with dessert. It seemed a good idea.

While he waited, he stared at the drawing. He decided he'd frame this one and put it in his office. Someday when she was a great artist like her mother and grandmother, he'd get her to sign it, but for right now, he needed to look at it and remember that people are not always what they seem.

Some are short-stout giants and others are fairies in disguise.

Chapter 15

POST OFFICE

THE LETTER DIDN'T SHOW UP IN THE STACK UNTIL SHE'D almost finished sorting. Ronelle set it aside, knowing she had a delivery to make. Yesterday she'd been too frightened to go out and was relieved there had been no mail for Marty Winslow. But today, she told herself, she was ready to face him. Somehow he didn't seem so frightening knowing that he worked with numbers. Her mother had never mentioned that serial killers were usually great at math.

Numbers were like the words in her crossword puzzles. They couldn't hurt her or embarrass her. Numbers and words populated a safe world.

At a quarter till noon, she put on her official coat and the wool cap her father used to wear when he walked a route. She'd found his old mail pouch and decided to wear it strapped over her coat even though she had only one letter to deliver. Ronelle now thought she looked very official.

As she moved past the main office, Mr. Donavan smiled at her. "You making your delivery?"

She nodded and fought to get the first word out. It was always the hardest. "I can take the mail for the fire station too, if you want."

Donavan looked surprised. "All right."

He watched her leave. She didn't know if he was more surprised that she'd offered to do extra work, or that she'd talked to him. She did talk to the man now and then when she had to. He'd probably be very surprised to know that she said more words to him than she did anyone else most days.

The wind blew out of the north, brushing against her cheeks like tiny icicles.

Today she'd stop by Marty Winslow's place first, then the fire station, then the diner. She'd have the Tuesday special of meat loaf and mashed potatoes.

She liked the diner on Tuesdays. It was never quite as busy thanks to all the business club luncheons. If she went home for lunch, her mother always welcomed her by saying she'd have to fix her own lunch; after all, this wasn't a quick-order place. When Ronelle usually left after eating a peanut butter and jelly sandwich, Dallas would yell from the living room something like, "You better not have left a mess for me to clean up."

The letter to Winslow wasn't special delivery, but she knocked anyway.

"Come in." His bark didn't sound any friendlier than the first time.

She pushed the door open and walked into what she thought of as his cave. "Mail," she said simply.

He raised his open hand and waited for her to cross the room. His dark eyes studied her as before. "What's your name?" he asked as he studied her.

"Ronelle Logan," she managed as she tried to keep her hand from shaking.

He frowned at her for a moment, then said, "Thank you for bringing it in. Jerry usually leaves it in the box by the road."

She got the picture. It couldn't be easy on snowy days to go down the ramp and get letters.

He barked a laugh. "Maybe it's because I usually tell him to shut up and get out when he brings it in." His gaze locked on hers. "I'm guessing you feel the same way about him."

It was a statement, not a question. He'd read her mind, she thought.

When she turned to leave, he said, so low she wasn't sure he wasn't talking more to himself than to her, "I'm not going to blow my brains out, you know, despite what your mother said Saturday. If I were prone to suicide, I would have done it two years ago."

She looked back at him, realizing he must have heard every word her mother said. As always, she wanted to apologize for Dallas. As always, she didn't.

To her surprise, he smiled. "I asked around. That was your mom, right?"

She nodded.

"I guess we all have our cross to bear. Most of my days are too dark to even be aware of people like her. I probably wouldn't have noticed her if you hadn't been near her. I saw you the moment you walked in. You did a good job of ignoring me and everyone else."

"I . . ." Backing up, she tried to think of something to say. "I didn't want to be there. I wasn't ignoring you, just the world."

"I understand."

She was almost to the door when the motorcycle thug came barreling in. "I got the table and chairs"—he froze when he spotted Ronelle—"you ordered," he finished.

She backed as far away as the little corridor space would allow. If the tattooed youth hadn't been blocking the door, she would have run for her life.

"Border, this is the mailwoman, Ronelle Logan." Marty rolled toward them. "Ronelle, this is Border Biggs. He lives next door with his older brother, Brandon. I couldn't ask for better neighbors."

She had no idea what to say. The big kid obviously didn't

either. He gave her a confused look like he thought she might be a bug he needed to squash.

Marty laughed and touched the arm of her coat sleeve. With gentle pressure, he moved her to the side. "Get out of the way, Border. You're frightening the lady."

Border frowned. "Hell, Marty, did it ever occur to you that she might be frightening me?" He wiggled the chair he carried along the corridor, allowing her enough room to go around him. "In those clothes I didn't even know she was a woman. I thought she was just a short mailman."

When Ronelle made it to the sidewalk, something made her turn and look back. Marty had pulled one of the drapes aside and was watching her. He looked as if he were sorry to see her go.

Absently, she brushed her sleeve, still feeling the warmth of his touch.

She walked to the fire station and delivered their mail to Hank Matheson, the fire chief. Most women in town thought Hank was the best-looking man around. Folks said his heart had always belonged to the sheriff, Alex McAllen, who had stolen it when she was a kid. Ronelle had never talked to either one of them, but she considered them the guardians of the town.

"Thanks," Hank, said turning back to his work.

"You're welcome," she managed in just above a whisper.

Hank glanced up and touched the end of the letter to his forehead in a kind of salute.

She turned away and smiled, thinking maybe next week she'd ask Donavan if she could deliver the block all the way to the diner.

Chapter 16

❦

DALLAS, TEXAS

DENVER SIMS HAD TAKEN A FLIGHT LAST SUNDAY OUT of DFW three hours after Claire Matheson left his room at the Hyatt. He thought of her every spare minute as he moved from flight to flight doing his job. Three days later he found himself back in Dallas for one night. He couldn't stand the thought of staying at the Hyatt without her, so he booked a room farther from the airport.

After a shower and clean clothes, he checked her schedule and was surprised to find she was due to be in Fort Worth lecturing at the university on trends in today's art world. He rarely called her because she was always surrounded with family or friends. Probably would be tonight as well, but he rented a car and drove out to the lecture site in hopes of at least seeing her on stage.

When he got to the lecture hall it was already packed. Denver pulled his Stetson low and watched the crowd.

She'd told him once that she sometimes traveled to the Dallas area for talks or meetings with potential buyers, but only rarely did she spend the night. If she wasn't planning to meet him, she usually drove home.

Denver didn't like the thought of her driving half the night, but he couldn't say much. Claire wasn't the kind of woman to take suggestions, much less orders.

When Claire and four others walked on stage, the audience settled. Each member of the panel said a few words, and then the questioning began. Denver stood in the shadows and watched her. He paid little attention to what was being said while his eyes drank her in like a man dying of thirst; his ears didn't work at all. He memorized everything about her but couldn't quote one word she said. Every time she stood, he slowly undressed her in his mind.

Tonight she wore a wine-red pantsuit almost the color of her hair. To the world she must have looked very proper, almost distant, untouchable, but he saw far more. He knew the way she felt beneath the very proper suit. Warm, almost as if she had a slight fever, and soft in all the right places.

The talk ended, and people filed by to ask questions or to gush over how much they liked her work. The room was almost empty when he saw her recognize him in the back. Her back straightened slightly and he didn't miss the anger flaring in her eyes a second before she turned away.

When he moved to shake her hand, she didn't greet him, but only whispered, "Why are you here?"

"I thought I'd walk you to your car," he answered as he gripped her hand hard, not allowing her to move away. "I'll be waiting just outside the door."

She shook her head, but he only smiled. He knew Claire. She'd argue with him and herself, but she'd step right into his arms.

He walked outside and waited just beyond the steps. The night was chilly, not cold, but he barely noticed.

Ten minutes later she walked out alone. Tall and beautiful. When she didn't move, he took the steps two at a time until he was almost within reach. Then, slowly, as if he thought she might bolt if he moved too fast, he raised his hand and waited.

"Come on, darlin'. I'll walk you to your car."

She didn't take his hand, but she walked down the stairs and along the sidewalk toward the parking lot. The sidewalk was shadowed by evergreens on either side and silent in the evening air. Somewhere deep in the campus a clock tower chimed the hour.

Halfway to the parking lot, he suddenly circled her waist and pulled her into the darkness.

She didn't make a sound, but she tried to wiggle away from him and when her hands shoved at his chest they were balled into fists as if she were about to fight.

Cupping the back of her head, he brought her lips to his and kissed her hard. Like he knew she would, she slowly melted against him and her mouth opened.

His hand moved along her body, petting her gently as her arms circled around his neck and drew him closer. When he broke the kiss, he felt her warm breath against his throat.

"Do we have to go through this every time, Claire? Can't you just come to me?"

"I . . . I . . ." she whispered, brushing her mouth against his.

Denver forgot the question and kissed her again. This time with tenderness, silently showing her the love he felt but couldn't say.

A couple walked by; their giggles brought him back to his senses. He couldn't make love to her here. Breaking away from her, he took her hand and walked her to a bench.

"I can't stay the night."

He didn't ask why. He could guess. Claire had a daughter to take care of, family responsibilities, and a hundred other reasons. He didn't care which one pulled her away from him this time . . . every time.

"I've missed you, darlin'," he whispered as he pulled her against his side.

"You saw me three days ago."

"I know, but I've never been good at rationing passion where you're concerned."

She nodded as if she understood.

"I'll be home in a few days. Promise you'll come to my house. I don't care if you come late and leave early, I want to be with you. I want you to see what I've done to the place." He almost added *for you*, but didn't dare. She wanted—no, craved—passion from him, nothing more. No gifts. No promises.

"I'll try," she whispered.

He knew trying to push her wouldn't work. He kissed her gently on the cheek. "If you come, I'll make love to you in every room of my house and then we'll start all over again." He added, close to her ear, "There's no one else there, Claire. You won't have to bring a change of clothes. We'll hang up what you wear in when you get there, and you can put it back on when you leave. In between we'll have wine in front of the fireplace and eat breakfast in bed."

She laughed then, something Claire Matheson rarely did.

As they stood and walked toward her car, she whispered, "I'll come as soon as I can." She laughed again. "And I plan to see every room."

"I'll be at the farm waiting."

Chapter 17

TWO DAYS AFTER HE HAD BREAKFAST WITH HANK MATHE-
son, Tyler Wright did all his paperwork at the funeral home
and left for the hospital. A part of him hoped the woman had
already gone. He didn't remember much about her, except
that she was tall and thin, dressed like a teenager, and had
seen him at his worst.

When he walked into Autumn Smith's room, he remembered the half bushel of dirty-blond hair as well. The
woman was curled up in the hospital bed sound asleep. He
took the time to study her. There was something hard about
her face, almost as if she'd been pretty once, really pretty,
and then life had beaten her down, changed her. There
were worry lines along her forehead, but no laugh lines
around her mouth or eyes.

He guessed she'd had a hard time, and he hadn't made
it any easier for her. Her cheeks were damp. She'd cried
herself to sleep. The nurse told him when he asked about
her that the doctor had said she could go home tomorrow.

Tyler knew without asking that she had no home to go
to. He looked around the room. She'd been in the hospital
four days, yet there were no flowers in the room, not one
card on the shelf. Not one get-well drawing by a child or
one balloon wishing her a quick recovery.

When he looked back her blue eyes were staring at him.
"Who are you?" she said, in a voice sounding dry and
scratchy.

"I'm sorry," Tyler said, moving closer to offer his hand.

"How about getting out of my room, Sorry," she said,
coming fully awake like a wild animal.

"I'm sor . . ." he almost said again. "I'm Tyler Wright."

"You're the man who almost got me arrested." She looked
at the bruise on his face. "From the looks of you, I must have
won the fight."

He smiled. "You did. I landed on icy rocks and hit
myself in the head with my flashlight. You, on the other
hand, landed on something soft. Me."

She didn't look like she trusted him, but at least she had
stopped snarling at him. Tyler considered that progress. "I
wanted to drop by and see how you are and to tell you I'm
sorry for any trouble I caused you."

"They impounded my car, thanks to you." She pushed her
hair away from her face. "Tell them to give it back and we'll
call it even. I'm ready to get on my way. It's my car. I made
every payment even if it is registered in a dead man's name."

"Oh," Tyler said. He didn't like hearing about problems
he could do nothing about. This young woman should be
talking to Jerry Springer, not him.

"Forget it," she snapped. "Not your worry. You're just
the cemetery patrol, right?"

He ignored the insult. "Is there something you need that
I could bring you? I'd be happy to help any way I can."

Tyler didn't know if he meant what he said, but it felt like the right thing to say.

She stared at him a minute and said, "Any chance you could get my stuff out of the Mustang? If I can't have the car, I'd like my clothes and books."

"I could try. I know the sheriff and it seems like a reasonable request."

She shrugged and leaned her head back onto the pillow. "Whatever," she whispered as she closed her eyes. "So long, Mr. Wright. Don't let the door hit you in the butt on the way out."

Tyler straightened. He wanted to tell her that people never talked to him that way, but he figured she wouldn't care. Glancing into the open closet as he walked out, he saw no warm robe. No slippers. Only a folded hospital gown and a cheap comb. A pair of muddy tennis shoes. A sweatshirt with what looked like dried blood on it lay across muddy jeans on the closet floor.

He could see why she would want her things. He didn't know much about women, but he knew, poor or rich, they all wanted their things around them. Walking out to the lobby, Tyler tried to decide how involved he wanted to get in the business of someone who obviously wasn't expecting much. She sure didn't seem to like him.

Tyler figured he must attract women who didn't like him much. Willamina had left without a word, Kate seemed to have lost his e-mail address, and now Miss Autumn Smith didn't want anything to do with him. If a female serial killer ever passed through town, she'd probably stop at the funeral home first.

With a shrug he turned into the gift shop. "Morning, Mrs. Lovelady," he said to the sweet little lady who'd been volunteering at the hospital for thirty or more years.

"Morning, Mr. Wright, and how are you this beautiful day?"

Tyler glanced out the window. Rain had been threatening to fall all morning, and the wind whipped between buildings, almost knocking folks down, but to Mrs. Love-lady, the days were always lovely.

"I need your help, please," he began. Immediately he saw excitement in her smiling face. "I'd like to send a few things to a woman who is stranded here because of an accident. I don't think she has any family, or at least none who know she's here. She doesn't know me, but I think she could use some cheering up, so just tell her the gift is from a friend."

Mrs. Lovelady got her pad. "Were you thinking flow-ers? We have some nice potted plants."

He shook his head. "She's leaving tomorrow; she'd have nowhere to put them, or balloons for that matter."

Mrs. Lovelady tapped her pen against her bottom lip. "A card or a book, maybe a stuffed animal."

"No. I think something useful would be better."

"We have a nice set of bath soap and lotions. Every woman can use those." She led him toward a display of personal items. "Does she have a robe?"

Tyler frowned. "I don't think she even has a toothbrush. Could you just make up a basket of everything she might need on these shelves?"

Mrs. Lovelady looked thoughtful. "If I add our best fluffy robe and gown, with slippers to match, it'll be a big basket. You'd be wise to just buy the suitcase to put it all in. It's a little expensive, but it would do her far more good than a basket."

Tyler reached into his pocket for his money clip. He peeled off two hundred-dollar bills. "Will this cover it?"

The lady shook her head. "For another hundred I'll throw in a nice jogging suit. And of course, the bow and card for free."

"What a deal," he said as he handed her three Franklins. "Send it up to room three eleven, Autumn Smith."

"Oh, the woman who was sleeping behind the ceme-tery."

Tyler should have been surprised that Mrs. Lovelady knew hospital gossip, but he wasn't.

"I'll toss in some chocolate where there's room. When I was pregnant I always liked chocolate."

"She's pregnant?"

Mrs. Lovelady nodded. "Dr. Spencer was here all night the night they brought her in. I heard one of the nurses say the poor thing almost lost the baby."

Tyler walked out of the hospital and ran to his car. He might have had nothing to do with Autumn Smith getting pregnant, but he definitely had some part, no matter how small, in her almost losing the baby. He felt terrible.

AUTUMN SMITH WATCHED THE STRANGE LITTLE CHUBBY man running to his car. He'd been all dressed up in a suit like some kind of lawyer. Maybe she was in more trouble than she thought. She swore. That wasn't possible.

The Mustang might still have her father's name on the title, but he'd been dead five years, so he wasn't likely to have claimed it as stolen. She'd been sixteen when she'd picked it out all shiny and new. He'd had to sign for it, but she'd made every payment. He'd said he'd change the title when it was paid for, but before she could make the last payment, he died and no one thought of the paperwork on her car. He died on her eighteenth birthday, leaving his little farm to a common-law wife Autumn had never gotten along with.

Autumn had packed everything she owned in the back of her car and driven away with her almost-stepmother waving from the porch. There was nothing left for her in Tennessee.

"Five years," she whispered. "Five years of trying to make a living, of trying to keep body and soul together." She didn't want to think about how badly she'd failed at love, at life, even at surviving. And now, she carried the baby from a man she barely knew and had never liked. He'd said he wanted her, needed her. She'd gotten pregnant before she realized that he was lying. His kind of want and need had nothing to do with love.

Autumn couldn't take care of herself. How was she ever going to take care of a kid? But she couldn't end the baby's life any more than she could end her own. Somehow, deep down inside, she had to believe that things would change. She knew life would never be easy, but did it have to always be so hard?

Chapter 18

❧❧

SIMS PLACE

DENVER SIMS THOUGHT THE RINGING WAS IN HIS HEAD for a few times before he realized it was the phone beside his bed. He opened one eye and smiled, realizing he was home in Harmony and not in some hotel between flights. His house on Lone Oak Road was the only place he felt like he could let his guard down. He might have remodeled and had it furnished in Mission-style décor that looked more like it belonged in New Mexico than West Texas, but this place was very much his lair. The place he went when he needed to rest, to hide out.

The house phone sounded again.

With a loud groan, he frowned and climbed out of bed. Home didn't have wake-up calls. Who'd be phoning him before dawn? Claire had promised to try to drop by one night, not at sunup.

"Hello. This better be important!" he snapped in a voice he hadn't used since the army.

"Denver, you awake?"

"I wasn't." Denver sat on the edge of the bed as he recognized the voice of his best friend and only neighbor within shouting distance. "Is it time for the babies to come, Gabe? Are you on your way to the hospital?"

"No, we're still five weeks out," Gabe answered with a laugh. "But since you're awake, there's something I want to talk to you about."

"I'm not helping you name the twins." Denver had thought his friend was an intelligent, talented guy until his wife got pregnant. Gabriel Leary could write a book, and illustrate it, on how not to be an expectant father. "And I'm not, I repeat not, having a discussion about breast-feeding again. I couldn't even look at a woman from the neck down for a week after our last talk."

"Forget that," Gabe said. "It turns out I don't have a vote on the breast-feeding question, and after my last suggestion on the names, Liz and her mother both agree I don't get a vote on that either."

Denver knew he'd be sorry he asked. "What did you suggest?"

"Well, after Thing One and Thing Two didn't go over, I thought Thor and Loki. After that, I was told to stop thinking period. Apparently, my role in this whole thing is sperm donor and nothing more."

Denver smiled, having a hard time feeling sorry for the luckiest guy he knew. "So, since your job was over more than seven months ago, why are you waking me up today?"

Gabe paused a moment as though he were starting to lose faith in his ideas. "I think we should practice a few runs into town. You know, run surveillance to make sure there is nothing in the way that will slow us down when labor starts and we're on our way to the hospital. This time of morning there should be no one on the roads, but just to be on the safe side we could do runs at different times."

"Gabe, we're five minutes from town, another five to the hospital. If we start when the contractions start, that's maybe one or two contractions before we're there."

"I read they sometimes start closer together than that. What if they start three minutes apart? Liz will have a half dozen before we can get her inside the hospital."

Denver saw that there was no reasoning with the man who'd saved his life in combat more than once. He figured he owed him one. "Why don't you get a room at the hospital and just leave Liz there the last few weeks?"

"Great idea!" Gabe shouted. "I'll be over to get you in five. We'll go in and see if they have any openings we can book ahead."

Denver tried to argue, but the phone went dead.

Before he could find his shoes, he heard Gabe's pickup flying into his drive.

Denver walked outside barefooted and yelled, "I don't want any credit for this dumb idea. You've already got every Matheson woman including little Saralynn thinking you're crazy. I don't want to be guilty by association."

Gabe shrugged. "Maybe it's not a good idea, but we could ask. What harm could it do to just ask about booking a room?"

An hour later, when Dr. Spencer threatened to call the sheriff if they didn't leave, Denver decided to physically drag Gabe out of the hospital corridor.

"Lets go to the diner and have some breakfast," he suggested as he took Gabe's keys.

Gabe nodded as he continued to mumble death threats under his breath. When he climbed in the passenger side of his Jeep, he frowned. "I don't know what they were getting so excited about. All I was going to do was canvass the area and see if a few of the older patients might be willing to check out a little early to make room."

Denver fought down a laugh. "I think it might have been the term *check out* that upset them. Maybe you should have used *go home*."

Gabe shook his head. "Touchy people." He rolled down the

window, ignoring the fact that it was freezing. "I'm not sure that Dr. Spencer is old enough to be a real doc. We've both seen more blood in battle than she'll probably ever see. She's so young I wouldn't be surprised if she parks a tricycle in the hallway when she makes her rounds. She does have small hands, though. That could come in handy if the baby . . ."

"I don't want to know." Denver shot out of the parking lot. "How about we make a deal? We don't talk about anything related to being pregnant or having a baby while we eat."

"You got it, Lieutenant."

The years of being a soldier seemed a long way away, but the fact that they had the same shared history would forever bond them as friends. More than friends. Brothers.

Denver tried to help. "If you're worried about the five minutes it'll take to get to town, how about you and Liz moving over to Winter's Inn? It would cut the time in half."

Gabe shook his head. "I don't think I could take sweet old Martha Q for more than a day. I think the last time we ate over there with Hank and Alex, the old lady patted me on the bottom."

Denver laughed. "She's interested in you, I guess."

"No." Gabe shook his head. "I think she was just testing to see if I was fat enough to eat yet. I swear she was the role model for the witch in 'Hansel and Gretel.' For years she made men miserable by marrying one after the other. Now, she's fattening them up to eat."

Denver didn't argue. "Speaking of man haters, what do you hear from Liz's sister, Claire?" Denver always tried to work Claire into the conversation when he could without being obvious. He would have liked to talk to Gabe about her, but Claire wanted their relationship kept secret from her family, and half the town was either part Matheson or married to one. As far as the Matheson family knew, he was just Gabe's friend who came to dinner now and then at the ranch house. They all seemed to like him, but Denver wouldn't be surprised if Alex, a Matheson by marriage, hadn't had a background check run on him. Alex Matheson was the best sheriff he'd ever seen. Little got past her.

"From what I hear from Liz's mom, Claire is home working like crazy," Gabe said, between telling Denver how to
drive. "Only comes down every night to eat dinner with Saralynn and help her with her homework. Then by nine she's
back working. I heard her last painting was of a businessman
face down in the mud with the shadow of a plane over him.
The caption read: FASTEN YOUR SEAT BELT, PLEASE. Her agent
says she'll get twenty or thirty thousand for it. She's sketching
out one with a guy lying dead in a parking lot. Huge black
crows are pulling bites off him. She's calling it *Picnic in the
Park*. You might be careful, Denver. I swear this new guy in
the painting looks a bit like you."

Denver frowned.

Gabe didn't seem to notice. "Claire's getting richer
every day and more of a recluse. If her agent didn't make
her travel, I swear she'd never leave the house. She tolerates
me, but it's obvious that woman doesn't like people and
hates all males. Liz says her sister was never boy-crazy as
a teenager, but when she came home after her marriage
broke up, she'd changed inside. Like something had died
and would never return."

"Look who's talking, Gabe. Before you met Liz you
lived around here five years without more than a handful
of people speaking to you."

They reached the diner and got out. Neither seemed to
notice the wind that almost knocked them down. They'd
lived on the plains long enough to ignore wind.

As always, Gabe picked a back booth and the two talked
about their army days and how different life was now for
them. Gabe always asked about Denver's job, which he considered cushy: flying around the country, keeping an eye
out for trouble on planes.

Denver told him about a drunk who started yelling one
night on a flight out of Chicago. He wanted the stewardess
to sit on him to hold him down so he wouldn't float off the
plane when they lost gravity. A steward appeared and took
over the job, ignoring the drunk's complaining.

On the way back to the farm, Gabe talked about his

work, but Denver didn't understand much. The only graphic novels Denver had read were Gabe's work. He knew his friend was good. Money hadn't been an issue when he'd built a house overlooking the canyon. It wasn't big, but the views were outstanding and he and Liz lived in every room.

Denver shared Gabe's confusion over people who built rooms in a home that they never went in. Maybe their feelings came from spending so many years in tents where they thought they had luxury if their feet didn't hang out. Life in Harmony seemed not only a world away from what they once were, but a lifetime as well. The two soldiers who once thought only of staying alive were now talking about diapers.

But with Gabe and Liz, life was blessed and their lifestyle was reflected even in their home. Their house was open, flowing from his study into a living area and an open kitchen. Denver got the feeling they couldn't stand to be separated by even the walls. Liz could stand in the kitchen and watch him work and he could watch over her when she slept on the couch or in the sunroom. Denver caught himself feeling a little jealous of that kind of love.

The house phone was ringing as he waved good-bye to Gabe and stepped back inside. For once he knew it wasn't Gabe.

Pirate, the mangy dog who'd seemed to come with the house he bought, appeared from the hallway.

"You could have answered it," Denver said as he rushed past. "Maybe taken a message."

The dog didn't look like he cared.

Denver grabbed the phone. "Sims here," he said, reaching for a pen to write down the time of his next flight. He wasn't due to work for two more days, but he usually took shifts when they came along so he could build up comp time.

There was a pause before a woman's voice whispered, "Denver?"

He felt his heart slow. "I'm here, Claire."

"I saw you with Gabe at the diner on my way home from taking Saralynn to school. Is everything all right with my

sister? I wanted to call her, but I was afraid that if everything is fine, I'd wake her this early, and if it's not she'd be
too busy to talk."

"Everything is fine. How about I promise to call the minute something does happen?" He figured Liz would call her
sister when it happened, but she and Claire were not close.
Maybe because there were too many years between them,
or maybe just because they were very different people.

"I'd appreciate it," she whispered, telling Denver she was
probably calling from the Matheson Ranch. With all the
women living in that place he was surprised she'd found an
empty room.

"It's Thursday," Denver, said trying to keep her on the
line. "Doesn't Hank take Saralynn to school?" He made a
point to remember every detail about Claire and her family.

"Usually, but he and Alex were called in early. There's a
dawn meeting at the courthouse about a disaster plan. This
year everyone wants to be prepared if a tornado comes our
way. Alex as sheriff and Hank as volunteer fire chief both
had to be there."

"So you had to get up early." He lowered his voice.

"Yes," she said, without emotion.

"Can you meet me?" He slammed his fist against the
door frame, wishing he didn't sound so needy. *Keep it light*,
he reminded himself. *Keep it casual.*

"I . . ."

"Where?" he said, without giving her time to say no.

"It's dangerous here at home. Someone could see us.
Everyone knows us."

Denver wanted to yell that he didn't care if the world saw
them. "How about the Buffalo Bar and Grill? We could just
happen to bump into one another there."

"No. I don't ever go there."

He couldn't really see her going into the bar either, but
it was the first place he thought of. It was a popular hang-
out, but not for an ice princess like Claire. "The roadside
lookout?"

"It's too cold."

He knew she probably wouldn't come to his place, even though she'd said she'd think about it.

"I have to fly out of Dallas Monday; any chance I could see you before then?" He tried to keep the bitterness out of his tone. They were both single. Why did they have to both leave Harmony to connect?

"Liz and Gabe are coming to Sunday dinner. Why don't you come along? I could see you then."

"All right. Sunday dinner." He got the picture. Sunday dinner with the two great-aunts sitting between them. With Claire rarely even looking his way. With her daughter, Sara-lynn, asking questions in rapid fire.

If she didn't want to see him, then she should just tell him. Sometimes he had the feeling Claire was torturing him like a cat playing with a mouse before she had him for dinner.

"Good-bye, Denver," she whispered.

"Promise me something before you hang up."

"All right," she said.

"Promise there will be a place and time for me to hold you."

"I will try," she said, and the phone went dead.

He was beginning to hate those three words as well as himself for accepting them from her.

Chapter 19

THE THREE DAYS IN THE MEMPHIS HOSPITAL FOR NOAH McAllen turned into six. Reagan stayed by his side while the doctors looked for the cause of the constant pain in his back.

Finally, on Friday, they told him to go home. Maybe the pain would pass when the other parts of his body healed.

While Reagan packed his few things, Noah called his parents.

"Hi, Mom," he said, forcing himself to sound better than he looked. "How are things? I thought I might come home for a few weeks."

He listened, ignoring the nurse who came in to run a final check.

"That sounds great, Mom. No, don't even think about

canceling the trip. I'll just make a few more stops and be home in March. Then you'll have pictures of your trip to show me. Have a great time."

He paused to listen, then added, "Tell Dad I'm doing fine. My card's filling up. Yeah, I miss you guys too. Good-bye."

When he clicked his phone closed, he looked at Reagan. "They're taking a month-long vacation. Plan to see California and then fly to Hawaii for ten days. This time of year is pretty much the slow time for Dad's trucking company."

"Why didn't you tell them?"

"Because I know them. They'd miss probably the best vacation they've ever planned. I'll go home and stay alone. I'll do fine."

"Nonsense," Reagan said. "You'll come home with me. In fact, my uncle told me the night you called to bring you back with me. He said our house is starting to look more and more like a hospital every day. You might as well be there recovering too."

Noah's grin was there for a moment, reminding her of the boy who'd bugged her when she moved to Harmony.

"You inviting me to move in, Rea?"

"Yes. I'll call and have Foster order another hospital bed. We can have the dining room table removed and you can sleep there."

"I was hoping we'd moved to being friends with benefits."

"We have," she laughed. "I'll see you recover and hide your truck keys so you can't get back on the road too soon. I've got Foster Garrison and his wife living with me. He'll help you do your therapy and Cindy will fatten you up on ginger-apple pancakes and buttermilk pie. If you like, you can share the parlor with Uncle Jeremiah, but you're not sharing my room."

"You've grown from a mean spitfire of a girl to a cruel woman, Reagan Truman. The only time I can get you to cuddle up close to me is when I'm hurt."

"I'm sure on the road you've had far prettier girls than me."

He shrugged. "Maybe. Definitely nicer and more willing, but better, I don't know. Maybe one of these days you'll let your guard down and we could give it a try, just for comparison's sake."

She laughed. "That's about the worst line I've ever heard. To think I was worried about you sleeping with a different girl every night. With that kind of logic, I shouldn't have worried. I'll bet you were living a monk's life."

Handing him his jeans, she turned around as he tried to slide them on with one hand. When he hit her with his hospital gown, she grabbed his shirt and faced him. Noah's chest and shoulders were more scarred than she remembered, and far more hairy. He was so thin she could see his ribs, along with deep bruises that hadn't completely healed from other rides.

With his arm in a cast, she had to help him with his shirt. When his face was close to hers, he whispered, "Thanks for the offer, Rea. Even without benefits, you're the best friend I've ever had."

She wanted to cry. When she'd come to Harmony at sixteen she had no friends and didn't plan to make any. Noah "Preacher" McAllen called everyone in town his friend. Everyone loved the wild, happy-go-lucky kid—everyone still did, but he no longer saw it. Noah had left Harmony, but the people still talked about him, asked if she'd heard from him. Men young and old dreamed of doing what Noah was doing. They'd be surprised to see him now. Even now, after seeing him like this for almost a week, Reagan was still having trouble blending the boy who left with the man coming home.

"I booked the late flight home tonight. We'll be landing after ten and it'll be after midnight before we get home. If you like, no one has to know you're even in Harmony. That way you can rest."

He smiled. "Protecting your reputation. Don't want folks to know you got a cowboy's boots under your bed."

She smiled. "Don't want to see girls from seventeen to thirty lined up outside my door to take your temperature."

He shook his head. "I doubt anyone will remember what

I look like. The two days I was home for Christmas I had to show my ID to buy a drink at Buffalo's one night."

With the nurse's help, Noah forced himself to move from the bed to the chair. By the time they got to the airport, he looked exhausted. He barely noticed the nurse who helped him move onto the plane. Reagan had hired her to fly with them to Dallas and make sure Noah got on the plane to Amarillo. After that, Reagan figured she could handle the fifty-minute flight. Foster would be waiting in Amarillo.

Noah stretched out in his first-class seat beside her and reached for her hand as the plane taxied out. Before they were in the air, Noah was asleep, but he never turned loose of her hand.

He woke up in Dallas complaining of pain, took two pills, and went back to sleep. He seemed drugged when Foster made him comfortable in the back of a Suburban he'd rented. Reagan made the last leg of the trip home listening to Noah's snoring as Foster drove through the night.

When they arrived home, the dining room had been cleaned and removed of all the clutter. The space looked more like a hospital room now with all kinds of supplies and equipment neatly stacked.

While Foster got Noah settled in and comfortable for the night, Reagan checked on her uncle, took a shower, climbed into her thickest PJs, and curled up in her favorite chair beside his bed.

"He'll sleep through the night," Foster said as he pulled up the railing on either side of the bed.

"I know. I just wanted to sit with him for a while."

Foster nodded, but she had no idea if he understood. "Call me if you need anything else."

Reagan pulled the blanket over herself, realizing how exhausted she was. Within a few minutes the house grew silent, but sleep couldn't find her. She wiggled, first thinking it was too cold in the room, then deciding it was too hot. She got up twice to make sure the drapes were tightly closed. She went to the kitchen for milk and then for a sandwich that she took only two bites of.

Finally, Reagan lowered the railing on one side of Noah's bed and crawled in beside him as she had once in the hospital when he'd been hurt. Barely touching him, she placed her hand on his heart and felt the beating. Closing her eyes, she took a deep breath and tried to match the beat of her heart to his.

Within minutes she was sound asleep.

Chapter 20

POST OFFICE

RONELLE WAITED UNTIL ALMOST ONE TO PUT ON HER COAT to make her delivery. She'd hoped the weather would warm some, but the day had stayed cloudy, holding the frozen earth captive.

As she walked toward the duplex just off Main, she saw no one out. Today seemed a good day to huddle in. Not even the wind blew by. Moisture hung in the air, not rain or snow, but damp, depressing, like an icy compress on her face and head.

When she knocked on Winslow's door, no one answered.
She knocked again.
To her surprise, the door swung open.
Marty rolled back a few feet and snapped, "Come in. It's about time I got some mail."
She stepped inside and pulled his letters from where she'd stuffed them inside her coat so they wouldn't get wet. One

looked like it might be something important. The other was only an ad addressed to *Occupant.*

"You look half frozen," he said, still none too friendly. "Where's that dumb hat you usually wear?"

She didn't answer. She wasn't sure if he was worried about her or just insulting her again.

"Go over by the fireplace. I'll get you a coffee."

She stood watching him roll away, not sure what to do. Did mailmen accept coffee? She had a feeling that if anyone in town offered Jerry something to drink, like a stray dog, he'd stay the winter.

More from fear of what he'd say if he came back to find her still standing at the door than from any real need to get warm, Ronelle walked into his front room. A fire was going in an old Rookwood fireplace, and it made the room not seem so drab with light dancing over the red of the brick.

"Take off your coat and hang it over the back of one of the chairs." His voice came from a room away.

She looked toward the windows and saw the table and chairs the thug had delivered a few days ago. They were thin wood, the kind that she'd seen for sale at thrift stores. She pulled one chair closer to the fire and removed her wool coat, surprised at how wet it was. Another few minutes outside and the dampness would have reached her shoulders.

She'd just pulled the other chair close to the fire and sat down when he entered. He rolled toward her, two cups of coffee on a tray across his legs.

He frowned and offered her one cup. For a few minutes, they both watched the fire and drank their coffee.

Finally, he said, "You didn't have to come. My mail would have waited."

"It's my job."

Silence lingered between them.

"You heading to the diner to eat?"

She shrugged.

He took a drink. "I've seen you walk that way. Border says you always eat alone at the diner. You take the worst table, by the door, and you turn your back to everyone."

Ronelle looked up, not sure she liked anyone watching her.

His dark eyes studied her as if he were trying to figure her out without asking questions. The only sounds came from the crackling of the fire and the tapping against the windows as watery snow turned to ice.

He took a deep breath and said, "Look, don't take this the wrong way, but if you want to eat here, I've got plenty. It'll save you marching to the diner and back and by the time you eat, your coat should be dry enough for you to make it to the post office before you turn into a snowman."

"Snow woman," she corrected, and was surprised when he smiled.

"Snow woman," he said. "How does chili sound?"

"Great."

"I'll check the corn bread if you'll pull the table over here by the fire."

She watched him disappear before she moved the table. She'd pulled two chairs up before she realized they'd only need one.

When she stood at the kitchen door, she was surprised at the room before her. Everything, from cabinets to a sink, had been built to accommodate a wheelchair. "This is nice."

He looked up, then handed her a plate with a bowl and spoon atop. "Yeah, it's why I rented the place. Only one I could find in this entire town made to fit me that wasn't in a retirement home."

"Why here? Why Harmony?" she asked as she held her plate out for a ladle of chili. "Folks say you're not from around here."

"Why not? I liked the name," he answered, then added in a lower tone, "This town was as good a place as any to come to die."

"You're dying?"

He looked up at her. "Lady, I'm half dead already." He must have caught the sorrow in her eyes, because he added, "But looking at you without that bulky coat on reminds me I'm also half alive."

She lowered her eyes as his gaze moved down her body.

"Stand up straight, would you?" he requested more than ordered.

Without looking at him, she straightened, knowing she'd just added a few inches to her already too-tall frame.

"Much better," he said, and filled the other bowl before handing it to her.

She took both plates while he balanced the corn bread basket on his legs. They made their way to the table by the fire. Neither said anything for a few minutes, and then she whispered, "This is good. Really good."

"I can cook," he said without bragging. "When I lived in Dallas, I got so tired of eating out that I watched the food channels until I could pretty much cook anything I wanted. What's your favorite food?"

She shrugged. "I don't know. I like the meat loaf at the diner." She could think of nothing she liked that her mother fixed. It all tasted about the same.

He handed her a piece of corn bread. "I know you like corn bread."

For a moment she didn't understand how he knew anything about her, and then she remembered how she'd stolen the slice from the table at the fire station last Saturday.

She couldn't look at him as a warmth that had nothing to do with the fire spread up her cheeks. She couldn't tell him that she'd eaten the corn bread so that if the food was poisoned she wouldn't be alive and alone with her mother.

They were almost finished eating when he asked, "Would you mind if I call you Ronny? It seems to fit you."

She looked up at him, thinking that he'd just asked the strangest favor in the world. People didn't usually call her anything. He watched her, obviously waiting for an answer.

"I wouldn't mind," she said. "Thank you for the lunch."

"You're welcome, Ronny." He said her new name slowly. "Will you come again, next Friday, say? I haven't had a guest since the accident."

She didn't have to think about it, but she wasn't sure what to say, so she only whispered, "Yes." He hadn't been very friendly. Most of the time they were silent, but it was the nicest meal she'd ever had.

He rolled back, and she knew it was time for her to leave. Standing, she pulled on her coat and walked toward the door.

He followed. When she turned, with one hand on the knob, he said simply, "Thanks for not asking questions, Ronny."

Without giving it much thought, she did something she hadn't done to another human being since her father died. She leaned down and kissed his cheek, then stepped out into the cold before he had time to react.

All the way back to work, she smiled. Finally, after all these years she'd accidentally bumped into someone like her. Despite all her mother's efforts, she'd found someone she could call a friend.

Chapter 21

TYLER WRIGHT HAD A FUNERAL ON FRIDAY THAT KEPT him busy most of the morning. He'd gone by on Thursday and talked to Alex Matheson about getting Autumn's car out of lockup.

Alex didn't think it would be a problem. Though it was registered to a woman in Tennessee, when they'd called her she'd said she didn't want the Mustang or anything to do with the woman driving it. She said she knew an Autumn Smith five years ago and wasn't surprised the police were checking up on her. According to the Tennessee woman, Autumn had been wild and good for nothing.

On Friday afternoon, Alex gave Tyler Autumn's keys and added, "I only talked to her for a few minutes. I've heard of folks that don't have a friend in the world, but until her I don't think I've ever met one. You want to take her the car? She's getting out of the hospital this afternoon when Dr. Spencer does a final check."

Tyler nodded. In a bigger town law enforcement would

never hand over someone else's keys, but here in Harmony judgment sometimes overruled procedure. He took the car and had it washed and filled with gas. The least he could do for her, he decided.

Most of the clothes in the back looked dirty, so he dropped them off at the laundry and asked if they could have them finished in an hour. Most of the books in the back looked like mysteries. He stopped at the bookstore and bought a few more to add to her collection.

He felt like he was trespassing on her life when he opened the trunk. More books, an old computer ten years out of date, and a box of dishes and pots. Not enough to stock even a small kitchen, but enough to survive. Tyler had a feeling these few things were all Autumn owned.

When he got to the hospital, he found her waiting for the final checkout. She wore the jogging suit that had been hanging in the gift shop window a few days ago. It looked too big on her, but at least it was clean and warm. Rick Matheson was sitting in a chair a few seats down from her. He looked like a kid who was still growing into his grown-up lawyer suit.

Autumn seemed disappointed when Tyler joined them.

Rick smiled. "Afternoon, Mr. Wright, good to see you."

"Nice to see you too." Tyler offered his hand. He didn't know Rick well. He remembered the boy, but Rick had been away for years at college. "How's the family?" Asking that one question of any Matheson in town could start a half-hour discussion.

"Fine." Rick kept it short.

"Your cousin Liz must be due any day." Tyler thought it better to talk to Rick and give Autumn time to warm up to him. "I hear Gabe Leary is so excited he's driving everyone nuts. Alex told me he called in an emergency complaint about that bump in the road near the bridge. It's been there for twenty years, but Gabe thinks it should be removed immediately. Seems it's on his route from home to the hospital."

"That's what love will do to a guy." Rick laughed. "First

you get married, then the little wife gets pregnant, then you get crazy."

Autumn stared at them. "Do you two think you could have your little family reunion somewhere else? I'm not interested in hearing it and I've already told you twice, Matheson, that I don't need a lawyer." She moved her gaze to Tyler. "Or an undertaker."

Rick frowned as he stood, but not before Tyler saw something in his eyes. Rick was like his cousin Hank, the fire chief; he simply cared about people, all people, and whether Autumn wanted any help or not, the young almost-lawyer wanted to help her.

"I was just telling Miss Smith that I'd be happy to take her over to the shelter. She could rest up there until she gets her strength back, but she's not convinced it's safe."

"I know it's not safe," she corrected. "I've stayed at a few shelters over the years. Fellow guests will rob you blind. The food is no good. Folks who run it try to save you and get you to mend your wicked ways. I can't afford ways, wicked or otherwise."

Tyler wanted to remind her that she had nothing worth stealing, the food was good at the Harmony shelter, and as far as he knew, "getting saved" wasn't painful. But, he didn't comment. It felt safer to let Rick take the fire.

"I just want to get on down the road. I keep believing like a fool that somewhere else is always going to be better than where I am." She tried to push her hair out of her face, but like always it just bounced back. "I've been a waitress or cook in half the towns on Interstate 40. There's always a truck stop with a HELP WANTED sign out. I'll find something."

"I filled your car with gas." Tyler hoped she'd be happy about that, at least.

"I can't pay you," she snapped, "but if you'll give me your address, I'll send back money as soon as I land."

Tyler fished in his pocket for his card and handed it to her. He thought of telling her to forget it, but he had a feeling he'd hurt her pride.

The nurse came in. Rick took the opportunity to leave. Tyler couldn't help but wonder if he'd come on his own or been sent by Liz. The Mathesons, since they were one of the founding families, always thought it was their duty to watch over the town. Tyler couldn't decide if Rick considered himself part of the welcoming committee or a guardian at the gate.

"Funeral director, not undertaker. I see you're the big cheese Mr. Wright from Wright Funeral Home," Autumn said as she held up Tyler's card. "You hoping to drum up business hanging out at the hospital?"

"No, just delivering your car."

The nurse pulled up a wheelchair and said it was policy that Autumn ride out. Tyler followed, pulling the suitcase he'd bought for her.

When they reached the door, he handed over the keys to the Mustang. "If you'll follow me a few blocks around to the square I'll take you to the laundry where I left your clothes."

She didn't look comfortable saying it, but she thanked him anyway. He walked her to her car, put her suitcase in the trunk, and watched her follow him as he drove downtown.

When she parked beside him, Tyler rolled down his window and told her to wait in the car. He'd get her clothes. The wind had started to kick up and her jogging suit didn't look near warm enough.

When he came back out, her Mustang was still parked beside his Rover, but she had vanished. For a moment he circled, looking for her, and then he spotted her in the bookstore. He walked inside in time to hear her asking if there were any job openings.

The manager shook his head. Tyler watched her shoulders round in defeat.

When she walked back toward the door, he said, "I thought you hated this town. I figured you'd want to be out of here fast."

"It doesn't really matter where I go. I just need a job. One place in hell is as good as any to stop." Autumn straightened. "But, looks like I will be moving on. I tried every café, diner, and truck stop around here when I came in. The bookstore was a long shot. I don't know why I even tried."

Tyler smiled. "Maybe because you love books."

She glared at him. "How do you know that? Did you rummage through all my stuff?"

Tyler wasn't in the habit of lying. "Yes."

She looked more defeated than angry. "Well, I guess you know I've nothing worth selling and I need money. That tank of gas you loaned me might not last long enough to find a job, and once it's gone I'll be looking for another place to park."

"You want to know what else I found out?"

"Sure, why not."

"I found out you don't drink . . . no empty bottles. You don't smoke and the only drugs the sheriff found in the car were vitamins."

She laughed. "Maybe I can't afford any."

"Or, maybe you're trying to take care of yourself for the baby's sake."

"You know about that problem as well." She didn't look surprised that he'd found out about the baby. "I'm not doing a very good job of it, but that's not your problem. Thanks again for the help, Mr. Wright, but it's time I hit the road. You're okay, you know."

Tyler didn't think. He acted. "I do have a favor to ask if you'll allow me."

"I'm not a prostitute, so don't ask," she snapped, the anger back.

He held his hands up. "No, no, nothing like that. I was just wondering if you would be interested in filling in for my housekeeper for a few weeks at the funeral home. The pay is fair and there is a room off the kitchen." When she hesitated, he added, "With a lock. Room and board are free and the housework is light, but the cooking will keep you busy."

"Would I have to touch any dead people?"

He smiled. "No. Though most of my employees are old, they're still breathing. Once in a while, Willamina, my housekeeper, makes a simple lunch if we're busy or it's snowing, and she usually keeps desserts in stock in the break room." He was making it up as he went; Willamina hadn't done much cooking. "You'd buy the groceries, cook me usually two meals a day. I'd let you know when I'm going to be out and won't be eating in. The kitchen and quarters you could use are on the first floor with the business offices. I live on the second floor."

It occurred to him that he might not have always told Willamina when he was eating out. He wondered how many times she must have cooked supper for him and he never made it in.

"I don't know. I'd be working in a funeral home around dead people."

"Look at it this way. Most folks die in hospitals and you just spent a week there. In four generations I don't think one person has ever died in the Wright Funeral Home. I could show you the quarters and kitchen, and then you could decide."

She looked tired. "I guess it wouldn't hurt to look. But if you're not on the up-and-up, I'll make sure this whole town knows about it."

Tyler almost told her that the whole town would know anyway. The only crime in Harmony that people seemed to get away with was exaggerating.

An hour later she'd opened every cabinet in the kitchen, examined Willamina's bedroom and small sitting area, and asked a dozen questions. Finally, she agreed she'd take the job on two conditions.

"What?" he asked, still a little unsure about hiring someone he barely knew. But, in truth, he had no idea who else would want the job. Autumn was tall, but looked frail. No one else would probably give her a chance to work. He couldn't help but wonder how long it had been since she'd had a good meal. Her paperwork said she was twenty-three, but the anger in her eyes almost seemed a defense masking fear, and the bruises along her arms seemed layered over time.

"I'll need a desk in my quarters," she said, as if testing to see if he'd call off the offer.

"Done."

"And I want that dog to stay away from me." She glared at Little Lady, who sat politely in the doorway leading to the front foyer. "I have no use for dogs. Don't expect me to feed her or get up and let her in when she starts yelling outside."

Tyler almost laughed. Little Lady would never yell. "I'll take care of the dog, but her bowl of food and water will remain in the far corner of the kitchen."

She looked like she was thinking about it, then finally agreed.

"I have one more question before we begin."

She braced herself as though she expected bad news.

He hesitated, not sure how to ask. Finally, he said simply, "How far along are you?"

"Ten weeks, I guess. Dr. Spencer told me to come in to see her next week and we'd run some tests. When I missed my period I figured I was pregnant, so I stopped drinking and started taking vitamins. When I missed another one a few days ago, I had no doubt. There was no need for the pregnancy test; I couldn't afford it anyway."

Tyler could feel the blush crawling up his neck. He'd never discussed a woman's period. "What about the father?"

"Not in the picture. He didn't want a baby, or me when he found out. After he yelled at me for a few days, his only comment was that I'd probably lose the baby sometime soon. The night before I left, I got the feeling he aimed to make sure it happened." She looked down and added, "I told him I'd take care of it, but he said he didn't want me having a kid and the law coming after him for child support someday. He knew I was planning to leave him as soon as I could, but I don't think he figured I'd run. The last time he got rough, I could tell he was trying to make sure most of the blows landed in my middle. I didn't fight back. I just took it, and then when he went to sleep, I packed what I could and left." She glared at him. "Anything else you're dying to know about me, Mr. Wright, or do you want more details?"

Tyler closed his eyes. "No," he said. "That was more than enough, Autumn." He'd always thought he wanted children. He couldn't imagine someone who wouldn't. "I'm sorry."

Autumn shook her head. "He was nothing special. Just somewhere to crash when I was down." She hesitated. "I guess I'm nothing special either, Mr. Wright, but if you're offering me a job, I'll do my best while I'm here."

"I'll have Calvin help you unload, and tomorrow he'll bring a desk up from the basement. You can park your car around back. Get settled in and rest tonight and we'll talk about details in the morning over breakfast at seven." Tyler walked over to the cabinet by the stove and pulled out a wooden box. "There will always be two hundred dollars in this box. When you buy groceries, put the receipt in here and I'll replace the cash. From this point on, consider the kitchen yours. Buy what you want and cook what's needed around here."

She nodded and he left, wondering if the box and Autumn Smith would be in the kitchen come breakfast. Smiling, he looked at the bright side. At least he knew she wouldn't be taking Little Lady along with her.

After working until dark, he went out for a pizza. When he came back, he entered through the back and crossed the big kitchen. Autumn's door was closed, and probably locked. The remains of a sandwich and an empty bowl of soup were on the counter. He grabbed a beer and headed for his office, thinking that he might have to hire someone to clean up after the housekeeper.

As always, when he turned his computer on, he checked his e-mails. For the first time since he'd taken Kate to the airport, there was a note. It said simply:

Ty:
Haven't heard from you. Hope all is fine. Figure you're working hard.
Kate

He leaned back in his chair. Nothing personal. To his surprise, Tyler realized he hadn't thought of Kate or worried about her all day. Maybe the way to keep the sadness away was to stay busy. When Kate came back, he'd be waiting, but until then he had to get on with life . . . and life for him was working.

THE NEXT MORNING, TYLER ENTERED THE KITCHEN HALF expecting the money and Autumn to be gone. Instead, Autumn was standing by the stove wearing the bottoms to her jogging suit and an old T-shirt in worse condition than the rags they used to polish the hearse. Her feet were bare and her hair was pulled back. The smell of sage sausage and French toast filled the room. He took a deep breath, figuring he must have been the first person to die here and had gone straight to heaven. Or else this was a dream.

"Get your juice, Mr. Wright, and have a seat. I'll serve up your breakfast."

He did as told and was surprised when she put two plates on the kitchen table. Then she sat down across from him, her legs folded in the chair. "I don't know how this works, so I'll make up the rules I don't know. When you eat in the kitchen, I'll join you. If you tell me to take a meal up to your rooms, I'll put it on a tray and leave it. If you ask for it delivered to your office, I'll knock before I come in just in case you're busy with grieving folks. Sound fair?"

"Sounds fine," he said. When he'd finished half his breakfast, he added, "Where'd you learn to cook?"

"When I was a kid, my mom always took me with her on wheat harvest. She'd cook for thirty men three times a day. It didn't take me long to learn. Then she died, and my dad let the witch move in. By then I was twelve and the witch thought cooking and housecleaning were my jobs. She didn't care if I went to school, but she sure was picky about everything being clean." Autumn smiled. "If we'd had a fireplace for me to sit by I would have been a Cinderella, I guess. During the days all she did was yell at me or slap me around just for the hell of it, but once my dad got home she was real sweet in front of him. Too bad no Prince Charming came along. I could have used one. When my dad died, she kicked me out and I've been moving from town to town ever since."

"So, you've seen the world." Tyler decided he liked not having breakfast alone. Autumn's story was sad, but she told it with humor and an honesty he found fascinating.

"I can do pretty much everything but pick men. Some women go for the tall ones, some the wild ones, I go for the bastards. Show me a man who'll treat me bad, take any money I have, or leave me pregnant and I'll head straight toward him already puckered up for the first kiss." She shook her head. "I'm telling you, Mr. Wright, it's a real dangerous habit bringing stray sons of bitches home."

Tyler laughed. He'd never been around anyone who talked like she did. He'd never eaten a meal with the cook sitting across from him. He wasn't sure he felt comfortable, but if she stayed around, he might get used to it.

When she smiled, she looked younger. He knew she was in her early twenties, but right now he would have guessed her age in her teens.

Standing, he said, "You need anything, just ask Beth in the office. She'll probably be in sometime today to introduce herself. Mrs. Stella McNabb might drop by. She works in the evenings when we have someone here for viewing."

Autumn looked worried, so he added, "They're nice ladies. Bake them something sweet and they'll love you. Bake the guys in the basement anything and they'll like you. Calvin will talk to you, but Dave never says a word. The other groundsmen come by now and then."

"So the rule is feed anyone who walks through the kitchen?"

"That's about it."

She smiled for the second time. "You know, Mr. Wright, I love to cook. I think I can do this job."

He was at the door when he turned back and added, "No one is going to treat you badly here, Autumn. No one will ever yell at you." He'd never said anything like this to an employee, but he felt it needed to be said. "You're safe here. You've my word."

She looked skeptical. "We'll see."

By ten there were hot rolls and butter in the break room, and by noon she'd made soup and corn bread for everyone. When he left to go to the bank, his bookkeeper was running off recipes for Autumn.

Chapter 22

⮑⮑⮑

SATURDAY
FEBRUARY 27
BUFFALO BAR AND GRILL

BEAU YATES LOWERED HIS HEAD SLIGHTLY SO HIS HAIR shaded his eyes as he tried to act like he was out of his teens. He didn't like confronting people, but this time, whatever it took, he wasn't backing down. If he had to fight his way up, he might as well start with Harley at the Buffalo Bar and Grill. No one in this town believed in him, but Beau knew he had a destiny and it was time he got on down the road a few steps.

"Now I'm telling you boys for the last time, I don't hire underage kids to perform no matter how good they can play." Harley Moreland leaned over the bar and yelled at Beau and his best friend, Border Biggs. "You two look like you belong in a country-western bar about as much as earrings belong on a pig."

"What if we play for free?" Border said. "That shouldn't be illegal. Or, you could lock us in that cage of a stage you got and we wouldn't actually be in the bar."

"Hell, that's probably more of a crime." Harley snorted. "I swear, just having you two clowns walk in here is probably breaking one or two laws right now. Why don't you do us both a favor and get out. Maybe drive over to a big town and see if McDonald's needs a band in the kiddie area."

"But . . ." Beau started.

"Ain't no *but*s about it, kid. Besides, I've already got a man hired to play tonight. He's been coming once a month for ten years. He's a drunk, but as long as he can stand, he can play. By nine o'clock, when the crowd gets here, it's so loud nobody's listening, they're just stomping to the beat and calling it dancing. Some nights by midnight the dance floor looks more like drunk foreplay than waltzing."

"We can play waltzes and 'Cotton-Eyed Joe' and lots of the oldies," Beau promised. "Give us a chance."

Harley glared at Beau. "You two don't look like you could play nothing, but when you turn twenty-one come on in. I'll serve you that first drink."

Border tried again. "I've been learning to play, but Beau here was born with a guitar in his hand. Besides, everyone tells me I look twenty-one."

Harley looked at Beau. "I don't remember you. How old are you? You don't even look like you're shaving regularly yet."

"Nineteen," Beau lied.

"If you're nineteen, I'm Hank Williams. Get out of here."

Border yelled as he walked backward, "If your one-man band doesn't show up, will you give us a shot?"

"Sure, kid, but Eddy Bailey always makes his gigs. Once a month he plays in Clinton on Friday and here on Saturday. I wouldn't be surprised if he's got his van already parked out under the trees, sleeping out the day so he can play the night away. Time was he was good enough to make it in Nashville, but the drinking and drugs got him. Now he's happy to play one weekend a month."

Border jerked Beau through the back door.

Beau shrugged Border off. "What's your hurry? I'm not sure Harley was finished with his preaching."

"I got a plan," Border said as soon as they made it to the parking lot. "All we got to do is get rid of this Eddy Bailey."

"Are you nuts?" Beau said. "I'm willing to do whatever it takes to make it in the music business. I even taught you to play and that was no easy job, but I'm not willing to murder anyone."

Border smiled as if Beau had just given him Plan B. "I was thinking more on the lines of being nice. Delivering the man a gift. But I guess killing is an option."

"What kind of gift?"

"A bottle of good whiskey." Border reached in the pocket of his leather duster and pulled out the bottle.

"Where'd you get that?"

"I picked it up at the bar when Harley was yelling at you and you were telling him how old you're not."

"You stole it?"

"Don't look at me like that. You're the one wanting to kill the guy. I just want him too drunk to stand. Besides, we can write it off Harley's payment against tonight's performance." He looked over in the trees at the back of the Buffalo Bar and Grill. Sure enough, an old Dodge van was parked on the slope that led down to the dried-up creek bed.

"What do you say we go down and give the man his gift?"

Beau grabbed the bottle. "I'll deliver it. If he looks out the window and sees you, he won't open the door." He took a few steps and grinned back at Border. "You know, this just might work."

Border shrugged. "What have we got to lose?" He'd shaved his head this morning for luck and regretted it instantly. Even his big brother Brandon told him he looked like the poster thug for most-likely-to-sell-drugs. Border liked people for the most part. He also liked his leather jacket and spiked cuffs. He'd long had the feeling that people could take him like he was or leave him alone. For the most part, they left him alone.

He watched Beau take the bottle to the van and walk back a few minutes later without it.

"What do we do now?" Border asked.

"We go to your place and practice until the crippled neighbor complains."

Border swung on his motorcycle while Beau opened the door of his old car. "Don't call him that. Marty's a good guy. Besides, he's not home today. He's always gone on Saturday. I'm not sure where, but I usually hear his car leaving early and he's never back before dark."

"He can drive?"

"Sure, you'd be surprised what he can do."

"You sound like you're his friend."

Border shook his head. "I don't think he wants friends. Sometimes, when my grandmother drops over with a meal, my brother invites him to join us, but he never comes. Once when I couldn't get my bike started and was just about to go back to bed and skip school, he came out and offered me a ride. I wasn't too happy about making school that day, but it was interesting watching him drive with his hands."

They started their engines and headed the few blocks to the duplex. After downing half a cold pizza, they went to work. Neither considered whether they looked, or played, much like a country band, but by nightfall they planned to be able to play a half dozen songs. Border had the easy part with chords and Beau could usually play anything he'd heard a dozen times.

They were an odd match for friends. Beau, raised by his father who let him take lessons so he could play in church, and Border Biggs, who'd been wild all his life. When Border checked into Harmony High School two years ago, he'd been picked on and called trash. Beau, who'd never fought in his life, stood up for him and got hit in the mouth for his trouble. After that, Border taught him to fight and Beau taught Border to play music. Since Border had no dreams, he decided he might as well follow along with Beau's.

By dark, they were standing in the shadows at the back of the Buffalo Bar. Eddy Bailey hadn't climbed out of his van. As always on busy nights, the back window in the kitchen was open. Beau and Border could hear everything being said. The place was packed. The cook complained that they might run out of wings if the music didn't start soon. Once couples start dancing, they give up eating in favor of drinking.

The owner, Harley Moreland, came in telling the cook to use the frozen frog legs if the chicken wings ran out. He claimed that after a few drinks, no one could tell the difference and the frog legs had been in the freezer far too long.

A half hour later Harley stormed back into the kitchen and yelled for someone to go get Eddy out of his van.

The kid who washed dishes ran out the back door so fast he didn't notice Beau or Border in the shadows. They waited in the dark, listening to the kid pound on the van door. After a few minutes, he marched back inside the kitchen.

Beau listened as Harley swore when he learned that his entertainment for the night was too drunk to stand.

"Do we go in now?" Border asked.

"No, we let him stew a few more minutes, and then we go in."

Border wore a trail in the grass behind the bar before Beau picked up his guitar case and knocked on the kitchen door. "I'm not working for free no matter what you said," he whispered to Border. "We're at least getting supper out of this deal or we don't play."

"Don't order the chicken wings," Border whispered back a moment before Harley opened the back door and jerked them inside.

"You boys got your first gig," the big man yelled, "but I'm keeping the lights low so no one'll be able to see you. Stay in the cage. I don't want you coming out till midnight."

Beau slung his hair back. "Then you'll deliver us a meal when we finish the first set?"

Harley looked like he might spit, but he nodded and led them through a back hallway, past the restrooms and storage room, to what everyone called the cage . . . a small stage surrounded by chicken wire.

Border unpacked his guitar and a small keyboard for Beau. "I feel like the world's largest trapped pigeon."

Beau lifted his guitar as he glanced around. Prison hold-ing cells were probably cleaned more often than this place. Mud, blood, and beer seemed caked on the floor. The cage had been built to protect the musicians from drunks. Beau had a feeling he might need that protection.

From his dark spot behind the dance floor he looked out. The place was packed with cowboys with their hats shoved far back, bikers in their leathers, and a few men in white business shirts. The women seemed to come in every size and age. Most had their hair puffed too high, their blouses cut too low, and their laughs turned up too loud.

Beau smiled, feeling right at home. The ladies reminded him of his mother, who'd run off with a trucker one night. Someday he'd write a song and dedicate it to Mom. He'd call it "Wild at Any Age," and then he'd try to find her to play it for her. His Bible-thumping father always said he hoped the Lord would take her in because no man in his right mind would.

"You sure you want to do this?" Border asked.

Beau took a deep breath. They were going to either love him or hate him, but either way he'd play his first gig tonight. "I was born to play," he answered with a laugh.

As they plugged in, the lights went down and the dance floor came alive with fairy lights reflecting off the unfin-ished ceiling onto a polished wood dance floor.

"Any advice?" Beau looked at Harley.

"Yeah. Play loud. The less they talk, the less trouble we seem to have. If a fight breaks out, just keep playing. Make sure the first few are fast to warm everyone up and get them thirsty, and the last one needs to be slow so the newly found lovers cuddle up on the dance floor and think of going home or at least to the privacy of the parking lot."

Beau turned to Border. They held their guitars down like rifles at rest. "Ready, partner?"

"Ready."

Harley pulled the mic to his mouth and yelled, "Ladies and gentlemen, welcome a new band to Buffalo's. The Part-ners!"

A moment later the music rolled like a wave over the bar. Loud, fast, and strong. Beau closed his eyes, afraid of what the reaction might be as Harley stepped out of the cage. When he finally ventured a look he was surprised. No beer bottles hitting the cage. No screams for him to turn it down. Only couples moving toward the dance floor far more interested in the touching that was about to happen than the music.

Border's steady chords became the heartbeat while Beau moved from keyboard to guitar. He slurred his way through a few country songs, then played a few more. No one on the dance floor seemed to notice the difference. They just danced and yelled and bumped into one another. They all thought they were the stars of the show tonight, and he was just the background.

As he played he studied the crowd. Border's brother, Brandon Biggs, was near the back of the bar. He had a beer in his hand, but he was listening, not drinking. Beau noticed a few girls still in high school. They couldn't be more than seventeen, but they were dressed up and made up like they were older.

At the end of the night, Harley was the only one outside the cage who looked sober. He'd forgotten about bringing them a meal, but he gave each a hundred dollars and told them they could have Eddy Bailey's one night a month if they'd learn more than six songs.

Beau thought about telling the bartender that he was probably the only one who noticed, but he didn't want to press his luck.

Chapter 23

MARTHA Q PATTERSON DRESSED ON SUNDAY WITH HER mind set on finally getting her new lonely hearts club in motion. She'd already talked a few people into at least coming to the first meeting. Rick Matheson as an advisor; Dallas Logan and her daughter would come, of course. Dallas never missed any kind of meeting in town that didn't lock her out. She also had one of the waitresses from the Blue Moon and two guys from the phone company who promised to come. Three widows answered the ad Martha Q had put up in the beauty shop. But they were all over seventy. One had a brother who lived with her, whom she said she'd bring if she didn't have to bring a dessert.

The numbers were good, but not good enough. Martha Q figured if she could rope in a few eligible men, the women would come. Only problem was, any man in Harmony over twenty and still single had learned to run like a rabbit.

Martha Q was proud of herself for keeping the club rules simple. One, anyone in the club had to think positive no matter how homely they were. Two, draw aim on one prospect at a time—the shotgun approach always leaves you the last one at the dance. Three, practice between meetings— talking, kissing, acting interested.

She picked up the basket of homemade muffins Mrs. Biggs had baked for her and walked to her car. She planned to stop at the fire station first. The men there were a little young, but at least they were single. Then she'd walk across to the sheriff's office. One of the dispatchers was in his thirties and newly divorced. Finally, she decided she'd stop at the roping corrals where the ranch hands gathered on Sunday afternoon if the weather was good. They'd be all smelly and tired from roping, but they might like a muffin and an invitation.

Martha Q set off on her hunting trip with great hopes, but by midafternoon, she was tired of talking and her feet, crammed into her *good* shoes, hurt so badly she was sure one of her toes had died from lack of oxygen and two others had committed suicide in protest.

When she passed the funeral home she decided to stop in and talk to Tyler. He knew everyone in town; maybe he could giving her some advice. Plus, he was single and of a good age for picking.

She went to the side door so he'd know it wasn't a professional call.

Martha Q knew Tyler lived alone above the business. Kate had told her that his apartment was probably over two thousand square feet and furnished beautifully. Martha Q found that hard to believe. What wife in her right mind would want to live above the business? But then, there had been three generations of Wright women who had, and if Tyler ever married, his wife might do the same.

"If Tyler ever married?" She laughed as she climbed out of her car. Men like him rarely did unless they were

lucky and married young. He wasn't that bad looking or
that overweight, but he had the curse. Tyler Wright was too
nice. Every woman in town saw him as a friend, a shoulder
to cry on, a man to depend on, but Martha Q would bet her
pantyhose that not one of them saw him as a lover.

She pushed the bell at the side door. She'd have to ask him
to come to Dreaming and Scheming, but she wouldn't push.

To her surprise a young woman wearing sweatpant bottoms and half of a T-shirt answered the kitchen door. For
a moment all Martha Q could do was stare at the bare skin
showing from just below her breasts to her belly button.

"May I help you?" the woman said, making little effort
to appear friendly. "If you need Mr. Wright, you need to go
to the front door."

Martha puffed up. "I'm not here on business, but on a
social call. Would you tell him Martha Q Patterson has come
for a visit?"

"Sure," the girl said, leaving Martha Q standing in the
doorway.

Martha Q watched the young woman closely. She wasn't
special, but more medium in every aspect except her hair.
The girl seemed blessed with a double dose of hair that
wasn't light enough to be blond. As she talked into a phone
by the kitchen counter, Martha Q noticed wonderful smells
floating her way. The girl was baking, not one, but several
things.

Tyler swung through the door that must lead to the business office beyond. He held a stack of papers in one hand
and his glasses in the other. When he saw Martha Q, he
smiled. "Come in, please. This is a nice surprise. Have you
news from Kate?"

Martha put all the pieces together and figured out what he
hadn't said. First, he obviously hadn't heard from Kate. Second, he'd been working, and third, the girl worked for him or
he would have introduced her at once. Martha Q organized
his problems. She couldn't hit him with all the truth at once.
A young girl around would never do. Tyler needed an old
housekeeper with maybe two or three unmarried daughters.

Somebody needed to tell the man that he should forget about Kate. If she'd wanted him she would have let him know a year ago. And, of course, at some point Martha Q had to bring up the subject about him being so nice.

She decided to start out in neutral. "I thought I'd come by to ask your advice about my club if you're not too busy."

"Of course not." He glanced back toward his office. "I'm afraid my office is a mess. I'm working on taxes. If Autumn doesn't mind, we might have coffee in the kitchen." He pointed with his glasses. "Mrs. Patterson, I'd like you to meet my new housekeeper, Autumn Smith."

The cook nodded, a bowl tucked into the crook of her arm as she stirred.

"Nice to meet you, Autumn. Please, call me Martha Q."

Autumn nodded once and turned to face Tyler, her words hesitant. "I could get you two coffee from the break room as soon as I take out the next batch of cookies."

"Don't bother, I'll do it, and I bet I can talk Martha Q into trying a few of your warm cookies." He smiled at the girl in his kind way, then turned back to Martha Q. "Autumn agreed to fill in for my housekeeper starting Friday and I think she's been cooking ever since. Last night she put four dozen cookies out for the family visiting, and not one was left. Today she says she's getting prepared for Monday, when we'll have two funerals, and last night she made the best stew I've ever tasted."

When the girl looked up, Tyler added, "My staff thinks we may have found a treasure."

Martha Q took a better look at the girl as Tyler went to fill the coffee cups. "So you're a cook, are you, girl?"

"I guess so. I can read a recipe and the staff around here isn't too picky. Mr. Wright says it's not usually this busy on the weekends."

"You interested in getting married?"

Autumn finally stopped stirring and looked up at her. "No."

"Why not?"

Tyler came back in talking when he hit the door. "So what's this visit all about, Martha Q?"

Autumn turned away without answering the question, and Martha Q decided right then and there that she didn't like this young woman. Too much past piled into too few years of living.

Martha Q asked what he thought about a few things as the girl listened and cooked. Tyler seemed distracted and was of little help, although he did suggest she contact the churches that had singles classes.

After downing a half dozen cookies, Martha Q decided to postpone her talk with Tyler. She waddled out of the kitchen and headed home. If she'd known starting a club was going to be so much trouble, she would have taken up quilting instead.

Chapter 24

❧

TRUMAN FARM ON LONE OAK ROAD

NOAH SPENT MOST OF THE DAY SATURDAY SLEEPING IN the quiet old house. He remembered meeting the nurse who talked about starting therapy on Monday and his wife, Cindy, who told him several times that he needed to eat. Reagan was around, but she didn't say much. He couldn't tell if she was glad to have him back or not.

That first night Noah had a dream that she crawled in bed with him, but he knew it had only been a wish.

Sunday he spent the day dozing and eating a little more. Late in the afternoon he thought he heard someone knock, but he couldn't tell if it came from the front of the house or the back. His room, the former dining room, was halfway between them and had no view of either.

A few minutes later he heard Rea whispering to someone in the hallway just beyond a door.

"Thanks for coming by to check on Uncle Jeremiah," Rea said.

"I figured he'd be fine. It's you I'm worried about."

The voice was low and rough. Noah knew he'd heard it before, but he couldn't quite place it.

"I'm always worried about you, Rea. You're doing too much trying to run this place, taking care of the old man and going to school full time."

"I'm fine, Brandon. I just need a little rest."

"How about I take you to the show Wednesday night? We could eat Mexican food first." He laughed. "If anyone sees us together you can always claim you were kidnapped."

She must have shaken her head because Noah thought he heard Brandon swear, then add, "By the way, where were you last week? I came by twice and both times Foster, the palace guard, told me you'd gone to the hospital to pick up something."

"I had," she said.

"Well, how am I going to date you, Rea, if we never go out and I only see you five minutes every weekend?"

"I told you, we're not dating, Bran. I don't have time right now."

"I know. I know. Jeremiah's sick. You have to study. The orchard needs work. I've heard it all. Just promise me one thing. When your world does settle down, you'll go out with me on a real date. Assuming I'm not married with five children by then."

Noah heard Rea laugh and say, "You got a deal."

Then he heard shuffling in the hallway and a door open and close. Then nothing.

Noah leaned back, staring at the ceiling. In the two years he'd been on the road chasing rodeos, he'd never thought that Rea might be dating. He had no claim on her. In fact, he had more in common with Brandon. She didn't want to date him either.

Only she hadn't mentioned to Bran that she'd brought a broken-down cowboy home from the hospital. He knew

she wouldn't, but he wasn't sure she would have lied if
Bran had asked her directly.

He closed his eyes when Rea came into the room. He
didn't want her to know he'd overheard her conversation
with Bran.

She moved around his bed, straightening his covers,
picking up the tray from supper. When she turned down the
light, he slowly opened his eyes. She was standing by the
window staring out into the side yard, where she had hung a
dozen wind chimes. Direct wind couldn't reach the area, but
the chimes still tingled softly. They reminded him of her,
never allowing life to touch her directly, always living in the
shelter she'd found here on the Truman farm.

Noah remembered a poem once about a desert flower
blooming so far away that no one would ever see its beauty
or smell its perfume. Reagan was like that. He'd just never
noticed until now.

Hell, he didn't care if she was friends with Brandon Biggs.
The big guy had always seen the worth of her. Bran was
probably a better friend than Noah would ever be. Only
problem Noah saw was that he didn't want Brandon being
more than just a friend.

Late in the night he woke as she climbed into bed beside
him. He didn't move until he thought she was asleep, and
then he circled her with his arm and pulled her close. Part
of him wanted to protect her from Brandon—obviously
the big guy was attracted to her—but another part of Noah
wanted to call Bran and ask the man to protect her from
him. Noah knew he wasn't near ready to settle down, and
staying in Harmony for more than a visit would be torture.
He would break her heart if he let it go beyond friends
because he knew she'd never leave this farm.

Chapter 25

❧

MATHESON RANCH

DENVER MADE SURE HE RAN INTO LIZ AND GABE ON SAT-
urday, and as always, they invited him to Sunday dinner at
the Matheson ranch. He'd been there for dinner so many
times he probably could have just gone. Except for Claire,
the whole family made him feel like he was one of them.
Aunt Pat even made him help with the salad and Saralynn
always acted like he'd come to see her, but Denver ached
just to see Claire. He needed her more than air.

As usual, all the Mathesons were there: Claire; her brother,
Hank, and his wife, Alex; her sister, Liz, and Liz's husband,
Gabe; Claire's mother; and the two great-aunts, of course. To
round the number out to a dozen Saralynn had invited her
friend from school, a cute, chubby eight-year-old named Violet, who constantly giggled. The girl's mother came along.
No one really knew why. Violet and Saralynn were having

a sleepover, so the mom could have simply dropped the girl off, but she'd settled in.

Before the dinner bell rang, Denver figured it out when Violet's mother told Gabe that she wanted to be a writer.

Gabe flashed his best friend a look that said *Save me*, but Denver had no intention of giving up a chance to talk to Claire. He knew all he'd have to say to the writer-to-be was *What do you want to write?* and she'd be talking for at least an hour.

When they all went in to dinner, Violet's mother took Denver's usual chair next to Gabe. Denver hesitated, feeling like the last one standing in musical chairs. Then he spotted an opening. The chair next to Claire. As casually as he could, he slipped into the seat.

She didn't even look at him.

As the meal progressed, with two or three people always talking at once, Denver slid his hand along the side of Claire's leg. She jerked a little and pulled her leg away. When he didn't advance, she moved her knee against his, silently asking for more.

Denver grinned, thinking that maybe if he quit advancing, she'd come to him.

Above the table they nodded and laughed as everyone else talked. Most of the time they weren't even looking in the direction of the other. But under the table he was memorizing the feel of her long, perfect leg.

When they both stood to help with cleanup before dessert, he whispered, "Next time wear a skirt."

The aunts and Claire's mother were in the kitchen listening to Violet's mother talk as they ate their pie. Gabe and Hank pulled their wives into the living room to cuddle and watch a rerun of the Texas Tech game. Saralynn and Violet vanished into Saralynn's room to play Chutes and Ladders.

Denver picked up Claire's dessert and waited to see where she planned to light. Wherever she settled, he would be in the same room.

"Everyone seems busy," she said, so calmly he was almost fooled into believing she hadn't thought of him at all. "Would you like to see my aunts' new greenhouse?"

He stared at her and smiled. Without drawing any attention, he followed her out the back door and along a walk to a small glass greenhouse. The Matheson place already looked like a village with Claire's mother's pottery studio, a huge barn for horses, a tool shed big enough to work on more than one car at a time, and several other sheds and garages.

Following Claire down a path to the new greenhouse, Denver noticed rows of flower beds ready for spring.

"They start growing from seeds about this time of year, but of course, the perennials that were clipped back in fall are now given light and full attention. By the last of April they'll be beautiful and ready to set out."

She sounded cold as a tour guide, and Denver hated it. If he weren't carrying two slices of pie, he'd remind her that they were definitely not strangers.

When she opened the door he set the pie down on the first table as she searched for the light pull.

"Leave it dark," he ordered as he pulled her hard against him with one hand and locked the door with the other. He felt like he might die of hunger for her, and when their lips touched he knew she felt the same. He pressed her against him, loving the way she trembled at his touch and how her warm breath came in rapid gulps against his throat when he broke the kiss.

"Wish we were in a hotel room, darling. Even in the dark a glass house doesn't feel safe." He closed his hand over her hip and felt her straighten, pressing her breasts against his chest. "I need you so much, Claire," he whispered.

He had half the buttons of her blouse undone when someone knocked on the door.

Claire jumped away and pulled her blouse together.

"Mommy," Saralynn said as she knocked again. "Are you in there? I want to show Violet the baby flowers."

Denver raked his hair back and picked up the pie. When Claire pulled on the light, she'd managed to button her blouse. She flipped the lock as he walked to the center of the room and downed two bites of pie.

When the girls came in he watched Claire. Her face was flushed, her lips were plump, and the buttons were mismatched with their holes, but he didn't think the little girls noticed. They moved though the rows of tables.

"Don't touch anything," Claire said calmly. "And turn out the light after you've looked around." She picked up her plate and walked out of the room.

In the darkness between the greenhouse and the back door, Denver held her pie as she rebuttoned her blouse. "We have to meet someplace where we can be alone," he whispered. "I'm about to die from the need for you, and don't bother lying to me and saying you don't feel the same."

She nodded. "What time are you leaving tomorrow?"

"Dawn. Can you make it over tonight?"

She shook her head.

"When are you traveling again?" He wanted to touch her, but with a plate in each hand that was impossible.

"Not for another month."

"I'll be back a few days next week. I'll let you know my schedule." He always did when he was home, but she never came to his house.

They heard the girls moving slowly down the path. Since Saralynn had been told she only had to use one crutch, she'd doubled her speed. Denver moved on and Claire stayed to offer any help Saralynn might need.

When Denver reached the kitchen, he found Gabe waiting for him. "Alex said she'd take Liz home. It appears my sister-in-law wants to see the nursery. They didn't seem to want us along." Gabe glanced over at Claire, then back to Denver. "If you're ready to leave I thought I'd catch a ride with you."

"Sure." Denver knew if he stayed any longer it would look odd. "Let me thank the aunts for the meal and I'll meet you at the car." He wouldn't have any more time with Claire. They were lucky to get the time alone they'd had.

A few minutes later, when he climbed in beside Gabe,

Denver didn't have time to buckle up before Gabe said, "How long are you going to let this thing with Claire go on?"

"What thing?" Denver played dumb even though he knew Gabe wouldn't fall for it.

"You think I'm nuts," Gabe mumbled. "Everyone knows how it is with you two. We see the way you look at her, and worse, the way she looks back. Aunt Pat even said one day that she thought you two were smitten."

"Hell," Denver swore. "What do you suggest I do? And giving her up is not an option."

Gabe shrugged. "Tell her you love her. Ask her to marry you? Take her to bed? I don't know. Do what you have to do before you both explode with longing."

"I've tried everything to get more time alone with her. I can't even get her to go out to eat, much less drop by my house. I haven't spent enough time talking to her to know how I feel about her or how she feels about me. All I know is I'm addicted to her. I haven't looked at another woman since I met her." Denver figured he probably looked as miserable as he felt. He looked out into the night and added, "What do you suggest next?"

Gabe slowed the car in the middle of the road and looked at his best friend. "How about stop trying."

Denver shook his head. "I can't give her up."

"I didn't say that." Gabe grinned. "Maybe if you stop chasing her, she'll stop running."

"That thought crossed my mind." Denver let out a long, defeated breath. "How long has *everyone* known?"

Gabe laughed. "Since the first night you went to dinner. You both disappeared for a while and when you came back you looked like you'd been in a fight and she looked like she'd just stepped out of an open-air jet."

"I don't suppose the old aunts know too? I'll probably never be invited to the Matheson dinners again."

Gabe smiled. "They're holding the bets on what will happen, and to my shock everyone is in your corner. How do you think you just happened to get the chair by Claire tonight?"

"Does Claire know you all know?"

"No," Gabe admitted. "We all decided you could tell her after the wedding. She'd be mad at the whole family if she thought we even suspected."

"Why'd you tell me?" Denver wished he didn't know.

"Because you saved my life a few times and I thought I'd return the favor. Stop chasing her, Lieutenant, and give her a chance to come to you."

Denver stared out into the lonely night. The only sound he heard was a coyote's howl. He might as well give his best friend's idea a try; otherwise it was only a matter of time before he stood on the nearest mound of dirt and howled at the moon.

Chapter 26

WRIGHT FUNERAL HOME

WHEN HE FINISHED WORKING FOR THE NIGHT, TYLER Wright walked from his study to the kitchen wishing Kate had e-mailed a note. He left his coffee cup in the sink and made sure Little Lady had plenty of food and water, but his mind was full of worry about his hazel-eyed friend Kate. He knew her assignments could be anywhere in the world. He didn't like to think of her traveling alone, going to strange cities, working in places where the streets might not be safe.

As he reached to turn the kitchen light out, he noticed Autumn cuddled in the bay window where Willamina always watched her soap operas. The old housekeeper must truly be gone for good; she'd taken her twelve-inch TV with her.

"Everything all right?" He half expected Autumn to say she was working too hard at this job and planned to quit. He'd reminded her both Saturday and today that she could take either day off plus any one weekday except Monday.

At this rate Autumn would have her forty hours a week completed within four days.

The girl turned when he spoke and stared at him.

"Something the matter, Autumn?" he tried again.

"I'm sorry. I didn't hear you, Mr. Wright, I was just looking out at the night. It looks so calm, so peaceful. The whole town seems asleep."

"Yes." Tyler could think of no better answer.

"I have fun cooking here. I've already tried a few new recipes. This place isn't like what I thought it would be. All the staff are nice, and near as I can tell no ghosts wander the halls. I guess I should say thanks for the job even if it will only last a few weeks till your real housekeeper comes back."

Tyler felt bad about lying to Autumn. "If she doesn't return, would you be interested in the position for a longer term?"

"I think I would. I feel like Snow White. I've found the cottage hidden in the woods and no evil can find me here. I know it won't last, but this is a good place to stop running for a while."

Tyler had never spent much time with fairy tales. His parents weren't prone to reading them, and he'd never had a niece or nephew to buy them for. "I'm glad you feel safe. Good night, Autumn."

"Good night, Mr. Wright, I'll see you at seven."

As he climbed the stairs with Little Lady as his side, he thought of how simple life would be if all you wanted was to be safe. Safety seems like such a little concern when you have it, but it's all that matters when you don't.

Chapter 27

RONELLE NOTICED THAT EVERY FRIDAY MR. DONAVAN SPENT the morning at the front desk. When he wasn't talking to customers he did what he called his accounts. She'd watched him do it so many times she could have parroted every step. He always began with counting the change drawer and ended with getting all the stamps in order. No matter how many or how few people came in and interrupted him, he always finished before lunch and never left his post.

Ronelle knew she wouldn't be disturbed in the back until Jerry came in around noon, so she always set her crossword puzzle aside and began what she called seeding.

A year after she'd started work, she'd been looking for something to do to pass the time. At first reading the magazines and postcards had been enough, and then she began working some of the crosswords in magazines she knew wouldn't be read . . . those going to the funeral home, for example. As time passed, she noticed things, she remembered things, and finally, she changed things.

For example, Mrs. Perry Lynn Davis at the nursing home always got a card from her sister in California the first week of the month. The sister, Miss Alice, also with a nursing home address, often said she'd never be able to visit, but she needed to know Perry Lynn was well. So postcards passed back and forth each month between the two women in their nineties. When Ronelle read Miss Alice's card saying she hadn't heard from Perry Lynn for over a month and feared something might be wrong, Ronelle called the nursing home in Harmony.

"I'm afraid," the head nurse said kindly, "Mrs. Davis has mentally slipped away. Though she still holds the cards to her chest, she's no longer in the present enough to respond."

Ronelle hung up the phone. Without the postcards, she had a feeling Miss Alice wasn't long for this world. Ronelle saw only one logical answer.

She began writing Miss Alice. Each month Mrs. Davis got a postcard to cherish and Miss Alice got a printed card in what looked like her sister's handwriting that said she was doing fine. They exchanged weather information and love. That seemed enough for both.

Then, as she kept sorting, there were others Ronelle worried about. Mr. Jetters, who came in complaining he never got mail, for example. Ronelle signed him up for every free magazine she could find. Miss Pat Matheson got all the free seeds every spring that Ronelle could find to offer. She even signed her mother up for the *Women Serving Time Behind Bars* quarterly. Dallas Logan complained every time it came, but she read it anyway.

Only today, Ronelle hurried through her seedings because she had someplace to go for lunch. Marty Winslow was cooking for her. Imagine that. He'd invited her to lunch.

She'd had his stack of letters at the corner of her table all morning. As soon as Mr. Donavan told her she could go to lunch, she would be off. She'd told herself a hundred times that this was no big deal. One loner asking another to share a meal wasn't exactly a date. But she had washed her hair and made sure her clothes were first-day clean. Any more would have drawn her mother's attention.

At twelve forty, the postmaster poked his head in the back and waved her gone. She picked up the mail for the fire station and both duplex apartments and hurried out.

Ronelle hardly noticed the cool air as she hurried to make her deliveries. Halfway to the fire station, she wished she'd taken the time to put on her coat, but she wouldn't turn back. She hadn't delivered any mail to Marty Winslow since Wednesday, and then he'd been on the phone and hadn't spoken to her.

What if he'd forgotten about asking her to lunch? She'd feel like a fool walking in expecting to eat. She decided to just deliver the mail and wait for him to say more. If he didn't say anything, she could just walk out like she usually did.

Only the moment she stepped into his house, she saw that the little table by the window was set for two.

"That you, Ronny?" he yelled from the kitchen.

"Yes," she said as she placed his mail on his desk.

"Take off your coat and come back here. I've almost got it ready."

She took a deep breath. Something smelled wonderful. Her mother had given up cooking years ago in favor of cans, frozen dinners, and takeout. Their kitchen at home only smelled good when Dallas lit a candle to mask the cat box odors.

Ronny stood in the kitchen door and watched him moving about in his wheelchair. "What are we having?" She forced herself to unknot her fingers.

He looked up at her and almost smiled. "My mom used to make this on cold nights. An easy mixture that took me a dozen tries to reproduce after she died. Onions, green and red peppers cooked in with ground beef, then add macaroni and a few cans of tomato sauce and you've got

Winslow Goulash." He stirred the boiling skillet. "Except, of course, for the secret ingredient." He grabbed a bottle of ketchup and poured.

Ronelle laughed. "I'll never tell."

While she sliced bread, he dipped them each a bowl full of goulash. They carried everything to the table as if they'd done this simple task together many times.

After she took her first bite, he reached over and stuffed a cloth napkin in the V of her shirt. "Wouldn't want you returning to work with sauce all over you."

His touch had been light, almost impersonal, but she froze.

It took him a moment to notice, and then he asked, "What's wrong? Don't tell me you hate it."

Ronelle shook her head. "It's great. It's just that . . ."

He frowned at her. "What, Ronny? I don't have enough time left on this planet to have people not speak their minds around me."

She swallowed and forced herself to take another bite.

He waited, and she knew he wouldn't let it pass.

After she swallowed her second bite, she blurted out the truth. "It's just that no one touches me."

Marty raised an eyebrow. "No one?"

"No one."

He leaned back in his chair and drank his coffee. "Because you want it that way, or because it just is that way?"

She relaxed, glad to have told him the truth. "Because it just is that way, I guess."

He buttered a slice of French bread and handed it to her, then made one for himself. "I meant nothing personal."

"I know," she answered, unable to look at him. "Would you mind if I had some more of this stuff? It's wonderful."

"Help yourself."

While she was in the kitchen, Ronelle tried to relax. She was way out of her comfort zone here. For years she'd watched people talk at the diner, sometimes even eavesdropped on their conversations. Now, she was almost having one.

When she walked back to the table, he was finished. She sat, her head down, her hair curtaining most of her face as she ate. He sat, his hands steepled in front of his chin as he studied her.

As she watched, he stretched his hand slowly toward her until his fingers trailed along her temple and moved a few strands of her hair behind her ear. She didn't even breathe.

"Are you all right with me touching you?"

"I'm all right." She smiled, liking the honesty between them. "I'll tell you when I'm not all right about something."

"Good. I've been hollow for so long I think I've stopped seeing people." He sat for a minute, then added, "It's good to see someone again, but I don't know if I've enough left to be much of a friend."

Ronelle felt a tear slip free and drift down her cheek. How could she tell him that *not much of a friend* was more than she'd ever had? Her father had touched her, talked to her, seen her, but her mother never had.

He lifted the corner of his napkin and brushed the tear off her cheek. "I fell away from life two years ago, but you've been asleep all your life." He moved his knuckle gently along the side of her face. "I wonder if waking you might be too painful?"

She couldn't move, much less speak.

When he moved his hand away, his words turned conversational once more. "I guess you liked the meal. Want to try another sample of my cooking next week?"

She nodded without meeting his gaze. "I'd better be getting back."

As he had before, he followed her to the door.

When she turned, she said, "I left your mail on the desk."

His hands were on the wheels of his chair. "Thanks," he said.

From his tone they were back to being strangers again.

Without a word, she leaned and kissed him on the cheek as she had before. Only this time, when she pulled away she saw something in his eyes she hadn't seen before, and she knew Marty Winslow was like her in another way. He was a person never touched.

"Lean down, Ronny," he whispered.

When she did, he touched his fingers to her chin and turned her head slightly, then lightly brushed his lips against her cheek. "Thanks for coming."

She smiled as she straightened. "Thanks for lunch." When she knew he had given her so much more.

Ronelle didn't feel the cold as she walked back to the post office. Again and again she touched her cold fingers to the spot on her cheek where he'd kissed her, as though she could still feel the warmth.

That night her mother served frozen dinners for supper on TV trays in front of her favorite crime show. Ronelle ate it, remembering the goulash Marty had cooked. Just for fun, she pushed the corner of her paper napkin into the V of her shirt.

At the commercial, Dallas looked over at her. "Get that napkin down in your lap where it belongs," she snapped. "I swear, Ronelle, if you don't get any brighter they'll fire you for sure. Then what will I do without your hundred a week? We'll starve, that's what."

Ronelle pulled her napkin to her lap. When she'd started at the post office, her father had told her to tell Dallas she was paid a hundred a week and bank the rest. At first it had been more than half her take-home pay, but as the years went by Ronelle took correspondence classes and slowly advanced. Her savings had been building and building. She'd opened her account at a credit union in Oklahoma City and made her deposits by money order. When the statements came, they were marked *General Delivery, Harmony, Texas*. Dallas would never see them.

She'd worried that Dallas might figure out that she was making more money, but her father had been right. Dallas had no head for figures. He'd set up a trust fund that paid the bills. The house was paid for and Dallas drew her husband's social security. Ronelle had the feeling that her mother thought if she asked too many questions about her income, Ronelle might ask what Dallas did with her father's retirement checks.

"Would you mind getting me some ice cream since

you apparently aren't watching the show anyway?" Dallas broke into her thoughts.

Ronelle got up without answering. It hadn't been a request but an order.

While she got the ice cream, she thought about Marty. Maybe she could ask him what to do with her money? That would give them something to talk about.

When she returned with the ice cream, her mother complained that it was too much, but she ate it all anyway. Ronelle sat back down and picked up her crossword puzzle book and wished it were Monday.

Chapter 28

WRIGHT FUNERAL HOME

TYLER SAT ON THE TINY SECOND-FLOOR BALCONY OFF THE back of the funeral home. The legend in his family was that his grandmother had the balcony built because she hated the smell of the cigars her husband smoked. She wanted the space big enough for the three brothers to sit out on, smoke, and talk business, but not big enough that people would expect to have a party on the balcony. When Tyler was a boy, he remembered meeting old folks who had known his great-grandparents. They said everyone in town called the balcony "the compromise."

Now Tyler might not smoke, but he went out almost every day to think and watch evening move across his town. He was a man of order and routine. It brought peace to his life, and balance.

More than two weeks had rushed by since he'd picked

up Kate for her weekend visit. Two weeks since he'd curled around her and held her on his bed. She'd never mentioned it and he'd only referred to it once. He wished he could e-mail her a long note and tell her what that one hour had meant to him, or better yet, he wished he could forget all about it if it was never to be repeated. Holding her, if only for an hour, left a memory across his heart dear and painful.

"You want your supper out here?" Autumn asked from the doorway of the balcony. Tonight she wore a big knit top that hung off one shoulder and jeans with more holes than material, but as always, Tyler pretended not to notice.

"No, thanks, I'll have it in my study downstairs as usual."

She nodded and walked away.

Autumn was still too thin to look healthy. No one would guess she was pregnant. Most of the time she seemed more like a ghost around the place than a housekeeper. He'd expected her to interrupt his world, but surprisingly she'd melted into the woodwork like lemon oil. She moved easily with the pattern of his days. Learning when to interrupt him with questions, when to leave the food on warm, and, most important, during his longest days she knew just when to bring milk and cookies. He'd also noticed she was making the kitchen hers. Little changes were everywhere. A new spice rack over the sink, pots moved from one cabinet to another, and a huge wooden bowl of fruits and vegetables on the counter. She'd even started a small spice garden in the bay window with tiny little pots lined up in an order only she understood.

Autumn Smith didn't know much about the protocol for being a housekeeper. She ate breakfast with him in the mornings, sometimes in her wool pajamas. She appeared now and then in his quarters without knocking, and she wore clothes that looked more like they belonged at Buffalo's Bar than here, but the woman could cook, really cook, and Tyler decided to overlook the rest.

In the days she'd been here, Tyler *had* noticed other small changes. His employees, even the two who worked at the cemetery, had all started gathering for coffee at ten in the break room. They tended to stay until whatever she baked was eaten. And, to his surprise, the afternoons around the place were silent. He wasn't sure what she did but, as soon as lunch was over and she'd put away the dishes, Autumn vanished into her room and didn't come out until it was time to start dinner.

Also, the constant sound of the TV had vanished. Whatever Autumn did on her afternoons off didn't include watching soaps. Maybe she read. Maybe she slept. He didn't really care. He just enjoyed the silence.

Tyler walked downstairs and noticed she'd put his tray beside his desk. Grilled chicken atop a salad and chocolate pie she'd made with a sugar substitute. He'd told her he liked to eat light at night and, unfortunately, she'd believed him.

He flipped on his computer and started his meal with his dessert. When he noticed there was no e-mail from Kate, he ate the rest of the pie and tried to think of something to say to his Kate that would encourage her to answer back.

Finally, he simply wrote,

I miss you, Kate. Wish you were here for me to talk to. Ty.

As he finished his dinner, he gave up waiting for her to reply and turned on the news. If Kate didn't e-mail him, they obviously wouldn't be chatting either. He wondered if she missed it as dearly as he did. He told himself she was probably working or maybe in flight somewhere she couldn't talk about. He told himself anything to keep from admitting that she might just have forgotten to check in with him.

A rapid pounding on the front door startled him out of his chair. They had no funerals pending, so he'd locked the door earlier than usual. Now, someone seemed very impatient to get in, and no one was ever in a hurry to get into a funeral home.

Tyler rushed to the door. As he twisted the lock, he was almost knocked down by a man pushing his way in. The bull of a man tumbled to his knees, suddenly disoriented. He was rough looking, as if he belonged more in a bar than a formal foyer. His clothes were dirty and his hair hadn't been washed in days, maybe weeks.

"May I help you?" Tyler asked out of habit.

"I'm here to get Autumn Smith. I'm taking her back where she belongs." He puffed up like a rooster as he stood. "And nobody, including you, old man, is going to stop me."

Tyler was taken off-guard by the stranger's manner and by being called an old man. "What makes you think she's here?" he asked, stalling for time while he tried to figure out what to do. No one had ever stormed the gates before.

"I found out her car had been impounded and they said she was in the hospital. The cop didn't want to tell me where the hospital was until he found out I was her husband." The man looked around as if trying to figure out what planet he was on. "One of the nurses at the hospital said she was working here." The rooster glared at Tyler. "What kind of a place is this anyway?"

"It's a funeral home," Tyler said. "And I'm the owner."

"Well, you don't own Autumn. She lives with me and it's time for her to come back where she belongs."

"I wasn't aware she had anywhere to go. She never mentioned a husband." Tyler tried to stay calm, but the man looked like he belonged on a WANTED poster. His hands were fisted and blood pumped rapidly in the veins of his neck. Tyler wouldn't have been surprised if he snorted like a bull and charged forward. "I would think if she wanted to live with you, she would have called you to come get her." Tyler felt like he was trying to reason with a post.

The stranger made a move toward Tyler. "I'm through talking."

Tyler jumped backward, hitting his leg hard against the hallway table and knocking a lamp over. The hundred-year-old glass shade shattered into tiny diamonds over the polished redwood floor.

"Autumn!" the man yelled. "You'd better get your butt out here before somebody gets hurt!"

Autumn appeared from the hallway leading to the kitchen. She looked frightened, but she carried a broom like a weapon.

"There you are, bitch!" He forgot Tyler and took a step toward her.

"I'm not going back with you, Leland." Her voice shook as she raised the broom. "You are not my husband. You just moved into my place and started ordering me around like I was some dog you found on the street."

"That's bull. We were sleeping together. If you didn't have me, you'd have nobody!" he screamed. "Your own family kicked you out!"

She shook her head. "You raped me the first night we met. Thanks to you, I was so drunk I didn't even fight, and the second time when I said no, you hit me. After that I was too scared to fight and too dumb to run. But I'm not scared now. I don't want to go back." She swung the broom. "Do you hear me? I'm not going back."

Tyler pressed against the wall, trying to choose his time. His hand brushed over the hallway phone no one ever used. Slipping the receiver off, he dialed 911, then moved to where he thought he could dive in front of this stranger if he got any closer to Autumn. Tyler had no hope he'd win in a fight, but maybe he could give Autumn time to run.

Leland smirked. "That was no rape. I just like it a little rough and you played along. I told you I'd let you keep that bastard you're carrying." He took a jab at her, hitting her hard in the stomach. "If you carry it full term."

Tyler reacted. He jumped at the man, knocking him to the ground. On his side, Leland couldn't swing, and Tyler managed to get off two blows before the bull made it to his knees and grabbed Tyler around the neck.

As Tyler fought for air, he heard the fire truck bell ringing and a police siren. Both were only two blocks away and must have reacted at once to his 911 call.

Leland heard them also because he dropped Tyler and tried to stand. "Come on!" he shouted at Autumn. "We're getting out of here. I came looking for you, not trouble with the law."

"No." Autumn swung the broom at Leland, connecting with a loud *thud* across his back. Once. Twice, before the broom cracked and splintered.

Tyler gulped for air, then charged hard, as he'd always thought he would if he had to fight for his life. He caught the bull around his knees and pushed his whole body weight forward.

Leland wavered as if in a strong wind and toppled forward, leaving a head-sized dent in the paneling.

Tyler wasn't sure in what order everything happened after that. It seemed to avalanche over him all at once. Two firemen, Willie Davis and Brandon Biggs, he thought, shoved their hands beneath his arms and picked Tyler up as if he weighed nothing. They must have carried him to a chair in the parlor, but he didn't remember much about that part. Suddenly they were working on him like he was a dummy at first-aid training.

He could hear a deputy reading Leland his rights.

When Tyler turned his head enough to look, he saw Deputy Phil Gentry sitting on the bull of a man as he cuffed him. The EMT named Charlie bumped his way inside and yelled, "Do we have a real emergency, or are these two just ice-skating again?"

Phil told him to shut up and see about Autumn.

Tyler didn't see Autumn at first, and for a moment he thought she'd done what he'd hoped she would do and run, but then he saw her bushel of hair at his knee. She was kneeling beside his chair crying.

"I'm so sorry, Mr. Wright. I'm so sorry."

Tyler felt like every spot on his body hurt. Besides his throat, and the leg that hit the table, he had scrapes all over him. But he managed to ignore all that and say calmly, "This wasn't your fault. Let the EMT check you out. Don't worry about this; right now we need to worry about the baby."

"Baby?" both the firemen said at once.

Tyler looked at both the young firemen. In the few years they'd been volunteering, a few kitchen or grass fires were all they'd probably handled. "The intruder"— he felt no need to say anything about Autumn's personal situation—"hit her hard in the stomach."

Autumn looked up at both. "He would have killed me,"

she said with tears streaming down her face, "if Mr. Wright hadn't stopped him."

Deputy Gentry stood, pulling Leland to his feet. He pointed with his head toward the firemen. "Do you think you two can help Charlie get her and Mr. Wright to the hospital? I've got my hands full with this one. Any man who'd hit a pregnant woman is going to get our special cell." He shoved Leland along. "Sorry I haven't had time to clean it since the drunk threw up in it last night."

Tyler wanted to say he didn't need to go to any hospital, but he was fighting to keep the room from spinning.

Willie knelt beside Autumn and asked her if she'd like him to carry her to the ambulance. He promised her it would be easier on her than trying to ride on Charlie's gurney. Brandon Biggs helped Tyler stand, but didn't offer to carry him. Phil shoved the handcuffed intruder out the door, telling him how much he hoped the guy would try to run.

Autumn slipped her hand into Tyler's for just a second and whispered, "Thank you." Then she let the firemen carry her.

Two hours later they were back in the Wright Funeral Home kitchen. Tyler had enough painkillers in him not to feel anything. They'd x-rayed him all over. Dr. Spencer told him simply, "The good news is you'll live. The bad news is you're going to feel like hell tomorrow." Then, the very proper young doctor grinned and added, "Heroes often do, I understand."

He'd frowned at her, wondering what she meant. He wasn't a hero. If the firemen and deputy hadn't arrived, it would have been only a matter of minutes before Leland stepped over Tyler's body and took off with Autumn.

About the time he was beginning to think Dr. Spencer was all right, she'd added, "Mr. Wright, I suggest you take off a little weight. The next time you get in a fight, you might be in here with a heart attack."

Next time, he thought. He'd lived forty years without getting into a fight. What were the chances he'd get in another one? But he'd told her, "I'll do that." Now, over a homemade chocolate-pecan pie, he was trying to come up with a weight-loss plan.

The two young firemen were eating and talking to Autumn as if Tyler were invisible.

"Autumn, you really need to learn self-defense," Willie said. "Then you wouldn't have to take any crap off some ex-boyfriend."

"Yeah," Brandon said. "Willie and me would be happy to come over and teach you."

"I couldn't ask for your time." Autumn almost glowed beneath their attention.

Willie downed another bite. "You could pay us back in food. I've never tasted a pie this good. I've been living at the fire station for three years eating my own cooking, and it's bad."

"Believe him, Autumn." Brandon added, "Trust me. It's really bad. You'd probably be saving his life by having him skip a few meals he's cooked."

Autumn smiled. "Well, self-defense couldn't hurt, I guess, and the doc said I need regular exercise."

"Seems like a really good deal," Brandon encouraged. "You feed us some evening and we'll give you a lesson. Even a woman your weight could throw a man my size if you know a few tricks."

Autumn looked at Tyler, and he nodded slightly. It seemed like a good idea right now to have two more men close. None of his staff would have been of any help even if they'd been here. For the price of a few meals, he'd like to have these boys around.

He saw that Little Lady was sleeping in her dog bed. When he clicked his fingers, she rushed over and waited for a treat. "Where were you, Lady, while the fight was going on?"

Willie laughed. "Maybe she's a lover and not a fighter."

"Yeah, like you." Brandon poked Willie in the shoulder.

When Brandon poked him back, Willie and the hundred-year-old chair Tyler's grandmother had brought over from Italy toppled.

Everyone laughed, including Tyler. Maybe it was time for a change, he decided. Might as well start with the furnishings.

Before he had a chance to slip Little Lady a treat, Autumn dropped a bite of something from her fingers. Little Lady instantly snapped it up. For a woman who wanted nothing to do with the dog, she was acting as if sometime this week the two had formed a truce.

Chapter 29

❧

TRUMAN FARM

REAGAN WATCHED NOAH SITTING OUT IN THE YARD IN one of Uncle Jeremiah's ancient lawn chairs. Everyone else had wandered back into the house for supper after watching the sun set, but Noah remained alone in the dark.

Jeremiah stood beside her, leaning heavily on a cane. "Winter's about over. I imagine we'll be getting into spring tornadoes before long. They say men half a world away run with the bulls through the streets. Out here on the plains we do the same thing every spring, only with twisters."

She smiled at him. He always pointed out the downside to every season. "You'd think you would be able to predict the weather after watching it for ninety years."

"Not true. I didn't start watching until I was in my twenties. Give me a few more years to study it. I'm already as good as those guys on TV."

She put her arm around his waist, steadying him. In a few minutes Foster would come with the chair and make him sit, but Jeremiah was tough; he pushed his time on his feet as far as he could every day.

Tonight, he let her help him a little as he continued to stare at Noah. "You know, during the war, I saw men who acted like your feller has this past week."

"He's not my feller, he's my friend," she corrected. "But that's not important. What do you mean?"

Jeremiah just watched for a while, then said his thoughts. "He's mighty brave, don't you think?"

"Foolishly so. There aren't many who'd climb on a bull one time much less several times a week. He's had so many cuts and broken bones he carries a medical folder with him, just to save the emergency rooms time."

"Does he talk about going back?"

She nodded. "Constantly."

"Does he talk about when?"

She paused, surprised by the question. "No," she finally said. "He doesn't. Foster says he's healing fine, so it shouldn't be too long." She frowned. "Though he still says his back keeps him awake even if the doctors can't figure out what's wrong. For Noah, rodeoing was always his dream. Now it's his life. Maybe that's why he seems so sad. He can't wait to go back to it."

Jeremiah patted her shoulder. "When I was in the war I saw men brave like Noah. They were always up, always helping others make it, always ready for the fight. Then, one day, one battle, they snapped. For some of those soldiers their wounds weren't all that bad, but one day they just couldn't go back into battle. Maybe they saw the end."

"What happened?"

"Some went home. Some got talked back into staying in the fight. They ran into battle just like before, yelling and fighting their hearts out."

"What happened? They became heroes?"

"A few. Most became dead. I think if you see your end

and don't change your fate because of honor, or fear, or maybe just because you can't see another road, you might as well run all-out toward it."

Reagan gulped down a sob. "What can we do?"

Jeremiah shook his head. "I think that's why he wanted to come here. To figure it out. To find another answer. He's got a lot of pressure to go back on the road. Living up to his father's reputation, having the whole town thinking he's living their dream, knowing he might never get the money to have that ranch he's always planned if he doesn't ride."

Reagan knew her uncle was right as she watched Noah cuddling his broken arm and staring out into the night . . . into nothing.

"If he weren't brave and proud, it wouldn't be such a choice."

Reagan turned her face into her uncle's worn flannel shirt and silently cried. "You're wrong about him leaving. You're wrong." She whispered the words, wanting to make them true. "He wants to go, he just doesn't know when. He's not afraid."

He patted her shoulder. "I hope so, child. Lord, I hope so, but for some, young or old, when the death drum sounds there ain't nothing to do but march to the beat."

Chapter 30

<THURSDAY>
THURSDAY
MARCH 11

DENVER DIDN'T MAKE IT BACK TO HARMONY FOR ALMOST two weeks. He felt like he'd flown around the world and back. Part of his delay was work, but most, he admitted to himself, came because he didn't like the possibility that his grand affair with Claire might be over. If her family all knew, it was only a matter of time before someone let it slip. He wasn't sure what she'd do, but he had a feeling whatever happened wouldn't be good.

Claire liked being a person of mystery. It was both part of the image as an artist and part of her personality.

She'd left one message on his phone about being tied up for a while. Saralynn was going through another surgery, minor this time, and Claire wanted to stay in rehab with her.

Denver talked to Gabe and was told the family held out little hope that Saralynn would ever walk on her own.

They'd been through this a dozen times. New doctors, new hope, and never more than slight improvements. Claire was the only one who never gave up, and Saralynn . . . well, for Saralynn, it was just a way of life. She never complained.

For the first time Denver realized that he wanted to be with Claire and Saralynn during this time. He wanted to hold Claire's hand and make Saralynn laugh. Only he hadn't been invited. Gabe checked in every few days, keeping him up on how Liz was coming along with the pregnancy and letting Denver know that Claire and Saralynn were back home.

A little after nine on Thursday morning, Denver called Gabe as he drove from the airport to Harmony.

"I'm inbound," Denver said simply when Gabe picked up the phone.

"Glad to hear you're back. Liz went with her mother for a doctor checkup and then they planned to eat lunch over at Winter's Inn." Gabe sounded frustrated. "So I'm home worrying about her."

Denver laughed. "Do you ever let her out of your sight?"

"No," Gabe admitted. "Not if I can help it. She's threatening to file charges on me for stalking. I tell you, some days it's hell being married to a lawyer."

"I've got to pick up some groceries." Denver laughed at how pitiful Gabe sounded. "How about meeting me in an hour at Buffalo's? We'll have some wings and beer and I'll catch up with what's been going on in town."

"Sure," Gabe said. "That's the one place in this town I know I won't run into my wife or mother-in-law. Buffalo's sounds a great deal better than the B&B."

He laughed. "Any other day I wouldn't be too sure Martha Q wouldn't be at Buffalo's. Years ago she was the queen of that bar. They say she picked up more drunk cowboys there than the bouncer. Word was once they sobered up and didn't run fast, she married them."

"Surely not sweet little old Martha Q?" Denver used his best southern drawl.

"You haven't been around here long."

Denver didn't argue. Two or three days home at a time

was usually all he got. This time he had until Monday. "Do you think Claire knows I'm home?" Somehow it felt good to be able to talk about her directly with Gabe.

"Sure. I mentioned it to Liz this morning and she'll tell her mother, who, of course, will say something in front of Claire." Gabe laughed. "I swear, Lieutenant, only women should be in the CIA. They got a network you wouldn't believe. To give one example, Aunt Pat found out that Noah McAllen was hiding out over at the Truman place because he didn't want his sister to know he got hurt again. Pat didn't tell Alex because she knew the McAllens were on the first real vacation they'd had in years and Alex was bound to call and tell them. So Aunt Pat climbs in the cart when that nurse, Foster Garrison, comes over to the ranch house to start Saralynn's exercises. She rides over to old Truman's farm and says she's there to help."

"That was nice of her." Denver was barely following the story. Aunt Pat was a Matheson, and the Matheson ranch bordered the Truman farm.

"You don't get it." Gabe said. "Aunt Pat sent Jeremiah a Dear John letter in WWII and he hasn't spoken to her since. But Pat said it was her duty because Noah's sister is a Matheson now, so she had to cross onto Truman land. They're like warring family. Old Aunt Pat crossed into hostile territory."

"And . . ."

Gabe waited a moment, then said, "She hasn't been back home and that was three days ago."

Denver laughed. "Well, either the old man killed her, or they're shacking up. Do you think you could stop gossiping long enough to meet me for a beer?"

"I'd better. My brain is turning to oatmeal. I've been around too many women too long. I love my wife, but I miss those quiet days with just me, the dog, and a security system that kept everyone off my land."

"Any idea if the twins are boys or girls?"

"Liz made the doctor swear not to tell us. She wants it to be a surprise, but I'm telling you if it's girls I have a feeling I'll be re-enlisting about the time they learn to talk. With all the Matheson women around, I already feel like I'm sleeping in the enemy camp."

Denver hung up, bought his groceries, then drove to Buffalo's Bar. He'd just taken his first swallow of beer when a tall woman dressed totally in white walked in. She was so out of place all three people in the bar stopped what they were doing and watched her cross the floor.

He tried not to move, but he couldn't stop the slow smile that spread across his face.

When she was a foot in front of him, she stopped, took his beer, and gulped half of it down without saying a word.

"Morning, Claire." Denver tried to keep his voice low. "Do you come here often?"

"I do when your car is parked out front."

"Want to join me and your brother-in-law for lunch?"

"No. I'll be at your place in ten minutes. If you're not there, I'll be gone in eleven." She sat the bottle down and walked back out.

Denver threw a twenty toward the bartender. "You know Gabe Leary?"

"I know him."

"Well, I'm buying him a beer and wings when he comes in."

"Who do I say it's from?"

Denver grinned. "Tell him it's from his friend who just went over to the enemy."

He drove eighty all the way down Lone Oak Road. When he reached his house, Claire was stepping out of her car. She'd parked at his front door so anyone driving down Lone Oak Road would notice her car.

She leaned against the hood of her car waiting for him.

When he reached her, he took her hand in his and tugged her toward the front door. "About time you came," he said, more to himself than to her.

He pulled her in front of him, pressing her back against the door frame as he unlocked his home and reached in to flip off the alarm. With one arm tightly around her waist, he lifted her inside and into his arms.

His hands slid beneath her white coat and moved across

the silk of her blouse as he kissed her with all the bottled-up need he'd been saving for far too long.

As always, she hesitated, tried to pull away, break free. But she'd come to him this time, and Denver wasn't interested in playing games. As always, when he finished one long kiss, she'd melted into him.

He pulled away and looked down at the one woman in the world he couldn't seem to turn away from. "How long do you have?" he asked.

"Until I pick Saralynn up from school."

"Good." He smiled down at her. "I'm starving. I'll open a can of soup and we'll have lunch. I want to talk to you and then show you the house, one room at a time."

She tugged off her coat. "What do I do while you're cooking?"

He smiled. "Take off your clothes."

She pouted, and he knew she'd never be a woman who took orders. He walked outside, hardly noticing the cloudy day as he grabbed the bags of groceries. They needed to talk, to make plans. From the public display she'd made in Buffalo's Bar, he guessed she was open to the idea of them becoming a couple. He liked the idea too.

When he walked back inside and closed the door, Claire wasn't there. In the shadowy house, he didn't see her for a moment, and then he saw her tall, slim silhouette against the long windows of the living room. With the low brooding clouds behind her and the earth tones of her surroundings, she looked more like a painting than a woman.

She was beautiful. And she was nude.

Denver forgot all about the soup and the tour of the house.

Chapter 31

❧

THE NEXT MORNING, DENVER WAITED IN THE BLUE MOON
Diner for Claire. A heavy March rain had kept many of the
regulars away. He half expected her to stand him up. Yesterday they'd spent the afternoon making love and hadn't
said anything that needed to be said between them. He
thought of how little he knew about her, and he couldn't
remember a single question she'd ever asked him.

He was on his third cup of coffee when she walked in. He
stood and waited for her to take her seat across from him.

"You've got the drowned-rat look about you," she said.

He shook his still-wet hair. "When it starts raining, my
plan is usually just to run. I don't think I own an umbrella."

"Because you always travel light?"

He grinned. "Because I always travel light." At least she'd listened to one thing he'd told her about himself. "You, however, with your raincoat and umbrella, look terrific." The thought crossed his mind that in another month the rain would be warm enough to make love outside on a rainy night. The hammock on his back patio might be the perfect place. They could finish off a bottle of wine first to warm their blood, then strip so neither would have to worry about getting clothes wet, then . . .

Denver slapped himself mentally. He had to stop thinking about her that way all the time or he'd never be able to carry on a conversation. "What looks good?" He tried distraction as he picked up the menu. "This time maybe you'd like to order your own food instead of just eating mine."

She didn't look at the menu. "All right."

The waitress showed up to fill her coffee cup and they ordered, then just stared at one another.

Denver had never been one to waste words, and he didn't now. "So, we're going public, me and you?"

"It's on the table for discussion."

"When I'm here in town, you'll come over to my place so we can spend some time alone. I'll come to your place, maybe watch a game or cook out. I like being around your family; except for you, they all seem to enjoy company."

She pouted and he almost leaned across the table to kiss her.

"We could take Saralynn with us to the show, and I'll go to anything she has at school. We'll just be an ordinary couple as soon as we figure out what ordinary couples do."

She shook her head. "It sounds so boring."

He laughed. "It does, doesn't it?"

"Maybe Saralynn and I could meet you in New York or Dallas one weekend? She's getting stronger and she's already old enough to travel well. We could see a few shows, take a carriage ride in the park."

"Sleep in separate rooms," he added, then smiled. "I could handle it as long as I get to see you."

"It would be hard on me too, but Saralynn is my life. If we're to go public, she has to be a part of that."

"I agree. I love talking to that kid. She may be only eight, but I got a feeling she's smarter than both of us." He raised one eyebrow. "But after a weekend of seeing you on a hands-off basis, promise me time alone next. I've become addicted to you."

She nodded as if she understood. They both seemed to have the same addiction.

The conversation died there. He couldn't think of anything else to say, and Claire didn't seem interested in small talk. Denver just stared at her. Every woman he'd ever met could carry on a conversation even if all he did was nod now and then, but not Claire.

When the waitress brought their food, he managed to comment on how hers looked better than his, and she claimed his might taste better. Without another word they began eating off each other's plates. Sharing the eggs, fighting over the sausages. As the food disappeared, they got in a sword fight over the last bit of pancake.

Denver laughed as he let her win. He watched her eat her prize bite and whispered, "You're so beautiful, darlin'. Any chance you'd consider sliding under the table and making love right now?"

"That's why I wanted to meet you somewhere for breakfast. If I'd gone to your house, I'd be naked and starving right about now."

"I love you naked and starving. Remember last fall when we were snowed in near the D.C. airport? No planes were in the air, but we didn't care. We'd make love and order room service, then do it all over again. I think we had breakfast brought up three times that day."

"Four." She winked at him.

He'd made enough memories that day to keep him in daydreams for a month. "I love the way you make love, but I want to know more about you, Claire. I want to know everything about you."

"I'm not sure."

He saw the worry and the fear flash in her eyes. "I swore I'd never get involved with a man again. Maybe all we have is this attraction, nothing more. Maybe all the rest would just be boring details."

"Maybe. But if we could have more, isn't it worth the risk?"

She looked down and the world went silent for him. They could debate all day, but if she wasn't willing to try, she wouldn't try.

Denver waited as long as he could, and then he stood. Dropping bills on the table, he reached for her hand. "Walk with me, Claire."

She glanced out the window. "It's still raining."

"I don't care."

He didn't let go of her hand until they were at the door. She lifted her umbrella as he put his arm around her shoulders. Claire was tall for a woman and with her heels they were now almost the same height. They fit, he thought. A perfect match.

Walking in step, he held her close as they rushed in the rain past stores and offices, past the town square, past the funeral home and along the tree-lined streets everyone called the old part of town. Neither said a word, neither seemed to care that they were getting soaked to the bone. They just walked.

Finally they reached the city park, long forgotten in winter. Leafless branches waved over brown grass. A trash can rattled in the wind as if fighting to escape the chain that bound it to the ground, and empty swings jerked as if angry that they'd been forgotten.

Denver pulled her into a corner of one of the buildings that surrounded the public swimming pool. The space was dark and littered with trash, but it was dry. She lowered the umbrella and moved into his arms.

For a while he just held her as she shivered.

When she raised her head, she laughed. "This is crazy."

"I agree." He kissed her cold cheek. "So, why'd you come?"

Without hesitation, she said, "Because you asked me."

And, just like that, for the first time since he'd met her, Denver believed it might work between them.

Chapter 32

WRIGHT FUNERAL HOME

TYLER LIT THE FIREPLACE IN HIS OFFICE FOR WHAT HE hoped would be the last time this winter. After all, it was March; spring had to be just around the corner. He watched the firelight's reflection off the beveled cut-glass window. Rain ran in tiny rivers along the outside of the glass. He'd had to cancel two funerals for today, which would probably mean working all weekend. Tyler didn't really mind, but if he didn't get his paperwork done on Saturday he wouldn't allow himself to take his Sunday drive. Even with the rain, he hated the thought of missing it.

He loved the long drives where he could take forgotten trails and back roads. Only with the rain, it would probably still be too muddy on Sunday to venture too far off the highway. He knew every road mark and back path in this part of the state.

Lightning flashed, mirroring the flames.

Autumn poked her head inside his office. "You busy?"

"No," he said, smiling. He'd told Autumn several times not to interrupt him unless it was important, but in the days she'd been with him, he'd learned that her "important" level and his were vastly different.

She took one step into the room. "Don't you find this place a little scary when it's storming like this?"

"No," he answered. "Maybe a little gloomy, but not scary."

She took another step inside. "You know, Mr. Wright, you should rent this old building out for one of those horror films where a group of people are trapped for a night and picked off one by one. Some evil spirit would have a field day in this place. I found a passage in the back of my closet that drops down to the basement."

Tyler grinned. He'd forgotten all about that hole in the floor. "Years ago when they used coal, the housekeeper could lower a bucket from there and the guys in the basement would fill it with coal. She'd stomp her foot three times and they'd send up enough to supply the stove in her bedroom. My father took the stove out when he put in central heating. I guess he forgot about the hole in the closet."

She moved a little closer to his desk. "Speaking of scary things, Leland is due to make bail today. Willie told me last night that one of the deputies told him that Leland's mother was wiring him the money. If they let him out, this town will never see him again. When they call his name at his hearing, he'll be three states away."

"That's fine with me." Tyler just wanted him gone, but he figured Autumn might want justice. "Of course, for your sake, I hope he pays for his crimes."

She sat on the arm of an overstuffed chair. "As long as he's gone, I think I'm all right. I think I was just a thing to him, not a person. He didn't hit me any harder than my step-mom used to when I was a kid." She brushed her hand over her middle. "I swear I'm never going to do that to this child."

"I'm glad." Tyler smiled. "But just in case Leland doesn't leave town, I've told everyone to make sure the doors are kept locked except for the front door during business hours. You're in charge of checking the kitchen door."

"I won't forget." She stood and started for the door. "I'll bring in your lunch in about half an hour."

"I thought we agreed that today would be your day off."

She grinned, guilty. "I know, but it's so cold and I don't have anywhere I wanted to go in this rain. If I hadn't cooked, everyone who works here would have to go out. Besides, stew is easy."

"You're very thoughtful, Autumn."

She looked like she didn't want to take the compliment. "Oh, one more thing. I asked Willie and Bran if they wanted to drop by. I have a feeling it will be around lunchtime."

Tyler smiled. "I'm always happy to feed the fire department. You sure we have enough?"

She grinned. "Sure. I baked an extra pie. I figured they could split it."

Autumn was gone before he could comment.

Tyler sat down at his desk, smiling. He wasn't too worried about Leland showing up. Men like him tended to pick on women they think are helpless and alone. Autumn was no longer either. Even Calvin in the basement set a shovel beside the back door and bragged that he'd just like to see Leland try to get past him.

Tyler also suspected the two young firemen would be circling by today if Leland did get out on bail.

He wished Kate would contact him so he could tell her all about his little adventure, but he guessed she was off working somewhere and hadn't had time to check her mail.

Chapter 33

POST OFFICE

RONELLE LOGAN DELIVERED THE MAIL TWICE DURING THE week. Both times Marty was working. When she handed him his letters he held the phone away from him and said, "See you Friday, right?"

She nodded and left.

One lunch hour she spent her time looking for a new blouse. Her mother had told her more than once that top-heavy girls like her only looked appropriate when well covered, but Ronelle wanted something new. But on Friday she walked to his house in the same old clothes she always wore, telling herself he'd simply invited her to lunch, nothing more. It wasn't like a real date.

The afternoon was stormy. She wore a plastic rain slicker that was held together with duct tape. She delivered mail to the fire station and then stopped in at the diner and ordered the takeout special and two slices of pie. No one noticed her.

At the corner she turned toward the dried-up riverbed. After glancing around, she opened the takeout meal and left it beneath the bushes where she'd seen a mother cat. Then she stuffed the pies in her satchel and walked to the duplex.

Marty was waiting for her, the table already set. "You're late," he said without greeting her. "I thought you weren't coming." His mood seemed as dark as the clouds.

He looked out the window, not at her. The strong line of his jaw was clamped closed. She couldn't help feeling that something haunted him. He seemed a man in a prison of his own making. She guessed he was angry, but not at her.

She walked all the way across the room and held up the pies. "I brought dessert."

The corner of his mouth lifted slightly. "If you think you can bribe me into a better mood, you're out of luck. I only have two moods, dark and darker."

"That's all right. I hate cheery people."

He winked at her. "Me too. Promise me we'll never try to cheer each other up. Promise to always be straight with me, Ronny. If I get too moody, curse and yell, but don't spread false sunshine."

"I promise," she answered, knowing the weight of such a request.

She relaxed into the warmth of his smile. She was learning him. He'd sounded angry, but maybe he'd been just worried or in pain. The thought that he might care about her feelings, even a tiny bit, made her comfortable.

"You look like you're dressed up for Halloween as a trash bag."

He watched her as she pulled off her slicker and wool coat and hung them on the back of one chair, and then he added, "Better, much better."

Ronelle wished she'd bought the blouse she'd shopped for, or even new shoes. Most of the time she felt like a watercolor done only in grays.

He reached over and shoved the chair out on his right,

then left his hand on the back of it as she sat down. When she settled, he brushed her shoulder lightly. "I'm glad you came."

"Because I brought pie?"

"That's it, Ronny." He leaned back. "I never make desserts, and since I don't get out much I rarely have them. What kind did you bring?"

"One apple. One chocolate. Which one do you want?" She reached for the bag, but his hand stopped her.

"Later," he said. "If I see them now, I won't eat lunch."

His hand remained over hers as he studied her for a moment, and then he asked, "Why haven't you asked me what happened with my legs?"

"It doesn't matter."

He shoved her hand away from him. "You mean an accident that almost killed me isn't important?"

She shook her head. "I mean the chair, the reason you're in it doesn't matter to me. It's not the reason I'm here."

He remained silent a while before saying in almost a whisper, "Why are you here, Ronny, and don't tell me it's for the cooking."

She straightened. "I'm here because you asked me. Girls like me don't get asked even to lunch all that often."

"What do you mean, girls like you?" His question shot out like a whip snapping an inch from her face.

She closed her eyes, knowing she couldn't list her shortcomings, not even to him. He could see who she was . . . what she was. Dull, boring, painfully shy, and as she'd been told by her mother all her life . . . plain, simply plain. Brown hair, brown eyes, too tall, too big in the chest to be fashionable, too awkward, and a hundred more faults. Her mother's advice was always the same: *Try to be invisible, Ronelle; just try to be invisible.* Sometimes Ronelle thought if she managed it and really did vanish one day, no one would notice.

"Open your eyes," Marty said as he tilted her head up. "Look at me."

She did, very much aware of his thumb moving along the line of her jaw as he looked at her.

"I wish you could see what I see," he whispered, moving so close she thought he might kiss her.

She shook her head, not wanting him to feel sorry for her. "No false sunshine, remember."

He moved away. "Eat your soup while it's still hot," he snapped, then added, "You are either the dumbest woman I've ever met or the smartest. Either way, I'm probably so out of practice at reading people I'm too dumb to tell."

She lifted her spoon, trying to figure out what he was trying to tell her. As before, they ate in silence.

"Finished?" he asked as he shoved his plate back.

She nodded and set down her spoon.

"Then let's see the pie."

She opened the sack and pulled out two small containers. Opening them both, she asked, "Which one do you want?"

"I'll take the apple." He took one bite and said, "No, let me try the chocolate."

Before she could taste the apple, he traded plates and took a bite of the chocolate.

Ronny lifted her fork and watched the apple pie before her disappear as he mumbled, "No, I think this one is better. Maybe I should give it another try."

She laughed as he ate both pieces of pie.

When the plates were empty, he shook his head. "Really, neither one of them was very good; maybe you should bring different ones next time."

"I'll remember that."

He glanced down at both plates. "Oh, I'm sorry, did you want any?"

"No." She smiled. "It was much more fun watching you eat both."

"Maybe next time you should bring a whole pie."

"Next time." She liked the sound of that. "We'll do everything the same. You'll cook and I'll bring dessert, only I promise to try to find one I like and you don't."

He shoved his chair back from the table and rolled beside her. "No," he said simply. "We won't do everything the same,

Ronny. I don't want you kissing me on the cheek at the door anymore." He let his fingers rest over her arm.

"All right." She ripped up the paper napkin in her lap. Nothing this nice could ever remain. She shouldn't have even hoped.

His hand moved over the sleeve of her sweatshirt. "I want to kiss you when we're at eye level, if you've no objections."

She looked up. "What?" She'd heard his words but couldn't believe them.

He laughed. "Like this, Ronny." He leaned close, his hand still gripping her arm as if he thought she might run.

His mouth closed over hers. She didn't move as his tongue slid along the seam of her lips. When she didn't react, he straightened away.

"You didn't like it?" His eyebrows went together as if he were surprised he'd read her so wrong.

She didn't answer.

His tone turned dark. "All you have to do is tell me, Ronny. I've no intention of doing anything that you don't want. Hell, it didn't mean anything. You don't have to look at me like I just stole your mailbag. I'm sorry I grossed you out so completely you can't speak." He shoved away from her.

"I . . ." she started, knowing she had to say something. "I don't know if I liked it. I've never had anyone kiss me like that before."

He looked like he didn't believe her, then finally said, "Never?"

"Never."

"How old are you, Ronny?"

"Twenty-seven."

"That's impossible."

"What?" she said. "That I'm twenty-seven or that I've never been kissed."

"Both, I guess." He plowed his hand through his black hair. "I was guessing you were about twenty, maybe twenty-one. No one gets to be twenty-seven without being kissed. You've got to be lying."

She stood suddenly. She'd always thought of herself as

strange, not like others, but now he seemed to want to dwell on just how strange he thought she was. "I said I wouldn't lie." Words seemed to hiccup from her. "I have to go."

"Fine. Will you come back next Friday?"

"I don't know." She was out the door before he could ask any more questions.

Halfway to the street she realized she'd forgotten her coat and the old satchel. She turned around and stormed back inside.

He was still sitting by the little table, his head down. When he looked up at her he reminded her of a dark hero in a novel. Strong, brooding, handsome.

"Did you forget something?" The angry man was back.

"Yes." Ronny pulled her chair beside his and sat down facing him. "How you hurt your legs doesn't matter. The wheelchair doesn't matter because I don't see the chair. I see the man. A man who is like me, who doesn't like being around many people, who wants to be honest but the words don't come easy." She gulped for air and added, "I see a person I'm not afraid of because he sees me."

"Anything else," he grumbled, "now that you've finally decided to talk?"

"Yes. I don't lie. I don't know how to kiss. I don't know a lot of things, but I'd like to learn."

"You want me to teach you?" He now looked far more surprised than angry.

"Yes," she whispered, as her entire body shook with fear. She'd never done anything so insane in her life. If her mother learned of this she'd have her committed. "I want to feel and not just walk around asleep. I want to talk to someone who listens. I want you to care about me, but I don't know how to start."

He sat back in his chair and watched her for a minute, and then a slow smile spread across his face. "Give me your hand," he ordered gently.

Ronny lifted her hand. He gripped it in strong fingers. "Why me? There must be a dozen men in this town who'd love to teach you how to kiss and a lot more. All you'd have to do is dress up and step into Buffalo's Bar one night and they'd be standing in line."

She shook her head. "Not true."

"It is too, but that's not important. 'Why me' is." He laced his fingers through hers and held on so tightly it was almost painful. "Nothing but the truth, Ronny. No manipulation, no lies between us."

"Because you're the only man who ever made me sorry I didn't know how."

"Lean forward, for me, would you?" He tugged her to the edge of her chair.

He raised her hand and rested it on his shoulder. "Close your eyes." His hand moved to her chin. "Wet your lips."

He cupped her face in his hands. "Now, open that beautiful mouth."

She blinked.

He smiled. "I'm not kidding, honey. You got the kind of mouth made to be kissed. The fact that you haven't learned tells me the men in this town are all blind." He rubbed his thumb over her bottom lip, pressing slightly in the middle. "Now, lets start over. Close your eyes."

He pressed harder against her lips. "Now, open your mouth slightly." When she did, he lowered her bottom lip and moved his thumb against the moist inside of her mouth.

As his thumb circled her mouth, she heard his voice, low and very close to her ear.

"Relax, Ronny, nothing about this is going to hurt. I'm just going to kiss you, nice and easy." His thumb moved over her mouth once more. "And you're going to love it."

His hand moved to the back of her neck and tugged her closer. She jerked when his tongue began to brush her lips as if tasting her, but he didn't let her pull back. "Now," he whispered while his lips touched hers. "Just like before, open your mouth and let me inside."

When she did, she felt his lips move over hers and his tongue brushed the inside of her bottom lip.

Then, as simple as that, he was kissing her and she was lost in the pleasure of it.

When he finally pulled away, she waited, her mouth wet and slightly open.

"That's lesson one." He smiled as she opened her eyes. "We're going to take it one lesson at a time. Now, do I need to repeat lesson one?"

"Yes, please," she whispered.

The second kiss was bolder, and she almost cried for more when it finally ended.

She slowly stood, pulled on her coat, and walked toward the door.

"Ronny." He stopped her with a word. "Come back Monday. I don't want to wait a week to kiss you again."

"All right." She touched her fingers to her mouth. "To answer your question from before, I liked being kissed. I liked it very much."

She was at the door when she heard him say, "So did I."

Chapter 34

TRUMAN FARM

REAGAN SPOTTED NOAH WALKING ALONG THE ROAD WHEN she drove back from the Truman orchard. The muddy pot-holed lane was slippery, but he didn't seem to notice. He walked like a bull rider, she thought. That kind of slow swing as if pushing his hip bones forward in a loose way while one of his powerful shoulders hung lower than the other. She'd heard an announcer say once that rodeo cowboys were a breed apart, and bull riders were the wildest among the wild.

Every group seemed to have a few like that. Pilots had their barnstormers who risked death every time they climbed to the sky. Skiers had their hotdoggers. Soldiers had their Special Forces. From the beginning of time they'd been the heroes, the legends . . . the men who came home on their shields.

The whole town talked about Noah McAllen like he was a star, but Reagan just wanted him back as her friend.

"Noah!" she yelled over the thunder. "What are you doing out here?"

"I couldn't take your uncle and Miss Pat arguing any longer. When I left they were rehashing a fight they had before the war. Sixty years and they still can't settle it. I suggested dueling pistols and the only ground they found in common was to order me out."

Reagan laughed. Almost from the moment Pat Matheson moved in to help, uninvited, she and Jeremiah had been arguing about everything. Though they drove everyone crazy, the two senior citizens seemed to be having a ball. Jeremiah hadn't looked as good in months. He refused to use his chair. He'd had Reagan trim his hair. If she didn't know better Reagan would think the two of them were courting again.

"Get in!" Reagan ordered Noah. "I'll run away from home with you."

He laughed and swung into the cart. "I don't care where we go, just get me out of here."

"I know just the place." She drove to the garage and they switched to her old pickup.

In ten minutes they were turning onto the old McAllen ranch, which Noah's father had given him the day he turned eighteen.

Noah stiffened.

Reagan slowed and looked at him. "I thought you'd like to drive over to your land." She could see that she'd made a mistake.

"It wasn't meant to be mine, you know," he said, more to himself than to her. "Dad always said he'd split it right in half and give Warren and me each a share. He thought we'd run it together, and Alex would eventually get the house in town.

"I don't remember much about when the family lived here, but Alex and Warren used to talk about when we all lived out on the ranch before Dad and Mom separated. Dad loved it out here, but I don't think he ever loved ranching. For him it was the rodeo, and when he gave up the blood and the mud, he couldn't seem to make a go at just ranching."

Reagan slowly moved toward the ranch house. "How old were you when your brother, Warren, was killed?"

"Thirteen. Sometimes when I think back to the days after he died, it seems like I was just standing in a corner watching. Alex had just finished her master's in criminal justice and was home celebrating. Warren had only been a highway patrolman for a few years and he was so proud of her. He was on a late call the night she got home. Walked up to a parked car and was shot in the face, probably by a drug dealer. That's all I remember. He and Alex were so much older than me, I thought of them more as a second set of parents than my brother and sister. Even now, if she knew I was home she'd be over here telling me how to run my life."

Reagan pulled up to the abandoned ranch house. "Where are the couple who lived out here and kept the place up?"

"They moved on. I told Dad to sell the few cattle to pay the taxes, and last I heard Hank and Alex were looking after my horses." Noah looked over the winter landscape, watching tumbleweeds blow in the wind. "You know, Rea, I think this place is jinxed."

"It's beautiful. It's your land. How could it be jinxed?"

Noah shook his head. "My sister doesn't want any part of it but that little cabin down by the brakes. Warren never wanted it; his goal was to be a Texas Ranger. Mom and Dad always fought over it. The only square I'll ever really feel like is mine will be the square I'll be buried on."

Reagan cut the engine. "Let's walk."

"It looks like rain." Noah gripped the window frame with his hand as if he thought about refusing to move.

Reagan ignored him and climbed out. She walked to the front of the pickup and stared out at the beautiful open land.

When he finally climbed out, she took his hand and pulled. They walked across land that had been owned by McAllens for more than a hundred years. The corral gate was down. Tiles had blown off the roof of the main house and were scattered around, baked terra-cotta planted in forgotten gardens.

Reagan fought down tears. She didn't care how run-down the place looked; it had once been Noah's dream. He'd talked for hours about what he was going to do with his land when he won big money in the rodeo and came home. He'd said he'd have hundreds of head of cattle and rough stock for all the little rodeos around. He'd laughed and said he wanted a houseful of kids to help with the chores.

"What do you dream?" she whispered. "What do you still dream, Noah?"

He shook his head, knowing what she was asking. "Nothing," he finally said. "Nothing about here. I used to love riding across this place, but now I don't want to even see the few horses I still own. Hank can have them for all I care. I dream of making the best time at the next rodeo. Of drawing a good bull. Of having enough gas to make the next town in time, but I don't dream of coming home any more."

Reagan put her arm around his waist and hugged him as they walked. Finally, he stopped and stared out over rolling hills and brakes that he once thought would make the perfect horse ranch. For as far as they could see there was nothing but his land. Abandoned land. Forgotten land.

"Like Dad, I can't sell this place, but I can't see living here like I used to think I would. I'm no longer that guy."

"No bars around for a drink. No buckle bunnies wanting to two-step," she teased.

"Believe me, the nights were not as wild as the old-timers talk about."

"What do you dream?" she asked again.

He shook his head. "I used to dream of the lights and the money at nationals, but lately I'm not even sure I want to go back." He was silent for a moment and said, "I'm not sure I can go back, Rea. The fear of climbing back in the chute makes me shake. And worse than that fear is the realization that I don't know what I want any more, and that scares the hell out of me."

Noah rubbed his eyes and swore at the damn mist in the

air. "I once dreamed of me and you, Rea, but now I feel lucky to have you as a friend. From the very first you saw right through all my BS, and you still do."

She couldn't stand to see Noah broken. He'd always been the one to help her stand up. He'd always been her anchor, her friend. "Stop it." She poked him in the ribs.

He groaned and she almost apologized. "If you talk any more I'll have to write everything down for your obit. We both know I had to stand in line in high school just to get to talk to you. Half the guys in town wish they were you right now."

He turned to face her, anger flashing in his eyes. "You're right. I'm sorry to unload on you, but you started it. You brought me here." He leaned down and kissed her hard on the lips. Not a sweet kiss, or a loving kiss, but a challenge.

"That's what I think about, Rea." He stepped back, still angry. "That and a whole lot more. I think about you."

She watched him, more confused than mad. Who was this man and what had he done with Noah? Slowly, the truth sank in. Noah was no longer a kid. Part of her had kept him in her mind and heart as the boy she'd first met, but this man before her was different.

When she didn't move, he broke the silence. "Forget what I said. Hell, forget that I kissed you. Let's go back and see if old Jeremiah has his sweetheart from over sixty years ago in bed yet."

She laughed, glad to have the Noah she knew back. The man she'd glimpsed was too unsettling. "Stop it. I don't even want to think about Aunt Pat and Jeremiah that way."

"Trust me, Rea, fighting is just one step away from fore-play. Her support hose might already be around her ankles."

Rea took off running.

"What's your hurry?" Noah smiled. "It's going to take them a while."

"I've got to stop it. What if Aunt Pat gets pregnant?"

The old Noah was almost back as they drove home. He made all kinds of jokes about the old couple and what the families would have to say about them rolling in the hay.

Rea knew Noah's joy was forced, but she didn't care.

She had her best friend back for a time. Maybe he'd forget about the kiss he'd given her. Maybe she would too.

When they reached the house it was almost dark. Rea jumped out of the pickup and looked back at him still sitting in the cab. "Aren't you coming in?" she asked. "Cindy's making smothered burritos."

Noah slid over to the driver's side. "I think I'll go for a drive if you got enough gas in this old thing."

"It's standard. Can you handle shifting with your arm in a cast?"

"I'll manage." He shoved the gearshift into reverse and was gone before she could offer to go with him.

Reagan watched him drive out onto Lone Oak Road. When she walked back to the porch, Jeremiah was sitting in his favorite chair.

She sat down next to him, knowing better than to ask him how he was feeling.

"That Noah?" he said after a few minutes.

Reagan nodded. "I don't know where he's going, so don't bother asking. He makes me so mad. One minute he kisses me and the next minute he can't get out of my sight fast enough."

Jeremiah stared out at the sunset. "Ain't nobody who can make you mad, kid. You have to get there by yourself."

"You're right." She thought of adding that she planned to stew in her bad mood a while, so he could keep his advice to himself.

After a while he added, "I'm guessing the same is true of kissing you. Nobody better even try unless you want them to."

She didn't answer. She wasn't willing to admit she wanted him to, but she hadn't stopped him.

Finally, Jeremiah unfolded from the chair. "Come on, girl, let's go eat. Don't worry about him. A man's got to fight his own demons. You can't do it for him."

Reagan pulled her knees to her chin. "I don't understand why he came back here. He's not happy and he doesn't seem to want to talk about it."

Jeremiah chewed on that for a minute, then answered so low his voice blended into the wind. "Maybe he came back here to fall. Maybe right here is the only place he knows he'll be safe if he crashes. Funny thing about rodeo heroes, or any kind for that matter; when they fall it's sometimes farther to ground than they thought."

Reagan decided her uncle was slipping. Noah had relatives all over town and a family who spoiled him. He could have gone back to any of them and been welcomed.

She stood and helped her uncle inside. Before they reached the kitchen, she said, "I didn't let him kiss me. I just didn't stop him."

"Oh," Jeremiah says. "Makes perfect sense. What you planning on doing next time . . . let him or stop him?"

"I don't know."

"Might want to make up your mind, 'cause I got a feeling next time will be coming."

Chapter 35

BUFFALO BAR AND GRILL

BEAU YATES AND HIS FRIEND BORDER BIGGS CLAMBERED in the back door of the Buffalo Bar and Grill with all their equipment.

Harley, the owner, stood with his arms folded over his massive chest waiting for them. "'Bout time you boys showed up."

Beau set down his keyboard. "We got here as fast as we could."

Harley nodded as if to apologize. "I guess you did. The band out of Lubbock called half an hour ago saying they were having car trouble. This was the second and last time they'll be canceling on me."

"Can we have their slot?" Beau asked.

Harley laughed. "You got more than six songs?"

"Sure, we got eight."

"Good enough for this crowd. I'll pay you the same money and you now have two nights a month."

"And a meal at break," Border said. "I didn't have time to eat before we loaded up."

Harley nodded. "Give the cook your order before you climb in the cage and I'll make sure he delivers it on break."

Ten minutes later they broke their first song to an almost empty bar. One table of cowboys in from one of the big ranches for the evening was talking so loud they could have been playing the theme to *Sesame Street* and no one would have noticed. Two couples more interested in each other than dancing and one lone man at the back booth with a cast on his arm.

Beau watched him as they moved from song to song. He never looked up except to wave for another beer. He was young, probably only a few years older than Border, but he looked hard. Like he didn't care about anyone or anything but the beer.

As people finally started to get up and dance, Border's brother came in. Like before, he sat at the bar and ordered one beer. Brandon still had his construction clothes on. He nodded at a few people, but mostly he just smiled at Border playing away. Beau knew his friend didn't have any parents, but he sure had one big brother who was proud of him.

When they took their break, Harley brought them food and Cokes. "You boys are getting better. I'm starting to recognize a few songs."

"Thanks," Beau said, wondering if it was a compliment or not. Border didn't seem to care. The steak burgers and fries had totally distracted him.

Brandon Biggs pushed away from the bar and headed over to say hello, but he stopped when he noticed the man at the last booth.

Beau couldn't hear what the two men were saying to each other, but it didn't look too friendly. Finally, the guy with a cast on his arm half stood and took a swing at Brandon.

Brandon ducked, then lifted the cowboy over his shoulder as if he were a sack of grain. With Brandon gripping his good arm, the guy had no chance to fight. Brandon carried him out of the bar and no one seemed to notice the kidnapping.

Beau wasn't about to say anything. He had only five minutes to eat before he had to start the next set.

NOAH WOKE UP WHEN REAGAN'S RATTLING OLD PICKUP turned off Lone Oak Road and hit the dirt trail heading toward the Truman farm. He'd driven it so many times in high school he recognized every bump, and right now every one felt like a hammer pounding in his head.

Only Rea wasn't driving; she knew when to swerve right or left. For a moment, in the dark of the cab, he didn't recognize Brandon Biggs. He and Bran had fought off and on for years. Biggs had lived in a few towns around Harmony. They'd butted heads in football and during after-game fights.

The strangest thing seemed to be that Bran and Reagan were friends. A mismatched pair if he'd ever seen one. She didn't come to the middle of the big guy's chest, but Noah had seen her poking him with her finger and yelling when she thought he wasn't listening to advice. Funny thing was, the big guy always backed down.

Reagan was petite and would probably get carded until she was forty. Bran, on the other hand, must be inflatable. Every time Noah saw the thug he seemed to get a little bigger. Not just taller or fatter, but bigger all over from head to foot.

Noah gulped down the need to throw up and said, "She call you to come get me, Bran?"

"Who?"

"You know damn well who. Reagan."

"I haven't talked to her. I just went in to watch my little brother play at Buffalo's. Didn't take much when I saw her truck to figure out you were the one driving it. Since you're too drunk to drive, I'm just taking you with me while I take her truck back to her."

Noah didn't believe Bran. Reagan had been watching

over him like a mother hen since she brought him home. "I'm not staying with her," he admitted. "I'm just staying out the Truman place."

Bran smiled. "I figured that out too. She's got you on some kind of pedestal, thinking you're a hero, but I'm giving you fair warning: When you let her down, and you will let her down, I'll be there to catch her."

Noah thought of slamming his fist into Bran's smiling face, but either they'd run off the road and hit one of the evergreens old Jeremiah had planted after the prairie fire a few years ago, or Bran would pull up and beat him senseless. Drunk and with one arm in a cast, Noah didn't think he'd put up much of a defense. In fact, he almost wished the thug would pound on him a while.

"Let me out at the side door." Noah said. "And much as I hate it, I guess I should say thanks. I would have been really embarrassed if my sister had stopped me driving drunk."

"You could have killed yourself."

"No such luck." Noah climbed out of the pickup and headed up the stairs. He had no idea how Bran planned to get back to town, and he really didn't care.

A half hour later Noah stepped from the shower. His body was healing. The bruises had faded and his arm no longer ached, but now he felt like something was wrong with his mind. Any other time, when he had to sit out a while to recover, he'd counted the days until he could go back. Now, he seemed to be mourning each day as being one less day he could stay here.

Getting drunk didn't help a thing, not that he thought it would.

He stepped out into the hallway and slowly felt his way to his room. Halfway down, his hand encountered something soft along the wall. Something breathing.

Noah gently felt the body. A mass of curly hair. Short. Rounded. "Rea?" He was surprised she hadn't slapped him. He quickly pulled his hand away.

"I wanted to say something before we both call it a night, if you're sober enough to listen."

"I'm sober enough," he said.

"About that kiss this afternoon . . ."

"I shouldn't have done it," he admitted. In truth he didn't even know why he had. She'd just asked him what he dreamed about, and she was definitely one of his favorite dreams.

"You're right, you shouldn't have kissed me," she whispered. "I want to give it back."

She placed her hand on the side of his face and slid her thumb to his mouth. A moment later, her lips replaced her touch and she kissed him.

At first he didn't react. He couldn't react. If he'd been less drunk, maybe he would have thought what to do. If he'd been more drunk, he might have just relaxed and enjoyed it. She ended the kiss before he could decide.

"There," she said, sounding disappointed. "Don't kiss me again unless I ask you to, and you'll die of old age before I ask."

She was gone so fast he bumped against the wall reaching for her.

Chapter 36

SUNDAY
MARCH 14

SUNDAY AFTERNOON WAS ALWAYS THE SAME. RONELLE went to church with her mother, cleaned the kitchen after lunch, and slipped into her only pair of jeans and an old T-shirt of her father's. Dallas usually commented that Sunday was a day of rest, so while her mother napped, Ronelle did the list of chores Dallas always left taped to the fridge.

When she finished, she settled down at the kitchen table and began a new crossword. Clouds gathered in the sky outside the kitchen window and Ronelle wondered if rain was heading in again. The days were changing from winter to spring, but the air still had a chill to it.

As the clock struck five, her mother hurried in, re-dressed in her Sunday best. When leaving, Dallas was always in a rush, as if her days were so full she barely had time to move from one important appointment to another.

"I'd like to take you with me tonight," Dallas shouted as though Ronelle weren't three feet away. "But this is an important meeting to plan my high school reunion. If you tag along they'll think I have dementia, like Freda May Willis. Her daughter is the only one at the meetings who really doesn't belong, but no one says anything because poor Freda can't remember her own name half the time."

Ronelle put her pencil down and looked like she was listening.

"I have to go or you know all they'll do is talk about me. I'm sure that's what they do if I'm late or leave early. I know it even though I let them think I don't."

Ronelle was only half listening. In her mind she was reliving for the hundredth time how Marty had kissed her.

"Why don't you walk down to the diner and get you something? Your cooking skills are so poor a rat would starve around here if you did the meals. I didn't have time to even buy frozen dinners yesterday what with my hair appointment. Now with that endless wind my hair will probably be a mess by the time I get there. They scheduled the meeting all the way out at Hilltop Baptist Church and, of course, Betty insisted we all bring a salad. By the time we eat and get the meeting over with, I know it will be late, but if I miss it they'll screw up this year's reunion as badly as they did last year's."

Ronelle knew better than to do more than nod.

"The walk to downtown will do you good. You've been sitting around all day. Be sure you're back before dark. It's a dangerous world out there, Ronelle. You're lucky you're not a woman men take a second look at or you'd find out just how dangerous." Dallas pulled her lettuce and apple salad from the refrigerator. "Don't forget to lock the doors when you get home. I don't want to walk into a bloody crime scene when I get back home."

Dallas left, still talking and totally unaware that her daughter hadn't said a word in two days.

Ronelle thought about putting on her pajamas and eating the last of the chocolate ice cream, but she didn't want to stay home, and the soup she'd had for lunch had left her hungry. The evening was still and so cold the bare branches crackled in the old elm trees. She'd enjoy a walk.

She tied her hair up in a knot, slipped her jacket over the white T-shirt and left out the back door. No matter where she walked in town, there was always the chance her mother's friends might see her and report in, but if she walked the old dried-up creek bed that ran behind her house on its way across town, she could be alone.

Once in a while, when Dallas Logan went to bed with one of her headaches, Ronelle would walk the creek after dark. Then she could hear the music from Buffalo's Bar and Grill on summer nights, and even cross into the shadows of downtown and window-shop in stores locked up for the night.

She slid down the five-foot slope and felt her feet crunch on long-dead leaves. To her this place had always been like a secret wonderland. She loved the rare times she walked its windy trail while there was still enough daylight to see all its wonders. Sometimes she'd imagine that she had stepped into the first days of Harmony when the town was little more than a general store and a livery stable. Harmon Ely owned the town and all around. Three men worked for him: a Matheson, a Truman, and a McAllen. All three men brought their families west, but Harmon's never came. In the end, when he knew his family wasn't joining him, the old man left everything to the three families. The creek bed had been a river then. Ronelle could almost feel the ghosts of all those early settlers surrounding her as she walked.

Once she'd found a plate, old and broken into a half dozen pieces in the mud of the creek bed. She'd hidden the pieces away and each time she returned to that spot, she'd stop and put the plate back together like a puzzle she'd worked many times. Somehow the pieces held her to the history of the place.

Ronelle passed the steps behind Winter's Inn and knew Martha Q had them built so she could also walk the creek bed, but it was far too cold for anyone her age to be out this late. Ronelle assumed the plans for the club Martha Q wanted to start were still being ironed out. It didn't matter. She couldn't see herself going, and she knew her mother wouldn't insist. After all, if Ronelle found a man, that would leave Dallas alone.

When she reached the trees behind the Blue Moon Diner, Ronelle decided to stop in for her dinner. The wind was starting to kick up and she didn't want to be out when it started raining or got too dark. She was halfway up the slope when she spotted a couple arguing near the back door of the diner.

Ronelle slid back down the slope, kicking up rocks and dirt as she moved. She didn't want to interrupt the couple. Retracing her steps, she walked about half a mile and decided to climb up where a small bridge crossed over the creek bed. The concrete was old and crumbling in spots. She'd heard the city council arguing about when to replace it, but *later* always got the most votes.

A cloud blocking the weak winter sunset and shadows of trees made it hard to see just where to step or grab hold. She managed to get to the street and reached for the piping running along the side of the bridge.

Just as she stepped forward, the piping gave and Ronelle jumped up toward the road. Her foot slipped on the crumbling edge of the bridge and she hit her knee hard. A second later she yelled in pain and rolled. The stinging on her knee, the roar of a motorcycle, and the screech of tires all blended together.

Ronelle closed her eyes and tried to think of herself as invisible so no motorcycle would find her, but the steady pounding of footsteps coming toward her told her she'd failed.

"Lady, are you all right?" someone yelled.

It took her a second to remember to breathe. Slowly, she opened her eyes and looked up into the face of the tattooed thug she'd seen at Marty's duplex. He'd shaved his head, making him even more frightening, but up close she saw that he was younger than she'd thought. Maybe only eighteen or nineteen. Marty had introduced him as Border Biggs.

"I swear, I didn't even see you or feel the hit. It was just like one blink the road was clear and the next you were there."

She let him help her to her feet. "You didn't hit me. I fell." She limped when she tried to move her leg. "I'm glad you were able to stop before I became a speed bump."

Border looked relieved. "You're the mail lady, Marty's friend. I didn't recognize you without your hat."

Touching her knee, she felt the blood through her jeans.

"You sure you're all right, lady?"

"I'm fine. I just skinned my leg."

"I could take you home."

"No." If the neighbors saw her pull up with Border Biggs, it would give her mother a heart attack when she found out.

"At least let me take you to Marty's place. It's only a few blocks. He knows all kind of things about patching people up. The last time my brother and I got in a fight, he came over and patched us both up."

She tested her weight on her knee. Blood ran down her leg. Then, as if someone had dumped cold water on her, she began to shake. The horror of what could have happened filled her thoughts. If she'd been hit? If she'd been killed?

"All right." She gave in. It would take her forever to limp home, and besides, she needed to get the wound cleaned as soon as possible.

When she climbed on the motorcycle behind Border, Ronelle pulled her hood down to cover most of her face. Her mother would think that she was insane, but Border had given no indication that their conversation was pre-killing banter. He knew Marty and he'd offered to help. If he headed out of town to a good murdering spot, she'd fall off the bike. After all, she was already bleeding; how much more damage could she do in a fall?

But he didn't speed up. He drove slow and easy the few blocks.

When they climbed off the motorcycle he watched her

limp a few steps, and then he picked her up and carried her to the door. Without letting her down, he banged on Marty's side of the duplex.

He twisted the knob, saw it wasn't locked, and walked in talking without waiting for an invitation.

Marty looked up from his computer and frowned.

"Now before you start yelling, Marty, I didn't hit her with the bike, I swear. She just fell on that lousy road by the bridge."

Ronelle looked at Marty, and it seemed to her that his face had gone pale.

Border stood before the desk, still holding her in his arms. "I don't think nothing's broke, but hell, I don't know. I offered to take her home, but she said to bring her here."

Finally, Marty moved. "Put her on my bed. I'll get the first-aid kit."

Border took a deep breath, obviously happy to have a plan. He walked her into the bedroom and gently set her down on a slim military-style bunk. "I'm real sorry you're hurt," he mumbled.

"I'm fine." She tried to smile. "Just a skinned knee." She moved her leg as if to prove nothing was broken.

Border nodded and backed a few feet away.

"Thanks for bringing her here," Marty said from the doorway. "Mind closing the door you left open?"

"Sure. I'll be right back."

Marty didn't move from the doorway as he stared at her. "How about I have a look. I made an A in first-aid. My specialty at the time was skinned knees."

He yelled back at Border. "Mind bringing me a big pot of hot water and a couple of kitchen towels?"

"Glad to," Border answered. "I'm fine as long as I don't have to look at blood."

Marty moved closer as she sat on the edge of the bed and tried to pull up the leg of her jeans, but they wouldn't go more than halfway up her calf.

"You'll have to take them off," Marty said. "Or I could cut

them off above the knee." When she didn't move, he added, "We need to clean that wound, I can see the blood dripping."

"I'll take them off," she said. "Turn around."

As she untied her shoes Border came back with the water and some towels. "If you guys are all right here, I need to be moving on. My brother's expecting me over at Winter's Inn. We promised to help Martha Q and my grandmother get Easter decorations down from the attic. The old witch will yell at us the whole time, but my grandmother will have supper cooked, which kind of balances it all out, I guess." He hesitated. "But I could stay if you need me."

"We'll handle this. Go." Marty opened a first-aid kit and began spreading supplies out on the bed.

Border was gone before Ronelle had time to tell him thanks.

She looked around the room. Except for the half-bed, the room looked more like a gym than a bedroom. There was even a bar above his bed and machines everywhere. The room was the same size as the living area, but it seemed cramped.

"Nice job of decorating," she said.

"Thanks. Take off those jeans."

"Turn around."

He met her stare. "Ronny, I'm going to see your legs anyway."

"Turn around."

He swore and whirled until his back was to her. While she unbuttoned her jeans, he asked, "What were you doing walking? It's freezing out there."

"I just had the chance." She didn't want to tell him more. She removed her jacket, then her shoes, and last her jeans, knowing they were ruined, but she folded them on the floor anyway. "You can turn around now. I'm ready."

He turned to face her and took his time looking at her bare legs before he ordered, "Put your foot on the footrest of my chair."

To her surprise he moved his foot off the rest without using his hands.

"You can move your legs," she whispered.

"A little. That doesn't mean I can walk." He wet a corner of the kitchen towel and brushed it over the long thin cuts at her knee. "Not so bad. I think we can clean this up in no time."

She sat completely still as he cleaned the wound and spread Neosporin on it. "Doesn't look too bad. The bleeding has pretty well stopped. The main problem will be infection, so keep it clean and wrapped for a few days. At night let it breathe all you can."

"You sound like a doc."

"I made it to the first year of med school before the thrill of skiing pulled me away. Then there were several times my skills came in handy on the slopes."

He put his hand behind her knee, lifted her leg up, and straightened it out over the arm of his chair. As he wrapped the cuts, his hands moved over her leg, touching her.

When he taped off the gauze, he rested his hand just above her bandaged knee. "Lie back, Ronny, relax a few minutes. You've been through a fright."

She leaned back against his pillows.

"Now, breathe deep, honey. Let your muscles relax."

She took deep breaths and let her heart slow. He lifted both her legs and she stretched out atop his bed. "I'm right here. You're safe here."

He placed his hand just above her knee, lightly stroking her skin.

She believed him. Her mother always told her the only safe place in the world was home, but she'd lied. The big kid with the tattoos hadn't hurt her. Marty hadn't hurt her. They hadn't yelled at her or told her what a fool she was.

Without opening her eyes, she asked, "Why do you call me honey?"

She heard him laugh. "I knew those lips would taste like honey even before I kissed you." His hand brushed her skin. "I've been thinking about the feel of your mouth all weekend, but I never guessed . . ."

"What?" she said when he didn't continue.

"Never mind."

"No." She rose to her elbow. "What did you never guess?"

"That you'd have such a body under all those baggy clothes."

"I don't," she started.

He rolled suddenly forward, his face only inches from hers. "The hell you don't."

"But I've seen models . . ."

"Men don't want models, honey, they want women. Real women." He moved his warm hand up to her hip.

The look in his eyes told her just how beautiful he thought she was.

Before she could argue, he kissed her. His arm circled behind her as he pulled her closer to him. Against her lips he whispered, "You got a body that would drive the men in this town crazy if they ever got a look at it."

The kiss that followed was hard and fast. When he pulled away, he whispered against her ear. "You ready for lesson two?"

She nodded slightly. Afraid and excited.

He held her head at just the right angle and waited until she closed her eyes, wet her lips, and opened her mouth lightly. Then he kissed her long and tenderly. When she relaxed, he lowered her head in the crook of his arm and began kissing his way down her throat while his hand made lazy circles over her abdomen. The thin T-shirt made his touch almost skin on skin.

When he straightened, he leaned back and watched her move slowly, trying to figure out where her arms should go and where her head should rest against his arm.

When she looked at him, nervous and embarrassed, he said simply, "Keep moving, Ronny. I love watching you just move." He fisted her shirt, pulling it tightly across her breasts. "You're a work of art in motion."

She didn't say a word, but she began to shake. No one had ever talked to her this way.

"Cold?" he guessed. "You've had quite a shock."

She nodded, for lack of anything else to say.

He pulled the covers over her gently.

After he'd tucked her in, his fingers pulled her hair free of the knot and gently combed it back away from her face as he lifted her head to the pillow.

"I better be going . . ."

"No." He stopped her. "Stay just a minute longer." He brushed her arm. "Stay and let me look at you."

She didn't answer. She couldn't. If she'd said a word she might have cried. No one ever saw her.

He raised her arms above her head to the pillow, and then slowly moved his hands beneath the covers and brushed his fingers along her sides. "Are you still cold?"

She closed her eyes, thinking his touch was warming her to her toes. "I'm fine. Just fine, thank you."

His hand slid along her arm, slowly caressing her. "I don't know where you got the idea that you're not beautiful, Ronny, because you are. Looking at you is almost as pleasant as touching you."

She caught her breath when he moved his hand to her waist and tugged her T-shirt up a few inches.

"Any objections, honey?"

"None," she whispered.

His warm fingers spread out over her middle and she bowed with the pleasure, then settled back, hoping for more.

She heard the wheelchair move slightly and felt his breath on her cheek. "You all right with me touching you? Because if you're not, we stop now," he asked as he pulled the bedspread up higher with one hand.

"I don't want to leave," she whispered as his mouth brushed against her cheek. "I want to be with you."

He tucked the covers around her. "Stay then. Rest. I'll wake you in an hour."

Ronny drifted to sleep to the rhythm of his touch. His strong fingers gently brushed over her with calming, loving strokes.

The room had grown dark when he whispered, "Wake

up, sleepyhead, and get out of my bed. The least I can do is feed you after all the pleasure you brought me."

"Pleasure?" she mumbled, more asleep than awake.

"It's been a million years since I've touched a woman, and even in your sleep you moved to my touch." He leaned close and slowly kissed her, deepening the kiss as she woke.

When he broke the kiss, she felt his hand patting her hip. She sat up with a start. "I didn't mean to sleep. Did you . . . did you touch me all over?"

"Would you have minded if I did?"

Tears bubbled in her eyes. "Yes. I don't want to miss it."

He laughed. "You didn't miss it, honey. I felt the weight of your breast in my hand and the nice roundness of your hip, but I want you awake when I touch some parts of your body."

She nodded, scrubbing away her tears, and sat up. "You must think I'm an idiot."

"No. I think you've been asleep maybe all your life. You're just waking up. At a point in my life when all I wanted to do was disappear from life, watching you is like pulling back the curtains and letting light in for the first time in a long while."

Tears started falling down her cheeks again, and she shoved them away.

He pulled her hands away from her face and didn't let go as she began to talk to him, really talk, like she'd never done to anyone on the planet. When she finally stopped she sat for a while, then laughed. "I'm sorry."

"It's okay, Ronny, you can drop by anytime. I could drive you home anytime you're ready."

"No." She stood, brushing the bandage as if she could brush away the pain. "I can walk." She reached for her shoes.

He laughed. "Put on your pants first."

"No." She shook her head. "They're bloody. Mother might see them and go nuts."

He seemed to understand. Rolling a few feet to a shelf, he pulled out a pair of black jogging pants. "Here, wear these. They'll be too big, but they'll keep you warm until you get home."

She didn't have time to debate. Her mother was probably already on her way back from the meeting. Pulling on the pants, she slipped into her shoes and grabbed her coat. "Thanks, I have to run." At the door, she turned. "I'll see you Friday for lunch."

"No," he yelled. "I don't want to wait that long. Try for Monday."

"Lunch?" She smiled.

He nodded. "And lesson three."

She would have run back and kissed him good-bye, but she remembered his demand. No kissing when she was standing.

At his door, she paused. "Marty?"

"Yes," he said.

"Could we do that again sometime . . . even if I don't need first aid? It felt good to have you touch me lightly like that."

He smiled. "I'll look forward to it."

She darted away, embarrassed that she'd been so bold to ask.

Ronny ignored the pain and jogged her way home. She'd just slipped into her pajamas when she heard the garage door. Shoving Marty's jogging pants under the bed, she hurried to the kitchen.

When her mother walked in carrying an empty salad bowl, Ronny looked up from her crossword.

"Have you been sitting there all night? I swear. Couldn't you at least move into the living room and watch TV? Working those little crosswords will ruin your eyes. When you're sitting around with glasses thick as safety glass you'll wish you'd listened to your mother."

Before Dallas could rage on, Ronny asked, "How was the meeting?"

She never said another word as Dallas talked herself into exhaustion. Even when they'd retired to separate bedrooms, she could still hear her mother mumbling in her sleep. Ronny knew that her mother thought the world would go to hell in a hatbox without Dallas Logan to explain everything.

Dallas would never take the time to see where her daughter was going.

Ronny smiled. She'd made up her mind. She was going to fall in love.

Chapter 37

TRUMAN FARM

AFTER SPENDING ALL DAY SATURDAY IN HIS CLOSET OF A room trying to figure out what parts of his drunken rage had been real and what came from the bottle, Noah elected to just sleep. He didn't want to see Reagan. Every part of his body hurt, but if what he thought had happened in the hallway hadn't happened, he decided he didn't want to know yet. The truth might hurt worst of all.

Lately, when he drank, he drank slowly all day long. He hated being drunk, but he liked the dull feeling of being halfway in-between. Not sober enough to do any serious thinking, not drunk enough to do anything stupid.

When Reagan brought him orange juice on Saturday, he pretended to be asleep; later that night someone set a tray by his bed, but he didn't eat anything.

Sunday morning he knew he'd have to face Reagan.

Bran had probably told her the details of how he'd found
Noah passed out in the bar anyway.

When Noah got downstairs, everyone smiled at him and
said hello. Foster even asked how he was feeling, but no
one, not even Reagan, asked him any questions.

Aunt Pat, whom he seemed to have inherited when his
sister Alex married Hank Matheson, was reading to Uncle
Jeremiah, who looked to be sound asleep. Noah wandered
into the kitchen and found Rea setting up to make pies. He
sat down and watched her for a while, then asked, "Why do
you love making pies so much?"

She shrugged. "I don't know. Maybe because when I lived
in children's homes between foster homes, we never got pies,
not real ones. I find it hard to believe anyone would want to
eat a store-bought one after tasting homemade."

Noah had never given it much thought. "What are we
having today?"

She smiled. "Chocolate. Both Pat and Jeremiah are having a little trouble with their teeth."

"And they can gum chocolate."

"Right."

Noah looked down at his hands. "You mind if I borrow
your pickup again? I need to go to town and thank someone
after I say I'm sorry. It won't take me thirty minutes."

"I don't mind. Bring Bran back for lunch if you like."

Noah studied her. "How'd you know I was going to see
Brandon Biggs?"

"I saw him drop you off at the back door and start walking back to town. Foster picked him up about the time he
got to Lone Oak Road and took him home. He probably
thought if he knocked he'd wake everyone up." She paused
and then added, "Like you did stumbling over everything."

Noah watched her closely. She wasn't mad. She just
looked busy. He almost asked if she'd kissed him in the
dark hallway, but he wasn't ready to hear the truth.

"Tell Bran we're having baked pork chops. He likes
those."

Noah lifted the keys and started to say something, but

then he thought better of it and grabbed his hat. He'd much rather beat the tar out of Brandon Biggs than apologize, but Noah knew he wouldn't feel good in his own skin until he made it right between them.

Bran had done him a favor and, like it or not, he wouldn't feel even until he paid the guy back.

He found Brandon Biggs on the front porch of a duplex near the old downtown square. He was drinking a beer and offered Noah one without a word when he walked up.

Noah sat down on the porch railing, but before he could say anything, a terrible banging racket came from the open front door.

"That's my brother, Border," Bran yelled. "He's practicing."

"He do that often?"

"He's been doing it since just before I started drinking." Bran laughed. "After a few beers he gets better." They both took a long drink and he added, "After five beers you start dancing to the music."

Noah found that hard to believe. "About Friday night . . ." he began.

"Forget it. You would have done the same for me."

Noah wasn't so sure he would have, but he nodded. "I owe you one."

Bran smiled. "Next time you get the urge to slug me, promise me you'll take a step back."

"Fair enough."

They listened to the band practice while they finished off their beer. When the boys took a break Bran asked, "You hiding out at the Truman place?"

"I guess. I didn't really think of it as hiding, but you may be right." Noah found it strange that the one person he really didn't like knew his secret. "Rea told me to invite you to Sunday lunch, but I guess you're busy."

"No such luck." Bran smiled as he stood. "I'll be there before you can get that old pickup started."

Noah watched him leave, then poked his head in the apartment to tell the boys how good they sounded. Friday night he hadn't paid much attention to the band, but now he decided they must have added to the headache he had yesterday morning.

Border Biggs was a carbon copy of his big brother. The kid named Beau, on the other hand, had something about him. Noah had seen it in bull riders. Something in the way they stood or maybe something in their eyes that said they were going to be somebody someday and nothing would stop them.

Noah took the time to drive around the town square before heading back to the Truman farm. When he was away from Harmony he thought he might never come back, but now when he was home he realized how dearly he'd missed the town. It was as if one windy day the soil got in his lungs and no matter where he went for the rest of his life there would always be a piece of this town in him next to his heart.

He took his time driving home. When he passed his folks' house in town, he could tell it was all closed up. Most people were sleeping in or already in church. The First Baptist and the First United Methodist Church were across the street from one another. Every Sunday they'd fight over the parking spots along the street. The Methodists won in the end because they always started five minutes before the Baptists. Noah figured they'd still be racing on their way to the Pearly Gates one day.

He drove past the bank, the post office, and the town hall. In an odd way he felt like he had to see them all, just to make sure nothing had changed.

A half hour later he walked into the Truman kitchen and found Bran kissing Reagan right in the middle of her pie making.

He took one step, his fist ready to fire, and then Reagan broke the kiss and looked at him. Noah expected her to look startled or even shocked into fear, but no, she simply looked bothered.

"What in the hell do you think you're doing?" After all, she'd just kissed him two nights ago. At least he thought she had.

Reagan smiled and moved back to her pies. "Comparative shopping," she answered.

Noah glanced at Bran, and the big guy looked as confused as Noah felt. A half hour later, they sat down across from one another. Each looked at the other, and Noah had a feeling Bran felt the same way he did. They were in the same boat, and someone had taken the oars.

Chapter 38

SIMS PLACE

SUNDAY MORNING, DENVER WAS PACKING WHEN HE HEARD a car drive up in front of his house. The part of him that had lived far too long in a war zone came alert. He walked to the front window and flipped the security system he'd just set on rest to full cover.

A moment later he flipped it back off and ran for the door. Claire had just stepped from her car when he grabbed her and swung her around. Before she could even say hello he was kissing her.

The feel of her in his arms made him realize just how much he missed having her close. He felt like all of him wasn't there, wasn't working, wasn't breathing, when her skin wasn't brushing against him.

When he finally broke the kiss to let her breathe, he whispered against her cheek, "I've missed you."

She laughed. "You saw me last night at dinner."

"No, I saw your family and, much as I like them, I didn't want to rip their clothes off. I want you." Since their rainy walk in the park he'd seen her twice. Once when he'd taken her and Saralynn to the show and on Saturday night with everyone around watching them. She might be taking their going public seriously, but he wanted the private back.

"I thought I'd come over and drive you to the airport."

"I don't have to leave for another hour." He kissed her neck as he talked.

When he pulled back, waiting for an answer, she just smiled and he understood. They might have trouble carrying on a conversation, but they had no problem communicating.

"I'll race you," he whispered.

An hour later they were both trying to find the clothes they'd tossed on the way to the bedroom. Both knew it was time to leave, but they couldn't seem to stop touching one another.

"We're worse than Saralynn's rabbits." Claire laughed.

Denver caught her and kissed her again, and then she insisted they leave.

Since he was heading east, they drove to the Will Rogers International Airport in Oklahoma. His hand never stopped touching her on the drive. He thought of telling her that he was falling in love with her, but using the word *love* was something he never did. Denver had always felt like that one word opened the relationship up for a world of hurt.

They talked of little things and listened to music. He told her how to drive and she told him to shut up. They argued over which road to take, but all the while he was caressing her hair, trying to memorize the feel of it.

"Next time," he whispered in her ear, "I'll hire that crazy pilot who lives in Harmony. What's his name, Wild Derwood? He could have me to OK City in half an hour, and then I'd have longer to stay home and make love to you."

Claire laughed. "Derwood is nuts. He smoked too much

weed in the sixties. Half the time he flies my mother to Dallas, she has to tell him which way to go. I think his method of navigation is the same as the Wright Brothers—follow the train tracks."

"It would be worth the risk," Denver whispered. "I didn't get enough of you, Claire. How about pulling over?"

"There's not even a tree left between here and Oklahoma City. I'm not pulling over."

He kissed the side of her throat and she sighed. "I'm hiring Derwood next time," he whispered. "And I want four hours at home alone with you before we start playing the couple to everyone. Four full hours, Claire."

"I'll try," she answered, her hands white-knuckled on the steering wheel. "But I was thinking more like six. I'd like to take it slow for once. Very slow."

"You got it, beautiful."

When they got to the airport, he checked his luggage and then held her. For several moments he felt like he couldn't let go. Something had happened in the few days he'd been home. Maybe it was the "going public" thing, or maybe they were just getting to know each other's world, but Claire had gone way beyond being a woman he had an affair with when they both had the time.

Somehow this complicated woman who made him mad as often as she made him laugh had climbed into his heart. A heart he would have sworn had turned to stone years ago.

"Call me," she whispered.

"When?" She'd never before asked him to call.

"Anytime after nine. Any night."

He pulled away enough to see her, to know if she was serious.

What he saw shocked him. Claire Matheson had tears in her eyes and she was holding him as tightly as he held her.

Denver smiled and kissed her nose. "Promise you won't paint any pictures of me."

"No deal. You have your work and I have mine."

He laughed, thinking he'd probably see his likeness shot out of a cannon or stapled to a barn door when he got back.

She kissed his cheek and ran from him as he turned toward security check.

He watched her go, knowing that he'd finally gotten to her. As he began to toss his coat and keys into the tray, he whispered to himself, "I love you, Claire."

Chapter 39

MONDAY
MARCH 15

RONELLE WENT BY THE DINER ON HER WAY TO WORK MON-
day and picked up a pie. Marty had told her they'd be having
lunch today. It seemed like only a few hours since she'd seen
him. Maybe it was, because every waking moment since
he'd kissed her last night she'd been thinking of him.

She'd been very careful at breakfast not to favor her left
leg. She'd even dressed early so her mother wouldn't see the
bandage through her pajamas. The only thing she hadn't
had time to do was wash her jeans and his jogging pants,
but they were safely tucked under her bed. If she had to wait
until her mother's Saturday hair appointment, it wouldn't
matter.

A little after noon, she walked up the steps to Marty's
duplex. A fancy car was parked outside and she wondered if one of the Biggs boys had stolen it. They'd always

seemed nice enough to her, but her mother and Martha Q both thought they were prison bound.

Just before she knocked, Ronelle heard voices, angry voices.

"Stay out of my life, Kerri," Marty shouted. "I'm telling you no for the last time."

"Don't be ridiculous," a female answered. "You're rotting in this town. I've come to load you in my car and take you back to Dallas. Your father agrees, you belong in a rehab facility, not out here. End of discussion."

Ronelle didn't know what to do, so she just stayed where she was.

Marty's voice came angry and low. "I'm thirty-three years old, Kerri. I've been running my life for years without your or my father's advice. The accident didn't change that. Just because I can't walk does not mean my brain cells have died."

The woman changed her tactics. "But Marty, how could you possibly be happy here? There's not even a decent place to eat in this town, and this apartment is drab as a prison cell."

"Good-bye, Kerri. Tell my father I'm fine. I don't want or need anything from him."

"He sent money. Cash this time, since you didn't cash the checks."

"I don't need it."

"You're not yourself, Martin. I told your dad you're probably hooked on drugs or something. Otherwise, you'd see reason."

"Of course I'm hooked on drugs. They're called painkillers, but I only take half of what I did when I was seeing all those doctors. If I'm dying, I at least want to be able to count the days."

She must have stomped her foot. "I'm not leaving without you."

"Morning," someone said from behind Ronelle, almost making her jump off the porch. "How's the knee?"

She turned around and saw Border grinning at her.

He might not look any less scary in the daylight than

he had last night, but he'd helped her and she did need to thank him for that.

"I . . . I wanted to thank you for last . . ."

"Oh, forget it. Glad I could help." He looked down at her. "You planning to deliver the mail or just stand out here till the postage rate changes?"

She smiled. "Mr. Winslow has company."

Border pounded on the door. "He won't mind the interruption. He said for me to come on over when I was ready to go to school." The overgrown kid smiled. "I slept in this morning on account of I had to practice late last night. I'm in a band, you know."

"Really." She would have guessed a gang before a band.

"Yep. We have real gigs and make real money. I'll let you know the next time we play at Buffalo's, and maybe you and Marty will come listen."

"Maybe." The clear picture of her mother having a heart attack flashed in her mind. "I'd love to."

"Love to what?" Marty snapped as he appeared in the doorway.

Ronelle could see a beautiful woman in a fine silk suit standing a few feet behind him. The visitor looked like she'd stepped out of a fashion magazine.

Border didn't seem to notice the woman. "Ronny says you and her might show up to one of my gigs. I'll tell you the songs we know and maybe you could request one."

Marty smiled and met her eyes. "We might, if she'd go out with me. A real date might be nice."

Ronelle felt his gaze moving over her as if she didn't have on enough clothes. Compared to the woman in silk with high heels and pearls, she must look like a Goodwill mannequin. But he wasn't looking at the woman. In fact, he seemed to have forgotten she was even there.

"Martin, I'm not going to stand here and be ignored. Are you coming with me or not?"

"No," he said, without even looking at her. "I have a lunch date." He shoved the door open. "Ronny, if you'll wait here, I'll take Border to school and be right back."

He motioned Ronny in, and Border followed behind like a pet bear.

"You're having lunch with the mailman?" Kerri snapped.

"Mailwoman," both guys said at once.

"I'm sure we've plenty for three, if you want to join us," Ronny said in little more than a whisper. "I didn't mean to interrupt your business."

"Don't be ridiculous." The lady in silk shoved her way out the door. "This wasn't business, this was personal. Something I'm sure you wouldn't understand."

As she stormed toward her car, Border yelled, "Sorry about that dent, my bike fell over when I was trying to start it."

When the woman climbed into her car, Ronny swore she heard several hiccupped screams.

Marty and Border disappeared out the back door, and Ronelle was suddenly left alone.

For a few minutes she didn't touch anything, but as she warmed she took off her coat and began to walk slowly around the room. His desk was covered with papers, most with numbers and charts. She looked into his bedroom, where she'd been for a while the night before. Workout equipment. Shelves full of clothes, but no drawers. A bed made perfectly in military style.

Nothing personal, she thought. Not one picture or notebook, nothing. Everything in Marty's world was in black and white and chrome. It crossed her mind that maybe he saw himself as nothing but a machine. Sometime after the accident he must have stopped living and started just surviving.

Silently, she crossed into his perfect kitchen. He'd said this place had the only kitchen and bathroom in town that were handicap friendly. But the house didn't seem to fit him. She set her bought pie down on the polished counter. Like him, everything was clean, spotless. Ronelle looked down at the ink stain on her hand and the spots on her baggy pants where she'd accidentally spilled bleach. A man like him would have a friend like the lady in pearls, not someone like her.

When she heard his car pull up at the back ramp, she ran into the office area and waited by the fire. Everything about her was mousy. She didn't belong near a man like Marty Winslow.

She could hear him banging his way into the kitchen, then down the hall and into the office.

"Take that ridiculous hat off," he snapped, obviously still in a bad mood.

Ronny gathered her strength. She wouldn't have anyone else ordering her around; everyone in her life already did. "It's not ridiculous. It was my father's. When he died he gave it to me, and Dallas let me keep it because she didn't want it and she said stuff like it doesn't even sell in a garage sale."

Ronny turned toward the fire, seeing just how stupid the hat did look in the reflections on the brass frame of the grate. The only good thing about it was that it seemed to match the rest of her outfit.

She knew he was behind her, but she didn't turn around. She expected him to yell at her again, or maybe order her to sit down and eat, but he didn't. He just reached for her hand and tugged it toward him.

Her knees almost buckled when she felt his kiss against her palm.

"I'm sorry," he whispered, so low she barely heard him. "You're the only person in my world who doesn't make demands on me, and yet I can't seem to be nice to you."

She knelt beside his chair. He tugged her hat off and looked at it. "A fine hat," he declared.

"Don't make fun of me," she said.

"I'm not. I'm the only clown in the room." Then, as if he'd done it a hundred times, he leaned forward and kissed her gently on the lips. "If you don't mind, honey, take off your coat and I'll get the salads. We can eat by the fire if you like."

She nodded. While he went for the food, she pulled off her coat and then her sweatshirt. She wore a simple button-up white shirt with cap sleeves. It was the nicest thing in her closet.

When he came back, she saw his slow smile and straightened as if she were wearing a ball gown.

He laughed. "No one would mistake you for a mailman now. Sometimes I think you must be a diamond wrapped in burlap so the rest of us won't look so bad."

They ate and talked. She didn't ask about the woman in silk, and he said nothing. When she mentioned that she had savings but didn't know what to do with it, he told her to find a good brokerage house. They'd advise her, but never should she give all her money over to one person.

"What do you want to do with it? Buy a car? Take a trip? Invest it for old age?"

"I don't drive," she admitted. "Dallas says there is no need."

"How long have you called your mother Dallas?" he asked between bites.

"For as long as I can remember I called her that in my mind. I used to read fairy tales with a wicked stepmother and, even though I knew she was my real mother, I liked to think she was my stepmother."

He laughed. "You've got a wicked imagination, Ronny."

Then she told him about the seeding she did with magazines and postcards. He laughed so hard she finally joined him. Anyone else might think she was crazy, but he saw the seeding for what it was . . . her way of caring for people.

When she finally glanced at her watch, it was after one. "I have to go."

"No, please stay. How about calling in sick? You do have sick days, don't you?"

"Yes, but I've never used one. If I stayed home I'd be there with Dallas."

"I get it." He smiled. "Just call and leave a message. I'll tell you what to say. When the postmaster gets back from his lunch, I'm sure he'll get along without you for one afternoon. I'd like to take you for a drive."

Ronny was so nervous she stuttered though the entire message. She'd never played hooky; that wasn't an option for homeschooled kids. If Marty was really sick, maybe dying, she wanted to be with him. Maybe he'd just said that to the lady in pearls, but his words hung in the shadows of her mind like damp spiderwebs.

When she hung up, he pulled her onto his lap and laughed. "You're free, Ronny. For one afternoon we're both free."

They did the dishes and he showed her a few of the cookbooks that had taught him to cook. Ronny felt like she'd been saving up things to tell someone all her life, and finally she'd found someone to listen.

He pulled a book off a low shelf beneath the bar. "I want to pay you for the pie."

"No. It was my contribution." The book in his hand opened like a box. A secret storage place. He pulled an envelope from the side of his chair and stuffed it in the box, then pulled out a few bills from the bottom of the box and stuffed them in his shirt pocket. "Well, then I can at least buy you supper."

The afternoon was cold and cloudy when they climbed into his Volvo that had been built for someone in a wheelchair. She watched him brace against the car door and frame. Slowly, he stood and folded up his chair, then lowered himself into the seat.

"Where shall we drive?"

"I don't care."

He grinned. "Then pick a direction and we'll head that way until we spot a Dairy Queen. Then we'll turn left. If we always do that, we should end up back home."

"Makes sense to me."

He tossed her a few books from the backseat. One explained every historical marker in Texas and another told about sites not to miss in the area. She read and explained as he drove. She'd always thought there was nothing much to see in the panhandle, but suddenly everything looked interesting.

On a long stretch of road he rolled down the windows and drove ninety. When they were both half frozen he closed the windows and explained to her that he felt like he was skiing again. She listened as he explained the thrill of it, the adventure. "It's like," he said all excited, "it's like flying. You're one hundred percent alive for that moment. You can feel every ounce of blood in your body pumping. You know what I mean?"

"No," she admitted. "I don't know."

He looked at her as if he didn't believe her. "Ronny, tell me about one time in your life when you felt totally alive, so alive that you could die and wouldn't have to go anywhere because you were already in heaven."

She looked at him. "Right here. Right now."

He pulled off the road on a lonely strip where truckers sometimes pulled off to sleep. There wasn't a tree or another car in sight. He pulled her into his arms and just held her for a long while, and then he didn't say a word as he set her back in her seat and buckled her seatbelt.

They drove home singing songs with the radio. Light faded behind the clouds. Ronny knew it was time for her to head home, but she couldn't bear to end the day. Her mother was having afternoon tea with Martha Q, so she probably wouldn't be in until late. The two liked to move from tea and sweets to wine and cheese.

When Marty asked if she wanted to come in and help him finish off the pie she'd brought for lunch, she nodded. A few more minutes. No matter how much Dallas yelled when she got home and found out Ronelle hadn't started heating dinner, it would be worth it to stay a few more minutes with Marty.

Ronny ate her buttermilk pie with her feet propped beside Marty's knees. His hand rested on her ankle as they talked about all their likes and dislikes. She was growing used to his casual touch and guessed that he liked touching her almost as much as she loved having him near. With Marty she wasn't homely and he wasn't crippled. They were just two people enjoying being alone together.

Finally, he said, "I know I have to let you go, but first I want to thank you for the best afternoon I've had in a long time. You make me forget about things."

Ronny smiled. "And you make me feel pretty."

He frowned. "Climb on," he said, reaching his hands about

her waist and pulling her onto his lap. "I've got something to show you."

He rolled them toward his bedroom. A minute later, they were before a floor-to-ceiling mirror. He took her face in his hands and turned her to face him. "Look deep in my eyes and tell me how I see you."

She tried to pull away, but he wouldn't let go. Then she looked into his eyes and saw his honesty, his caring. She saw that he cherished her. "You see beauty. To you I'm pretty, but you don't see me. Not the real me. Not the me everyone else sees."

"No, honey, you have it backward. You don't see the real you. I've known lots of women. Girls who know how to use makeup, the lighting, flattering colors, everything to their advantage, but in the morning with no makeup or frills, believe me, they are not as beautiful as you. A few times I've slept with a beautiful woman and felt like I needed to introduce myself in the morning.

"They stand poor in comparison. They don't have your shy honesty, your gentle kindness. Believe me, no matter how stunning a woman is, if she's lying to you, she's turning bone ugly."

Ronny smiled.

He kissed her, deeper than they'd ever kissed.

When he pulled away, he said, "You've got to go. It's bound to be after six."

She shook her head. "Not before I have that lesson you promised."

Marty laughed. "Oh, one other thing I forgot to mention. You're demanding." He began rolling backward. "I'll give you the lesson, but not here. If we're going to do one a visit, we'd better not start in the bedroom or the lessons might run together."

He took her back to the fireplace and she sat on a chair facing him. As she met his eyes with only a few inches between them, he whispered, "Put your hands behind you, Ronny. I don't want you tempted to touch me."

She moved her arms until her hands caught the bars of wood at her back.

"Now close your eyes and take a deep breath."

She could feel her heart pounding, but she followed his orders.

"When I begin to kiss you, I want you to move closer as the kiss deepens. Can you do that?"

She nodded and waited. Very slowly she felt him growing closer until his lips brushed over hers.

Ronny caught her breath and he broke the kiss.

"Closer," he whispered, and touched her cheek with his knuckles. "Move your body closer."

The kiss continued and she did as he said until her breasts brushed against his shirt.

"Right there," he said against her lips. "Now hold it right there and take a deep breath."

He wasn't touching her anywhere but with the kiss, but she pushed lightly against him each time she breathed and his kiss made her breathe deeper and faster.

Finally, he pulled away and laughed. "Now you know how to drive a man crazy."

Ronny blinked. "Really. Did it drive you crazy?"

"Honey, you've been driving me crazy since you walked into my life. I would have never guessed insanity came special delivery."

He took her hand and they talked while the wind whipped violently around the duplex. For a second, she thought she heard someone running, and then a whistle sounded from out back. Someone was circling the side of the house.

Before she could act, Marty tightened his grip on her hand. "Something is going on outside. Don't move."

A pop of shattering wood sounded from the kitchen a moment before the unlocked front door slammed against the foyer wall.

Ronny screamed as men carrying guns rushed in from both the front and the back. In the firelight they seemed like approaching demons.

"Freeze, Winslow!" someone yelled.

Men stormed forward from the shadows. Men with guns. Men wearing the brown uniforms of the sheriff's office and the blue of the highway patrol.

She glanced at Marty. He sat stone still, but she saw no fear in his eyes, only anger.

"What's going on here?" Marty snapped.

A deputy she'd never seen stepped forward. "We know you've got a child here. Where is she? Her mother informed us the girl was kidnapped, brought here, and held against her will." Men began to spread out, searching.

Phil Gentry, the deputy who always brought mail in at the office, stepped forward and lowered his weapon slightly. "Ronelle? What are you doing here?"

Ronelle gulped down her planned scream. "Having pie." She said it so innocently the other deputies began to look confused. "No one is here but us."

"I'll try again. Deputy, what's going on here?" Marty asked, calming his voice as they both figured out that somewhere along the line the cops had made a mistake. "There's no child here. There never has been while I've rented the place."

A younger deputy stepped forward. "A woman called about an hour ago saying that her little daughter had been kidnapped. She said this duplex was on her route and one of the two criminals living here must have kidnapped her."

Phil Gentry holstered his gun. "What was the woman's name?" he said in the same tone one might say, *Slug me, I deserve it.*

"Dallas Logan."

Phil swore. "Put up your guns and stand down, boys. You're looking at Dallas Logan's only child, and I've known Ronelle all her life. What are you, about twenty-six or -seven?"

Ronelle looked down. "Twenty-seven."

Phil stepped closer. "We're real sorry to have bothered you folks. These guys didn't know your mother, and they overreacted. You're not a child and it doesn't look like you're being held against your will."

"No, sir, but I didn't call my mother to tell her where I was."

Phil laughed. "You're a grown woman. You don't have to call your mother, but for our sake, now and then, you might. Sorry to have bothered you folks. I think I'll run by your mother's house and let her know what might happen to people who file false reports. She's had half the town out looking for a child."

Ronelle nodded. "My mother still thinks of me as a child."

Phil held his hat in his hand as he backed away. "I'm sorry to have bothered you both. I'll have someone come out and secure that back door we kicked in, Mr. Winslow."

Marty didn't smile. "You might think about knocking next time."

After the police left, they talked for a while and then Marty insisted on driving her home. He wanted to go in with her, but Ronelle wouldn't have it. She'd been embarrassed enough for one night. She could face her mother far easier than she could face what her mother would say to Marty.

"If it gets bad, call me and I'll come get you."

She nodded, barely hearing him.

He gripped her arm. "If it gets bad, walk out. You don't have to take anything. You can always walk away."

"Where would I go?" she whispered.

"To me," he answered. "To a hotel. To friends."

Ronelle stepped out of the car. All her life she could never remember wanting to go home, and she didn't want to go now.

She walked into the house that had never seemed like her home. It had always been Dallas's. She and her father were simply guests following Dallas's rules.

To her surprise, her mother wasn't there. Two gym bags she'd bought once at a garage sale were left on her bed. Ronelle walked over and tried her mother's door, but it was locked. She knew without trying that Dallas wouldn't answer even if she pounded all night. In the kitchen her TV dinner had been tossed in the trash along with her crossword puzzles.

She emptied out all the junk her mother had put in the bags and packed one change of clothes, her toothbrush, and a picture of herself and her dad taken when she was five. Then, without looking back, she walked out of the only house she'd ever lived in. Dallas had said all she needed to say. Ronelle was trash and she wanted her out.

For a block she thought she might go back to Marty, but she didn't want to force her problems on him.

Finally, she knew there was only one place she could go. To the one other person who'd ever seen her in the shadows. To the man who'd given her a hug when she'd most needed it, at her father's funeral.

Ronelle Logan turned toward the funeral home as the last of the gray light of day faded.

Chapter 40

~⚮~

WRIGHT FUNERAL HOME

TYLER SAT AT HIS DESK FINISHING OUT THE PAPERWORK for the day. He'd been putting off e-mailing Kate. For days after she flew away she hadn't written, and then last week when Martha Q found out about Autumn taking the house-keeper job, she took it upon herself to write Kate.

It seemed, according to Martha Q, that Tyler had got-ten himself in a mess with a homeless woman who wasn't married, was three months pregnant, and almost got him killed when he stepped between the wayward girl and her drug-addicted boyfriend.

Though Martha Q's summary was fairly accurate, Tyler wouldn't have described it the way the old innkeeper did.

Tyler didn't even know where to start with an explanation to Kate and, more to the point, didn't think he needed one. Martha Q had the facts, but not the truth. The old busybody had left out facts, such as the fact that Autumn was on the run from being abused, and he wasn't just taking her in, she was working for him. Everyone at the funeral home had taken the time to stop by and tell Tyler they thought he'd done the right thing offering her the job. Beth, in the office, said Autumn was always willing to run errands when she left for the store. Calvin said she helped him bring in the flowers and was already better than him at arranging them at the front of the chapel. Even Dave, who never commented on anything, told Tyler the girl should have a raise because they'd never find anyone who could cook like she did. Tyler suspected Dave had been bribed with chocolate chip cookies.

He typed *Dear Kate*, then stopped. Part of him didn't want to explain anything to Kate. He was a businessman who'd been running his own life and a business for more than twenty years. He didn't want Martha Q, or even Kate, telling him what he should do. He'd done the right thing helping the girl.

Tyler pressed the delete button just as he heard the front doorbell chime.

Adrenaline shot threw his veins. The memory of Leland showing up was still too raw in his mind to make a guest at night welcome. There were no family times scheduled for tonight.

When he reached the hallway, Autumn was already there in a robe that looked like it might have been left by Willamina. The girl had the broom in her hands as if prepared for battle.

"Should I dial 911?" she whispered.

Calvin came running up from downstairs. "I heard the bell. You don't think it's . . ."

Dave bumped into Calvin, almost knocking him down with the snow shovel he carried.

Tyler couldn't panic; the job was already overstaffed. He had to be the voice of reason. "Autumn, get the kitchen phone. If it's trouble, dial and set the phone down. The boys will be here fast when the Caller ID comes in at both the station and the sheriff's dispatch. Calvin and Dave, stand in the shadows in case you're needed."

Tyler moved to the door as the bell chimed again. He felt like a general riding in front of the troops. "Everyone stand ready. It's not that late. Maybe someone thought we'd still be open."

He flipped the lock and slowly opened the door. As he saw who it was, he raised his hand as if to tell the troops to stand down and let out a long breath.

"A little late for a delivery." He smiled, letting Ronelle Logan in. "But a postwoman is always welcome. Is there something I can help you with?"

Ronelle nodded. "I need a place to stay. I think I just ran away from home."

Autumn moved forward. "Well, from the looks of you, I'd say it's about time. Mr. Wright, you want me to get out the cookies and milk?"

"Yes." He was grateful to his new housekeeper, as he had no idea what to do in a situation like this. No one in the hundred-year history of Wright Funeral Home had ever had one, much less two runaways in residence.

Chapter 41

TUESDAY
MARCH 16
BLUE MOON DINER

TYLER BARELY MADE IT TO BREAKFAST WITH HANK THE next morning. By the time he and the girls had finished talking while eating cookies and milk last night, Autumn and Ronelle had bonded and Tyler had gained five pounds. The girls made up the hide-a-bed in Autumn's sitting room for Ronelle, and Autumn filled her in on the schedule while Tyler put away the milk. They all agreed she should stay with Autumn for a few days before making any big steps.

He'd left the girls in the kitchen, thinking he didn't even want to think about what Martha Q would have to say about his new situation. Maybe he should change the sign out front. WRIGHT FUNERAL HOME AND HALFWAY HOUSE FOR RUNAWAYS.

When he sat down at the Blue Moon a little after dawn,

Hank looked like he was already on his second cup of coffee. They ordered and Saralynn settled into her drawings.

"You hear about the mess at the sheriff's office last night?" Hank didn't wait for Tyler to answer. "Seems one of Alex's new deputies overreacted to a call from Dallas Logan. He had the whole panhandle out looking for a girl who'd been kidnapped . . ."

"I heard," Tyler said, before he had to listen to the entire story again.

Hank raised an eyebrow and waited.

"Ronelle knocked on my door last night. I don't know if Dallas kicked her out or if she ran, but she says she's not going back. She's staying with my housekeeper."

"I can't blame her for leaving. It would take a real gentle soul to put up with Dallas for that long. What is she going to do?"

"I told her I'd help her find a place to live, but she's welcome to stay till she gets her footing." Tyler shook his head. "I don't know if I can stand it. Having Willamina around all those years was like living with a ghost. She rarely even spoke to me. On the first of every month, I walked into the kitchen and handed her a check and her only comment was always, 'About time.' Now I've got Autumn, who never stops talking, and Ronelle. They're both young enough to be my daughters; maybe I should adopt them. I'm not used to women around."

"Welcome to my world. Now you have one day of my life. When my father died I was trapped on the ranch with a mother, two sisters, and two old aunts."

Tyler got over his pity party. "How are all the ladies in your life?"

"Well, Aunt Pat's been gone for days. She went over to the Truman place and Aunt Fat hasn't stopped talking about the scandal of it all. I expect Jeremiah to crawl out of his deathbed and bring her back home any minute. She's a real dear, but after forty years in the classroom she can't seem to stop teaching. Sometimes I think she and Aunt Fat take turns at the podium. She's eighty-four and apparently, according to Aunt Fat, has decided to live in sin with the neighbor."

"How is old Jeremiah?"

"Doing better, I think. He'll probably outlive us both."

"Sir Knight?" Saralynn patted Tyler's hand with sticky fingers. "Can I come live with you too? I don't have a daddy and you don't have a kid."

"Wouldn't you miss your mother and grandmother?"

"I could bring them too."

Both men laughed, but it was Hank who answered. "You know, Saralynn, I need you at the ranch. You're the only one who keeps up with what day it is. And who would feed your rabbits?"

She sighed. "You're right. Sorry, Sir Knight. I got to stay home."

"It's all right, Princess." Tyler smiled down at her. "I'll just have to settle for being your knight and you being my princess. Maybe one day the right man to be your daddy will come along."

"How will I know him?"

Tyler thought for a minute and whispered, "You'll see a twinkle in his eyes that says he thinks you're something. If he's the right man, he'll love your mother and he'll protect you just like your uncle Hank and your uncle Gabe and I do now. He'll ride in and save you if you ever get trapped in the castle."

She smiled and went back to her coloring.

Hank's voice was calm. "Alex told me Leland, Autumn's boyfriend, is long gone. You don't have to worry about him."

Tyler picked up his coffee cup. "I think I'll keep my doors locked after hours just in case, for a while."

They talked on about Hank's family and about the people of town. To Tyler they were all family, except maybe Martha Q. After getting to know her, he was surprised at least one of her seven husbands hadn't killed the woman. He couldn't tell if she was trying to get Kate and him together or rip them apart.

A nagging possibility tugged at his thoughts. Maybe he

and Kate were never a couple except in his mind. If so, Martha Q's meddling wouldn't have much effect at all.

After breakfast, he walked over to the post office as he did every morning. Ronelle was there in the back. Rumor was Dallas Logan hadn't stepped foot in the post office since her husband died. Tyler guessed Ronelle was betting on her mother not showing up today.

When Jerry Donavan handed Tyler his mail, he whispered, "That's a good thing you did, Mr. Wright, a real good thing."

"How's she doing?" Tyler nodded toward the back.

"A little jumpy when the door opens, but good. She asked me if she could stay in the back all day today, and I thought it was probably smart. I've known Dallas for thirty years and I swear if she was bottled wine, she'd be pure vinegar by now."

Tyler picked up his mail and nodded. He didn't know Dallas Logan all that well and hoped that fact would remain the same. He walked out to his car, as always planning his day.

Beth and Stella McNabb were in the main office when he got back to work. A family who lived in Harmony years ago had called and wanted a graveside service for their father on Thursday. Stella thought that maybe since the family was small and had no church affiliation, she would put together a meal for them in the conference room after the short service.

Tyler started to say that funeral homes don't cater, but Autumn walked in, handed Tyler his coffee, and offered to help cook.

"I just heard on the radio that a storm's coming in Thursday," she said.

Stella agreed. "Bob's been tracking it since yesterday. What with bad weather and a funeral, it would be nice to have a quiet lunch before they head back."

While the women talked, Tyler slipped into his office.

As Tyler sat down at his huge desk he decided he had time to check his e-mail while he opened his regular mail.

He flipped his computer on and noticed Kate had sent two messages.

The one from last night said, *What's going on, Ty? Martha Q says you've got trouble.*

The other came an hour ago and said, *I'm on my way home. Will call as soon as I know my flight.*

Tyler laughed. Apparently all he had needed to get his Kate to come see him was have two young women move in with him. The world was getting more confusing by the day. All his life he'd told himself he liked order. He grinned, realizing he was wrong. It turned out, he loved chaos.

Chapter 42

POST OFFICE

AT NOON, RONELLE UNWRAPPED THE SANDWICH AUTUMN had made her for lunch. She wanted, more than anything, to walk over to Marty's place, but she didn't dare. She hadn't had a chance to tell her mother why she'd been late getting home. But in this town there was little chance Dallas hadn't figured it out.

Knowing Dallas, she was circling the post office waiting for Ronelle to come out. With luck, she hadn't heard where her daughter had gone after she'd packed her things last night, but someone was bound to tell someone, who in turn would call her mother.

Ronelle picked up the phone on the back desk. She never used it except for official business, but maybe Mr. Donavan wouldn't mind this once. She dialed.

"Hello."

"Marty," she whispered.

His voice changed from hard to caring in an instant. "Ronny, are you all right?"

"I walked out of my mother's house last night." She said the words without shaking. She was getting used to the idea and there was no going back. If she did, her mother would spend the next thirty years reminding her what a fool she'd made of herself.

"Where are you?"

"I'm at work. I spent the night with a girl named Autumn at the funeral home. She works there and has a small apartment beside the kitchen. She said I could stay for as long as I needed to."

Marty was silent for a moment. "You've got a lot of growing to do, Ronny. It's not going to be easy, but the woman who is going to come out the other side of this mess will really be something."

"You think so?"

"I know so, honey."

She smiled. All she'd been thinking about was the chaos she was in. He gave her hope that there was an end to this dark tunnel.

"Want me to pick you up after work? We could get a hamburger and talk about it. Maybe drive over to Bailee, where no one would know us."

"I think I'd like that very much. Pick me up out back of the post office. I didn't take much last night. I may need to do a little shopping."

"You got it," he said. "And Ronny, I'm sorry to be the cause of all this, but you did the right thing."

"You weren't the cause. I should have moved out a long time ago." She knew what he meant by growing. Fear tangled with excitement in her blood.

"After we eat, I'll find a back road and start teaching you to drive. If you're going to be on your own, I have a feeling you'll want to go a lot farther than you can walk."

"Really? You'd teach me?" She wasn't sure she wanted to venture farther than the back room of the post office right now, but being with Marty and learning something new would be fun.

"Sure, honey. There isn't much I wouldn't do for you. See you at five." He hung up.

Ronny pulled a driver's ed manual she'd found at a garage sale and spent the rest of her lunch hour reading.

Mr. Donavan poked his head in the back room about three. "Ronelle, I heard you moved out last night."

She nodded.

"You need any money or anything, just let me know."

"Thanks." She looked up. "Mr. Donavan, do you think you could call me Ronny? I've hated Ronelle for most of my life."

He grinned. "Sure, Ronny."

When he left, she pulled her small pocketbook from the bag she carried her crosswords in. She had four hundred twenty dollars in cash. Tomorrow she planned to buy a few new clothes; after that, she had no idea what to do. The reality of thinking everything out for herself took a great deal more figuring than just going along.

Chapter 43

WEDNESDAY AFTERNOON
MARCH 17
TRUMAN FARM

NOAH FOUND REAGAN CURLED IN A BLANKET IN ONE OF
the lawn chairs in the Truman front yard.

"Mind if I join you?" he asked, not really sure where he
stood with her anymore. Since Sunday he'd been busy with
therapy, and she'd had lots to do running the farm. She still
talked over everything with the old man, but Noah had the
feeling Reagan was taking the reins of the operation.

"Of course not." She didn't look at him when he sat down.
Her eyes were on the sky. "There's a storm coming in. Uncle
Jeremiah says it's going to be a bad one."

"Your uncle a weatherman now?"

She shrugged. "I guess he could be. He's been watching
long enough."

"Rea." Noah waited until she looked at him. "I don't

want to talk about the weather. I want to talk about me and you."

"Okay," she said, giving him her full attention.

Great, he thought, now he didn't know where to start. He did what he always did. He ran straight out. "I hadn't meant to kiss you the other day when we were at the ranch. It just happened and I can't say I'm sorry because I'm not. I've been thinking about kissing you for what seems like half my life."

"All right," she said with a worried look in her eyes, like she was trying to put a puzzle together.

He tried again. "But when you kissed me in the hallway I was half drunk and didn't react like I should have."

"What are you trying to say? Just say it, Noah."

"I'm saying, if you're doing comparison shopping I'd like to have another chance."

"Why?"

He shot up. "That right there is what drives me crazy about you, Rea. You're always asking questions, digging at some truth. Hell if I know why."

She stood and walked to the edge of the yard, where shadows were already gathering. "Well, Preacher, do you want to kiss me again or don't you?"

"I do, but only if you'll cooperate. No surprise kiss."

She took another step beneath the branches. "All right."

The wind whipped up. He barely heard her. The tree above them began to sway, blocking anyone's view from the house.

Noah moved up in front of her. He would have liked to put his arms around her, but with the cast, he couldn't hold her. If she wanted to step away, she'd have no trouble.

He leaned down and slid his hand along the side of her neck and into her curly hair. He'd kissed her before a few times when he was more kid than man, but this time he wanted to kiss her completely.

She looked up at him as if expecting a trick, and he saw more of the girl in her than the woman, but when his lips touched hers the woman in her seemed to come alive. She leaned into him and crossed her arms behind his neck like she had no intention of letting him go.

Their kiss mirrored the approaching storm. Wild and reckless. Unlike any kiss he'd ever had or thought about.

The surprise, the feel of her against him, the depth of feeling running through him almost buckled his knees. He circled one arm around her waist and held on tight as he lifted her off the ground. This wasn't just his best friend in his arms, this was about to be his lover for the rest of his life if he got lucky.

When he finally broke the kiss, he breathed her in deep, loving the way she felt against him. All the rodeo queens and bar babes disappeared in his mind. She was what he wanted . . . she'd always been what he wanted.

"The storm's starting," she whispered.

"Yeah," he answered, thinking only of kissing her again.

"Noah, put me down." She struggled in his hold. "We'd better run for the house."

She was gone before it dawned on him that it was raining. He took off after her.

They hit the door at the same time, laughing and shaking off water like wet dogs. He wanted to kiss her again, but they were no longer alone.

The moment, the magic, was gone.

Chapter 44

WEDNESDAY AFTERNOON, MARTY DROVE RONNY ALL THE way to Amarillo. They went shopping at the mall and bought Ronny clothes she never dreamed she'd be wearing. Long skirts and sandals. Jeans that fit and western shirts that she tucked in. A double-breasted raincoat that looked like she could be a spy in it—and boots. Red cowboy boots that looked great with the jeans.

"Now when we go to Buffalo's to listen to Border and Beau, you'll fit right in at the place." Marty grinned. "I don't know when I've had so much fun. What do you say, let's toss the bags in the trunk and go back in to buy another round."

"No, I only have a few things to pick up and then I'm starving."

She had him wait in the car while she ran into Target to pick up a few personal things she needed. While she was there she picked up Autumn a few new books. When she ran back to the car with two bags Marty wanted to know what she bought, but she wouldn't tell him. How could she explain how much fun it was to buy little things like lip gloss and panties without her mother looking over her shoulder?

They made a stop at a bank branch where she'd been sending her extra money for nine years. She signed up for a checking account and got a debit card.

They ate Mexican food at a place called The Plaza on Interstate 40 where Marty claimed he had the best stuffed sopapillas on the planet. As he ate all of his and half of hers, they planned what she would do. Ronny wanted to just coast for a while, but he loved details. She'd never seen him so excited, so happy. He might want to drift in his life, but he saw lots of roads she could go down.

They were back in Harmony by nine. Even in the shadows she could tell he was tired.

When he pulled up to the funeral home, Dallas Logan's car was parked out front.

"I could drive you to the back," Marty offered, "or take you home with me. I wouldn't mind that at all."

She had a feeling she'd be asking too much if she asked for his help now. "Take me to the back, and then I'll walk out front and talk to her. I'm not afraid of her anymore."

Marty nodded.

Ronny took her bags in through the kitchen, then slipped on a sweatshirt and walked to the front hallway.

Tyler was there. "Do you need help?"

She shook her head. "This is something I have to do alone."

Ronny knew he was watching her as she walked down the steps to where her mother sat beneath the streetlight. Dallas Logan could have been a stuffed dummy in the car. She didn't move, but faced straight ahead as if she couldn't hear the tapping of new boots coming toward her.

"Hello, Mother," Ronny said.

Silence. Dallas saved silence for the worst times. Those rare times when she got too angry to even speak.

"How are you?" Ronny tried.

Nothing.

Ronny waited, knowing Dallas wouldn't be able to hold in her rage for long.

Finally, it came fast and hateful. "I'm so embarrassed at what you've done. I'm the laughingstock of this town to have a daughter like you. I may never live down what you've done." She gulped a breath and delivered what she'd come to say. "I have no daughter; you're as dead to me as everyone else in my family. Never contact me. Never speak to me if you pass me. Never. Do you hear me? Never."

Ronny was sure everyone within two blocks heard Dallas. All her life Ronny felt like she'd always said she was sorry for everything, but not this time.

She stepped back from the car and smiled. "Good-bye, Dallas."

She turned and walked back up the stairs as Dallas slammed the car into gear and drove off.

Tyler still stood in the doorway, as if silently letting her know that he had her back. They walked inside and closed the door. He gave her one of his great hugs and said good night.

Autumn had already gone to bed, so Ronny took a shower and slipped into one of her new gowns. After she turned out the light, she tiptoed to the front of the house and stood in the darkness. Dallas Logan never made mistakes, so she'd never take back her words. A part of Ronny's life had ended as quickly as a branch snaps beneath the weight of an ice storm. A tear rolled down her face. It had taken her mother twenty-seven years to abandon the child she never wanted.

The place was silent as Ronny let tears fall. Little noise could pass through the thick walls, but tonight it wouldn't have mattered. Ronny climbed into her bed and pulled the covers over her head, and cried for the first and last time for her mother.

Chapter 45

THURSDAY
MARCH 18

TYLER WORKED THE GRAVESIDE SERVICE, THEN DROPPED
the family off at the funeral home for the lunch Stella and
Autumn had prepared. He had about an hour to kill before
he had to start setting up for a full funeral at four, and the
bad weather was already giving him headaches.

As he drove through town trying to decide where to eat
lunch, he worried about the tent Calvin and the men at the
cemetery were fighting to get moved to another site by four.

The wind had been kicking up dirt all morning, making
the sky look hazy, and now clouds were gathering. There
would be two hundred people at the next funeral and the
weather was getting worse by the minute. He'd have all his
people out to help with the funeral; even Stella had promised to help Calvin with moving the flowers to the church

and then setting up everything before people started arriving. The family said folks would be coming from three states. On top of the numbers and the weather and the mud they'd be fighting if it rained, the man who'd died was a rancher. He wanted a riderless horse to lead the funeral procession from the church to the cemetery. Tyler had already borrowed two extra family cars from Gray's Funeral Home over in Bailee and wasn't sure he'd have enough.

He'd been doing funerals since he was old enough to go with his father and stay quiet. Tyler had a feeling about the four o'clock funeral and it wasn't good.

His cell sounded about the time he'd decided to skip lunch and just sit in the car and worry.

"Hello."

"Ty?"

He didn't have to ask who it was. He knew Kate's voice. "How are you?" He'd talked to her so very few times on the phone he didn't know what to say. "Are you all right?" He never knew what she'd been through when she was gone.

"I'm fine. I just pulled into Harmony. I'm parked in front of the B&B. Any chance you can break free and come over here for lunch? I know Mrs. Biggs, she'll have something in the fridge."

Tyler fought down a groan. He'd love to see Kate, but he knew Martha Q had meddled in his business and he didn't want to see her. "I'm really busy, Kate. We've got a big funeral at four and we're all scrambling to get ready."

"Okay," she said slowly, as if thinking as she spoke. "Need some help?"

Tyler closed his eyes. She'd never offered to help, hadn't even wanted to go by the cemetery to lock up when she visited. Now she made an honest offer. He felt like he was standing in a six-foot hole daring her to toss dirt. "Sure," he said. "Meet me in fifteen minutes back in the kitchen downstairs from my apartment. Come in the back."

He hung up, not even sure if he'd said good-bye. His Kate was going to help him with a funeral. He couldn't believe it. In all the years they'd had dinner together, e-mailed back and forth, driven around the countryside, talked and talked, she'd never shown more than a passing interest in his work.

He stopped at the florist to make sure all the flowers for four had been delivered, and then he headed home.

The family was still visiting in a small conference room beside his office. He crossed down the back hallway so as not to interrupt them. When he reached the kitchen, Kate was already there . . . talking with Autumn, who was putting away serving dishes.

"Hello, Kate," he said, leaning to kiss her cheek. "I would have picked you up at the airport if I'd known what time you were coming in."

Kate smiled, but wasn't too friendly. The little major was back, he thought, all business and proper.

Autumn pointed a serving spoon at him. "Mr. Wright, you didn't tell me you had a girlfriend."

"What makes you think she's my girlfriend?" The last word stuck to his tongue like peanut butter.

"She told me she was." Autumn shrugged, her attention already moving like a flea on a sweaty dog. "Those people in there didn't eat much of anything. I got chicken salad running out my ears."

Tyler didn't see that as very appetizing.

She added, "You two want some?"

Kate made a face only Tyler saw, then politely said, "I'd love some."

Tyler grabbed a couple of cold waters, and Kate took the bowl and two small plates from Autumn. They moved over to the kitchen table by the bay window and began to eat.

For once Autumn didn't join them. She finished cleaning up and disappeared into her room, smiling at them with a kind of silly smile people usually reserve for babies.

When she was gone, Tyler laughed. "She thinks we're a couple." Kate had always gone to extremes to make sure people knew they weren't. He had no idea why she let Autumn get the wrong impression now.

She took a bite, chewed, then took a long drink and said, "We are."

Tyler had always figured that once he got in a real relationship, he'd be the first to know, or at least the second. He was surprised to find out in his forties that belief wasn't true. "We are?"

Kate nodded. "Unless you don't want to be?"

"That depends." He frowned. "Where are you staying tonight?"

"I thought I'd stay in one of your extra bedrooms upstairs, unless your quarters are already full."

"They are not."

She grinned. "That's what I figured out three minutes after I met Autumn. She thinks you're great, but she calls you Mr. Wright."

He shook his head. "You've been listening to gossip."

"Guilty and not proud of it. According to Martha Q, some gold digger moved in and had you under her spell. I expected to meet a schemer, but all I found was a frightened young woman looking for a place to hide away from harm for a while. I guess you didn't need rescuing after all."

He should have been mad, but his Kate was moving in, at least for a few days. "I'll get your bag. Got anything black to wear to the funeral? We need to get going."

"Black's my favorite color. If you'll get my suitcase, I can be ready in ten minutes."

Tyler almost ran to the rental car. They walked up the stairs together. He waited while she dressed. He tried to figure out what was going on. He thought maybe he should send Martha Q flowers. He had no idea what would happen tonight, but it didn't matter; anything would be better than saying good night to Kate on the porch of Winter's Inn.

When she walked in the living area of his quarters, she looked very proper in her black suit, white shirt, and sensible shoes. He explained a few of the things that had to happen at the church before anyone arrived. Memorial programs, a memory book to sign in, tissues in every pew, flowers arranged to frame the casket, and a dozen other little details.

"If we have the service here at the chapel, we have everything in order, but when we go into the churches we've learned to expect the unexpected. One funeral at a church that had a mother's-day-out program taught me a few lessons. Just before people started filing in, the four- and five-year-olds came into the hall for a Bible story. The teachers hadn't had time to read the memo. It wouldn't have been so bad, but each child carried a pair of paper animals to put in Noah's ark. The kids were shuffled out, but I was picking up camels and sheep scattered everywhere."

Kate smiled. "This is going to be interesting."

"I hope all goes well. The dearly departed was a long-time rancher. Most of his friends are coming in on the Shady Days nursing home bus and ranchers are driving in for miles. I've been asked to set up two extra mics for the cowboy poets who'll be reading."

Thunder rattled the sky as they climbed into a long black family car. "And," he said, looking up, "just to make it more interesting, it's going to rain."

To his surprise Kate's offer to help wasn't an idle promise; she was a quick learner and turned out to be a great help. She stood back to watch how he greeted people, and then set to work. When he pulled out the huge black umbrellas and waited as people pulled up near the door, she did the same thing.

When the service started, she stood beside him, silent as a soldier waiting for the next order.

When the funeral ended, rain pounded hard against the two-story stained glass. Most of the people elected not to go to the graveside, but a few family members and the minister climbed into the family car. Tyler drove while Kate sat next to him. They followed a saddled horse with a mounted escort on either side all the way to the cemetery. By the time they climbed back into the car, everyone was soaked.

While Calvin worked beneath the tent to cover the coffin, Tyler drove the family back and hugged each one goodbye. When he climbed back into the car, he couldn't tell if Kate had rain on her face or if she was crying.

"You do this every day?" she whispered.

"No. Every day in this business seems different. Some funerals are small; some, like this one, are big. Sometimes we go a week or even two without a funeral. What we did today is just what people see, there's more to it. I'll spend tomorrow doing paperwork."

She was silent on the drive home, and Tyler wondered if his profession was too much for her. There was nothing glamorous about it. He wasn't solving mysteries or saving the world. She was probably sitting beside him now trying to figure out how to say good-bye to him forever. He wished he could tell her not all men were born to be a soldier or a cop or CEO of some big company.

They didn't bother with the umbrellas when they got back to the funeral home; they just ran through the rain to the kitchen entrance.

Autumn took one look at the two drowned rats and ordered them upstairs.

"How old is that girl?" Kate asked as they dripped on the elevator carpet.

"Twenty-three, but she's been bossing me around since I met her."

Kate giggled. "And to think I was worried about you. The truth is, she's too old for you."

They separated at the living room. He went to the shower off his room and she went to the shower next to what was now her room. The two rooms on the north side of his apartment had been empty for so long he couldn't remember the last person to stay there, but out of habit he kept them ready.

Tyler couldn't stop smiling as he peeled off wet clothes. It was odd to have someone else in his apartment. He took a quick shower, not wanting to use all the hot water, then dressed in his favorite jogging suit that he always wore on Sunday mornings.

When she appeared in the living area, she was dressed almost exactly the same, only she had on fuzzy pink socks with her navy blue jogging suit.

"Pink," was all he said.

The very proper Major Katherine Cummings stuck her tongue out at him.

They were laughing when Autumn brought up a tray of soup and sandwiches. She set them down on the coffee table. "I didn't know what kind you liked, so I made three different ones. Hope you like hot cocoa, but if you want coffee I'll bring a pot up."

"I love cocoa, especially on a night like this." Kate smiled at the girl. "But don't you worry about us or go to any trouble because of me."

"Oh, I didn't. I had to cook something for the two firemen hanging out in the kitchen, plus Ronny brought her boyfriend in. He's real good looking. Reminds me of that vampire on TV. You know, the good-looking one with long hair. I keep feeding him sweets, hoping he doesn't get hungry for blood."

"Maybe I should go down?" Tyler stood. "Ronelle, who apparently changed her name when she changed addresses, doesn't have a boyfriend that I know about and . . ."

Kate took his hand, stopping him. "Autumn, do you need us?"

Autumn shook her head. "We're fine. I can't remember a rainy night when I've felt so good . . . or so safe," she said to Tyler. "When you've got two firemen and a vamp downstairs, there's not much need to worry about someone knocking on the door."

He saw a tear roll down her cheek and wondered for the hundredth time how bad she must have had it to think this place was heaven. "Well, tell Ronny, and the firemen, and the vampire to have a good time."

"Yes, Mr. Wright." She smiled at him, making him feel very old.

When Autumn left, Kate laughed as if she'd just read his mind. "The kids will be fine," she whispered.

He lit a fire and they ate their supper on the couch watching an old western they'd both seen so many times they could say some of the lines with the actors. Halfway through, when the fire died to a glow, Kate pulled a blanket over them both.

When the movie was over, they talked quietly. He had

a feeling she had things she wanted to say, but it took her thirty minutes to get around to it.

"Ty," she started, her head down where he couldn't see her eyes. "I've never been good at getting close to people. When I was young, I was too involved in school and then in my career. Moving around with the army, it just seemed like roots never grew in one place. I very rarely even dated."

He didn't say a word. He had no idea what to say.

"But you're a good man, and I think I'd like to someday get close to you. The only thing is, I don't want you to hurry me. I may be in my forties, but a part of me still feels like I'm in my teens. Maybe it's too late for me to even start, but I'd like to try"—she took a deep breath—"with you."

"We've known each other for four years, Kate. I don't think either of us has been in any hurry."

"I know. If you don't want to wait any longer, I'd understand." Before he could say anything, she added, "Don't answer. Just think about it. We can talk more tomorrow."

She stood. "I'll say good night. It's been a long and interesting day."

She was gone before he could think of what to say. Somewhere his brave, strong-minded Kate was trying to change, maybe even mend. She seemed to be trying to let someone near for the first time in her life. She hadn't been an easy woman to get close to, but he had a feeling she'd be worth the effort.

Maybe all people were broken in some way by the time they reached forty. What he had to decide was, did he want to love her, broken and all? It seemed awfully cruel to close a door even though she'd only opened it a crack.

He got up and headed for his room, noticing her lights were already out. She was probably exhausted, flying halfway across the country today and then helping him with a funeral. She was right; there would always be tomorrow to talk things over.

Tyler crawled into bed, knowing he wouldn't sleep with the storm blowing outside. Most funeral directors hated the snow and the ice, but this time of year bothered him. Early spring storms, when the weather could turn deadly without warning. Though the earth still seemed cold and dead, the sky sometimes went to war above him.

He thought of how he'd loved having Kate working with him today. Slowly, he drifted into sleep, dreaming of what it would be like to have a partner not just in business, but in life.

An hour later he felt the bed dip and the covers lift. He didn't move.

"Ty," Kate whispered. "Can I sleep next to you tonight? This storm is keeping me awake."

He raised his arm and she slid in next to him. Neither said another word. For a long while he knew she wasn't asleep. Finally, he moved closer and put his arm around her waist. "Good night, my dear Kate," he whispered.

"Good night," she answered, and he felt her relax. In a few minutes she was sound asleep.

Tyler took a deep breath and drifted off, but he didn't dream. His only dream was at his side.

Chapter 46

FRIDAY
MARCH 19
TRUMAN FARM

REAGAN FELT THE TENSION IN THE AIR FRIDAY MORNING as soon as she woke. The wind and rain from the night before pulled everyone's nerves to the surface. No one at the farm had slept well.

Jeremiah and Foster looked like they'd been up for hours when she went in to make breakfast a little after dawn. The whole house still rattled from the wind.

"There's a bad one coming," Jeremiah mumbled over his coffee cup. "Did I ever tell you I was born during a terrible storm back in 1920? The wind blew the roof off the barn and we lost most of the grain that year, but my momma always said I came riding in on that tornado and she knew I'd be a wild one all my life. She wanted to name me Stormy, but then they'd have to stick with the theme.

Rainy and Sunny would have been all right, but if they had
several kids soon we'd be down to Cloudy and Haily."

Reagan smiled, knowing that her uncle's efforts at sto-
rytelling were aimed at making her laugh. Over the years
she'd guessed at least half of his memories were made up
on the spot.

Foster laughed at the story, but all Reagan could manage was a yawn. She'd been up listening to the rain most
of the night and planned to take a nap as soon as breakfast
was over. In this weather she could do little in the orchards.

Aunt Pat came in, moving slower than usual. Her arthri-
tis bothered her on rainy days, but she managed a smile for
them all. As she did every morning, she pulled on an apron
and wanted to help. Before Reagan could stop her, she got
out the eggs and set to work.

When no one seemed to want to talk, Pat said, "You know,
I've been thinking. It only makes sense for all of us to load up
and head over to my place. It's only next door, so it should be
no great problem and we've got a full basement to wait out
the storm in. I would make a big pot of coffee and we'd be
snug as bugs in a rug down there."

Jeremiah frowned. "I've been in this house all my life
and it hasn't crumbled down around me yet. I don't see any
point in getting wet moving from one place to another."

"Now, Jeremiah." She pointed a wooden spoon at him.

"Don't you 'now' me. I'm just fine where I am. You'll be
safe here too. That's the trouble with you Mathesons, you
always think what you got is bigger and better than what
other folks build."

"That's not true. I never built anything in my life, Jeremiah Truman, and you know it."

"No you taught school and everybody knows it's the
know-it-alls who think they can teach."

They argued while she cooked. No one else chose to step
into the ring with the two senior citizens, but they did wake
Noah up since he slept one wall away from the kitchen.

He came in wearing his pajama bottoms, stood right
between them, and called off the fight.

Neither of them listened to him.

When he tried again, Aunt Pat spatulaed a fried egg up against the side of his face, and Jeremiah laughed so hard they finally stopped yelling. Noah managed to eat half the egg off his face before it hit the floor.

He tried to sit down at the table, but Aunt Pat informed him that only wild animals eat before they're properly dressed and washed. He complained as loudly as Jeremiah had, but he left the room to pull on jeans and a shirt.

Pat yelled after him, "Are you sure you don't have some Truman blood in you, boy?"

"No," he yelled back. "Or Matheson, thank God. My family has had to put up with both of you for a hundred years and I'm telling you, from the stories I've heard it hasn't been easy."

"Hush your complaining," both Pat and Jeremiah yelled, finally agreeing on something.

The subject of relocating was tabled along with breakfast and everyone sat down to eat. Jeremiah told a story about how back in the dust bowl days, people used to eat as fast as they could so the dust wouldn't cover the food before they finished.

"It feels that way today," Reagan whispered. "Dust as fine as sand seems to be sifting through the floors of this old house, making everything and everyone seem like I'm looking at them through dirty glasses."

"It'll clear out soon." Foster smiled. "The rain'll come. Then we won't have to worry about dust. We'll have to watch for leaks."

Noah shook his head. "News says we might get tornadoes before dark."

No one spoke. They just ate in silence. Reagan remembered something her math teacher said a few years back. He compared living in Texas with being a hockey fan. If you sit in the stands long enough, you're going to get hit with the puck.

Halfway through the meal, Aunt Pat put her chubby worn hand on top of old Jeremiah's rough wrinkled fingers and said, "I know your house will stand, but I want to be near my sister if the storm worsens and tornadoes are in the area. She's always been afraid of them, Jeremiah. You know that. If the warning comes, will you come with me to make sure my family is all safe?"

To everyone's shock, Jeremiah nodded. "We'll all go. If it'll make you feel better, Patricia. Lord knows you've been worried about Fatilla all her life. I wouldn't expect you to stop now just because she's out of your sight." He stood and pulled up his walker. "I'll go watch the news. Everyone else get ready. If it moves from a watch to a warning, we load up the cars and move to the Matheson basement."

Pat followed him to the parlor, where the TV was already tuned in to the weather channel. They sat side by side.

"He gave in to her!" Reagan whispered in shock.

"Aunt Fat's name is Fatilla?" Noah added, but no one was listening.

"He loves her," Cindy said from the doorway. "I'd think all of you would have figured that out by now. She thumped Noah on the head as she passed him. "And don't call Aunt Fat *Fatilla*. She told me she's always hated her name."

"And she likes *Fat*?" Noah rubbed his head.

"I think it's kind of romantic," Reagan whispered. "After all these years they are together."

"Fatilla?" Noah glanced at Reagan. She looked like she might be the next to thump him so he stood, taking himself out of the line of fire. "I don't know about everyone else, but I'm getting ready. That cloud's too dark to be anything but a tornado mixer."

Foster nodded. "I think we can get everyone in the van. I'll take the meds; Cindy could you get blankets? If that watch turns to a warning, we'll be headed over to the next place. Since we can't take the path through the orchard in the van, we'll have to drive around."

Reagan felt a sense of panic at leaving her home, but she knew if Jeremiah went, she had to go with him. She locked away any important papers in the safe, turned off the gas just in case, and packed the pies she'd made. Other than that, she had no idea what to take to a tornado party.

When she walked back into the kitchen, everyone had gone but Noah. For a moment they just stood staring at each other. She felt close to him today, even though she hadn't said anything about it. They were so much a part of each other. All her memories since she came to Harmony, since she started her real life, were wrapped around him. She loved him in a way deeper than boyfriend and girlfriend, different than family, stronger than friends. He was a part of her, and she guessed she was a part of him.

He frowned. "You going to tell me what to do when you get that age?"

"Probably," she guessed. "Why?"

He looked like he wanted to cuss, but he just said, "I think it may take me a while to get used to the idea. I don't like following orders, so don't expect much out of me. Maybe you should look for someone easier to boss around."

"Shut up," she ordered. The one moment she thought fine lace bound them, he must have seen a rope . . . maybe with a noose on the end of it.

He hesitated, as if he planned to argue, then changed his mind and leaned across the corner of the kitchen table and kissed her. "I do like kissing you, Rea. Think we might make it a habit whenever I'm home?"

She shrugged, not liking the idea that he would be leaving soon. This was the first time he'd mentioned going back. Now that it was in his mind, she had a feeling it wouldn't be long.

When he pulled away, he asked, "You still comparison shopping?"

"Maybe." If he wanted to keep it light, she could too.

Chapter 47

WRIGHT FUNERAL HOME

TYLER SPENT THE MORNING GOING BETWEEN WORKING and checking on Kate. She slept late, and then about mid-morning he found her visiting with Autumn in the kitchen.

When he dropped by a half hour later he had the strange feeling he was interrupting their conversation, so he grabbed a few cookies and disappeared. When he returned to check on lunch, Kate was talking on the phone. A few minutes later he saw her heading up the stairs. When she came down all dressed, she said she was having lunch with Martha Q.

He tried to hide his disappointment. "I'll drive you. It's raining," he said.

"Thank you." She pulled on her raincoat and they hurried out.

Nether said a word in the car. After holding each other all night, they didn't seem to know how to break the polite silence between them. He wanted to say how much he loved her being next to him, but somehow he was afraid that words, any words other than simple nothing conversation, might frighten her off.

When he pulled up close to the Winter's Inn porch, he turned to her. "I'll be back in an hour. There's a tornado watch out. If it turns into a warning I'd like you to be back at the home with me. Those foot-thick walls will weather anything. I'm not so sure about Martha Q's house."

Kate nodded and leaned over to kiss him on the cheek. The kiss was awkward for them both, but they were forming a habit.

He watched her run onto the porch. "You are so dear to me," he whispered.

Sitting in the car, he felt like he'd been hanging out at a train station all morning. He wished he could have told her not to go, but just because they cuddled last night didn't mean he had any vote in what she did.

She'd kissed his cheek as if to say, *I'll see you in an hour, dear.*

Tyler smiled and went back to his work. He had no idea what was going on in Kate's mind, but one kiss on the cheek convinced him that everything would be just fine.

He'd just finished lunch at his desk when Alex called from the sheriff's office. Tyler picked up the phone thinking there might be some news about Leland. No one had seen or heard from him since he walked out after making bail. He'd simply vanished.

In the past few days Tyler had learned more about the man, and it was all bad. Alex told him about Leland's list of arrests since his teen years on everything from petty theft to assault. Apparently, Autumn was only one of several young women he'd tried to beat into line. His MO seemed to be picking up girls in bars who were too drunk to fight him off after he offered to take them home. Then he moved in without being asked and tried threats and finally beatings if they didn't want to play house with him.

Afraid there might be more bad news, Tyler tried to sound extra cheery when he picked up. "Good morning, Sheriff Matheson."

"Not so good, Mr. Wright."

He'd been the best man at her wedding. If she was calling him Mr. Wright, something was wrong. "What's up?" he asked.

"The National Weather Bureau has issued a tornado watch for this afternoon. They say a wall cloud is already forming north of here, so we may be in for an active afternoon. No sightings near ground yet, but I wanted you to know that if it gets worse, we may need you at the fire station to man the phones and radios."

"Of course." He could already feel his pulse speeding. "Just give me a call and I'll be there in five." Thanks to Alex and Hank's efforts, the town had a central place in times when both the fire department and the sheriff's office needed to be on full alert. A few months ago the emergency teams at the hospital had signed on as well. Tyler had offered to help and found himself at the phones relaying messages from one agency to another. Now it appeared he might get to put all his training to work.

He drove over to pick up Kate ten minutes early and, to his surprise, she came out as if she'd been watching for him.

"How was lunch?" he asked as she shook the rain from her hair.

"Fine. Martha Q wants me to help with Dreaming and Scheming, but I told her I wasn't sure I'd have time. When I'm here I want to give you a hand."

"Really?"

"If you'd like."

He pulled to the curb, leaned over, and kissed her lightly on the mouth. "I'd like that, dear. I'd like that very much."

She smiled, looking suddenly younger. "I'd like that too. In fact, the whole time I was having lunch with Martha Q, I was wishing I was back in your office having whatever Autumn brought us. I've got a ton of questions about your business. I guess until yesterday I really didn't see how much you help people. You're a good man, Ty."

She moved over until they were almost touching. Once he was driving again, she said, "Now don't pull over again, but I need to tell you one other thing about Martha Q."

"All right." Tyler knew whatever it was wouldn't upset him after she'd just told him she wanted to be with him.

"Martha Q is on her way over to your place. In fact I wouldn't be surprised if her car is following us."

"Why?" His first thought was that she wanted to plan a funeral, but as far as he knew no one around her was dying.

"I told her what you said about your place holding up if a tornado came and she agreed. She's decided to camp out with us until this is over."

"Great," Tyler managed without too much enthusiasm. "We'll make room for her."

Kate laughed and patted his arm. "At least she's not bringing Mrs. Biggs and her grandsons. Mrs. Biggs called her grandson who is still in high school and told him to meet her at the fire station. Her other grandson is already there working as one of the volunteers."

When he pulled in the drive his cell rang. Tyler answered and said simply, "I'm on my way."

Kate waited as he closed the phone. "I have to go man the phones. The tornado watch has moved to a warning. There have been sightings fifty miles from here, and it looks like they're headed this way."

"What can I do to help?" Kate was too much the soldier to look frightened.

At that moment Tyler Wright knew he loved Kate Cummings and he always would. "Get everyone downstairs. This building is probably the safest in town. There's a comfortable room below with couches and a TV. Beth doesn't like to go down there, but we have no one in the prep room right now so she shouldn't object too much. When it's over I'll call and let you know it's safe to come up."

Kate nodded just as the siren on top of the town hall began to sound the alarm.

"You'd better get inside." He touched her hand for only a second and then she was gone, running for the kitchen door.

Within minutes Tyler was at his station surrounded by volunteer firemen swarming in to be ready to help if trouble came. Bob McNabb took the seat on the opposite side of the table. With charts and phones lined up, they prepared. Every call had to be logged in. Every fireman who came in was listed and would be accounted for at all times. Tyler signed them in as they picked up radios and gave cell phone numbers.

Bob McNabb handed him a headset and Tyler took over. They'd stay in the bay with the phones ready unless a tornado came close, and then they'd all move to an underground storage room that was already set up like a bunker. Mrs. Biggs was in the kitchen. She'd have tons of coffee ready to pour into thermoses if men had to be sent out, and knowing Mrs. Biggs there would be double-fudge brownies for everyone when they came in after the storm had passed.

"Where's Stella?" Tyler asked as they set everything in place. Bob's wife was never far away from him. Sometimes when she helped out at the funeral home, Bob would sleep in the car waiting for her.

"She's got one of her headaches. I made her go lie down in the basement. It's quiet down there and if trouble comes I'll be right beside her."

Tyler's first call was from Gabe Leary, who wanted to know what was happening. His new house on the canyon rim was a dirt road mile from Timber Line Road. From there he could be in town within a few minutes. The problem would be the first mile getting off his land in a rainstorm.

"Load up that pregnant wife of yours and come on into town." Tyler didn't have time for small talk. "I'll call the hospital and tell her you're on your way. Tell Liz that her brother said the safest place for anyone nine months pregnant to sit out a tornado is in the basement of the hospital."

Hank was a few feet away organizing the others, but he

nodded toward Tyler. "Tell her I'll check on her as soon as this is over and tell that husband of my sister not to speed. I don't have time to go pull him out of the mud."

Gabe didn't respond when Tyler tried to talk. Apparently, when he'd been told to move, he'd dropped the phone and headed to the car.

Tyler smiled. They'd be at the hospital long before any tornado could get near.

Hank thanked him and added, "I've heard a change in the weather can cause labor to start. The water breaks and the woman has her bloody show before she even knows she's in labor."

"More information than I need to know, Chief," Brandon Biggs said as he signed in for duty. He asked Tyler about Autumn and seemed relieved to know that everyone at the funeral home was waiting out the storm in the basement.

Spotters began calling in reports of sightings and Hank marked them on the map. In this open country a tornado could touch ground a hundred times before it hit anything.

Everyone else at the station waited and listened to the weathermen telling people in the county to take cover. "We'll all ride this one out underground."

Chapter 48

DENVER TRIED TO CALL CLAIRE ON HER CELL TWICE AND at the Matheson ranch house a half dozen times during the day. He was moving from one plane to another, watching people, trying to not be conspicuous.

He followed the weather on his phone, always aware that storms or winds or even snow this late in some parts of the country could delay one flight and set his schedule off. While he watched the weather, he always checked Texas. Somehow it made him feel closer to her to know what the temperature was in her part of the country. A storm was moving in off the Rockies. Warm front coming up from the coast. The perfect mix for a tornado.

Denver never thought much about tornadoes. They were like earthquakes. Little or no warning. People who lived in tornado alley just did what they could, as fast as they could. No sandbags. No boarding up. No storing supplies. Just take cover. Be it underground or in a bathtub with a mattress over them, people prepared. Denver tried to picture Claire and her little Saralynn moving to an old game room in the basement. He had never thought to ask them what they did during the storms.

Only now, he had people he loved who might suffer. Gabe was like a brother and Liz would need help waddling to a storm shelter. And Claire, his beautiful, wild, sophisticated Claire. Who would be there to help her with her family? Who would be there to help her?

As the day passed and he couldn't reach her, Denver slowly went insane.

Chapter 49

MR. DONAVAN CLOSED THE POST OFFICE A FEW MINUTES after the tornado alarm sounded. He told Ronny she was welcome to stay in the back or he'd drive her over to the funeral home, but he had to get home to his wife before she went nuts with worry. She'd been in the Lubbock tornado in 1970 and hadn't stopped talking about it.

"I'll stay," Ronny said without hesitation. "I want to finish up with the mail, then I'll call someone to come pick me up."

Donavan remained at the doorway. "You want me to call and check on your mom?"

Ronny shook her head. "She always goes next door to the Carvers. He's deaf and his wife is losing her memory, which makes them good company for Dallas."

"I'm off then." Mr. Donavan waved. "I know you'll lock up if you leave."

She wasn't sure what she wanted to do. She had to think. Marty told her last night that he had a big showdown with his father this morning. Apparently, the family wanted him back in Dallas for another round of testing and operations. He said his old man had been trying to plan out his life since he was born and now, after the accident, Marty complained that he wasn't sure he could run fast enough to get away.

Ronny didn't want to take a chance of bumping into Marty's family, or the girl in silk and pearls. She'd noticed that when she was with Marty he always turned his phone off. When they were together it was like they had their own little world. The worry lines across his face vanished and she felt safe. Last night they'd cooked a meal together and she'd had her first glass of wine. She'd left early because she could see how tired he was even though he tried to hide it.

She finished up the mail and tried to read a chapter from one of the books required in her online course, but she couldn't concentrate.

When the sky darkened, Ronny could think of only one place she wanted to go. The little duplex halfway between her and the fire station. She put on her coat and the hat Marty hated, locked the back door of the post office, and ran all the way to his house. The wind whipped so violently, it threatened to knock her down, but she didn't slow.

The duplex looked dark, but maybe the electricity was out. There were no cars out front, so if Marty's family had come this morning they were gone now.

She tried the door and found it, as always, unlocked.

"Marty?" she called as she rushed in. "Marty?"

Ronny tried the kitchen first. He wasn't there, but she could see his Volvo parked out back. An uneasiness passed over her. The house felt empty, too empty. She ran to the bedroom, thinking maybe he was working out on his equipment. It was all there, the bars, the weights, now silent as a playground in snow.

She slowed, walking back through the house like a mourner. Something was wrong. Very wrong. He wouldn't have gone out in his wheelchair on a day like this, not even to pick up a paper. His fridge was stocked. The old house was drafty on cold days like this one. Marty always had the fire going in the main room, but not today.

The memory of the first time she'd stepped inside the place came back to her. There had been nothing personal. Nothing that said, *This is Marty's place.* There was nothing now.

Sitting at the little table by the window, she tried her best to curl into a ball. The cold of the apartment seeped into her. He'd been gone a while. Long enough that any heat from the house had cooled.

His computer and papers were missing from his desk, but the books were still scattered on the shelves as if someone had taken a few and thought the others worthless.

The wind rattled the shutters and seemed to seep into the room in little gusts. She wanted to cry but wasn't sure why. She wanted to scream that she needed him, he couldn't go anywhere without telling her first, but she'd never hold so hard to another person. If she did she'd be just like her mother.

Ronny tried to remember his last words. "When I'm feeling better I plan to teach you another lesson."

"On what?" she'd asked.

"On making love, honey."

Then he'd kissed her and told her to go home so he could sleep.

The slam of a door echoed from the other apartment, pulling Ronny from her thoughts. The Biggs boys were probably leaving. Taking shelter somewhere else till the storm blew over. She didn't care. The tornado could carry her away. She had nowhere else to go. She'd just wait here until Marty got back.

The front door rattled on its frame and for a moment she thought he might be back, but it was only Border banging his way in as always.

"What are you doing here, Mail Lady?" he asked, filling the room with his voice.

"I'm waiting for Marty," she managed. She no longer feared either of the Biggs boys, but she didn't want to talk to anyone. She just wanted to wait because, as long as she was waiting, she knew he'd come back.

"Radio says there might be a tornado heading this way.

My grandmother and brother are already at the fire station. I just came back for my guitar. I'm in my brother's truck if you want to ride along with me. Bran says the fire station is the safest place in town to be right now."

She shook her head. "I'll wait."

He set his guitar on the floor and crossed the room. For a moment he just stood there, and then he knelt beside her on one knee. "Lady, I don't think Marty's coming back. He banged on our door just after dawn and said Bran could have his old Volvo and I could have his weights if I wanted them. He left in a big car with several people surrounding him."

"Did he look ill?" Maybe he'd had to go to the hospital.

Border frowned. "He looked broken. Kind of like he always looked before you came along."

"He'll be back," she whispered. "He'll know I'm waiting."

"Come on to the fire station with me. We'll call his cell and let him know where you are." Border offered his tattooed hand. "It's going to be all right, lady. Marty would want you to be safe, wouldn't he?"

She didn't believe him, but she went with Border. For the first time in her life, she didn't want to be alone. She knew, deep down all the way to her soul, that Marty Winslow was gone, really gone.

Chapter 50

❦

TRUMAN FARM

JUST AFTER LUNCH, REAGAN STARED AT THE WINDOW AS the sky darkened. A warning came over the radio in the kitchen. Harmony and surrounding areas were now under a tornado warning. The alert sounded. Twisters had been spotted. Everyone should prepare to take cover.

She set the glass she'd been washing in the sink and left it there.

No one in the house spoke as they all moved toward the van parked at the back door. Foster had pulled it up close so that rain only dribbled on them as they moved one by one into the van. No one took much with them. The house would be here in a few hours when this was over, or it wouldn't. There was little time to think of anything else besides taking cover.

Reagan carried two of her pies packed double-decker in a tin carrier. Cindy brought a medical bag and a few blankets. Aunt Pat only brought her knitting bag. Foster packed the walker in the back. As he closed the back door, the lights blinked, then went off in the house. Reagan thought the dark house looked lonely on this stormy day. She missed it already, but she knew they all had to go.

Cindy flipped on the car radio to listen to the weather reports.

Everyone watched the storm blowing by outside as they drove off the Truman place onto Lone Oak Road and down two miles to the entrance to the Matheson Ranch. Reagan didn't like leaving her home, but Aunt Pat was right, this would be better. The basement at Jeremiah's place housed a huge heater and had rickety stairs the old man would never be able to get down. They also had a cellar out back built in the forties. The walls were dirt and Reagan had always been afraid to go down in it, even when Jeremiah had been able to check for snakes first.

"You okay?" Noah took her hand. He was the only one in the car who didn't look worried.

"Sure. I know it will blow over."

He nodded, but she could see he didn't believe her.

"What is it?" she asked, reading him easily.

"I called my sister. She said she already knew I was in town. Harley over at the bar told her, but she wanted to give me space if I needed it. I told her we were heading over to the Matheson place. She said Hank was already at the fire station on alert, so she was glad to hear we were going over to the ranch house. Alex said she didn't like to think of her mother-in-law and all the girls being there alone."

Aunt Pat turned around in her seat. "I'll have you know, Noah McAllen, that the Matheson women have been surviving on this land just as long as the McAllens and Trumans. That sister of yours is sheriff, she worries about everyone, but she's wasting it on us. She was probably thinking about someone watching over you during the storm. From the looks of all those scars you showed us before breakfast, you look like you've been riding tornadoes for a while."

"Bulls," he corrected.

She frowned. "Not much difference, to my way of thinking. I suppose you're going to climb right back on one as soon as you're able."

Noah had a feeling no one ever won an argument with this old schoolteacher. "You know what they say, when you fall off you got to get up and get back on as soon as possible. I figure that's what I'll do."

Aunt Pat was in no mood to be bothered. "You know what they call perfectly healthy young men who risk their lives for eight seconds of a quick thrill?"

"What?" He braced for words like *fool* and *idiot*, but she surprised him.

"Organ donors." She turned back in her seat.

Noah glanced at Reagan and saw fear in her eyes. He looked away. He didn't want to see it. Didn't want to think about it. On the road, when they were moving from rodeo to rodeo, no one ever talked about the odds of getting killed. It was all about the ride and the money and the ranking.

The Matheson ranch house appeared out of the rain. A huge old stone house built to stand anything nature tossed its direction. There were two huge elms in front, but the rest of the house faced the storm without buffers.

They parked in the Mathesons' garage and piled out. Hank's mother was there to welcome them. Within a few minutes, all were settled into the comfortable couches and chairs in the basement. Lanterns, handed down from generations past, were lit even though the electricity was still on.

Saralynn, Claire's daughter, was the only one not worried. She talked and laughed as she showed everyone how she could walk a few steps without her crutches. Claire complained that her cell phone wasn't working while Aunt Fat, as thin as a rail, ate two pieces of the pie Reagan had brought.

An hour passed. The radio announcer kept up the same warning. Everyone within twenty miles of Harmony was advised to take cover. Tornadoes had been spotted but none had touched ground near Harmony.

Cindy and Foster began to play cards with Saralynn. Jeremiah dozed in a recliner. Noah grew more restless. He paced back and forth from the couch to the stairs, sometimes going up to see the storm.

After watching him for a while, Reagan followed him up. They both knew that the last sign before a tornado hit would be the sound of a train coming. If they heard that, or the radio announcing a sighting close by, they'd have only seconds to take cover. All they needed to do was take a few steps backward and close the basement door. Then all would be safe.

When Reagan reached the top of the stairs, Noah was standing a few feet away watching the storm from one of the long windows running across the entry.

He didn't turn around, but he must have known she was there. "When I come back to my ranch," he said in a low voice, "I'll build a proper shelter."

She put her arm around his waist. "That sounds like a good idea."

He looped his arm over her shoulder. "You know, Rea, I'm good, really good at rodeoing. Being away from it has really given me time to think. I'm scared out of my mind sometimes, but when the ride's good and I win, it's a kind of high I can't explain. If I went back, maybe I could make it to the finals. Maybe I could make enough to get the ranch started right."

She studied him. "What are you saying, Noah?"

He turned her to face him. "I could die right here today. We get no guarantees in life. I hate the idea of going back, of leaving you, but if I don't, I'll always wonder what would have happened if I'd given it one more try."

"What if I asked you not to go?" She fought back tears.

"Are you asking?"

Reagan wanted to scream yes, but she shook her head. "No. I'm not asking. Go or stay, but do it because it's what you want." She couldn't be the one to kill his dream or the one to save him. He'd have to do whatever he chose on his own.

He pulled her close. "You know I love you, Rea."

"I know," she whispered against his chest. He was leaving,

maybe not today or tomorrow, but soon. He was leaving her again. She wouldn't tell him she loved him. He'd have to come back for good to hear that.

The wind whipped against the windows as if trying to break in. A branch from one of the elms blew past the window, almost as if it were floating on the rain.

"We'd better get downstairs." Noah took her hand. "Your hand is already shaking."

She didn't have the nerve to tell him that the fear rattling through her veins had nothing to do with the weather. She'd known fear all her life until she came here, and she'd not leave Harmony, not ever, but she couldn't hold him back. Noah needed to run. He needed the rodeo. If she tried, she might be able to stop him, but she wasn't sure the man who stayed would be the Noah she loved.

The storm outside, even the wind howling like a freight train running at full speed, couldn't keep Reagan from hearing her heart breaking. He hadn't asked her to wait. He wouldn't.

As they closed the door to the basement an announcer shouted. "This is one big storm coming, folks. To be safe, you need to be underground."

Reagan barely listened. Noah was going back; despite everything, he was going back.

Halfway down the steps to the others she heard a crashing sound. The house shook just before something hit the basement door so hard it shattered the wood.

Noah pulled her down so fast she lost her footing. He caught her just before she hit the floor.

Cold air blew in along with rain as the sounds of screams filled the basement.

Reagan looked back up the stairs. Branches from the huge elm in the front yard were now poking through splintered gashes in the door, and the entire tree seemed wedged in the only exit.

Chapter 51

WRIGHT FUNERAL HOME

IN THE BASEMENT OF THE FUNERAL HOME EVERYONE WAITED. With layers of thick walls between them and the storm, the threat of a tornado seemed far away. The women talked in the comfortable break room while Calvin drank coffee and Dave slept. Martha Q, Beth the bookkeeper, and Kate were talking about redecorating as Autumn thumbed through a magazine.

They'd been settled in for a while when Autumn stood. "Oh my God," she said. "We forgot the dog. Little Lady must be frightened out of her mind."

"I'll go get her," Kate offered.

"No, I will. I know all her hiding places around the kitchen. I'll be right back."

She was gone before anyone could debate.

Autumn ran up the back steps to where a panel in the back of the entryway opened. Anyone visiting would never notice the entrance, but she'd explored the hidden passages that allowed those who worked there to move from one room to another without ever passing through the public areas.

She was halfway across the kitchen when she saw a shadow cross the bay window. A man was wearing black and trying to look in the window.

Autumn darted for the dog as the shadow moved to the kitchen window.

Little Lady barked. The stranger's face pressed against the glass. Autumn backed away as she recognized Leland. He was standing just beyond the glass glaring at her.

Before a scream could clear her throat, he shattered the glass by the lock and was inside.

She backed up, hitting her head on a hanging pot.

"Looks like I finally caught you here alone." Leland smiled as he moved closer, like a cat cornering a mouse. "You should have guessed I wouldn't leave without taking you along."

Her back hit the counter, knocking the receiver off the phone.

Little Lady barked again and raced toward Leland as if to defend the property.

In the moment Leland swatted at the dog, she punched 911 and shouted, "Don't you dare hurt that dog!"

Leland looked up, ignoring the animal. "I didn't come to hurt no dog," he said in almost a whisper. "But I can't say the same about you. We weren't finished talking and now everyone in town is busy, I figure we might have our own little storm." He lifted his fist. "I'm going to rain down on you so hard there won't be a man in this town who'll look at you after today."

She moved around the center island, staying out of his reach. "Go away," she managed. "Go away and leave me alone."

"Not this time. I saw your boss run over to the fire station. I've been watching this place for two days. There ain't nobody here who can stop me, and with all the racket outside no one will hear your screams. Not even when you lose that bastard you're carrying." He laughed. "When we get through dancing, darling, I'll load you in the truck and take you home. I'd be willing to bet you don't give another thought to leaving me after today."

Autumn had to think. She couldn't panic. "I'll go," she said. "I'll go back home. Just let me get my things." She took a step toward her room.

He smiled. "You're not getting out of what is coming to you that easily, but if you want to pack up, I can wait. Take anything around here that looks like it's valuable while you're at it."

He backhanded her as she ran toward her room.

Autumn tumbled backward like a rag doll, hitting the floor hard. She crawled to her knees and managed to avoid a kick.

He grabbed her by the hair and pulled her to her feet. "I told you to go get your things. I don't want you leaving nothing here. As far as everyone knows you just left, like you always leave."

He was almost holding her off the ground. She grabbed at his hand, trying to make him let go of her hair.

He slapped her almost playfully as blood from her mouth splattered across the polished floor and counters.

The wind outside rattled the panes in the windows. He dropped her suddenly, and she crawled away as fast as she could.

"Hurry up!" he yelled. "I want to get out of this place before it gets any worse."

Autumn ran to her room, slammed the door, and threw the bolt. She knew it would never keep him out for long, but she only needed a moment.

Without looking back, she ran to the closet and closed herself in. Using her fingers to find the trap door, she opened the latch and slid down the old rope, pulling the trap closed behind her.

Halfway down, the rope broke, sending her sprawling to the concrete floor.

"Help!" she cried once before collapsing into tears.

Kate reached her first. For a moment she thought the girl had been hurt in the fall. As Calvin lifted Autumn up to carry her into the light, Kate's cell rang.

She answered it, knowing who it was. "Tyler!"

"Are you all in the basement?" he shouted.

"We are now. Autumn just came down."

"Good, lock all the doors and stay there. From what I just heard, Leland is upstairs in the kitchen. From what I heard he was beating Autumn. I'm glad she got away. I'll send the police as soon as possible. All hell has broken loose out near Lone Oak Road."

The phone went dead before Kate could ask any questions.

She followed the others into the break area. Beth and Calvin were holding Autumn up at the sink. She was crying and blotting her bleeding mouth with a towel, but she didn't look too badly hurt.

"Calvin," Kate whispered. "Lock the doors."

"They're already locked, except for the one Autumn used, and it closes automatically when someone goes through. No one upstairs will find it unless he knows how to open it."

"Good. We're safe enough." She left Autumn with Beth and crossed to the wide stairs leading to the hidden passage. From the bottom of the stairs she could see both the place where Autumn had landed from the trap door and the closed panel above. She'd know if anyone came down either way.

Martha Q joined her. "I never could tolerate a man who would hit a woman. That guy upstairs better pray he doesn't find the way down or I'll teach him a lesson he'll never forget."

Kate lifted the snow shovel. Preparing, like the soldier she was, for battle.

All seemed silent for a while except the wind wheezing through the cracks. She thought she heard footsteps. One, maybe two sets.

Then, like a bell chiming once, Kate heard a shot ring out from above.

Then silence.

Kate looked at Martha Q, knowing the others would be little help.

"Do we go up?"

Kate nodded. "We do."

Martha picked up a pipe.

Chapter 52

❧

HARMONY FIRE STATION

THE OUTSIDE LINE RANG NEXT TO TYLER'S LEFT HAND.
He picked it up quickly. All firemen were accounted for
except Brandon Biggs. He hadn't called or radioed in since
the first sightings of tornadoes touching down near Harmony.

"Hello. What is your emergency?" Tyler asked.

"Sir Knight?" came Saralynn's frightened voice. "Are
you or my uncle Hank coming to get us?"

"We're a little busy." Tyler tried to sound calm, but a
tornado had scraped along the cottonwoods fifteen minutes
ago and damaged most of the trailer park just outside town.
Every fireman they could spare had been called out except
Brandon Biggs, and as soon as Tyler could contact Biggs,
one more would be on his way.

The sheriff's office was setting up roadblocks. Right
now no one was getting down Lone Oak Road because of

scattered debris on the road. "Are you with your mother, Saralynn? Are you safe?"

One emergency at a time, Tyler reminded himself.

"We are all safe, but it's cold in the basement since the tree knocked down our door."

The Matheson place was several miles from the trailer park, but close enough that it could have taken damage from the hundred-mile-an-hour winds. "I'll get your uncle Hank on the line. Give me a minute."

Tyler stood and searched the bay area of the fire station. Hank had been loading up supplies five minutes ago, but now he was nowhere in sight.

"Saralynn, could I talk to your mother?"

"Okay," she said. "But don't forget to tell someone to come get us. I don't like it down here."

Tyler waited until Claire said hello, then asked, "Is everyone all right? Are you in any danger?"

"No," she said calmly. "Just frightened. The Trumans are here, and tell Alex her brother Noah is with us. We're trapped but unharmed."

"Good." Tyler wasn't sure what to say. "Hang in there. The road is blocked out your direction, but we'll get to you as soon as we can. Looks like the worst of it is over. I wouldn't be surprised if we're not seeing sunshine soon."

"I hope so," Claire answered. "Can you check on my sister and Gabe? I can't get either of them on the phone."

Tyler grinned, already knowing that answer. "They drove in an hour ago to the hospital. I think Hank tried to reach them also. When he called the hospital, a nurse told him cell phones were not allowed in the delivery rooms."

"We should be there."

The always-calm Claire sounded like she was beginning to shatter. Tyler wished he could help her, but there was nothing anyone in town could do.

Tyler could guess how it would feel being trapped. "We'll get out to you as soon as we can," he said again, hoping it would be sooner and not later. "Make sure everyone is warm." It was a dumb thing to say, but Tyler felt he had to give some advice.

She thanked him and hung up.

Tyler sat back down at his desk and tried one more time to call his funeral home. The line was still busy. It had been for twenty minutes. The 911 call had come in only a few minutes before everything happened. He'd picked it up, thought he heard someone scream and then nothing. A few minutes later he'd reached Kate, but in the storm he'd lost the connection.

Tyler answered two more calls of people reporting damage before he had a few seconds to dial Kate's number. No answer. She'd had her phone with her when she'd talked to him. She'd said they were all safe in the basement. No tornado had touched down inside the city limits. His home and business were safe . . . so where was everyone and who had called 911?

He was not a man who panicked, but he could feel his insides winding up for an explosion.

Hank called in to say they were transporting two people to the hospital from the trailer park. Another fireman reported that he was en route to the hospital with a man who might have suffered a heart attack.

Tyler took the calls, and relayed them when needed, but all the time he was worried about his people at the funeral home. Calvin and Dave were older; Beth should have retired five years ago. Autumn was pregnant. He thought of a hundred things that might have happened since he'd talked to Kate. He kept telling himself that Kate was there, she could take care of any emergency. She would call his cell if she needed him. They were safe in the basement where no one could get to them.

Five more minutes passed, then ten. The rain stopped pounding. Tyler glanced at the window. The sky was no longer black. People were still calling in. Some to say their electricity was out. Some to report damage. He'd put Ronny to work taking down reports. The girl had proven to be a great help, as had Border Biggs. Though he frightened a few people off, he was more than willing to do all he could. When folks saw his grandmother pass by and pat him on the cheek, they lost most of their fear of the kid.

Tyler needed to leave. He only had to go a few blocks and check on his people, but right now he had a job to do and he couldn't abandon his post until someone showed up to relieve him.

His cell finally rang. "Kate," he said as he answered. "I'm so glad . . ."

Kate's voice broke in. "We need an ambulance, Ty, as fast as possible."

Tyler picked up the other line and punched speed dial. "Who?" he said, mentally going through his list of employees who might be hurt.

"One man down. Gunshot wound. Life threatening."

Tyler's training kicked in. He relayed the message as fast as possible before asking any of the questions firing through his brain.

"It's on its way," he said to Kate. "Fill me in."

"Thank God." She took a moment to breathe before she answered. "Its one of your firemen. I think his name is Biggs. Leland beat Autumn up and when she escaped, the fireman must have come through the back door and surprised Leland. The fireman took a bullet in his chest, but near as I can tell it missed his heart because his pulse is pounding hard. Good vital signs, but he keeps asking for someone named Reagan. From his breathing, I'd guess he has a lung collapsed and he's lost a lot of blood."

Tyler gripped the phone so tightly he was surprised when it didn't shatter in his hand. "You and the others?"

"We're fine. Calvin and Dave tied Leland up. They're sitting on him now, so send a policeman when one is free. Autumn is still crying, but I think she's fine. How are you? We've been hearing the sirens. Was anyone hurt in the storm?"

Before Tyler could ask any more questions, she shouted, "I hear the ambulance. I'm going to the hospital with the fireman and taking Autumn along to have her checked."

She hung up before he could say anything. It took every

ounce of his strength to force himself to stay grounded in the chair. He called the sheriff and asked them to pick up an intruder as quickly as possible. The young dispatcher, who was barely trained, relayed him through to Alex, who was at the trailer park.

"Sheriff McAllen," she snapped.

Tyler explained as quickly as he could about Leland being tied up at the funeral home.

Alex said she was just leaving the park. Miraculously, no one had been killed. Trailers were scattered and trees down, but everyone was alive. It would be hours before they got even one lane of Lone Oak Road passable, but at least all were safe. The firemen and local construction teams were moving in now.

Tyler set the phone down and closed his eyes for a second, blocking out the noise around him. He turned to McNabb. "Can you handle the phones for a minute?"

McNabb nodded.

Tyler crossed the room to where Border was lifting supplies onto one of the trucks heading out. "Border, I need to talk to you a minute."

"Sure. How can I help you, Mr. Wright?"

Tyler put his arm around the big kid and walked him to the kitchen. "You're going to need to be strong right now for your grandmother's sake."

"All right." Border looked confused.

Tyler had to tell it straight. "Your brother is on his way to the hospital. He's been hurt."

Border shoved away. "No," he said, as if he could deny Tyler's words and make them untrue. "No."

Mrs. Biggs heard her grandson and seemed to feel his pain even though she hadn't heard Tyler's words. "What is it?" she asked, moving closer.

Tyler looked at her. "Brandon was shot. He's on his way to the hospital. That's all I know."

To Tyler's surprise, Ronny took charge. She wrapped her arm around Mrs. Biggs's waist and pulled her toward the side entrance. "Come on now. We don't know how bad it is. Border will drive us both to the hospital and we'll see for ourselves." She motioned for Border to follow.

Border just stood like a huge tree growing in the room. He didn't follow, and from the look on his face Tyler couldn't tell if he was planning to cry or hit something.

Before Tyler could get to him, Ronny grabbed his hand. "We have to go. Can you drive us?"

He nodded and followed her out the side door.

Tyler smiled. Silent Ronelle Logan had stepped in to help. He didn't know how, but the girl seemed to have woken up from a deep sleep and decided to join the human race.

Tyler sat back down at the phones. In an hour his job would be over and he could leave. He knew he'd go by home and check on everyone, and then he'd head to the hospital.

Chapter 53

DENVER CHECKED THE WEATHER AS SOON AS HE COULD turn his phone on. Tornadoes in the lower half of the Texas panhandle. Three spotted in open land and two close to Harmony. It might all be over before he could get there, but he would get there.

He called Derwood's Flight Service and Crop Dusting while his plane pulled into the gate. He got off and picked up his next assignment, then walked out the side door of the airport and across to a row of hangars where private planes landed.

Derwood was there by the time he finished a cup of coffee. Denver had tried Claire and the house twice during his wait and finally called the fire department. A man named Tyler Wright, whom Denver barely remembered, told him the road to the Matheson ranch was blocked.

Old Derwood finished gassing up and grabbed a bottle of pop. He must sleep and eat in his plane. The cockpit smelled like old barbecue sauce, but then so did Derwood.

Denver buckled in. Derwood laughed as he fought the wind to take off. "You were lucky. I was halfway to Amarillo dropping off vet supplies when you called."

Denver made his living on planes, but he'd never experienced anything like Derwood. If he didn't know better he would have sworn they flew low enough to do crop dusting on their way to Harmony.

Once they were in the air, Denver explained that tornadoes had taken out a few trees along Lone Oak Road and they needed to land on the hard packed lane that ran a quarter mile from the farm-to-market road to the Matheson house.

To Denver's surprise, the old pilot didn't seem to think it would be a problem, but he said it would cost an extra twenty for the wear on the tires at landing.

Denver closed his eyes as they lowered into the clouds looking for the Matheson place. He didn't open them until they touched ground. Derwood took him almost up to the front door of the ranch house. Or what would have been the front door if a tree hadn't been blocking the way.

Denver jumped from the plane and ran to the wreckage.

"Claire!" he yelled as he pulled splinters of wood and glass away from the entrance.

"I'm here," she yelled back. "We're trapped."

Denver laughed, loving the sound of her voice. "No kidding," he said.

Derwood walked up, his hands in his baggy pockets. "What a mess," he said simply. Rain lightly dribbled over him, making him look like a melting scarecrow left out long after Halloween.

Denver jerked his coat off, not caring about the cold. "Want to lend me a hand?"

Derwood was gone when he turned back to where the man had been standing. Apparently manual labor wasn't included in the charter price.

Pulling branches off as fast as he could, Denver worked his way to the trunk of the tree lodged between the porch and the door leading to the basement. Or what was left of the door. The wood had been shredded by branches as though it were the thickness of cotton.

"I'll get you out, Claire!" Denver yelled, but he didn't see how. He needed an ax or a chain saw.

"Denver?" a young man's voice shouted. "We'll push from this end if you can pull."

Denver didn't care who was below. He was happy to have the help. "All right. Push!"

Nothing moved. The tree was wedged too tightly.

The sound of a motor heading his way drew Denver's attention. Derwood pulled up to the porch in a tractor.

"Where'd you find that?"

Derwood smiled. "This is a ranch, city boy. They do have equipment on ranches. I looked in the barn."

Maybe Derwood hadn't destroyed all his brain cells smoking weed. Denver grabbed a chain and within minutes they'd pulled the tree away, taking most of the porch along with it.

One by one the people in the basement climbed out. When a man passed Saralynn out, Denver hugged her tightly and said, "I'm so glad you're all right. You mean the world to me, kid."

She smiled at him and whispered, "I knew you'd come." She wrapped her arms around his neck and let him carry her all the way through the living room with its broken windows to the kitchen, where everything looked just as it always had.

When Denver went back, Claire was climbing over the door frame. He offered her his hand and guided her out. For once he didn't hold her, didn't kiss her. He just smiled, and she seemed to understand. Just knowing she was all right was enough for now.

They carried Uncle Jeremiah out while he protested. When everyone was settled in the big ranch kitchen, Denver lent his cell to Noah, who called in to tell everyone in town that they were out and safe.

He reached Tyler, still manning the phones. "Tell my sister that there's no need to send anyone to the ranch. We're fine."

Noah listened, then said, "She's right here. I'll tell her."
He hung up while everyone waited silently.

Noah turned to Reagan. "Rea, Mr. Wright wanted me to
tell you that during the storm Brandon went over to answer
a 911 call and was shot. He's in critical condition. He's asking for you."

Reagan held her breath, fighting not to cry. "I have to go
to him." She turned toward Derwood, who was in a corner
finishing off the last of the pie she'd brought hours ago.

"I can't fly in," Derwood said, still chewing. "I just called
to check on the Harmony landing strip. One of the fellows
said the runway has tin all over it. Seems the roof on my
hangar blew off during the storm." He shrugged. "Appears
I'm stuck here for a while, folks. Hope you've got plenty of
food. I skipped lunch to go get him." He pointed with his
fork toward Denver.

Every Matheson woman groaned, including Saralynn.

"I have to get to the hospital." Reagan stood. "We could
take one of the cars as far down the road as we could get
and walk the rest of the way."

Noah shook his head. "It would take an hour, maybe
more in this rain and mud."

Derwood smiled. "Why don't you take a few of those
horses in the barn? You should be able to cross the open fields."

"My horses," Noah said. "Of course, they're here." He
glanced at Foster. "Can you help me saddle them? Rea, get
your coat."

Reagan started to object, but Noah and Foster were
already out the back door. She had to get to the hospital, but
riding a horse seemed like a crazy idea. Noah might have
grown up around horses, but she'd ridden only a few times
and never when it was raining with lightning still flashing
around them.

She walked out back, thinking this idea would never
work. They had to come up with another plan.

Noah hurried from the barn, leading two horses saddled
and ready.

"I can't ride," she said simply.

"Of course you can. I'll be right with you."

"No." She'd barely been able to stay in the saddle when the horse walked. She'd never make it.

"All right, Rea, we'll ride double." He helped her up and then swung up with his good arm and settled in behind her.

They were heading out across the open field toward the Truman orchard before she could say anything. The horse moved easily into a gallop, and Noah's arm cast felt like the bar of a roller coaster ride holding her in place. She wasn't cold or afraid. This time on a horse, she felt safe and protected.

He slowed when they reached the downed fence marking the entrance to the orchard. Years ago Uncle Jeremiah had made it easy for Aunt Pat to roll her little golf cart over the border between their land so she could collect all the apples she wanted.

Noah whispered in Rea's ear. "Do you think they used to secretly meet here under these trees? Who knows, maybe they've been lovers for years."

"I'd like to think that," she said. "I'm guessing that would give them both some happiness."

"Or sadness. Meeting now and then, but never being truly together."

"We'll never know," she whispered.

As soon as they reached the path, Noah encouraged the horse to pick up speed. They took Lone Oak Road as far as they could and then worked their way through the downed trees until they reached the edge of town. The little trailer park that had been there nestled among the old cottonwoods by the stream looked like a giant had taken his hand and stirred them all up. Some were on their sides, a few off their foundations. One was smashed completely, and a few looked like they hadn't even been touched by the wind. People were out everywhere. Standing, watching the sky. Helping others. A few were moving slowly about, picking up the pieces of their lives that had tumbled out of their homes.

When Noah crossed the bridge, he saw his first traffic. His horse panicked.

Noah held the reins and controlled the animal with soft

words and a firm grip. Within a few minutes they were crossing along the creek bed to the back of the hospital.

Noah's voice whispered against her ear, "You know, I'd
forgotten how much I like riding. It feels good to be sitting in a saddle that isn't bucking. I remember once when I
wanted to spend every day in the saddle."

He reached the entrance and lowered her to the ground.
"Go on in. I'll find you."

As Reagan ran into the hospital, she heard one of the
security guards yelling that Noah couldn't park that horse
at the entrance. Reagan smiled, thinking that if Brandon
was awake she'd tell him all about what she'd gone through
to get to him tonight.

People lined the hallway. Firemen, tired and dirty from
working; construction workers who'd heard Brandon was hurt.

She saw Martha Q standing next to Mrs. Biggs near the door.
"What's happening?" Reagan asked them both.

"The bullet went through. He's in surgery now." Mrs. Biggs
cried softly. "We'll know more as soon as they're finished.

"Where is his brother?" Rea knew Bran would be worried about Border. He might be only a few years older, but
he thought he was Border's parent.

"He's giving blood," Mrs. Biggs said. "They're running
short of O negative with all the injuries coming in."

Noah had stepped up behind Rea. "I'm O negative."

Mrs. Biggs didn't even have to ask; Noah was already
moving down the hallway looking for a nurse.

Reagan talked Mrs. Biggs into moving into the waiting
room. Martha Q came along.

She wasn't sure how long she waited; all Reagan knew
was that she couldn't leave until she'd seen Bran.

Mr. Wright came in. He looked around the room and
went straight to a woman Reagan hadn't recognized until
he hugged her. Major Kate Cummings, the arson specialist
who'd visited several years ago. To Reagan's surprise, Mr.
Wright kissed her on the mouth right in front of everyone.
They talked, their heads almost touching for a few minutes
before they seemed to notice there were people all around.

Reagan leaned back in her chair. The night was full of surprises. "How was Bran shot?" she asked Mrs. Biggs, but it was Martha Q who answered.

"I'm not sure. We think Brandon walked in and surprised Leland while he was robbing the place."

Martha Q leaned closer and added, "I was there right after it happened. When Kate"—she pointed to the woman still in Mr. Wright's arms—"came up from the basement of the funeral home, there was the Biggs boy bleeding on the floor and that man, Leland, rummaging through the silverware drawer.

"He looked up at us and yelled, 'What do you two old bags want?' Well, I wasn't going to take that kind of talk. I headed toward him, yelling that he needed to have a little respect and what had he done. I pointed my finger at him and began to give him a piece of my mind on beating women."

Reagan, along with several others in the waiting room, was listening to every word Martha Q said.

"I saw he'd left the gun on the counter and I aimed to get there before he did, but I'm not as fast as I used to be, even though I do work out at the gym now and then."

"What happened next?" Reagan pulled Martha Q back to her account.

"Well, he was getting madder and madder as we both moved toward the gun. Apparently he likes to be the one yelling, not the one being yelled at. I started waving my arms like I was planning to teach him a lesson. I had his full attention when Kate slammed the snow shovel up against the back of his head."

Everyone murmured, amazed at Martha Q's daring.

"He was stunned by the blow and by the time he recovered, she'd hit him in the back of the knees. He fell like a pine tree downed with one whack. When he could focus, he was looking down the barrel of a gun Kate obviously knew how to handle. She was in the army, you know."

Everyone around began asking questions, and Reagan moved away. When she looked for Mr. Wright and the major, they seemed to have vanished.

Chapter 54

HARMONY HOSPITAL

TYLER TOOK KATE'S HAND AND THEY WALKED TO A SIDE door off the waiting room leading to a courtyard. In summer it was covered with flowers and bird feeders, but now it looked dull and brown.

They stood a few feet beyond the door so the rain couldn't reach them. He hugged her again, needed to believe that she was safe. "You could have been shot, Kate. You could have been hurt."

"I calculated the risk. I wouldn't have charged in if I hadn't seen the fireman down. Plus, Leland wasn't trained and I was, though it had been a few years since I'd practiced combat." She patted his chest as if to calm him. "I also had a secret weapon. Martha Q as a distraction."

Tyler grinned. "I love you." He said the words before he'd realized his thoughts had tumbled out, but once said, he couldn't pull them back. "I love you," he repeated. "When I thought you were in trouble, I had to fight to keep from running to you."

"You manned your post, Tyler. That was exactly what you should have done." She patted his chest again. "And, by the way, Ty, I love you too. I have for a long time. I just didn't know how to say it."

Chapter 55

HARMONY HOSPITAL

REAGAN WATCHED TYLER WRIGHT AND THE MAJOR THROUGH the long glass windows looking over the courtyard. They were standing close, talking only inches apart. He leaned down several times and gave her a light kiss. She had her hand over his heart.

They were in love, Reagan realized. The forever kind of love that everyone else can see. A dozen dramas were going on in the waiting room, but just beyond the glass two lonely people had found one another. No, more than that, she thought. They looked like they'd found the kind of love that lasts a lifetime.

When they finally stepped back inside, Tyler held her hand in his.

Reagan moved toward them, sorry to be the first to step into their private world, but needing to know more about what happened to Bran.

When Kate greeted her with a smile, Reagan whispered, "I just talked to Martha Q. Is that the way it happened, Major?"

Kate winked at Tyler and said, "That's exactly how it happened."

Reagan doubted it somehow, but Martha Q was loving being the hero.

"Reagan," Tyler said in a low voice, "you don't need to call Kate *Major*. She's going to be retiring soon and joining me in the business."

"Really?" Reagan would have never guessed Mr. Wright would take on a partner.

Kate nodded. "I'll be just Kate," she laughed. "Or, of course you can call me Mrs. Wright if you want to be formal."

Reagan saw it then in their eyes, a kind of happiness that made them both shine.

"During the storm today," Tyler began, "we both figured out something. We don't want to be apart. Not ever again."

Kate laughed. "I've spent years looking for the right man. Who knew I could have just looked in the Harmony phone book to find the *Wright* one." She smiled at him and added, "The perfect one for me."

Before Reagan had time to say more than *Congratulations*, a nurse called her to the recovery room. Noah followed her in.

Brandon's chest was bandaged, but he didn't look near death, just groggy. "Thanks for coming, Reagan," he said. "I wanted to tell you I'm not dying. All I could think about while I was on that kitchen floor bleeding was to let you know."

"The nurse said you're going to be all right." She leaned and kissed him on the cheek.

"Yeah, that's what my little brother said when they let him in a few minutes ago. He gripes about me being hard on him all the time, but he was crying like a baby."

"The nurse says I only have a minute, but I want you to know there's a room full of people out there worried about you. I about went nuts with worry."

"I'll be around for a while." He noticed Noah standing by the door. "Thanks for the blood, cowboy."

"Don't go thinking this makes us blood brothers. I was just paying back a favor."

Bran laughed, then groaned in pain. The nurse moved in and told them to leave. Rea kissed him one more time and left before she started crying.

Noah led her down the hallway away from the others. When they were alone, he leaned down and kissed her gently.

"What's that for?" she asked, surprised by his sudden show of affection.

"For not crawling in bed with him. I may be leaving to catch the last of the spring rodeos, but you're my girl."

"What makes you so sure?"

"Because you climb up in bed with me when I'm hurt. And you're going to wait for me, Reagan Truman, no matter how much you hate it. You'll wait for me to finish rodeoing, and then we'll talk about the rest of our lives."

"You're light-headed from loss of blood."

He shook his head. "No. I think I'm seeing better than I have in a long time. The rodeo isn't my dream, it's just a gamble I'm taking that might pay off. But whether I come home with winnings or broke, you're still in my future."

He looped his arm around her shoulder. "You, me, the ranch, three kids. I see the whole thing clear as day."

Reagan laughed. Her Noah was finally back. "We'll see," she said, not wanting him to get too big a head.

Chapter 56

HARMONY HOSPITAL

THREE HOURS LATER, GABE LEARY WALKED OUT OF THE delivery room to a crowd of Mathesons and his friend Denver Sims. Everyone went silent, but Gabe didn't say a word.

Denver moved forward. "Well, Gabriel, what do you have?"

Gabe's eyes were wide like he'd been through the toughest battle of his life. Being a soldier hadn't prepared him for what he'd just faced.

Denver slapped him on the shoulder. "Gabe! What is it? What's wrong?"

Gabe stared at his best friend. "I've got two daughters. Girls. Little tiny girls."

Denver laughed. "Don't worry, they'll grow and then you'll really have to be ready for trouble." He glanced over at Saralynn, sitting beside her mother. "You know, I don't think being a dad is going to be half bad. I think I might give it a try. Little girls have a way of wrapping themselves around your heart."

Chapter 57

❧❧

THE DAY AFTER THE TORNADO, RONNY SLEPT LATE ON HER little bed in Autumn's sitting room. She was vaguely aware of Autumn crossing the room at dawn, and she could hear the mumbling of people talking beyond the door, but she didn't want to open her eyes. Yesterday had been too much for her. The tornado, then the wait at the hospital.

She'd left Marty five messages on his cell, and he'd never answered one. Apparently he'd stepped out of this one life and into another. She didn't know if he'd been forced or bribed to go back to Dallas, but she knew he didn't go willingly. The memory of him saying he didn't know if he had the strength to fight worried her. Had he given in to his father's plan of care, or had he simply given in?

She wanted to be there to help him, but he wouldn't

want her there to watch him die. Whatever had pulled him away, Marty wanted to deal with it alone, and she'd never know if he was forgetting her or somehow thought he was sparing her pain.

A part of Ronny thought if she just didn't get up today, she wouldn't have to face anything, but after fighting back tears for an hour, she knew that wasn't true.

Finally, when all was quiet in the kitchen, Ronny stood and slipped into her old baggy pants and T-shirt. She tiptoed out the back door of the funeral home and crossed to the muddy creek bed. Branches and trash cluttered the path now, making it look dirty and unwelcoming, but she maneuvered through the boards and pieces of roofing, not caring that her shoes were caked in mud.

The morning was bright, almost as if nature were smiling and saying, *Sorry about all the mess.*

Buffalo's Bar had lost most of the roof. The trailer park that had been down in the cottonwoods just out of town since Gypsies camped there in the 1890s, was pretty much destroyed. Tyler told her last night there were a dozen injuries, but no one hurt badly. A construction site over by the mall had had lumber and supplies piled up for a new restaurant. Most of it had vanished in the wind.

Ronny climbed the side of the creek bed a few houses from where Marty's duplex stood. Like several buildings, it had suffered damage. Most of the ramp Marty had used to get in and out of the house was gone, and one of the Biggs windows had been blown out, probably by flying lumber, Ronny thought. The old Mission-style duplex looked pretty much the same, considering the fact that it had probably stood years of winds.

When she reached the front door, Ronny bumped into Martha Q coming out of Marty's place.

"Oh." Martha Q looked surprised. "I didn't expect to see you here. If you're delivering the mail, the man moved out yesterday."

Ronny kept her head down and backed away. She didn't want to talk to Martha Q. Martha Q, on the other hand, seemed to have something to say. She closed in faster than Ronny could back away.

"I heard you moved out on your mother. I'm surprised you didn't think of it years ago. By the time I was your age I'd been married twice."

Ronny figured everyone in town had heard some version of the story, truth or not. Apparently, Martha Q hadn't heard that she'd been at Marty's place the night her mother caused all the trouble. That was all right; people wouldn't believe that a man like Marty would have anything to do with someone like her.

"About time you spread your wings," Martha Q huffed. "There's nothing wrong with your brain, is there? You can think for yourself, count money, open a can so you won't starve?"

Ronny almost laughed, thinking of how she'd flown once down a back road with the windows down. "What are you asking, Mrs. Patterson?" Just because Ronny never said a word when she was around the innkeeper didn't mean that something was wrong with her. She'd managed to get through three years of college online, and that hadn't been easy with her gaps in education after being homeschooled by a mother who thought math was a waste of time.

Martha Q stared at her. "You got enough money, girl? If I know Dallas, she didn't give you a dime."

"I have money." It crossed Ronny's mind that everything she said might be relayed to her mother. "I'll be fine. I've been gone almost a week and haven't had to eat a frozen dinner once. I can learn to cook when I have my own place." That she wasn't sure of, but she wasn't going to admit it to anyone.

"Oh, you can, can you?"

"I'm already collecting recipes. Stella, who works part time at the funeral home, was a home economics teacher. She knows everything about cooking."

Martha Q raised an eyebrow. "What are you doing here if you're not delivering mail?"

"Just looking around." Ronny had had enough of answering questions. She began to back up.

Martha Q wasn't finished. "Well, since you've looked around, do you want to rent this place or not? Mr. Winslow called me early yesterday and told me he was leaving. I told him he wouldn't get his rent back for the month and he said you might want to move into the place. I'd have to increase the rent by twenty-five dollars what with all the repairs I'm going to have to do, but I don't see any reason you can't move in and have the last of the month free since he already paid."

She looked into the apartment and saw Marty's cook-books still on the shelves in the kitchen. "What would I do with all the stuff he left?"

"Keep it or throw it out," Martha Q said. "If you take this place, you take it as is. I'm not paying to have it cleaned or painted."

"I'll take it."

Martha Q seemed to have second thoughts. "You do know who your neighbors are?"

"Yes."

Martha Q gave her a look that said she was questioning her mental capacity again. "I guess I could spare a few chairs and a dresser. Come over once you move in and we'll look in the attic."

"All right. I'll bring you the money for next month's rent Monday, but could I pay you two hundred now in advance? I'd like to start cleaning up from the storm."

Martha Q handed her the key.

Ronny paid her and walked into her new place. It needed everything—furniture, paint, a real bed—but none of that mattered. It was hers. She walked through the rooms and the memories, almost feeling Marty with her.

Border dropped by a half hour later and found her orga-nizing the books. "Mrs. Q told me you rented the place. I think Marty will be glad to hear that when he calls."

"If he calls," she added.

"He'll call. You'll see. Besides, he promised to come hear me play, and I've never known him to break a prom-ise." He walked through to the bedroom. "I'll get all the equipment out of the way."

"How's your brother this morning?"

"He's doing great. Autumn and Willie were with him this morning. Both say he's a real hero and I think my brother really likes hearing that."

She helped him carry a weight bench to the porch as he continued, "You know, I don't think I knew how many friends Bran had until last night. His room was packed. Even the boss from his construction site came."

"I count both of you as my friends," she said, thinking few would come to her room if she was hurt.

"Oh, you bet." Border went back for another load. "I'll be glad to help you out anytime you need some lifting. Bran said Marty was teaching you to drive and I should take out the Volvo and let you practice. I don't mind. I don't think I've ever taught anyone anything."

"Fair enough," she said as he hauled the last of the weights out.

He stopped and looked at her. "If Beau and I make too much noise for you, just bang on the wall. We'll keep it down."

"I don't think I'll mind at all."

She went back into the house. Even with some of Marty's things missing, she still felt him in the house. He'd liked the kitchen, and she had a feeling it would become her favorite room.

She brushed her hands along the row of cookbooks. She'd start here, learning everything he'd learned. She'd work on her classes every night on his desk, and she'd wait and hope. When he was able, he'd come back.

The book beneath the counter caught her eye. She pulled it out and opened the place where he hid his money. If he'd had any time before he left, he would have left her a message in the secret hollow book.

The white envelope lay on top. He'd written one word in a hurried hand. Hundred-dollar bills fanned out from inside as she picked the envelope up, but she barely noticed them.

One word. His last wish. His last hope for her.

Ronny ran her fingers over Marty's writing and said the word out loud.

Grow.

She lowered her voice to a whisper. "I will," she said. "I promise."

Keep reading for a special preview of
the next novel in Jodi Thomas's
heartwarming HARMONY series

JUST DOWN THE ROAD

SEPTEMBER

DR. ADDISON SPENCER STOOD BETWEEN THE EMERGENCY room doors of Harmony's only hospital and waited for the next wave of trouble to storm the door. The reflection of her tall, slim body dressed in white appeared more ghost than human in the smoky glass. For a blink, Addison feared she might be fading away like an old photograph facing the sun. When she'd been a child with light blond hair, her father had called her his sunshine; now there seemed little sunshine left. If it weren't for her work she'd have no anchor to hang on to in life.

Saturday night on a payday weekend always promised a full house in the ER, yet the wind just beyond the glass whispered change. She'd already been up since four A.M. delivering twins to a teen mother who yelled all the way through the birthing, but Addison's shift wouldn't be over tonight until the bars closed. If a fight didn't break out in the parking lot, maybe, just maybe, she could be in bed by two.

She thought of the silence at the little place she'd rented a few miles from town. An old four-room house with hand-me-down furniture from decades past. Nothing special. Nothing grand. Only the porch wrapped all the way around, and in every direction was peace. A single neighbor's place spotted the landscape to the south. Cornfields were to the east and rocky untamed land to the north and west. Closing her eyes, she wished she were already there.

"Dr. Spencer?" Nurse Georgia Veasey's voice echoed behind her.

"Yes?" Addison turned, trying hard not to show any hint of the exhaustion she felt. One of her med school professors had drummed into everyone he taught that a professional gives her best until she drops and can give nothing at all. He often ranted that a career in medicine left little room for life beyond the hospital walls, and for Addison that seemed perfect. One bad marriage had taught her all she wanted to know of the world outside.

"Harley phoned in from the bar." Georgia moved closer, as though looking through the night for trouble. "Appears we got a pickup load of roughnecks coming in all bleeding and cussing."

A year ago she wouldn't have known what the nurse was talking about. She'd learned that roughnecks were oil field workers. "Who'd they fight?" she asked, without any real interest. Half the time the drunks couldn't answer that question themselves when she asked.

"One man, apparently, but the caller said it was Tinch Turner. From what I hear, he never joins in a fight unless the odds are five to one."

Addison understood. "Get six rooms ready." She'd be stitching up the load of roughnecks and probably operating on the fool who took them all on. "I'll go scrub up. You know what to do."

The head nurse nodded. She'd start the staff cleaning up blood and giving shots while their drunk patients turned from fighters to babies. The nurses and aides would comfort the boys in grown men's bodies as they sewed them up and called someone to come get them. Addison knew Georgia would send the most seriously hurt one to the first room. She would be waiting there, ready to do her best one more time.

As she moved inside, Addison stopped long enough to pour a strong cup of black coffee. She hated coffee, but going into her twentieth hour on her feet, she needed something to keep her awake. Odds were good in a few minutes she'd be trying to save the life of some jerk who should have gone home to his wife and family after work.

Some doctors loved the emergency room and practiced there for their entire career, but Addison knew she'd finish out her contract here in Harmony and head back east somewhere. The problem that had driven her here was over. In four months she'd pick a new town on the map, find a hospital that needed her, and get back on her career track.

TINCH TURNER WAITED IN HIS PICKUP FOR ALL THE OIL field workers to pile out and go into the ER. They'd have a few black eyes, a few stitches, but he knew from experience that none of them were hurt bad enough to be admitted. Tinch just had to break up the fight as fast as he could, and sometimes the easiest way to get trouble's attention is to hit it between the eyes.

Next week he'd buy the boys a drink and explain to them that if they were in Harmony they needed to behave. Howard Samuels shouldn't have started calling them oil field trash, but every one of the roughnecks had been flirting with Samuel's wife. She was barroom beautiful and tended to forget she was married when she drank. Tinch had seen her flirt before, and he couldn't help but wonder if she wanted Samuel to be jealous or dead.

Closing his eyes, Tinch told himself he should have stayed out of it. Several others in the bar could have stepped in to help Howard. But Tinch had tossed caution out the window about the time he gave up on caring whether he lived or died. Somehow, taking a few blows reminded him that he could still feel.

Not that he wanted to. He wanted to die and lie next to his wife in the cemetery. He just wasn't able to kill himself. It bothered him that he was just one breath away from her. All he needed to do was not breathe and he'd be with his Lori. Only God had played a trick on them. He'd made Lori fragile and him strong as a bull. She couldn't make it to her twenty-seventh birthday and, with his bad luck, he'd probably live to be a hundred. Maybe if he kept drinking and fighting, one night someone would get lucky and put him out of his misery.

The blood dripping off his forehead bothered him enough to make him climb out of his pickup and head for the emergency room door. He didn't much care about the pain, but he hated bleeding all over everything. He'd get a doc to stitch up the cut and then he'd go back to his farm and drink until he washed memories away and finally slept.

Through the blood, he saw Nurse Veasey. She was frowning at him. Hell, he thought, she was always frowning at him. "Evenin', Georgia," he said, thinking she had that same look when she first saw him sitting next to her in the second grade more than twenty years ago.

"Shut up, Tinch. I don't even want to talk to you." She grabbed his shirt and pulled him toward the first little examining room. "Didn't I tell you I'd beat you up myself if you came in here after a fight again? I swear if there were two like you in this town we'd have to build another wing onto the hospital."

Despite a headache the size of a mustang bucking in his brain, Tinch smiled. "You did threaten me last time, Georgia, and the fear of it kept me away for weeks, I swear."

She slapped him on the arm and he thought of suggesting that might not be protocol for nurses, but Tinch decided to wait until he could see to run before he upset her more. He'd gone to school with her and her two sisters. All three were good girls determined to make the world a better place, or at least improve Harmony. Maryland taught school, Virginia married a preacher, and Georgia became a nurse. They were women on missions. The type Tinch had spent his life avoiding.

"Sit down on the table and keep quiet," Georgia said as she shoved his chin back and poked around the wound running the length of his forehead. "It doesn't look all that bad. If you had any brains, they would have dribbled out a long time ago. I'll send in the doctor."

"Aren't you going to give me something for the pain?"

She shook her head. "Judging from your breath, you've already had enough." She tossed him a towel. "Try not to bleed on anything."

Tinch grinned. "Thanks, darlin'."

"Don't you dare *darlin'* me, Tinch Turner. You're a walking one-man demolition derby. Stay here; I've got people who care about themselves to take care of."

She was gone before he could bother her more. Tinch shrugged. He liked *the states*, as everyone called her and her sisters, but he had a feeling they were passing around a petition to have him banned from town. Maryland had told him the last time she saw him that the way he drove was a bad influence on her high school students, and Virginia had been praying for him for so long, her knees were probably calloused.

Tinch lay back on the examining table, wishing he'd brought the rest of the bottle of whiskey with him. When the door opened, he didn't even look up. He was just about beyond caring for anything or anyone in his life.

"Mr. Turner, I'm Dr. Spencer," someone said as she moved close to the table.

Tinch opened one eye, but he couldn't see much through all the blood.

"Lie still and I'll take a look at that cut."

He didn't move as she cleaned the blood away with a warm towel. "Any chance it's fatal?" he mumbled.

The all-business voice answered, "Afraid not. You allergic to anything?"

He closed his eyes. "Work. Women. Hospitals." He felt a shot poke into his arm. "Silence. Snakes. And Wednesdays.

I hate Wednesdays. And kids." He thought of more things he was allergic to, but he couldn't seem to get the words out.

For a few moments he knew the doctor was still there. He felt her pushing his hair away from his forehead like Lori used to do. He could almost see Lori smiling at him, saying she wanted to see his beautiful blues better. She claimed she could measure his love for her in his eyes and he'd never doubted she could.

Lori's face faded and he dropped away into blackness.